the
SEA BEFORE US

SUNRISE *at* NORMANDY
ONE

the
SEA BEFORE US

SARAH SUNDIN

Revell

a division of Baker Publishing Group
Grand Rapids, Michigan

Published by Revell
a division of Baker Publishing Group
PO Box 6287, Grand Rapids, MI 49516-6287
www.revellbooks.com

Printed in the United States of America

Library of Congress Cataloging-in-Publication Data
Names: Sundin, Sarah, author.
Title: The sea before us / Sarah Sundin.
Description: Grand Rapids, MI : Revell, a division of Baker Publishing Group,
    [2018] | Series: Sunrise at Normandy ; #1
Identifiers: LCCN 2017036629| ISBN 9780800727970 (softcover) | ISBN
    9780800734879 (print on demand)
Subjects: LCSH: World War, 1939-1945—Fiction. | GSAFD: Historical fiction. |
    Christian fiction.
Classification: LCC PS3619.U5626 S43 2018 | DDC 813/.6—dc23
LC record available at https://lccn.loc.gov/2017036629

This book is a work of fiction. Names, characters, places, and incidents are the product of the author's imagination or are used fictitiously.

The author is represented by the literary agency of Books & Such Literary Management.

18   19   20   21   22   23   24   7   6   5   4   3   2   1

To my oldest son, Stephen—
Thank you for your support, encouragement,
and your steady strength . . . and for alerting
the world to the danger of squirrels.

Special Order of the Day
to the Officers and Men
of the Allied Naval Expeditionary Force

31 May 1944

It is to be our privilege to take part in the greatest amphibious operation in history—a necessary preliminary to the opening of the Western Front in Europe which, in conjunction with the great Russian advance, will crush the fighting power of Germany.

This is the opportunity which we have long awaited and which must be seized and pursued with relentless determination: the hopes and prayers of the free world and of the enslaved peoples of Europe will be with us and we cannot fail them.

Our task . . . is to carry the Allied Expeditionary Force to the Continent, to establish it there in a secure bridgehead and to build it up and maintain it. . . .

Let no one underestimate the magnitude of the task. . . .

I count on every man to do his utmost to ensure the success of this great enterprise which is the climax of the European war.

Good luck to you all and God speed.

Admiral Sir Bertram H. Ramsay
Allied Naval Commander-in-Chief,
Expeditionary Force

Prologue

Wyatt Paxton never realized coming home could be as bittersweet as leaving.

He climbed the wooded hill that overlooked Kerrville, his two younger brothers and their girlfriends behind him. After four years in college, he thought he'd be ready to become his father's manager at Paxton Trucking, and he thought he'd be over Oralee Bates.

He wasn't and he wasn't.

An oak branch dipped low in the pathway. Wyatt pulled it aside for the rest of the party. "When was the last time we boys came up here to our Celebration Point?"

"Two years." His younger brother Adler passed him with a smile. He and Wyatt had inherited fair coloring from Daddy and their mother, a woman they only knew from photos. "I was celebrating heading off to college."

"It was my high school graduation, Ad." Clay, the youngest brother, gave Adler a playful punch on the shoulder. His dark good looks hailed from Wyatt's stepmother and her Ramirez clan. "And the start of my servitude at the office. Now finished, hallelujah."

Wyatt grinned at Clay, who would soon be studying medicine.

7

All three sons had worked for Daddy for two years after high school to earn their tuition money.

"Wait up, boys. Ellen's got a pebble in her shoe."

For half a second, Wyatt noticed Clay's pretty blonde girlfriend fussing with her shoe, but then his gaze drifted to Oralee. Always to Oralee. Gentle and strong. And engaged to Adler.

He gripped the rough branch. Adler and Oralee had been together seven years. They'd be married in August. When would it stop hurting?

Ellen worked her shoe back on, and the ladies passed Wyatt.

"Thanks, Wy." Oralee smiled, her brown eyes sweeter than Mama's flan. Then the tall brunette darted to Adler, slipped her hand in his, and leaned against his shoulder, her sunny yellow dress swishing about shapely knees.

Wyatt released the branch and jogged to the head of the line. Better to have the lovebirds behind him than in front.

Adler chuckled. "Always have to be first, don't you, Wy?"

Wyatt's shoulders tensed. Adler should talk. From the moment he came out of the womb, he'd been nipping at Wyatt's heels. Besting him in grades, in home runs, at Paxton Trucking, and stealing the woman he loved.

He blew out a long breath. Not entirely true. Sure, Wyatt had met Oralee first, but while he was working up the nerve to ask her out, Adler swooped in, never hesitating, never failing.

Wyatt had to admit, Adler and Oralee were good together.

He rounded the bend and stopped. He'd forgotten about the footbridge. A chasm cut through the side of the hill, spanned by an old two-by-eight.

"Rats." They'd never brought the ladies up here.

"We don't have to cross this, do we?" Oralee stared at the plank. She and Ellen wore fancy dresses and heels from Wyatt's college graduation party this afternoon.

"You know, this is a good enough place right here." Wyatt swept

8

his hand to the west. "Got a clear spot to roast our marshmallows, and we'll be able to see the sunset just fine."

Adler snorted. "Good enough? Not when we've got the best view in the Texas Hill Country up yonder."

Oralee gripped her hands in front of her stomach. "It doesn't look safe."

"I'll go." Ellen gave Adler a saucy smile. "I'm not scared."

"See, darlin'?" Adler lifted Oralee's hands and kissed them. "Nothing to worry about. We've crossed this bridge hundreds of times."

"But there's nothing to hold on to and—"

"Come on, darlin'. For me?"

Wyatt's chest tightened. All his life, Adler got his way through charming people and cajoling them, and it wasn't right.

Oralee peered into the ravine, her forehead rippling. "I—I don't want to. It doesn't look safe, and you know how clumsy I am."

"You'll be fine. No reason to be scared. And wait until you see the view."

Indignation burned in Wyatt's gut. Why wouldn't Adler listen to her? "The view's fine here. Don't push her to do something she doesn't want to."

Adler dropped his fiancée's hands and stepped around her, his pale blue eyes narrowed at Wyatt. "Thought by now you'd have outgrown being a scaredy-cat."

Oralee hugged his arm. "Adler . . ."

Wyatt's jaw jutted out. "Thought by now you'd have outgrown calling people names."

"When it fits."

"It's not being scared. It's being cautious, protecting people."

"Hey . . ." Clay's nervous laugh filtered through. "We're supposed to be celebrating, not fighting."

"Yeah?" Adler's gaze stayed fixed on Wyatt. "Tell that to Mr. Busybody, thinks he knows better than everyone else 'cause he's two years older."

He took a step closer. "Maybe I do. If you think it's right to coax a girl to cross a little footbridge in high heels, then—"

"Stop it." Oralee stepped between them and pulled on Adler's sleeve. "Please don't fight."

Adler eased her aside, never breaking his gaze with Wyatt. "Out of the way, darlin'. This has nothing to do with you."

No, it didn't. It wasn't about the bridge. It wasn't even about Oralee. "You've just got to have your way, don't you?"

Adler closed the distance, his nose inches from Wyatt's. "And you don't? Listen to you, so high-and-mighty, marching around, giving orders."

"Orders?" Wyatt bumped his chest into his brother's. "I'm trying to protect her 'cause you won't. Can't you see she's scared? Can't you listen to someone else for a change?"

"Stop it!" Oralee's voice came from behind him, near the bridge. "Stop arguing."

"It's not your job to protect her. It's mine." Adler shoved Wyatt, his eyes ablaze. "Get out of my business."

Wyatt shoved him back. Felt good. "I will when you start treating your girl right."

"Stop it," Oralee cried. "He treats me fine, Wy. Just fine."

"You heard her." Another shove from Adler.

"Yeah?" Wyatt pointed to the rickety old plank. "If you love her, stop forcing her to do something she doesn't want to. Protect her for a change."

"Stop it, you two. Look, I'm going. I'll go. Please stop fighting." Oralee placed one foot on the bridge, a breeze lifting her brown curls.

"Oralee!" Wyatt yelled. "Don't. You don't have to."

She tossed her curls. "I can take care of myself, Wyatt Paxton."

"See?" Adler punched his arm. "She can do it. Can't you, darlin'?"

"I can." But her foot wobbled, and she barely caught herself. Wyatt lunged forward. "Oralee, don't."

"Leave me alone, Wy. I'm fine." Then her heel slipped, and she tottered, her arms seesawing.

"No!" Wyatt grabbed her hand.

"Stop it! Leave me alone." She yanked her hand free.

Then the fury in her eyes melted into terror, and she fell—away from him—her hand and her gaze and her scream stretching to him, but he couldn't—he couldn't reach her.

A crack ended her scream. Arms, legs, yellow skirt, brown curls rolled and bounced, then came to a rest, sprawled and twisted over blood-spattered rocks.

Wyatt's hand turned to ice, curled useless before him, and a guttural cry rasped over his throat.

"Oralee!" Adler screamed, and he scrambled down the rocks. "Oralee!"

"Careful." Clay followed his brother. "Don't touch her. You could make it worse. Wait for me."

What had he done? Wyatt stood, every muscle frozen. He wanted to protect Oralee, and he'd . . . he'd . . .

"Oralee? Say something, darlin'. Say something." About fifteen feet below, Adler hunched over her, hands spread wide, not touching, obeying the future physician.

"Oralee?" Clay gently brushed curls from her eyes, her wide, unblinking eyes.

"No . . ." Wyatt's chest convulsed. What had he done? What had he done?

Wailing rose beside him—Ellen, down on her knees.

Clay pressed his fingers to Oralee's neck, his head bowing lower and lower. "I'm sorry, Adler. You and I—we'll stay with her. Wyatt, go fetch the doctor, the sheriff, tell—"

"Noooo!" Adler roared. His arms, stretched in a benediction over the woman he loved, now arched, knotted, an eagle's wings rising to find prey. And he turned to Wyatt. "You did this."

"I—I wanted—I was trying to protect—"

"You killed her!"

As if that two-by-eight had slammed him in the chest.

Adler clawed his way up the ravine, his face twisted. "You—you always wanted her, couldn't have her, so you—" A primal cry ripped the air, as old as Cain and Esau and the brothers of Joseph.

Wyatt couldn't breathe, couldn't move.

That cry grew, and Adler burst over the ledge, gripping a rock the size of a baseball.

Adler Paxton's fastball had struck out the best batters in Texas.

Pain shrieked across Wyatt's left cheek, spun him sideways. He cried out, stumbled, fell to his knees, his hands braced on the rocky soil.

"Don't, Adler!" Ellen screamed. "You'll go to jail, to the electric chair."

Wyatt twisted his head, and a rusty taste filled his mouth.

Adler approached, a stone lifted overhead, his features unrecognizable in his grief and fury.

"Oh, Lord . . ." Wyatt didn't want to die, but he didn't want to live either.

"Don't!" Clay charged from behind and tackled Adler, slammed him to the ground. "Get out of here, Wy. Get Daddy. I'll hold him."

"Get off me, Clay." Adler struggled, but he was no match for the county wrestling champ. "Don't stop me. Get off."

Wyatt's breath returned, heaving humid air into his lungs.

"Run, Wy." Clay pinned Adler's arm behind his back. "Run!"

With one grateful nod, Wyatt lurched to his feet. His legs felt as loose as water, but he moved them, and he ran down that hill faster than the Guadalupe River during a flood, arms pumping, lungs hauling in survival, mind reeling, focusing, planning. Three things he had to do.

Get Daddy.

Get money.

Get away.

1

Second Officer Dorothy Fairfax slathered a thick layer of orange marmalade on the buttered toast and slid the plate in front of her father. "I had enough ration coupons for sausage and your favorite Fortnum & Mason's marmalade. If you don't eat your breakfast, I shall feed it to Charlie with no regret or shame."

Papa glanced from the *Daily Telegraph* to the Scottish terrier dancing by his chair. After an interminable minute, he took a bite.

Dorothy released her breath and sent a smile to Mrs. Bromley. The elderly housekeeper slipped back into the kitchen.

She spread a thin layer of marmalade on her unbuttered toast, her stomach hopping as gleefully as little Bonnie Prince Charlie. "I have the most splendid news. Quite a bit of change at headquarters. New commanders and staff are reporting—British and Americans, army and navy and air." If only she could tell him more about her duties with the Women's Royal Naval Service. Knowing the Allies would invade France in May might bring color back to those gaunt cheeks. But as a Royal Navy veteran, Papa understood the need for secrecy.

However, her news wasn't classified. "You'll never guess who's reporting to my unit."

Dorothy waited, but Papa kept reading the *Telegraph* as she knew he would. "Why, it's Lawrence Eaton."

The sound of his name was the sweetest music.

Papa looked her full in the eye.

The shock of it. When had he last looked at her?

His blue eyes clouded over, and Dorothy's heart shriveled. The wrong Fairfax child sat before him, and he couldn't abide the sight of her.

Then his brow wrinkled. "Lawrence . . . ?"

"Eaton." She brightened for her father's sake and at the name of the man she'd loved since she was fourteen years old. "You remember. He stayed with us on holidays. He was a Cambridge chum of—"

"I remember." The newspaper rose between them.

Dorothy bit into her toast, the marmalade sour on her tongue. She mustn't be hasty in speaking, not when she'd waited ten years for Lawrence to come back into her life. "It would be lovely to have him over for—"

"No." A page flipped.

Every muscle in her face wanted to assume an unladylike expression, but she restrained herself. If they could entertain Lawrence, he'd see she'd grown up, and his clever conversation would cheer Papa.

Or would Lawrence's presence only remind Papa of her brothers?

The newspaper rustled. "I do wish you wouldn't wear so much face powder. I thought I made my opinion clear on that matter."

She winced. "Yes, but the Royal Navy likes the Wrens to look smart." And Lawrence Eaton would never look at her if she were covered in freckles.

The sausage on her plate bent in an accusatory frown. He also wouldn't look at her if she were fat again.

However, it was against the law to waste food, so she finished her breakfast. "Will you be going to the office to—"

"No."

Papa only went to the office once or twice a week now. How did Fairfax & Sons stay afloat without Reginald Fairfax at the helm? James Montague was an excellent manager, but he shouldn't have to perform Papa's duties as well as his own.

Dorothy stood and straightened her double-breasted navy blue uniform jacket. "Have a good day, Papa." She kissed his forehead, his hair tickling her cheek. Once as brilliant red as her own, now graying and dulled.

He had been such a robust man.

Before the war.

LONDON
SATURDAY, JANUARY 15, 1944

Only $437.24 until Lt. Wyatt Paxton could go home.

He subtracted the cost of the Underground fare from his savings and tucked his notepad in the breast pocket of his dress blues. He hated to add to his debt, but how could he spoil his buddies' fun their first full day in London?

Besides, he'd always wanted to see these landmarks—Big Ben, Parliament, Westminster Abbey—all within his line of sight. Ancient spires disappeared in thick fog straight out of Dickens or Sherlock Holmes. Wyatt sank his gloved hands in the pockets of his overcoat and shivered from the privilege of being in this historic city. He didn't deserve it.

"Too cold for your blood?" Lt. Jack Vale nudged him as they walked down a sidewalk edged by carved stone pillars.

Wyatt would never admit it to his best friend, but the cold stung like yellow jackets. Nevertheless, he sent a grin over his shoulder to their fellow officers, Jerry Hobson and Ted Kelvin. "Dakota here's jealous that the sun prefers my home state to his."

Ted turned up the collar of his navy blue overcoat. "At least you two served in the Aleutians. You're used to the cold."

"You'll get used to it," Jack said. "If only we could get used to walking on the left side of the sidewalk."

Yep, Wyatt kept drifting to the right. The men turned the corner and strolled beside the Houses of Parliament. The area teemed with civilians and servicemen in every sort of uniform.

"Wonder what we'll do here." Hobson adjusted his officer's cover over his black hair.

"They'll brief us on Monday," Ted said.

"Think about it." Hobson gestured at Wyatt. "You were a gunnery officer. Jack, you were a communications officer. Ted, you fought U-boats in the Atlantic. And I manned a landing ship at Sicily and Salerno."

"That's enough speculating." Wyatt softened the warning with a smile. "Whatever we do, I have a notion it'll be big."

The other officers nodded.

Spring would arrive soon, the perfect time for the Allies to invade Nazi-occupied Europe. Now was the time to plan and prepare.

"A newsstand." Ted pointed ahead. "I need to get postcards for my wife and kids."

Wyatt hung back and checked his watch. Only one minute until the clock on Big Ben would toll twelve. He couldn't wait.

"Say, Wyatt, aren't you buying postcards for your family?" Ted held up a selection.

Wyatt's chest seized, and Jack shot him a look.

He couldn't explain. Not today. Today was meant to be fun.

"Say, Ted. How about this for your little boy?" Jack held up a card.

The distraction worked, and Wyatt thanked Jack with a smile. Soon he'd tell his new friends what Jack already knew. That he hadn't been home for two and a half years. That he hadn't written. That his family had no idea where he was or what he was doing.

He'd also tell them why. Daddy always said keeping secrets was as stupid as keeping gophers. All they'd do is pop up and poke holes in your life.

The familiar ache filled his chest. Boy, how he missed his family. By the time the war was over, he could pay off his debt. Maybe by then his brothers' grief and fury would dim enough to allow forgiveness.

At least God had forgiven him. *Thank you, Lord. Your forgiveness is all I need, but you know it isn't all I want.*

The Westminster chimes played, and Wyatt ambled over to the row of stone pillars, each pierced in the side with rusty holes. London's wrought-iron fences had been melted down for the war effort, and bomb craters and boarded-up windows added further testimony to the reality of the war.

For over four years, Hitler's Germany had bullied Europe, conquering and bombing and killing. But now thousands of Americans were flooding into Britain with tons of ships, planes, and weapons. The Allies were fixing to make things right, and Wyatt was supposed to play a part.

Long and low, Big Ben announced the hour, each strike resounding in Wyatt's soul with the enormity of the moment.

For the sake of freedom, Wyatt Paxton couldn't afford to be a failure again.

2

"Today's the day," Third Officer Gwen Hamilton whispered to Dorothy.

Third Officer Muriel Shaw set paperwork on the Wrens' work-table and gave Dorothy a sly look. "His office adjoins ours."

"Hush." Dorothy settled a firm look on her friends. "I mustn't look eager. And you simply mustn't tease me. Lieutenant Commander Eaton is a man of sophistication, and he likes a woman who is composed, urbane, and droll." What a gift it had been to overhear Lawrence discussing women with her brothers.

Gwen's gray eyes twinkled. "Jolly Dolly composed and urbane?"

"Hush." Her cheeks warmed. If only Gwen hadn't known her since they were schoolgirls. "I'm no longer jolly, and please don't call me Dolly. You know I've changed."

The door opened.

Lawrence? Not now when she was far from composed.

She spun around and stood at attention, and a sigh of relief and disappointment eased out. No, not Lawrence.

The new Wren commander, First Officer Julia Bliss-Baldwin, marched in with three American naval officers. The men's uniforms were almost identical to those of the Royal Navy, with a navy blue jacket, white shirt, and black tie. However, a gold star replaced the curlicue above the gold stripes on their sleeves.

First Officer Bliss-Baldwin had the quick-eyed, sporty look of a country gentlewoman. "Gentlemen, these are my Wrens—Officers Shaw, Fairfax, and Hamilton, and our enlisted ratings."

A brisk wave of her hand to the wall adorned with a map of the Norman coast. "They have been sorting photographs and postcards, which they then portray in maps and diagrams. Ladies, these gentlemen are attached to the Western Naval Task Force for the upcoming invasion. They're here to select targets for naval bombardment."

Dorothy's hand crept to the table behind her and cupped over her photo.

At the end of the line, a tall sandy-haired officer tipped his head as if asking her why.

Yankee impudence. Dorothy withdrew her hand and concentrated on her new commander.

Bliss-Baldwin raised her delicate nose. "Ladies, may I introduce Commander Marino, Lieutenant Geier, and Lieutenant Paxton?"

The last man was the impudent one, although he had a gentle look about his eyes.

"Very good, gentlemen." The Wren commander gestured to the door. "You do know the way back to Commander Pringle's office, do you not?"

"Yes, ma'am, and thank you." Commander Marino and his men departed.

First Officer Bliss-Baldwin faced the ladies, every blonde hair rolled in perfect order at the back of her head. "I would like to become better acquainted with my officers. Ratings, you are dismissed."

Dorothy remained at attention while the Wrens scurried to their maps.

"It is a pleasure to return to London." She spoke and moved with the grace of her class, the grace that made Dorothy feel like a plodding ox of a girl all over again.

"As you may know, I was amongst the first draft of Wrens sent to Singapore. We were able to escape directly before the fall." Her voice dipped low. "Then on to India and Egypt. I've had a smashing good time. Where have you served, ladies?"

Dorothy glanced to Gwen and Muriel. "London, ma'am."

"That simply won't do. Every Englishwoman dreams of seeing the glory of the Empire. I shall see to it that you have the opportunity."

Coldness seeped into Dorothy's veins. "Thank you, ma'am, but we have this assignment for a reason. We took our holidays in Normandy and are familiar with the land."

She clucked her tongue. "Such a shame. I'll see to it that you have your turn abroad. Carry on." She marched out of the office.

Dorothy sagged back against the table. "Oh dear."

"Don't worry, darling." Muriel's hazel eyes softened. "You have to volunteer for overseas duty."

"I know." Dorothy raised a feeble smile. Even if Papa barely acknowledged her, he needed her for his very existence.

The door swung open.

Lawrence Eaton! Even more handsome than she remembered, his uniform tailored to his form, his dark hair sleek, and his eyes . . .

Turning to her.

She stood at attention, keeping her face in the impassivity fitting an officer, while she struggled to control her galloping breath. Composed, urbane, droll. For years she'd practiced, and now the performance day had arrived.

"Lieutenant Commander Eaton." First Officer Bliss-Baldwin strode up to him. "Thank you for coming, sir."

She introduced the Wrens, and Lawrence responded with a nod to each lady, so genteel. Then he faced Dorothy.

He wasn't as tall as she remembered, not because he had diminished but because she had grown. "Surely this can't be Dolly Fairfax."

"I prefer Dorothy, sir." She kept her tone deep and modulated, her eyebrows high and her lids low. "I'm pleased to resume our acquaintance."

Had he noticed how much weight she'd lost? That her freckles had disappeared? That she was no longer a loud, overly dramatic schoolgirl?

A hint of a smile curved those finely formed lips. "A pleasure indeed. How long has it been? At least a decade."

"At least . . ." She trailed off as if she hadn't calculated the precise number of months. If only Papa hadn't been so inhospitable. She really ought to invite Lawrence to dinner.

His dark eyebrows bent. "I extend my condolences. I was so sorry when I heard . . ."

"Thank you." Time for that stiff upper lip. "I can't presume to take their places, but I'm serving the crown to the best of my ability."

A slow nod, then he stepped back. "I was honored when I received my orders, but after meeting such lovely and accomplished young women, I'm utterly delighted. Good day, ladies."

Then he was gone. But he'd return, and Dorothy could hardly breathe in her joy.

"Oh my." Muriel gave her the droll look Dorothy had been attempting to master. "He's rather good-looking, I do say."

"Rather." Gwen arched her blonde brows. "Titled family? Land?"

"Indeed." Dorothy turned to the blur of photographs on the table. He was everything she'd dreamed of in a man, so dashing and refined. Mum had often said Lawrence was the right sort of man for Dorothy, the exciting sort she needed to be happy.

And he'd be serving in the office next door.

For some reason, the parish rector's beatific round face came to mind, although she hadn't stepped foot in church in years. *"The hand of the Lord is upon you, my child."*

If she didn't know from experience that the hand of the Lord only slapped her around, she might believe him.

Luck, fate, or the hand of God—regardless, her dream was finally coming true.

ALLIED NAVAL EXPEDITIONARY FORCE HEADQUARTERS
THURSDAY, JANUARY 20, 1944

Wyatt followed Cdr. Joe Marino and Lt. Rudy Geier down a passageway in Norfolk House, their shoe leather slapping on the tile floors.

"I like what Eisenhower has to say," Commander Marino said. "They did well naming him to command the Allies in Operation Overlord. He's the right man."

Wyatt leaned closer. "He did a great job in the Med—"

"He did great work in the Mediterranean," Geier said. "North Africa, Sicily, Italy. Definitely the right man."

Marino looked over his shoulder. "Did you say something, Mr. Paxton?"

Wyatt wrestled back a grimace. "No, sir."

A long draw on his cigarette and Marino faced forward.

Typical. The hallway was wide enough for three, but Geier divided the space so that Wyatt had to walk behind, out of sight, out of earshot.

This past week, they'd visited Gen. Dwight Eisenhower's Supreme Headquarters and Adm. Alan Kirk's Western Naval Task Force Headquarters in London. They'd taken the train to Plymouth and Portsmouth and Southampton for still more headquarters. And all week Geier had edged him out.

Reminded him of Adler edging him out with Daddy at Paxton

Trucking. Geier even resembled Adler with his light blond hair, his social ease, and his need for the limelight.

Wyatt tamped down his jealousy. If Geier wanted the glory, he could have it. Wyatt just wanted to do his job.

If only he could, but today they'd returned to Adm. Sir Bertram Ramsay's Allied Naval Headquarters for more glad-handing.

"I swear," Marino said in a low rumble. "If I hear one more comment about how jolly good it is of us colonials to come help them out—well, I'll bop that man in the nose."

Wyatt chuckled. He hadn't heard the word *colonial*, and most of the British treated the Americans like true partners, but a few acted as if they were naughty children who'd come home late for tea.

"We'll spend the rest of today in intelligence. We'll work closely with them." Marino swung a door open.

Yeah, the room looked familiar. Teleprinters and maps and phones, Royal Navy officers and ratings, plus the "Wrens," like America's WAVES, wearing navy blue jackets and skirts.

"Commander Marino. Jolly good to see you." A dark-haired officer approached, but Wyatt couldn't remember his name. Never any good at names, unlike Adler. Much to Daddy's chagrin. *"Got to learn a man's name if you want his respect, son."*

Easier said than done.

"Lieutenant Commander Eaton." Marino solved the problem. "Good to see you too."

For the next half hour, Eaton described how his department interpreted intelligence from radio intercepts, resistance members, commando raids, and reconnaissance by air and sea.

Eaton had that upper-class sheen to him, but he was smart and fair and friendly. "You chaps can see the success of this operation depends on our work here."

Wyatt studied the map. The more information they had and the better they recorded it, the fewer men would die.

A familiar warmth stirred inside. He'd do his best to protect those men storming the beaches.

Eaton strode to the door. "Our Wrens are putting on a good show of it, plotting photographs and such from civilians. Come along."

"Excuse me, Lieutenant Commander Eaton?" a fresh-faced Wren called from a phone. "Commander Pringle wishes to speak with you, sir."

"Go on ahead." Eaton waved the Americans to the door. "I'll join you shortly."

Next door, the blonde Wren with the long stuffy name met them. "Welcome, Commander. We are thrilled you have come to aid us in our fight against the Nazis."

Wyatt stopped to gulp back a laugh. If Marino had known the next condescending comment would come from a lady, he wouldn't have promised a nose-bopping.

"Thank you, ma'am." Marino failed to keep his promise.

Geier tucked into a tight triangle between the lady and Marino. Wyatt would look ridiculous tapping on shoulders, like a pimply boy trying to cut in on the dance floor.

Instead, he circled the room, much like he'd done at high school dances, come to think of it. A map of the Norman coast covered the long wall of the room. Smart to select Normandy for the landings. The Nazis would expect the invasion in the Pas de Calais, where the English Channel was narrowest.

But Normandy . . . close enough for an overnight crossing to avoid detection, close enough for support from fighter planes, and close to the ports of Cherbourg and Le Havre.

"Would you like to see what we do here, sir?" A Wren stretched a string from a postcard on the wall down to a point on the map—the pretty redhead who'd set a protective hand over one of the photos in such a fascinating way.

The two light blue stripes on her sleeve cuffs identified her as an officer, but the Wrens had different names for the ranks than the men in the Royal Navy. And why couldn't he remember her name? "Yes, I would, Miss . . ."

"Second Officer Fairfax. And you are . . . ?"

His smile spread. At least she didn't expect him to remember. "Mr. Paxton."

"Mister? Oh yes, that funny American naval custom."

"You have to admit 'Miss Fairfax' would be less of a mouthful." After she smiled in acknowledgment, he gestured to the map. "So people just send in their snapshots?"

"The BBC put out a call under the guise of a contest, and we've received material from holidays all over the world, over a million photographs. This office concentrates on Normandy." Her face and voice were in constant motion as she talked, vivid and bright-eyed, and she had a mass of gorgeous red hair coiled in a knot low on her head.

Pretty little thing.

"For example . . ." She darted to the long table in the center of the room and handed him a black-and-white photograph. "Take a moment and study it."

A family of five stood on a beach, all wearing bathing suits, except the mother, who wore one of those shapeless dresses from the twenties. The father stood tall and beaming, his hands resting on the shoulders of two gangly boys of about ten or twelve. The mother stood to the side, gazing away from the camera. But the centerpiece of the picture was a plump little girl, standing on the seawall behind her daddy, with a big bow on her head. Maybe six years old, the little dumpling posed with hands on hips as if she were queen of the world.

"What do you see, Lieutenant Paxton?"

He tore his gaze from the dumpling to pretty blue eyes and back to the picture. "Um, a seawall, about five feet tall. A house in the background, not too far, two stories. A tree about fifteen feet from the house."

"Precisely. This shows the height and composition of the wall, and basic trigonometry tells us the distance from the house to the seawall. Piecing this together with other information, we can place this house here." She spun back to the map and pointed.

"That's fascinating, ma'am. And right useful."

"We can even tell the ground is shingle from how my brothers' toes dig in to the loose stones."

"Brothers?"

The vividness faded from her eyes, but then she pulled up that cute chin. "That's why I was attached to this unit. We used to take our holidays in Normandy, in that house."

This had to be the picture she'd protected. "So you're the little daredevil."

"I am." The words started on a high note of amused pride, then drifted to wistfulness. She returned the photograph to the table.

Had one of her brothers been killed in the war? Although Adler and Clay were still alive—as far as he knew—he understood that sense of loss. Wyatt opened his mouth to ask, but closed it. On board the troopship, he'd read *Instructions for American Servicemen in Britain*. The English didn't take kindly to personal questions from strangers, and he'd honor that.

The door opened. Eaton entered with two American admirals. Rats. Wyatt was on the wrong side of the room.

Second Officer Fairfax let out a soft gasp. Her fingertips fluttered to her cheek, and she smoothed her double-breasted jacket over her no-longer-plump belly.

Wyatt needed to meet the admirals. "Thank you, Second Officer. Very interesting."

"You're welcome." But she looked across the room.

Exactly where Wyatt needed to go, and he made his way around the long table.

Eaton passed him with a nod, then brightened. "Second Officer Fairfax. How are you today?"

"Fine, thank you, sir." Her tone changed, deep and languid, almost bored.

Strange. Wyatt glanced their way as he rounded the corner of the table.

The Wren rested her hip against the table, one arm draped along the edge, her eyes hooded like some model in a magazine. If Wyatt didn't know better, he'd swear that woman was Second Officer Fairfax's twin. "And how are you?"

"Better now that I've seen you. I never dreamed you'd grow up to be such a lovely woman."

So they'd known each other a while. Wyatt drew up behind the pack of officers by the door but didn't see a way in.

"Is that so?" Second Officer Fairfax drawled. "I never dreamed you'd grow up to be such a shameless flatterer."

Eaton gave a wry chuckle. "I believe in giving credit where credit is due."

He had the confidence and charm women liked. So did Adler. Oralee preferred it, and from the way the Wren leaned closer to Eaton, she preferred it too.

In the clump of brass in front of him, Geier said something, and the admirals chuckled.

A familiar tangle formed in Wyatt's stomach, and he fought to loosen it. That road only led to destruction.

3

"They have plenty of Weetabix this week. Would your grandmother like some?" Dorothy plucked two boxes of the cereal biscuits from the grocery shelf.

"Yes, thank you." Johanna Katin looked up with large brown eyes. "Thank you so much."

Dorothy clucked her tongue at her friend. "You mustn't thank me every single week. Papa and I are the only two people in Britain who don't consume all our rations. I'm happy to share, especially with your grandmother in poor health."

"Tha—" Johanna gave her darling slow smile and picked up a jar of mustard. "Ah, *Senf*. We haven't had any in weeks."

An elderly lady gasped and glared at Johanna.

Dorothy took her friend's arm and guided her to the next aisle. "How rude."

"I am used to it." Johanna settled the mustard in her basket, her black curls tumbling over her downcast face.

Heat simmered in Dorothy's chest. Johanna had been persecuted in Germany because she was Jewish, but her German accent drew suspicion in London. How terribly unfair.

"Let's see what other goodies we can find." She kept her voice cheery.

When Johanna had started working as a secretary at Fairfax & Sons in 1941, mutual grief had drawn Dorothy and Johanna to each other.

In 1935, Johanna's parents had sent her to London to live with her grandmother, but not one other Katin had joined them. Johanna hadn't heard a word in years and feared the worst, for good reason. The reports coming out of Nazi territory were horrific.

A grocer approached the counter with a tray.

"Eggs!" Dorothy was first in line. "I'll take two, please. And two for my friend. Do you have your book, Johanna?"

"Yes." She dug in her handbag.

Dorothy tucked the treasures into her basket. "Eggs are excellent for your grandmother's constitution, and Papa shall have poached eggs two mornings in a row."

"How is he?"

"The same." Dorothy trailed a finger down an empty shelf. "He's still losing weight, and he only went to the office twice this week. I can't imagine how the company is faring in his absence."

"Not well."

"Pardon?" Dorothy spun to her friend. "Not well? In what way?"

Johanna glanced away, her lips twisting. "It is only a rumor. Some say we are losing money although business is good. Very good."

"Oh dear." She pressed her hand to her stomach. If Papa's business failed, it would kill him.

"Do not worry." Johanna squeezed Dorothy's forearm. "Mr. Montague is a good man."

"I know. Thank you."

"Now, tell me, how is your Lawrence?"

"Hush. He isn't mine. But yes, he's as divine as I remember. And I know precisely what he likes in a woman."

"Because you spied on him, yes?"

"Eavesdropping, not spying. He likes a woman who is composed, urbane, droll—and that is the woman I've become."

Johanna didn't laugh, but her eyes . . .

Dorothy huffed. "All right, but I'm more like that than before, and when I'm with Lawrence I become that woman completely." It was the most glorious feeling.

"You did say you enjoyed playacting in school." Her voice lilted.

"I did, and I was rather good at it, I do say. My Desdemona brought the audience to tears." She flung back her head in a fake swoon, her wrist to her forehead.

"Composed . . . ?"

Dorothy laughed. "Oh, you."

After they paid the grocer and he stamped the ration books, they went out to the darkened street and said good-bye.

Dorothy shone her torch on the pavement, practicing her debonair ways. A long pace, chin high, eyelids low. The new Dorothy Fairfax thought carefully, spoke slowly, and was never excitable or impulsive.

She turned the corner, and a gentleman approached on the wrong side of the pavement. Dorothy dodged, caught her heel on a flagstone, and lost her balance.

"Careful." The man grabbed her arm.

Dorothy caught her breath. Thank goodness she hadn't fallen and broken the eggs.

"Sorry, miss. I wasn't watching where I was going." An American voice, like a cowboy in one of those Western films from Hollywood. A somewhat familiar voice.

She angled the torch toward his chest. He wore an American naval officer's uniform with two gold sleeve stripes for a lieutenant.

"Miss Fairfax? Second Officer Fairfax, I mean."

That shy officer with the soft gray-blue eyes and the startling scar across his cheek. "Lieutenant Paxton? What are you doing in Kensington?"

"Supposed to meet my buddies at a restaurant. They said I'd see it as soon as I stepped off the subway—I mean, the Underground. But I didn't. Reckon I'm lost."

"Did they say Kensington, South Kensington, or West Kensington?"

Silence, then a low chuckle. "Shucks. This is what happens when you set a country mouse loose in the city. Guess I'll head back to quarters. But wait—you've got your hands full. Let me help you."

If Papa didn't want Lawrence in the house, he certainly wouldn't want a stranger. But she could take the basket at the door. "Thank you, Lieutenant."

"You're welcome." He took the basket, leaving her with the torch. "I'm surprised they put you ladies up out here."

"Oh, I'm not billeted in the Wrennery. I live at home."

"Thought I spoke English, but I reckon I'm wrong. Wrennery— that's cute." Another chuckle. The Americans were always smiling and laughing.

Dorothy turned onto her street. "Is this your first time in London?"

"Yes, ma'am. Before 1941, I'd never left Texas. I've wanted to see London since the first time I read Dickens."

She sifted through the accent for the words. "There are many wonderful things to see, but I'm afraid most of the museum exhibits were moved to the country during the Blitz."

Lieutenant Paxton gazed at a gaping hole where homes had once stood. "Can't imagine how hard that must have been."

"We muddled through." She didn't miss the whine of the air raid siren, the roar of engines overhead, the searchlights slicing the night, the whistling bombs, the explosions, the shaking earth, the fires, the smoke.

The screams.

The ash-lined craters where mothers had once sipped tea.

Up with the chin. "We were glad when it ended. They send occasional nuisance raids, but they've learned their lesson."

Dorothy climbed the steps to her house and opened the door. She didn't call for Papa as usual but took the basket from Lieutenant Paxton. "Thank you for your help."

Something furry brushed past her ankle. "Charlie!"

"Well, hello there." Lieutenant Paxton stepped into the foyer and squatted. Charlie leaped at him, his little pink tongue darting and licking.

"Charlie, your manners. I do apologize. He's usually standoffish with visitors."

"I don't mind, ma'am." He ruffled Charlie's black fur. "Charlie's your name?"

"Bonnie Prince Charlie is his full name. He was my mother's dog. She loved Scotland and everything Scottish."

Lieutenant Paxton looked up, his square face quizzical and solemn.

Dorothy shouldn't have used the past tense. "She was killed in the Blitz."

"I'm sorry, ma'am." The compassion in his expression was deep and knowing, as with Johanna.

Tightness spread in her jaw, but she refused to let it quiver.

He stood, cradling the wiggling dog in his arms, and glanced to the table where her father displayed portraits of her brothers in uniform, but not of Dorothy in uniform. "Your brothers?" The hesitation in his voice said he already knew.

"Arthur was on the HMS *Glorious* when the Germans sank her, and Gilbert was on the *Hood*."

Lieutenant Paxton's shoulders slumped. Over a thousand sailors and officers had perished on each ship.

"I thought I heard voices."

Dorothy spun around. Papa stood at the top of the stairs outside his study, wearing a cardigan jumper and a frown. Oh bother. "Hallo, Papa. May I introduce Lieutenant Paxton? I met him at headquarters. He helped me with my parcels. Lieutenant, this is my father, Reginald Fairfax."

"How do you do, Mr. Fairfax?" Lieutenant Paxton tucked Charlie under one arm and shook hands with Papa after he made his way down the stairs.

"A Yankee."

No one would give Papa an award for hospitality. "Papa."

But Lieutenant Paxton chuckled. "Most of us Texans don't take kindly to being called Yankees. We prefer to be called rebels."

"As far as I'm concerned, all Americans are rebels."

"Yes, sir. We are. To make it worse, we're proud of it."

Dorothy held her breath.

Papa's frown shifted and reformed into something unfamiliar. Almost . . . a smile? "Honesty is a fine trait in a man. You'll be joining us for dinner, Lieutenant, will you not?"

She stifled a gasp.

"Thank you, sir." Lieutenant Paxton shot her an alarmed look. "But I just ran into your daughter, helped her, don't mean to impose."

"Nonsense. Dorothy, inform Mrs. Bromley—"

"I couldn't, sir." The lieutenant settled Charlie onto the floor. "I know rationing is tight and—"

"Balderdash. The Ministry of Food has too much power, but they cannot forbid me to entertain a guest. Dorothy?"

The alarm hadn't faded from the American's face, but Papa had insisted. She offered a polite smile. "Please stay."

"All—all right, then. Thank you, ma'am. Thank you, sir."

Papa gestured to the drawing room, and Lieutenant Paxton followed.

Dorothy marched to the kitchen with her groceries. Papa couldn't invite a family friend to dine, but he invited a stranger?

And how on earth would she and Mrs. Bromley expand the dinner to feed one more mouth?

She groaned and thrust open the kitchen door. This was not how she wanted to spend her evening.

4

Mrs. Bromley set a plate in front of Wyatt with a bigger portion of pie than on the family plates. He didn't dare protest. Better to consume more than his fair share than to insult a man's ability to provide. He smiled up at the white-haired lady. "Thank you kindly, ma'am."

She nodded and retreated to the kitchen.

Dim lamplight shone off the polished tabletop and china, and Wyatt studied his plate. Looked kind of like potpie.

"Lord Woolton pie, Lieutenant," Second Officer Fairfax said. "Lord Woolton was Churchill's first Minister of Food. The Savoy Hotel introduced the recipe and named it after him. None of the ingredients are rationed."

"Great." He forked some into his mouth. Potatoes, carrots, bland gravy. Could use some green chiles, but better than most of the food he'd had in England. "Very good."

Charlie bumped Wyatt's ankle. Maybe he'd sneak the little guy a bite. How many turnips had he dropped to Scruffy as a boy?

"How is your pie, Papa?" She pronounced her father's name with the emphasis on the second syllable—puh-PAW. Sounded classy with her British accent.

Mr. Fairfax glanced at his untouched plate, then took a bite.

Wyatt searched his brain for conversational topics—not his strength. "So what do you do, Mr. Fairfax?"

"Do?"

"He's asking about your business," Second Officer Fairfax said. "The carrots are nice and firm, the way you like them."

He took another bite without looking at his daughter. "What I do is run Fairfax & Sons. The company coordinates railway shipping for small manufacturers. We have offices in London and Edinburgh."

"Swell." Right up his alley. "I majored in business at the University of Texas."

Mr. Fairfax's eyes were the same blue as his daughter's but lacked their brightness. "Business at university? How unusual."

"It's practical. Accounting is what I like best. Working figures."

"It is rather practical." His face had a thin, sallow look, and he only seemed to eat when his daughter prompted him. Indeed, the redhead eyed her dad's plate with concern.

Maybe he could help. "Mighty good crust. Real hearty."

"Yes, it is. Mrs. Bromley has a nice hand with pastry." Mr. Fairfax took another bite.

Wyatt dropped the young lady a conspiratorial wink.

Her eyes widened, then one corner of her mouth flicked up. Mr. Fairfax never seemed to look at her, but if Wyatt had such a pretty, lively face in his home, he'd never stop looking.

"Why business, Lieutenant? Your family?" Interest sparked in his host's eyes.

Wyatt's neck stiffened, but the truth would come out eventually. "If we're going to talk about my life, y'all had better call me Wyatt."

They stared at him. Then the daughter cleared her throat. "White? Is that a nickname?"

He laughed. "Texas drawl. My name's Wy-att. And yours?"

She hesitated. "Dorothy."

"Dorothy. That's a fine name." He sampled his pie and smiled at Mr. Fairfax. "And this is fine gravy."

It worked. His host took a bite.

Time to wade into the swamp of his life. "I studied business because I'm the oldest son, and my dad expected me to take his place someday. He runs a trucking company, ships freight all over Texas. Similar to your company in many ways, I reckon."

"The oldest. Do you have other brothers?" Strange he didn't ask about sisters.

"Yes, sir. Two brothers, no sisters." His stomach constricted around his meal.

"Are your brothers Navy men as well?"

One more bite. He'd probably get kicked out soon. "I doubt it, sir. Adler will be needed in the business with me gone. It's vital to the war effort, so he should be exempt from the draft. And Clay should be studying medicine, so they won't draft him either."

"Should be?" Dorothy asked. "You don't know what your brothers are doing?"

"No, ma'am." His gaze fell away. "I haven't been home since '41, haven't been in contact."

"Why . . . why not?"

He forced himself to look at her, at her father. "It isn't a pretty story. Adler's fiancée died in a fall. It was an accident, but he blamed me and tried to kill me."

"Oh my goodness." Dorothy's face went white.

"I fled for my life." Wyatt's fingers coiled around his silverware. "First I drove home to tell my parents what happened. They agreed I should leave town for a few days, but after they left to fetch the doctor, I realized I didn't have any cash. I panicked. Clay had just withdrawn his college money from the savings and loan to deposit in a bank in Austin, and I stole it, all two thousand dollars. Worst thing I've ever done."

The silence accused him and his stomach shriveled, but he couldn't stop now. "I meant to pay him back as soon as I got settled in Charleston, but I let a friend talk me into starting a business. Thought I could double Clay's money in no time, but I didn't. We lost everything. That's when I joined the Navy."

The Fairfaxes stared at their plates, faces drawn.

"I save every penny I can. I've paid off our creditors, and I'll have Clay's money by summertime. But that doesn't erase what I did. I was wrong. I'm the Prodigal Son who squandered everything. Worse—I didn't squander my money but my brother's. That's why I can't go home. Not yet. Maybe not ever."

Mr. Fairfax didn't look up, but Dorothy did, her eyes watery with undeserved compassion.

Even though Wyatt hadn't eaten half his dinner, it was time to leave. "Well, Mr. Fairfax, when you said honesty was a fine trait, I doubt this is what you had in mind."

"No, it wasn't."

Wyatt folded his napkin and set it on the table. "Thank you for your hospitality. Please give my compliments to Mrs. Brom—"

"I didn't ask you to leave." Mr. Fairfax's watery gaze mimicked his daughter's. "When I said I admired honesty, son, I meant it."

A feminine gasp—from the statement or from the word *son*?

Wyatt swallowed hard. "Thank you, sir, but it's best—"

"It's best for you to finish your dinner." Mr. Fairfax sliced into his pie. "It takes courage for a man to admit his mistakes. It takes courage, humility, and honesty, and I admire those traits."

He deserved praise even less than compassion, but Mama always said turning down a compliment insulted the giver. "Thank you, sir." His voice sounded too throaty, and he coughed to clear it.

"You've lost a lot," Dorothy said in a tiny voice, her expression reaching, questioning.

The weight of mutual pain squeezed his chest. "The Lord pulled me through, holds me up every single day."

Dorothy jerked up her head and frowned at the ceiling. "Oh no."

Maybe he ought to leave after all.

Then a sound entered his ears, a low moan, climbing in pitch and intensity. "Is that—is that an air raid siren?"

"Nothing to worry about." Mr. Fairfax sipped his tea.

But Dorothy's gaze darted all over the ceiling. "I—I don't think this is a nuisance raid."

A long rumble swelled in the background. "Where do y'all go? Down into the Tube?"

Dorothy's gaze flew to him. "We have an Anderson shelter in the garden."

"Balderdash. No need to worry." Mr. Fairfax lifted his fork to his mouth.

Regardless, Dorothy looked worried. And that rumble was more than a handful of planes. Far more. "Dorothy, would you like to go to the shelter?"

"Yes—"

"You always nag me to eat, so eat." Mr. Fairfax pointed to Dorothy's plate.

Wyatt bolted to his feet. "Sir, I am taking your daughter to the shelter. Do you want her alone with a strange man, much less a Yankee, much less a thief? If you care about her reputation, you'll join us."

Mr. Fairfax gaped up at him, but Wyatt didn't budge.

"Come on, Dorothy. Show me the way."

"Fine." Mr. Fairfax shoved back his chair. "I didn't realize the Americans were a cowardly lot."

"Yes, sir. Cowards all. Why do you think it took us so long to join the battle?"

Dorothy strode down the hall. "Right this—oh dear. Charlie?"

Wyatt peeked under the table, but his little buddy wasn't there. "Where'd he go?"

"Oh dear. He hides in the larder under the shelves."

Thumps of antiaircraft fire added to the noise. "Where's the larder?"

Dorothy took her father's arm and headed toward the back of the house. "We don't have time, Lieutenant."

"Call me Wyatt, and where's the larder?"

She cast a surprised look over her shoulder.

He shook his head. "I won't leave him."

A sigh. "The kitchen's through that door."

"Thanks." Wyatt shoved it open. Nice big kitchen. An open door to his left—lots of shelves. And a whimper.

"Poor fellow." He squatted. "Here, Charlie. Come here, boy." There he was, wedged under a shelf.

A scared dog would bite.

A stack of towels sat on a shelf. Wyatt wrapped one around each hand, dragged out the squirming dog, and swaddled him. Cradling the dog to his chest, he found his way to the back door.

Outside, the war became real, even more real than shelling Japanese positions in the icy Aleutians.

Searchlights arced across the night sky, turning the clouds a sick shade of gray. The air raid siren keened, high . . . low . . . high . . . low. Airplane engines thrummed in a menacing beat. Antiaircraft guns thumped out a reply.

And the ground beneath him trembled.

Wyatt had watched the newsreels of the Blitz, when German bombers had blasted Britain almost every night for a year. He'd seen the footage of bodies in the rubble, of brave Londoners carrying on. But this was how it felt—small, naked, unarmed.

Charlie whimpered.

Wyatt pressed the dog's towel-covered ears to his head. "Come on, boy. Let's get you to safety."

That lump in the ground had to be the shelter. Earth had been piled over it, and a garden grew on top.

He scampered down stone steps and knocked on the corrugated steel door.

Dorothy flung it open. "Charlie? Oh, you naughty dog. Thank

you, Lieutenant—Wyatt." She took the dog, and the towels fell away.

"You're welcome." Stooping under the low arched ceiling, he shut the door behind him.

"Charlie, you mustn't hide. You mustn't." Dorothy hugged the pup and sank onto a cot beside Mrs. Bromley.

Wyatt sat on the other cot beside Mr. Fairfax and leaned his forearms on his knees. "Is this a normal raid or . . . ?"

Mrs. Bromley knitted by the light of a flashlight strung from the ceiling. She didn't answer, just kept humming.

Mr. Fairfax sat bolt upright, his face a mask. He didn't answer either.

And Dorothy rocked back and forth, murmuring to the dog.

Probably all she had left of her mama, and Wyatt's chest tightened.

Still the siren blared. Still the engines throbbed. Still the guns pounded.

This family had been fractured by death and grief, while his had been fractured by his own carelessness and sin.

An ache built inside, of loss and regret and a longing to help and heal and protect.

If only he could.

5

Teleprinters chattered and telephones buzzed, and Dorothy carried a stack of diagrams into the intelligence office. Generals Montgomery and Eisenhower had proposed landing five divisions for Operation Overlord rather than three, which meant postponing D-day from May 1 to June 1.

For Operation Neptune, the naval portion of the invasion, all plans had been thrown into disarray. More ships, more supplies, more convoy routes, and more beaches to survey.

Dorothy scanned the office, and her pulse fluttered. Where was he?

Lawrence and First Officer Bliss-Baldwin reviewed a report, standing too close for Dorothy's taste. An attractive woman and better bred than Dorothy.

And Lawrence hadn't asked Dorothy out yet.

Nonsense. She refused to obsess. For all she knew, Lawrence already had a girlfriend. Indeed, how could a man so handsome, charming, and cultured be unattached?

Dorothy greeted the officers and handed Lawrence her diagrams. "We're expanding our survey from Le Havre on the east to Cherbourg on the west with the most intense scrutiny between

Ouistreham and Quenelle." Thank goodness she'd excelled in French, her accent honed by summers in Normandy and Paris.

"Very good." Lawrence thumbed through the papers. "This work truly aids our analysis."

"Thank you, sir. We Wrens enjoy our duties."

"Very good, Second Officer," Bliss-Baldwin said. "Carry on."

"Aye aye, ma'am." She aimed a smile Lawrence's way—droll but professional—and turned toward her office.

A loud laugh in the corner. Lieutenant Geier held a rolled-up piece of paper, and he swung it in a giant arc as the Americans did in their game of baseball.

A Royal Navy officer plucked the fake bat from Lieutenant Geier's hand and demonstrated proper cricket batting form.

Dorothy shook her head. As much as she liked fun, they had work to do.

In fact, Wyatt stood by the wall map, taking notes. She'd over-looked him when she entered the office.

"Good afternoon, Lieutenant Paxton."

"Good afternoon, Second Officer Fairfax." His smile lacked surprise. He hadn't been so rude as to overlook her.

She'd have to make up for it, especially after his kindness on Friday. "Have you recovered from your first air raid?"

He dipped his chin and smiled. "I have. They say there were over four hundred bombers."

"They didn't do a terribly good job of it. Very little damage, scattered all over the south."

"And y'all shot down forty planes. Some of the fellows say they hope Fritz keeps this up. Then the Luftwaffe will be decimated before Overlord."

"Ah, you're learning the British black humor." She turned to the map. "You chaps must be busy with the change in plans."

"Yes, ma'am. We're concentrating on the two beaches to the

west. The British and Canadians are landing to the east—" He gave her a sheepish look. "You already know that."

She chuckled. "Carry on."

"First, we're locating the big gun batteries for the battleships to target—here at Morsalines, Quinéville, Émondeville, St.-Martin-de-Varreville, Maisy, Pointe du Hoc."

His French was atrocious. He pronounced it *point doo hock*. "Pwint doo oak."

He shrugged. "Too bad we're not invading Spain. I could pronounce those words just fine. As for these sites? I may not be able to pronounce them, but I can target them."

"That's what matters."

He tapped another spot. "Next come the cruisers and destroyers. They can come closer, target the smaller positions during the initial bombardment. After the landings, they'll be on call."

"And the spotter aircraft and the FOBs on the beaches will call for fire support."

"The Forward Officers, Bombardment? We Americans call them Shore Fire Control Parties, because we're rebels."

Dorothy crossed her arms and gave him a mock frown. "And you're proud of that."

"Yes, ma'am." Wyatt pointed to Vierville-sur-Mer. "This is the fun part of my job. For close fire support, we have to think like the Germans. Where will they hide machine-gun nests? Where will they erect barricades? Where will they concentrate their reserves? The more we can predict, the better we can prepare."

Dorothy didn't like how he focused on Vierville.

"For example, that picture of your family. There's a seawall, and right past that a little rise. If I were Field Marshal Rommel, I'd put a gun behind it."

She tucked in her lips, then stopped herself to protect her lipstick.

"Don't worry." His voice lowered. "We'll try not to hit your house."

"It isn't mine."

"But it's special to you, holds happy memories."

She hardly trusted her voice, but she raised a teasing smile. "See to it that you aren't as reckless with your guns as you are with your French."

That big grin again. *"Oui, oui, mademoiselle."*

Dorothy waved her hand as if she outranked him, which she didn't. "Very good. Carry on. At the double."

She strode toward her office and sneaked a glance at Lawrence. She'd acted rather silly with Wyatt, but Lawrence leaned over a map, his back to her.

Being sophisticated was hard work.

"Good evening, Papa!" Dorothy shut the door behind her.

He came downstairs from his study, as he had every evening this week. Usually he only called out his greeting. "You're late."

"I rang Mrs. Bromley, told her I had a sandwich at headquarters. We've been dreadfully busy."

"You received a letter in the post. I don't recognize the address or the hand."

"Probably an old school chum." She opened the envelope.

Dear Miss Fairfax,

I apologize for the subterfuge. This is James Montague from Fairfax & Sons. I used my daughter's address and hand-writing to send you this letter.

How odd. She'd best read this in private. "These shoes are pinching. I'll go change."

Papa fingered the hem of his gray wool jumper. "Did you see Lieutenant Paxton today?"

Dorothy blinked. He never asked about her duties, friends, or colleagues. "I did."

"When you see him next, invite him for dinner."

Dorothy removed her tricorn Wrens cap and set it on the coatrack. Of all the people for him to latch on to. "Papa, really. I don't want him to think I'm interested in him."

"I don't see why not. He's a nice-looking chap, I suppose."

She smoothed her hair. "If I liked the quiet sort, but I don't. Besides, you don't want me to fall in love with an American and move to the wilds of Texas. No more of this silly talk."

Papa marched to his study. "Invite him."

She had no intention of doing so.

Upstairs in her bedroom, she removed her uniform and put on an old tweed skirt and a thick creamy Scottish jumper with patched elbows, perfect for an evening with paint and easel in a chilly house.

Then she sat at her writing desk and read Mr. Montague's letter.

I hesitated to contact you, but I have little recourse. The company has been losing money over the last year or so, although business has been good. Rumors are circulating that someone is embezzling.

On the rare occasions that your father comes to the office, he is occupied with correspondence and I have little time to review the financial situation. When I do, he denies there is a problem.

I'm afraid someone will call an investigator. If there is wrongdoing, we could lose our contracts with the crown, which would ruin the company. I wish to resolve this situation quietly before a scandal breaks.

If you have any influence, I beg you to persuade him to return to his duties. Then he will see how dire the situation is and open a discreet investigation.

Please do not mention this letter to him. You may reply at this address. If you'd like, we can meet for tea to discuss the matter.

"Oh, Papa." Dorothy leaned back in her chair and pressed her hand to her stomach. If his company failed, it would destroy him. If a scandal broke, it would kill him.

But what could she do? He scorned her nagging, and she couldn't discuss the matter with him without admitting Mr. Montague had written her. Papa would be incensed at his manager's interference and would fire him. Then the company would be in even worse shape.

Since she couldn't reply to the letter in her unsettled state, she hid it in her desk drawer.

In the hallway, she leaned over the railing. Downstairs, pale light emerged from under the door to Papa's study, and her heart churned for her father.

How could she have any influence over him when he had no regard for her?

In the room she and her brothers had called the conservatory, she pulled on a paint-splattered smock and readied her supplies. She could do nothing for her father.

As a young girl, she would have prayed, her heart open and expectant.

Shades of brown and gray mixed on her palette, and she applied them to the canvas in stark, heavy strokes.

In those days, she'd believed the parish rector, a man with a glowing countenance, who talked about the Lord with boundless enthusiasm. She'd believed him, believed the Lord loved plump, freckled, loud little Dolly Fairfax.

Her youthful artwork had been filled with nonsense like fairies and ferns and flowers, all done in bright watercolors, the colors as wispy and naïve as her faith.

A tiny squeeze of red paint onto her palette, mixed with a dash of black and yellow.

Since the Blitz she'd favored oil paints, opaque and real. Now her stock was running low, and oil paints were dear with all the shortages.

Dorothy studied her painting. Once again, the subject was the house outside Vierville. This rendition was at dusk, muted and shadowy. The house stood off-kilter, with a scarlet hue in the windows. She hadn't decided if it was the glint from the sunset—or from a fire inside. She only knew it was red.

With the back of her hand, she rubbed her forehead.

This was her reality. The land she'd roamed occupied by the enemy. The house soon to be leveled by her allies. Her family shattered.

She was alone and unloved, without even faith to sustain her.

More red in the windows, but it blurred in her vision and she pressed her forearm over her mouth and nose to stifle the sudden sob.

What had gotten into her? "Nonsense. Chin up."

She hadn't given the Lord a second thought in ages, so why now?

More gray—more gray on the roof, the roof that was about to be blown to smithereens by naval shells.

She stood up straighter. Wyatt Paxton.

He talked about the Lord the same way the rector did, as if God cared. While Dorothy could dismiss the rector's faith due to his happy life, she couldn't dismiss Wyatt's faith the same way.

He'd lost his family as surely as she'd lost hers, with sin and personal failing on top, yet his faith remained.

Dorothy tore off her smock, balled it up, and tossed it into the corner, where it pinged off a string on Gil's Spanish guitar. Once this room had resounded with music and Shakespearean lines and spirited discussions over paint and canvas.

But not tonight, and never again.

Wyatt had lost his family by choice. She hadn't.

6

"Wish I had that report," Rudy Geier said. "I'd love to review it."

Wyatt turned right onto Grosvenor Square. If Geier had put any work into the report, he wouldn't need to review it. "Even if you had it, you couldn't read it in public."

Geier laughed. "See? That's why we make a great team."

Team didn't seem like the right word when Wyatt had written a good 90 percent of that report, but he only raised an eyebrow to ask for clarification.

Geier knifed his arm toward the gigantic block of buildings at 19 Grosvenor Square, longer than a football field. "You're like this. Every brick neat and in order. You're good with regulations and tables and charts, all those fussy little details."

Funny how the man made a compliment sound insulting. "Thanks."

"I'm like this." Geier swept his other arm toward the park that filled the square. Trees towered over green grass under a blue sky speckled with clouds. "Wide open, unplanned. I'm good with people, making connections, building bridges."

"We do have different strengths."

Pale blue eyes shone in the sunshine, and Geier clapped Wyatt on the back. "That's why we make a great team."

Wyatt smiled. True. Every man like Geier needed a man like Wyatt to do his work for him.

"Did you have a good weekend?" Geier could be plenty friendly when Marino wasn't around.

"Sure. Jack and I looked around near the Tower of London and St. Paul's Cathedral."

"No hot dates?"

"Nope. How about you?"

"Sure did." They entered the white-columned façade of 19 Grosvenor Square and removed their covers. As they traipsed down the hallway, Geier chattered about his date with a British girl he'd met on the Underground.

Last week Wyatt had considered asking Dorothy out. She intrigued him, so cheerful and strong despite all she'd lost. Although her father barely paid her any mind, she looked after him with care that seemed born of affection not duty.

He climbed the stairs, awful fancy for an office building.

Where could he have taken Dorothy anyway? He couldn't spend money on a date. That'd be stealing from Clay all over again. And a man without funds had no business asking out a woman like Dorothy Fairfax.

Just as well he hadn't asked. Yesterday, he'd dropped by Norfolk House for some data, and he'd overheard Lawrence Eaton invite her to dinner. She'd accepted, although she acted uninterested. However, as soon as Eaton left the room, Dorothy ran squealing to her girlfriends.

It was clear. Dorothy had known the man for years and had a crush on him.

At least Wyatt's debt saved him the embarrassment of rejection. And he could nip his own crush in the bud.

Wyatt opened the door to Commander Marino's office, crowded with his fellow officers.

Jack Vale joined him by the door, looking pale. "Ready?"

"Yep." He knew his material and couldn't wait to present it. "How about you?"

"Nervous." Jack ran his hand over his dark brown hair. "It's swell that Marino's giving his junior officers a chance to do the presentations, but this is an admiral. Admiral Kirk."

"You'll do great. You always do." He gave an encouraging smile.

"Ready to cover for Geier?" Jack said in a low voice.

"I don't mind as long as the work gets done."

Geier stood talking with Marino by the commander's desk. Marino looked over Geier's shoulder at Wyatt, then back to Geier and he nodded. What was that about?

Commander Marino worked his way to the door. "Let's go, men."

Wyatt and Jack followed the group of officers in dress blues down more hallways and up more stairs.

The Allied Naval Expeditionary Force had just released the Initial Joint Plan for Operation Neptune, and now Rear Adm. Alan Kirk, commander of the Western Naval Task Force, had requested reports from all divisions.

An amphibious assault on this scale had never been undertaken, and many interlocking components were required to make it work.

Ships needed ports, oil, and maintenance. Sailors needed food, housing, and training. Then the ships needed to be loaded and arranged in convoys. The shipping lanes needed to be swept of mines and protected from attack.

During the assault phase, the Navy would bombard and would guide landing craft to the beaches. Then in the build-up phase, convoys would ferry reinforcements and supplies.

It was a massive operation. Wyatt grinned at Jack. What an honor to play even a small role.

Marino led his officers into a conference room, where they met Adm. Alan Kirk. A trim man in his fifties with lean features, Kirk had experience as a military attaché in London, on destroyers, in intelligence, and in the landings in the Mediterranean—a perfect blend for Neptune.

The officers sat around a long table. Jack looked gray, so Wyatt sent him a smile. They frequently joked about how sociable Jack hated public speaking but reserved Wyatt loved it.

Marino introduced his division's work and called up Jack's team. They were coordinating communications with the Royal Navy, the Shore Fire Control Parties, and the RAF pilots who would serve as air spotters. Jack's team took turns presenting their report, sharing the credit as they'd shared the work. Despite a warble in Jack's voice, he came across as bright and knowledgeable.

When he finished, Wyatt gave him a discreet thumbs-up.

Commander Marino stood again. "Now we'll hear from Mr. Geier."

Wyatt winced at the oversight and scooted his chair back.

But Marino caught his eye, shook his head, and motioned for Wyatt to sit.

He obeyed because he was ordered to, but his jaw drifted low.

What was going on? Geier had only read the report once. He had no depth of knowledge and wasn't familiar with the background and details.

Geier stood with a confident smile, his blond hair sleek. He presented the report—Wyatt's report!—in a superficial way. He kept referring the officers to the report, kept saying, "I don't want to bore you with facts and figures," and kept up that cocky stance and breezy manner.

What a phony.

"Any questions?" Geier asked.

Vindictiveness knotted in Wyatt's gut. Now he'd get nabbed.

Admiral Kirk flipped through papers. "None at this point. The report is thorough and well written. Excellent work."

Geier bowed his head. "Thank you, sir. We worked hard on it."

That knot burned inside. *We?* Now he chose to be humble and inclusive?

More teams presented, but Wyatt couldn't listen, couldn't see, couldn't look at Jack or Geier or Marino, and he couldn't leave. But he had to control his jealousy. Had to.

Wyatt drew slow breaths, praying, cooling down, unraveling that deadly knot. It didn't matter who presented. It didn't matter what the other officers thought of him. The work was done and done well, and nothing else mattered.

At last they were dismissed. While the men chatted, Wyatt tucked his officer's cover under his arm and sneaked out.

"Wy! Wait for me." Jack jogged up beside him. "What happened in there? Why did Geier do the presentation when you did all the work?"

Wyatt's footsteps resounded in the hallway. "Most, not all."

"That's more credit than he gave you."

"Reckon Commander Marino thought he'd do a better job speaking." Was that what they'd conferred about in Marino's office? He could imagine what Geier might have said—how Wyatt was too shy, too awkward, too obsessed with numbers.

Wyatt flexed his fingers. It didn't matter, didn't matter one bit.

"Why'd you let him take credit for your work?"

"The commander ordered me to stay seated. And Geier didn't actually take credit."

Jack led the way down the stairs. "You've got to stand up for yourself."

He exhaled a long stream of air to calm down. "I refuse to let jealousy control me."

"Jealousy?" Jack stopped at the bottom of the stairs, eyebrows twisted. "What's jealousy have to do with it?"

Wyatt strode past his friend toward the front door. "Who cares if I get credit?"

"But if Commander Marino thinks Geier does all the work, he'll edge you out for projects."

"So what?" If he kept telling himself that, he'd come to believe it.

Jack shook his head. "You always say you don't want to fail. But if Marino gives a crucial project to Geier instead of you, and Geier fails . . ."

Wyatt sucked in a breath. Then the project would fail. Possibly endangering the invasion.

Nonsense. He was thinking too highly of himself again—the only man who could save the invasion, the only man who could protect Oralee.

He shoved open the door and slipped his cover onto his head. "Geier won't fail. He's plenty capable when he puts his mind to it."

"Hope you're right." Out on the sidewalk, Jack checked his watch. "Say, it's noon. Want to find some fish and chips? We have an hour before our next meeting."

His face scrunched up. "Transportation costs are killing my budget—"

"My treat and don't argue." Jack whacked him on the arm and marched across the street. "I was supposed to treat you for your birthday that night at the restaurant when you got lost."

Wyatt checked to the left and stepped off the curb.

A horn bleated at him, and he hopped back as a black taxi sped by—from the right. Kept forgetting to look the other way.

On the other side of the street, Jack spread his hands wide in mock exasperation. "You'd do anything to get out of doing something fun."

A glance to the right, and Wyatt jogged across to his friend. "I like fun. As long as it's free."

They stepped through a split in the hedge around the park. "I know you want to pay off your debt, but you have to stop punishing yourself."

Not until every penny was paid off, with interest and a hefty fine. "I miss them, you know."

"Your family?"

A huge silver barrage balloon lay limp on the grass, waiting for the next air raid. "Adler and I fought, but we loved each other. And Clay? He could do no wrong. The nicest kid. If anyone picked on him for being half-Mexican? Well, that's one time Adler and I always agreed. No one picks on our kid brother."

"Yeah. I have a little sister. I understand."

"That's why it hurts. I always stood up for Clay—until I betrayed him. That's why I have to pay him back. I want my family back. They may not forgive me, but I've got to try."

"You could write now, let them know the money's coming, send what you have."

"Nope." Wyatt picked up a pebble on the path and chucked it into the grass. "Every penny. I need proof that I'm sorry, that I know I was wrong and regret what I did."

Jack shrugged. "You should at least let them know you're alive."

Wyatt chuckled. "Once they have my address, I may no longer be alive. The Paxton boys—well, Adler has a hot temper. And Clay—he has a long fuse and a longer burn."

"And you?" Jack edged to the side with a comical look.

Wyatt winked. "You don't want to find out."

Jack laughed. "Still—"

"Nope. Absolutely not."

"Stubborn old Wyatt. Your theme song should be 'All or Nothing at All.'"

A slow smile. Yes, it should.

7

"I don't like all that paint on your face."

Dorothy suppressed a groan and studied herself in the mirror by the door. "It's the twentieth century, Papa. Women wear makeup."

"I don't care. I don't like it. I hardly recognize my own daughter."

That was the idea. Not one freckle showed, mascara made her eyes shine, and a burnished shade of lipstick complemented her hair color and would accentuate every droll smile.

"I wish you'd step out with Wyatt instead of Lawrence."

Why wouldn't he give up? With an affectionate smile, she faced her father. "I've adored Lawrence for years. He's so exciting."

Papa's face turned to stone.

Footsteps sounded on the front steps, and Dorothy's heart bounded. "Now, be kind, Papa."

She waited for the doorbell to ring, counted to ten so she wouldn't look eager, and opened the door.

Lawrence removed his officer's cap. "Good evening, Dorothy."

How could any man be so unspeakably handsome? "Good evening. You remember my father." She stepped back from the doorway.

"I do." His eyebrows sprang, but then he recovered and smiled. "Good evening, Mr. Fairfax. It's good to see you again, sir."

Papa returned his handshake but not his smile. "Lieutenant Commander Eaton. You don't seem changed at all."

"Thank you, sir." His hazel eyes shone. "That's a fine compliment."

"If you choose to see it that way. Good evening." He retreated to his study.

Dorothy glared after him. She worked so hard to save that man's neck, and now she wanted to wring it.

"Shall we?" Lawrence held open the door.

She glided down the steps to the cab and slid into the backseat. Lawrence joined her and tapped the back of the driver's seat. The cab pulled away.

Now she could apologize for her father's rudeness. She faced Lawrence, opened her mouth . . . and halted.

He leaned close, his expression intent. "Please excuse my impertinence, but there's something I must do."

He was so close she couldn't speak, this man she'd loved for a decade, and he pressed his lips to hers, smooth and confident.

All too soon, he pulled away. "Pardon me, but I couldn't think of anything but kissing you. Now it's taken care of, and I shall be able to concentrate properly on you over dinner."

Dorothy struggled to catch her breath. How was *she* supposed to concentrate on conversation? All she'd be able to think about was that kiss.

Somehow she had to be droll. "I'm glad we put that unpleasantness behind us." A tiny lift to the corner of her mouth to say she'd found the kiss anything but unpleasant.

A chuckle, and Lawrence settled back in his seat.

If only her friends could see how sophisticated she was acting. "Where are we dining?"

"At the River Restaurant at the Savoy."

Her breath stopped—for a different reason. "The Savoy? Isn't that near where the Nazis bombed last night?"

"The hotel wasn't damaged."

She clenched the strap of her handbag. Didn't he remember her mother had died in an air raid? "What if they come back tonight? They often do. They often target the same area."

"That's the fun of it—taking risks, flirting with danger." The darkness concealed his expression, but not the disappointment in his voice. "I thought you were the sort of girl who liked excitement."

Oh no. How could things have gone so wrong, so quickly? "I—I do like excitement. Very much."

"Ah, that's more like it." His voice warmed. "I seem to recall a girl who always wanted to join her brothers' escapades."

"I did." She made what she hoped was a charming pout. "But they always excluded me. Terribly unfair."

"Terribly wise." Lawrence laughed. "I'm afraid I was a rather poor influence on your brothers. Did they tell you about the time I absconded with some poor Frenchman's motorbike?"

She clucked her tongue. "You did no such thing."

"I did. And the three of us—all three of us on that motorbike—careened through the village—upsetting apple carts and such. I'm afraid we wreaked a bit of havoc."

She laughed at the amused regret in his tone. "Please tell me that was the end of it."

"If only I could, but I'm a frightful rogue."

He was, and she adored him. "Do tell me more."

For the rest of the cab ride, he regaled her with anecdotes. Not only was he a delightful storyteller, but his tales brought back happy memories of Art and Gil and Normandy. And when he did the talking, being sophisticated only required occasional clever comments.

They arrived at the Savoy, and Lawrence led her inside. "There was the time we found a bottle of Calvados—I won't say who found it or how—and the three of us drank it in one sitting. I believe a herd of goats was involved in that night's havoc, but I can't quite remember."

As he helped with her coat, she gazed up at him through her lashes. "I didn't realize what a naughty boy you were."

"But your father did. It appears he hasn't forgotten." He made an adorable hangdog face.

"If you can behave yourself, I daresay he'll forgive you."

"But I'm not behaving myself. I'm taking his daughter out on the town, and I'm not to be trusted." His eyes glinted.

A tingle shivered its way from her belly to her throat. He was sublime.

As they were escorted to their table, Dorothy tried not to stare at the elaborate furnishings and the well-dressed patrons. A sophisticated woman would be accustomed to such things, so she tried to look blasé. Since a woman in uniform was always well dressed, she refused to bemoan her lack of silk, lace, and jewels.

At the table, Dorothy studied the menu and ordered the *suprêmes de volailles Jeannette*.

"Speaking of your father . . ." Lawrence frowned at the candlestick. "I'm saddened to find him so altered."

She smoothed her serviette in her lap. "The war's been hard on him, I admit, but he's muddling through." No need for him to know how poorly Papa was doing or about the potential scandal at Fairfax & Sons.

"I'm glad you're stationed in London."

"I am too. I hope I can stay."

He tilted his head. "Why wouldn't you?"

"First Officer Bliss-Baldwin believes it's the duty of every Englishwoman to tour the Empire. She's determined to have me transferred. I've told her I don't wish to serve overseas, but she won't listen. She said she's going to draw up the papers for me, but I won't sign them."

His smile gleamed in the candlelight. "You'd like her to relent."

"Yes, but she won't."

"I'll talk to her. She'll listen to me."

Dorothy sat up taller. "Would you? I'd appreciate that. I told her my father needed me at home. She asked, 'Why? How old is he?' I told her he was fifty-four, and she said, 'Why, that isn't old at all. Is he an invalid?'"

Bliss-Baldwin's clipped tones were fun to mimic, and Dorothy added the woman's signature gestures. "'No, he isn't an invalid,' I told her. 'But he misses my mother and brothers, and I'm all he has.' Then she said, 'He needs a stiff upper lip. We have all made sacrifices in this war, and he mustn't hold back a good officer.'" She mimicked the imperious expression with a flourish.

Lawrence hailed the waiter, who brought over a basket of bread. He hadn't responded to her.

Her mouth went dry. What had she done? Jolly Dolly had reared her fat, freckled head.

While Lawrence buttered his bread, Dorothy pulled herself together. Composed, urbane, droll. "Now, Lawrence, you've told me about your mischief in Normandy. Surely you were better behaved at Cambridge."

He chuckled. "Surely you know better."

It was safer to let him talk. She leaned forward, listened, and responded properly, locking naughty Dolly back in her room where she belonged. If only being droll Dorothy weren't so difficult.

8

KENSINGTON GARDENS
SUNDAY, FEBRUARY 6, 1944

Wyatt drank in the scent of earth and grass and water. As much as he loved London, he pined for the country. Kensington Gardens helped fill that void.

"Who's up for a swim?" Jack pointed to the marble pools of the Italian Gardens. "Awful hot today."

Wyatt laughed and stuck his gloved hands in the pockets of his overcoat. It was maybe forty degrees. "Go ahead. Dare you."

Ted Kelvin leaned back against a stone urn. "Yeah, Vale. Bet you two bucks you won't."

"I'll toss in another two." Jerry Hobson crossed his arms. "It'd be worth it to see your teeth chatter."

Jack, the only one of the four men without an overcoat, glanced back at them with a gleam in his eye. "Four bucks? Easiest money I'll ever make."

Good thing Wyatt didn't have anything to chip in. Jack would take that dare, and Wyatt would have lost the money. But he could still egg him on. "He won't do it, fellows. He's full of hot air."

Jack took the bait. He plopped onto a bench and pulled off his black shoes and socks.

"Hey, if you frolic in that fountain, I'll even throw in a buck."

Jack squinted up at him as he rolled up the legs of his navy blue trousers. "You go too far. Frolicking is conduct unbecoming an officer. Unbecoming a man."

So was wading in greenish water among the lily pads, but Wyatt just grinned at his friend. Best entertainment of the month.

"Paxton's right. One toe in that water, and he'll go crying for Mommy." Ted curled his fingers before his chest, drew up one leg, and squealed like a little girl.

Wyatt flapped his arms like a chicken. "Bawk."

That pushed Jack over the edge. He marched to the nearest pool. "I'll show you who's chicken."

"Excuse me, young man." An elderly man strode up to Jack. "What in heaven's name do you think you're doing?"

"Um . . . wading, sir."

"Absolutely not. These are ornamental fountains and not for bathing."

"I beg your pardon, sir. I didn't know."

"Yanks." The Londoner marched away. "We fight off the Nazi invasion, and then we invite these savages right in."

Jack looked so chagrined, so disappointed, so ridiculous in his bare feet—Wyatt burst into laughter, Ted and Hobson right with him.

"Yeah? Go ahead and laugh." Jack sat on the bench and rolled down his pant legs. "You owe me four bucks because I was going in."

Something bumped Wyatt's leg.

A black dog sat in front of him and pawed his shin. A Scottie dog like . . .

"Charlie!"

He spun around.

Dorothy ran down the path, her unbuttoned coat flapping, one hand clamped on her cover and the other dragging a leash. She stopped at the bench, her mouth and eyes round. "Lieutenant Paxton—Wyatt?"

He laughed and squatted down to ruffle the dog's ears—and to conceal the breadth of his smile. "Second time I ran into you. We're out for a Sunday afternoon stroll. I promise I'm not following you."

She laughed too, such a pretty sound. "No, but it appears my dog is following you."

Better remember his manners. He scooped the pup into his arms and stood. "Second Officer Fairfax, these are my friends, Lieutenants Jack Vale, Ted Kelvin, and Jerry Hobson. Fellows, this is Second Officer Dorothy Fairfax—and this is Bonnie Prince Charlie."

Jack shook Dorothy's hand. "So you're the one who adopted the orphan boy when he got lost."

"I am." Then she glared at her dog. "And you are the naughtiest creature."

"I don't mind." Wyatt scratched Charlie behind the ears. "I miss having a dog."

Her eyes looked even bluer in the sunshine. "I don't know what got into him. He's usually so good. I let him off the lead to chase squirrels—he believes they're all Nazi spies—instead he abandoned his duties and chased after you."

Wyatt shifted his gaze from blue eyes to black. "Charlie and I are buddies—war buddies. Something special happens when men go through battle together, right, Charlie?" With those heavy black brows, the dog looked like a grizzled old sea salt.

"I suppose so," Dorothy said.

As much as he enjoyed seeing her, she was dating Eaton and he'd better get moving. But his friends had pulled to the side and were talking to each other. One more minute, and he'd make his escape.

"I don't believe I properly thanked you for bringing him into the shelter." She tucked a loose strand of hair into her bun. "I appreciate it."

"Shucks. It was the right thing to do." The Luftwaffe had bombed

London twice more since that evening—nothing big but still disconcerting. "How's your father doing?"

One cheek puckered. "The same."

"Well, I'm praying for him. At least the war is turning around. You know it better than most women."

Her lips bent in a sad smile. "I do."

"Say, Wyatt," Hobson called. "We're going to find a pub and get some chow."

"Teatime." Ted crimped his pinkie finger. "The British get two dinners. Why did we fight for our independence again?"

Wyatt's stomach sank. It would be rude to go to a pub and not order anything.

Jack knew he couldn't afford to go, but he was inspecting the polished toe of his shoe and didn't meet his eye.

"Sorry, fellows. I'll pass. See y'all back at quarters."

"Suit yourself." His friends didn't argue, didn't offer to pay for him, and they left. Jack dropped a quick wink over his shoulder.

What? Did they think they were helping, leaving him alone with Dorothy? He'd told Jack about her—but he'd also told him she was dating someone.

Wyatt handed the dog to Dorothy. "Well, it was nice seeing you two. Enjoy your afternoon."

She chewed her lips as if deep in thought. "My father keeps asking about you."

"That's nice of him."

"Do you suppose—I understand if you have plans—but would you mind stopping by for a little while? Only a little while."

That didn't seem wise. He needed to keep his distance. Yet her father . . . something about that man. "Sure, I could drop in for a few minutes."

"Thank you." Her face relaxed. "He's asked about you almost every day."

And this was the first time she'd mentioned it. He stepped over a stone curb and crossed a grassy strip to the path. Things like that would help him keep his heart in check.

"It's too nice a day for you to be in quarters anyway." She set Charlie on the path, his leash clipped back onto his collar. "Chilly, but not dreary."

"I like it. And I like this park. Almost forget I'm in a city."

"Isn't it splendid?" She strolled down the tree-lined path. "Charlie and I love to come here on walks."

"Hunting spies?"

"Oh yes. He's a member of His Majesty's Royal Highlanders, after all."

"I see." Boy, how this woman made him smile. He walked a good five feet from her so she knew he didn't see this as a date. Just to be safe, he'd mention her boyfriend. "So I understand you and that Eaton fellow go way back."

If only *his* name made her brighten so quickly. "We do. He and my brothers were Cambridge chums. He didn't like going home on holidays, so he often came home with Art and Gil. He even came to Normandy with us one summer."

Wyatt gave her a brotherly smile. "And now y'all are dating."

She gasped.

"Gossip gets around."

"It does. But it was only one dinner." Her dreamy look said otherwise.

"How was it?"

"Simply divine." She told him all about the fancy restaurant and the fancy food with long French names.

Wyatt could never afford a date like that, the kind of date she deserved, so he was glad he'd asked. She was crazy about Eaton, and now Wyatt could give his crush a proper burial.

If only she'd stop being so cute and animated and enthusiastic. If only she'd stop breaking into her musical laughter. If only she'd stop mimicking the people she'd seen. She sure didn't make it easy.

"Oh, look. Here's Peter Pan." She passed Charlie's leash to Wyatt and hopped up two steps onto the low flagstone pedestal. Peter Pan topped a bronze hill teeming with bronze fairies, rabbits, and squirrels.

Dorothy put her hands on her hips, looking for all the world like the little dumpling on the seawall—except she was trim and womanly now. "I always wanted to be Wendy."

"Why is that?" He led Charlie in a circle around the statue.

"Isn't it obvious?" She stepped up onto a bronze outcropping and grabbed a fairy's arm for support. "How thrilling for a girl to be spirited away by a dashing boy into a world full of adventure."

"For a little while, sure."

"A little while?"

"Yeah." He caught her eye from the far side of the statue. "It's no way to live. Peter Pan will never grow up. She had no future in Neverland. That's why she went home."

"You're a very practical sort of person, Lieutenant Paxton." Her Winston Churchill impression was spot-on.

"I am."

"Oh, I'm not. I'm just like my mother. I like excitement." She leaned away from the statue and swung one black-stockinged leg in front of her. Her foot wobbled.

"Careful there." Wyatt lunged forward and grabbed her arm as she landed. "Still the daredevil, I see. You all right?"

"I'm fine." She took back the leash and headed down the path. "That ankle is weak. I sprained it a few years ago."

"How'd that happen? Climbing statues? Trees? Seawalls?"

She gazed down at Charlie, his stubby legs in motion. "A word of advice. If you ever search for your mother's body in the rubble, do remember to wear sensible shoes."

Wyatt's heart and feet stood still.

Dorothy turned to him and sighed. "I'm sorry. You Americans aren't used to our black humor. It's how we endure."

"I understand." Wyatt resumed walking. To his left, a long lake flashed in and out of sight between the trees and bushes. A wide lawn opened up to his right, marred by bomb craters and sandbagged antiaircraft batteries, but brightened by older couples strolling, children playing, and British and American servicemen arm-in-arm with their girlfriends. "When your mama died—was that when your father shut down?"

One corner of her mouth tucked in. "We were never close—he was always closer to my brothers—but he was kind and warm. Then Art died, then Mum, then Gil. All within one year. Papa . . . he lost interest in everything."

Including his own daughter. "I'm sorry."

"He barely eats. It's hard to believe, but he was rather hefty before the war. And . . . well, he rarely goes to the office. I'm worried, and that's why I invited you today. He likes you, and he ate well that evening. Maybe you'll cheer him up, stir his appetite."

"Maybe I can talk him into going to work." He pictured himself wagging his finger at the older man, and he smiled.

"That would be lovely."

Wyatt shook his head and chuckled. "Don't know, but I'll see what I can do."

A squirrel zipped across the path. Charlie barked, loud and deep, and pulled at the leash. The squirrel scampered up a tree and chattered down at the dog.

"Hush now." Dorothy tugged on the leash and brought Charlie back to her side.

Kerrville, Texas, had a park, but nothing like this. Kensington Gardens stretched out in all directions, with city buildings peeking over the treetops in the distance. How incredible to be in a park where kings and queens had strolled for hundreds of years, to be surrounded by history in every blade of grass.

Rats. He hadn't spoken for a while.

But Dorothy hadn't either. Probably wished she were with Eaton. That man would have no trouble making conversation.

"Wyatt?" she said. "Didn't you tell my father you were an accountant?"

"Yes, ma'am."

"Could I ask you something? Your opinion? It's rather strange, and I can't puzzle it out."

"Well, sure."

She recounted a letter from her father's manager about how the company was losing money although sales were good, about rumors of embezzlement, the need for discretion, and the necessity of Mr. Fairfax returning to the office to handle the situation.

Sounded messy to him. "Too bad I can't see the books, see what's going on."

"Could you?"

He waved his hand back and forth to wipe the idea from her mind. "Just trying to figure it out. I think better when I see numbers. But it does give me an idea. Sometimes you look at things so often you can't see the obvious. Maybe Mr. Montague needs a fresh set of eyes."

"What do you mean?"

"Not me, of course, but an accountant from outside the company to look at the books and trace the money."

Her mouth scooted to one side. "I wish we could, but Papa would never agree. He's very proud. Our only hope is to convince him to return."

Wyatt would have an easier time with the books than with persuasion.

"Thank you anyway. And please don't mention this to anyone. Papa would be mortified."

"Wouldn't dream of it."

"Thank you." She pointed across an expanse of grass to an

elaborate monument. "That's the Albert Memorial, and Prince Albert Hall across the street. How Queen Victoria loved him."

She led him across the street and into the neighborhood, chatting like a tour guide, pointing out the Royal Geographical Society and the Royal College of Music and the Natural History Museum and the Victoria and Albert Museum, with colorful stories attached to each one.

He still couldn't believe he was in London, a city that had stood since Roman times. No building in Kerrville dated before 1850.

Soon she turned onto a smaller street, but he had no idea which one. He hadn't seen a single street sign. No wonder he'd gotten lost.

Pretty swanky neighborhood now that he saw it in daylight. The houses were crammed side-by-side, same as he'd seen in New York City before he shipped out. Each three-story house was built of tan bricks with bright white trim, complete with columns around the porch.

Dorothy trotted up the front steps and swung open the door. "Hallo, Papa! I found something in the park. Come see." She whirled to Wyatt with one finger pressed to her lips and mischief in her eyes.

He stepped inside quietly and closed the door behind him.

Dorothy unhooked Charlie from his leash, and the little dog trotted to a pillow in the parlor.

Mr. Fairfax leaned over the railing on the stair landing and broke into a smile. "Wyatt? What a lovely surprise. What a lovely surprise indeed."

"It's good to see you, Mr. Fairfax." Wyatt shook the man's hand after he came downstairs. "I ran into Dorothy in the park, and she asked if I could drop by for a moment."

"Yes, yes. Take off your coat and have a seat." He motioned to the parlor.

"I'm glad she asked, because I have a question for you." Keeping his coat on, Wyatt took a seat in a stiff upholstered chair. "As a businessman, I'm curious how British companies are run. I'm sure there are differences, and I'd love to see. I don't want to be a pest, but I was wondering if someday you could give me a tour."

"Brilliant idea. We'll arrange a date, next week perhaps." Mr. Fairfax sat forward in his chair and gestured to Wyatt's chest. "Why are you wearing your coat? You'll stay for tea, of course. Dinner too."

Wyatt fought a grimace and glanced Dorothy's way. "Thank you, but I just dropped by. Only have a minute."

"Nonsense. Where do you have to be on a Sunday evening? You'll stay, and I won't hear another word. Dorothy?"

Her eyes darkened, and her mouth pursed. "Yes, Papa." Then she marched away.

Swell. He'd made a big mistake. He took off his overcoat, hung it by the door, and glanced down the hallway in time to see Dorothy shove the kitchen door open.

"Excuse me, Mr. Fairfax. I'll be right back." He didn't wait for a reply but headed into the kitchen.

In the pantry, Dorothy yanked food off the shelf. No sign of Mrs. Bromley. Sunday had to be the housekeeper's day off.

"Sorry, Dorothy. I didn't expect the invitation. If you don't want me to stay, I won't."

"Nonsense. Why wouldn't I want you to stay?" But she kept her back to him and her voice cool.

"Well, you didn't act too pleased when he invited me, then you hightailed it out of there."

She passed him and laid the food on a table, her face averted. "You're a stranger. A complete stranger. And he shows more interest . . ." She shook her head.

Understanding sank in his gut. "He shows more interest in me than in his own daughter."

She didn't respond. She didn't have to.

"Listen." He motioned over his shoulder with his thumb, though she couldn't see him. "I'll tell him I forgot I promised to meet a friend for dinner. I'll stay half an—"

"Nonsense. You'll stay, and I won't hear another word." She ripped open a box.

The lessons of the past three years told him to leave. "Jealousy is a dangerous emotion. I know too well. I refuse to provoke it in others."

Her shoulders drooped. She faced him, eyes closed, and rubbed her forehead. "He smiled. Did you see? He smiled when he saw you. I haven't seen him smile for years."

Once again he'd stolen something that didn't belong to him, but how could he repay this debt? "I'm sorry."

She drew a deep breath and opened her eyes. "Please forgive me, and please stay. You make him happy. If I love him, I'll do what's best for him."

"Even entertain a rebel?" He tried a sheepish look.

Her smile rose, rueful but warm. "Even that."

9

ALLIED NAVAL EXPEDITIONARY FORCE HEADQUARTERS
MONDAY, FEBRUARY 7, 1944

If only Dorothy had an excuse to visit intelligence. She stared at the door leading to Lawrence's department and nibbled on the tip of her pen.

Those two kisses! The good-night kiss so delicious she forgot every morsel from dinner.

Her cheeks heated from the memory—and from the knowledge that she was daydreaming on duty.

She turned back to the diagram on her desk. The artist in her loathed the confining gridlines, but the officer in her knew the necessity.

With careful strokes, she marked the features between the D-1 and D-3 beach exits. Each rise and fall of land. Each tree. Each structure. Each gun battery. She'd redrawn this diagram several times, and she'd do so again as new intelligence arrived.

While her pen longed to add flourishes and skip unsightly elements, she stayed true to reality. In only four months soldiers would pour onto this beach, and the accuracy of her diagram could mean life or death.

"Excuse me, Second Officer Fairfax?" Leading Wren Stella Dodds held a stack of papers before her thin chest. "I finished typing up that list of new—"

"Lovely!" Dorothy snatched up the report. "I'll take it to Lieutenant Commander Eaton."

Stella's eyes widened, and she drew back. "Yes, ma'am."

Oh dear, she'd been rather loud and eager, hadn't she? Dorothy found her genteel smile. "Very good, Dodds. I appreciate your efficiency. Carry on."

The writer returned to her station.

Dorothy stood and took a deep breath to get back into character. The day before with Wyatt, she'd deliberately acted like Jolly Dolly to deflect romantic interest. She'd allowed herself to talk too much. She'd indulged in silly antics and mimicry. All good sport. For some strange reason, Wyatt didn't seem to mind.

Now the time for nonsense was over.

She glided to the door. On Friday, Lawrence had said he hoped for the pleasure of her company again. Well, she was free this coming weekend. If she hadn't been, she would have wiped her calendar clean for him.

The intelligence office throbbed with activity, but she didn't see Lawrence. Motion by the other door drew her eye.

Wyatt raised his hand and a shy smile.

She returned his greeting, but her stomach clenched. What if Lawrence saw her being chummy with another man? Wyatt understood where her affections lay, but would Lawrence?

However, Wyatt mouthed "Bye" and left.

Perfect timing. She strolled through intelligence, past the teleprinters and past men analyzing photographs with stereo glasses.

Thank goodness she'd laid aside her petty jealousy last night. Papa and Wyatt had talked about business until half-past nine. Papa had eaten every bit of his dinner, and this morning he'd chattered about his plan to give Wyatt a tour of his office on Friday. Then he'd gone to work—early!

The door opened. Lawrence held it open, and First Officer Bliss-Baldwin strolled inside, patting Lawrence's arm and gazing up at him through her lashes.

What was going on?

Bliss-Baldwin parted ways with Lawrence and passed Dorothy, her color too high for Dorothy's taste.

Then Lawrence beckoned Dorothy to follow him to his office.

She tamped down the impulse to scamper like Charlie, and she strolled into his office as if she didn't care. "I have the weekly report of the latest features we detected."

"Very good." He took the papers and flipped through. "Jolly good show."

"Thank you, sir."

He motioned for her to close the door and take a seat, which she obeyed a bit too quickly.

"Good news. I shall have First Officer Bliss-Baldwin eating out of my hand."

"Oh?" She crossed her ankles and her hands.

"We're having dinner on Friday. I'll explain your family situation and why you need to stay in London, with complete discretion, of course. I shall persuade her to relent." He leaned forward over the desk with that devilish smile. "I can be rather persuasive."

Her face tingled. Yes, he could. He'd persuaded her into a kiss before they'd even had dinner. Was that how he meant to persuade Old Blissy?

His gleam faded. "Is there a problem?"

"No. Absolutely not." But her voice squeaked.

Lawrence sat back in his chair. "You aren't the jealous sort, are you?"

Sophisticated women weren't possessive, so she lifted one shoulder. "Why would I be?"

"Good." He wrinkled his nose. "Jealous women are so tiresome."

She crimped one corner of her mouth. "As are jealous men."

He chuckled. "Very good, then."

Dorothy returned to her duties. Wyatt said jealousy was dangerous, and he was right. To win Lawrence and help Papa, she'd gladly set it aside.

LONDON
TUESDAY, FEBRUARY 15, 1944

Muriel Shaw patted an empty spot on the table in Dorothy's favorite tearoom. "Oh, to have sugar in my tea again."

Dorothy added her compassionate murmur to Gwen and Johanna's, but she didn't agree. Rationing had kept her figure trim for the first time in her life, and she didn't look forward to sweets tempting her from store windows again.

Gwen Hamilton took a cucumber sandwich from the tiered serving plate. "And this war bread. How I long for soft white bread."

"I don't mind." Johanna Katin selected an oat scone. "It is food, and I am thankful."

"As am I." Dorothy stood and lifted the teapot. "Shall I be Mother?"

"Yes, please."

She poured fragrant Darjeeling into each china cup. "Johanna, how is your grandmother? Is she home from hospital?"

"She is better, thank you. The doctor said she could come home tomorrow." The only woman at the table not in uniform, Johanna wore a shirtwaist dress in a burgundy wool that complemented her olive complexion. Since she was not a British subject, she was ineligible for military service.

"I'm itching to go dancing." Muriel poured a spot of milk into her tea. "Who wants to go out this weekend?"

"Not me, but thank you." Johanna stirred her tea. Her fiancé was fighting in Burma, and she avoided mixed social events.

Dorothy formed pretty white twirls with the milk in her tea until it blended to the right shade of brown. "I might, but it's too early to commit."

"If you're waiting for Lieutenant Commander Eaton to ask you out, don't," Muriel said. "Helen said he's taking her to dinner on Friday."

"Helen Woolford?" From Lawrence's own department? And Bliss-Baldwin the Friday before. Had Dorothy ruined her only chance with Lawrence with a silly monologue?

"I'm sorry." Johanna's face stretched long. "I know you had your heart set on him."

Gwen and Muriel giggled, and Muriel flapped her hand at Johanna. "It isn't over, darling. The lieutenant commander is a scamp. He doesn't think he's ready to settle down yet."

Dorothy forced a smile. "That's part of his charm."

"Charm?" Johanna asked. "I don't understand. Why would you want a man like that?"

Muriel sipped her tea. "It's jolly good sport."

Gwen's gray eyes softened. "He's perfect for her. She's talked of no other man since we were schoolgirls. It's no coincidence that they're serving together now. They were meant to be."

Meant to be. Dorothy's shoulders relaxed, and she sent Gwen a grateful smile.

Johanna fingered her scone. "A good man only loves one woman, and he's faithful to her."

"Oh, he'll get there." Muriel gave Gwen a knowing look. "Kicking and screaming, but he'll get there. And Dorothy's the woman to do it."

Dorothy found her energy again. "That's why he's so exciting. He's not easily won."

"But once Dorothy wins him . . ." Muriel snapped her fingers. "The love of a good woman will turn that scamp into a proper house dog."

"An unpredictable one, I hope." Dorothy gave her friends an arch look. How many times had Mum warned her not to repeat her mistakes, warned her not to marry a predictable man?

"You're doing so well." Gwen gave her a nod. "I never thought you could act cool and indifferent, but you're brilliant."

Muriel laughed. "Men can't stand indifference. They have to change it to adulation."

"He's watching you," Gwen said. "I've seen him. It's working."

Dorothy smiled and took a tiny bite of her watercress sandwich.

"The playacting, yes?" Johanna asked with a glow in her eye.

She gave her a teasing look. "I prefer to think of it as transforming rather than performing. I'm becoming the woman he wants."

Something sad flitted across Johanna's face, but then she smiled. "I'm glad you are happy. But . . . I am also glad I didn't have to change for Morris to love me."

Dorothy sipped her tea to conceal her expression. She had never been loved as she was, and she never would be. Change was her only hope. It was worth it to win the man she loved.

10

Wyatt sorted through the latest air reconnaissance photos, each labeled with grid numbers corresponding to the map.

German Field Marshal Erwin Rommel was building his Atlantic Wall defenses from Norway's North Cape to the Spanish border, and Normandy hadn't been overlooked.

At the American landing beaches, each warship would be assigned a sector to cover. Wyatt filled his charts with coordinates of the enemy's known and potential positions.

Geier's laugh hit his ears. The officer stood talking near Eaton's office with Marino and Eaton, looking over papers.

Wyatt frowned. Perhaps he should find out what they were discussing. Or perhaps he was being a busybody and it was none of his cotton-picking business.

Eaton waved over a Wren officer—Woolworth, was it? The pretty brunette flitted wren-like to Eaton and handed him a folder. He thanked her with a smile and a pat on the lower back, and the woman returned to her desk, beaming.

Something smoldered in Wyatt's gut. How dare Eaton flirt with another girl when he already had Dorothy's heart?

"Good day, Lieutenant Paxton." Dorothy sat beside him, holding photographs. "I'm glad you're here. You'll like this."

"Hi there." He studied her face, but she sifted through photos with a bright look about her. She must not have seen Eaton and the other Wren, thank goodness.

"Here." She brandished a photo, just some sand and grass and such. "Do you see that hillock? Doesn't look exceptional, does it?"

"No, ma'am." He hadn't even noted it on his chart.

"But look here." Dorothy set down a photograph of a little boy playing in the sand. "This was taken in 1939, a slightly different angle. And this . . ." A photo of two honeymooners lounging on the sand, heads together. "Same year, a bit closer, from the other direction."

It took a while to get his bearings, but a scrubby little bush oriented him. Then he saw. "No hillock."

"Precisely. Isn't it smashing?"

"Yeah. Wow." Wyatt compared the photos—a smooth lump of earth, about ten feet long and three feet high, plenty big to conceal a machine-gun nest. "You discovered that yourself?"

She nodded quickly, her smile luminous.

"Wow." He noted the information on his chart.

"Excuse me." She swept up the pictures and went to Eaton, of course. She showed him the same things she'd shown Wyatt, but with a cool, almost dull voice.

"Good show, Second Officer Fairfax. I say, you do have good eyes—and very pretty ones." He sent her away with the same pat to the lower back he'd given the other girl.

Dorothy returned to her office. When she passed Wyatt, she gave him a thrilled smile as if he were one of her girlfriends who'd squeal for her.

He didn't. But he managed a congratulatory kind of look.

More notes, his pen strokes too hard and dark. Eaton had tossed Dorothy a crumb of attention to keep her at his feet. And it worked. Why did some men—

"No," he muttered. No jealousy.

"Mr. Paxton?" Commander Marino called. "Are you done for the day? Would you walk out with me?"

He wanted a few more entries in his chart, but he could come back in the morning. "Aye aye, sir."

Wyatt straightened the photographs, gathered his papers into his portfolio, and grabbed his overcoat and cover from a hook by the door. In the passageway he fell in beside Marino.

With his overcoat slung over one arm, Commander Marino tapped a cigarette out of his case. "Mr. Geier showed me his report."

"His report?" Wyatt couldn't remember Geier writing one on his own. "Which one?"

"You ought to know. Mr. Geier said you compiled the charts listing targets by sector."

"Yes, sir." His mind spun. He'd worked hard on that report, and he and Geier were supposed to present it to Marino tomorrow. The smoldering in his gut flickered into flame. This wasn't jealousy. It was righteous indignation. "Sir—"

"Mr. Geier analyzed that data and the firepower of the British ships assigned to the American landing beaches, and he believes the bombardment will be insufficient. He says we need more ships. I concur."

Wyatt's jaw dangled. That was his analysis, his conclusion, and Geier was a bald-faced liar.

"I don't know how to say this, Mr. Paxton. In the Navy, every officer has to carry his share of the load."

Wyatt forced his lungs to squeeze out words. "Yes, sir. I do."

His commander winced and took a long drag on his cigarette. "That's not what I see. Mr. Geier tried to be diplomatic, but it's obvious he does the lion's share. All I see you do is fuss over charts."

"Sir, that isn't—"

"You need to carry your weight." He strode down the passageway. "You need to analyze the data, form conclusions, write reports, and present them. Come D-day, we'll need our officers on board destroyers applying that information in battle."

"I do all that, sir—honest. I've been in battle. I know what's needed."

Inside the main door, Marino paused and pulled on his overcoat. "Listen, I know you were an accountant in civilian life, but it's time to stop nitpicking over numbers and be an officer."

Wyatt fumbled with the brass buttons on his coat. "Sir, I *am* doing the analysis. I *am* writing the reports." He sounded like a whiny child saying he'd cleaned his room when he hadn't. Only he *had* cleaned his room—and Geier's too.

"I need to see more of an effort from you." Marino opened the front door. "Good day."

"Good day, sir." Outside, everything was gray, and a steady rain blurred the bare trees in the square across the street.

His work was supposed to speak for itself, but Geier was a ventriloquist who made the work speak for him instead.

Wyatt ducked his head and marched into the rain. Geier had turned him into the dummy.

Wyatt ran in place, harder than usual, as if he could sweat out his anger.

Jack jogged beside him in a ballroom in the hotel where they were quartered. Other officers also performed informal calisthenics in their gym shorts and T-shirts. "What's up, Wy?"

He didn't want to talk, but he was no good at lying. He shook his head as if too winded.

"You're about to hit that stubborn chin of yours with your knees. What's up?"

Why had Wyatt become friends with Jack anyway? Should have found a friend who didn't poke his nose into his business.

"Sit-ups." Jack sat on the floor. "I'll go first so you can talk."

Wyatt dropped to his knees, breath chuffing, and he grasped Jack's feet harder than necessary.

Jack lay flat on his back with his hands behind his head. "I'll count in my head. You talk. Don't try to get out of it. You'll only prolong the agony."

If only Jack would succumb to Wyatt's glower, but he just started his sit-ups. And Jack was no less stubborn than Wyatt.

While Jack did his fifty sit-ups, Wyatt related his conversation with Marino in a low voice. Didn't want the other fellows to hear.

"Fifty. Switch." Jack took his place.

Wyatt stretched out flat. Then he curled up to sitting, avoiding his buddy's gaze.

"I was afraid this would happen," Jack said. "Geier's walking all over you, and Commander Marino's buying it."

Wyatt clenched his jaw and continued his sit-ups, the muscles in his trunk warm and tense.

"You said you didn't want to let jealousy control you, but what does that have to do—"

"He's like Adler, all right?"

"Adler's a lazy, lying weasel?"

Wyatt blew out a breath and the truth. "No. No, he isn't."

Jack rearranged his grip on Wyatt's ankles. "So, because of what happened with your brother, you let Geier take advantage of you."

He'd lost count. Somewhere in the forties. He kept going, pushing himself. At last he rolled onto his belly. "Push-ups."

Jack got into the push-up position beside him. "You said it didn't matter who got the credit, but now do you see why it does?"

"I don't care." Wyatt shoved away from the earth, over and over, his words choppy.

"Now who's the liar?"

He glared at his friend but then sighed. "All right, I care. But I shouldn't."

"I think you should." Jack did a few push-ups. "What if your silence affects the work?"

"It won't." But an uneasy feeling wriggled inside. He collapsed to the floor and rolled onto his back. "Leg scissors."

Jack lay down and lifted his feet. "If I didn't know better, I'd think you didn't want to succeed."

Wyatt scissored his legs in the air. "I want the work to succeed."

"What about yourself? Don't you want to succeed?"

"Don't care about that. Don't want it, don't deserve it." His eyes flew wide open at the sound of his own words.

"Don't deserve it?"

Wyatt stared at the ornate ceiling. His gym shoes and his thoughts banged into each other as they crossed.

Jack got up to his knees, sweat dampening his dark hairline. "How long are you going to punish yourself?"

Unable to look his friend in the eye, Wyatt stood, swiped his forehead on his T-shirt sleeve, and stretched his arms straight in front of him. "Deep knee bends."

"Wyatt?"

He squatted until his rear end touched his heels. The pain felt right and good. The only punishment he'd received was the scar on his cheek, and it wasn't enough for what he'd done.

Jack puffed as he performed his knee bends. "Let me get this straight. You'd rather whip yourself than whip the Nazis."

Wyatt sucked in a breath and shot to standing.

"Wouldn't you?" Jack leveled a hard gaze at him.

"I'd never . . ." His body swayed from the force of the truth. If his inaction led to even one death in Operation Neptune . . . inexcusable. And he'd add even more guilt to his burden.

"Lunges, Wy."

Yes, lunges. Wyatt set his hands on his hips, stepped forward, and lunged deep. What was most important anyway? Allied victory. And victory required every man to do his best. For Wyatt to do his best, he had to stand up for his work. "All right. I've got to do something."

"Mm-hmm." Right, left, right, left. "Even if it means you succeed."

A chuckle escaped. "A risk I'll have to take."

"Toe touches." Jack planted his feet shoulder-distance apart and stretched his arms to the side.

Wyatt bent to touch his right hand to his left toes, straightened, then touched his right toes. "What do you think? Tomorrow, I'll talk to Geier, tell him we present the reports together from now on, tell him Commander Marino insisted."

"That's the way. Talk to Marino too. Tell him if Geier comes to him alone with a report, you respectfully request that he summon you."

Wyatt finished his toe touches. That might work. No whining. No blaming. At least he'd let Geier know he wouldn't be a pushover. "All right, then. I'll do it. Arm circles, backward."

Jack stood with his feet together and his arms to the side. "Any plans for the weekend?"

"See some sights, read a book." Wyatt made little circles with his arms.

A drop of sweat trickled in front of Jack's ear. "Why don't you go out with that pretty redhead from the park?"

He thought Jack had forgotten about her. "She's dating Eaton from intelligence."

"Eaton?" Jack barked out a laugh. "Who isn't dating him? Other than you and I, of course."

"Forward." Wyatt switched directions with his arm circles. "Why do you say that?"

"He dates a different skirt every week. All the men are in awe of him."

Wyatt grumbled. "I'm not."

"So you like her?" That stupid grin again.

"Doesn't matter one way or another. She's crazy about him, and a gal who likes a guy like that would never be happy with a fellow like me."

"Side stretches." Jack set one hand on his hip, the other up in the air, and he bent to the side. "My oldest sister was like that. She dated every bad boy in town. Finally, she came to her senses. Next thing we knew, she'd married the sweet quiet fellow who'd always doted on her. They just had a baby. Happiest couple you've ever seen."

Wyatt leaned to the side, tension dissolving from his muscles. "Good old Jack. Cheering me up."

"Are you kidding? I'm being selfish. Cheerful Wyatt is fun to have around. But grumpy Wyatt? I want to drop-kick him to France."

He laughed and stretched to the other side. But he did feel better. He'd only be in London a few more months, probably not long enough for Dorothy to come to her senses about Eaton. After all, she'd had a crush on him for years.

But why should Wyatt keep his distance?

If Eaton had been faithful, Wyatt would have stayed out of the picture. But by choosing to chase other girls, Eaton had thrown away his privilege.

Strength and purpose warmed his muscles. He was free to pursue Dorothy, not with Eaton's flattery and fancy dinners, but in his way. Slow and steady, as a friend.

Wyatt toweled off his face then smiled at his friend. "So, about this weekend . . ."

11

Dorothy gazed around the Queensbury All-Services Club at the uniforms from so many Allied nations. Since men far outnumbered women, she'd have plenty of dance partners. "I'm determined to have a good time this evening."

"As you should." Muriel patted her pinned-up brown curls. "Lawrence is out with Helen tonight, so find the handsomest man in the room, dance your heart out, and make him jealous."

"That never works. And he isn't here to see me anyway."

"Regardless, have fun. Maybe a Yank." Gwen nodded to the door.

Dorothy turned in her seat. Oh dear. Wyatt entered the ballroom with two of the officers she'd met at Kensington Gardens. If only Lawrence shared Wyatt's penchant for showing up unexpectedly.

"How about that tall cowboy?" Muriel said. "He's rather delicious."

"Wyatt Paxton?" She hadn't given it much thought, but he was quite good-looking in his own way.

"You're already friendly with him," Gwen said.

If only her hair didn't shine like a beacon. "He's very sweet, but

85

he's the sort who'd want his egg poached just so every morning. Life would be dreadfully dull. I need excitement."

Muriel glanced over Dorothy's shoulder. "That smile is all the excitement I'd need. I love the strong, silent type."

"Be my guest."

"Don't be daft." Gwen's voice rose as the band began to play. "He saw us, and he's coming over. He's the perfect chap to make Lawrence jealous."

"I refuse to use him," she said. "He's a nice man."

Muriel lifted a hand in greeting. "Good evening, Lieutenant Paxton."

"Good evening, ladies." He stood by Dorothy's chair and smiled down at her. "You remember my friends Jack Vale and Jerry Hobson?"

"I do, and you must remember my friends Gwen Hamilton and Muriel Shaw."

Lieutenants Vale and Hobson shook hands with Gwen and Muriel. Dorothy signaled to Muriel with her brows—*"Flirt with him. Dance with him."*

Muriel swung a beaming smile in the wrong direction. "Where do you come from, Lieutenant Hobson?"

"Dorothy?" Wyatt touched the back of her chair. "Would you like to dance?"

"Thank you. I would." A few dances wouldn't hurt, so she stood and took his arm.

As the band played "Moon Glow," Wyatt led her to the dance floor. "I may not be the elegant Lieutenant Commander Eaton, but I know a few dance moves."

"Oh? What sort of dances do they do in Texas?"

"Same as the rest of the US. Plus some square dancing. And Mama taught us the *jarabe*."

She simply couldn't decipher that accent. "Ha-ra-bay?"

"Roll your *r*'s. *Jarabe*. You may have heard it called the Mexican hat dance. Did I ever tell you Mama's Mexican?"

Dorothy studied Wyatt's profile as they threaded their way through the crowd. She didn't know much about Mexico, but the pictures she'd seen showed swarthy men in large hats dancing with women in black braids and colorful skirts.

He cracked a smile. "I love seeing people's reactions when I say that."

"Oh?"

In an open spot on the dance floor, he held out his arms, and she stepped into the dance position, careful to keep her distance. Wyatt's dancing might have lacked Lawrence's elegance, but he did know his steps.

Dorothy tried not to look into his face—the closeness made her jittery—but curiosity overpowered discretion. "One might say it's rude to provoke a reaction without providing an explanation."

Crinkles formed beside his eyes. "One might say"—he imitated a British accent quite poorly—"it's rude to inquire about a man's parentage."

It was, and her cheeks warmed.

But he chuckled. "I'll stop teasing. My mother died when Adler was born—I don't remember her. Daddy hired his manager's daughter to care for us boys, and they fell in love and got married within a year. A bit scandalous, but you've never met two people who love each other more."

Certainly not her own parents. Mum never said a kind word about poor Papa. "So your youngest brother—Clay? He's . . ."

Wyatt shrugged, making her too aware of the solidity of his shoulder under her hand. "Legally, he's my half brother, but I don't think of him that way. And Mama's my mama. She treated us all the same. Same love, same discipline. And believe me, when Mama reels out a long rope of Spanish, you run for the hills."

She smiled. "You do miss them, don't you?"

"Yep."

"Why don't you write them?"

The band shifted to the fast beat of "In the Mood," and Wyatt stepped back and grasped her hands. "You and I—we always talk about death and loss."

"We do have that in common."

"Well, tonight I just want to dance." He grinned and flew into a jitterbug, legs all over the place. The Americans had the wildest dance moves, even quiet Lieutenant Paxton.

She struggled to keep up, and laughter spilled out. What jolly good fun.

Wyatt pulled her close, spun her around, twirled her under his arm.

If only Muriel had kept her mouth shut. She didn't want to think of Wyatt as attractive, yet he was. He had a nice face and a charming way of dipping his chin when he smiled. And now he swung her around with strong arms. She'd always considered quiet men dull, but not Wyatt. Not this man who jitterbugged and knew how to do that *jarabe* dance. It almost sounded exciting.

No.

Lawrence, Lawrence, Lawrence. She'd adored him forever. Elegant and cultured and impossibly exciting, with the dark good looks she'd always preferred.

Wyatt spun her so fast, her feet left the floor.

"Oh my!" She couldn't stop giggling. "You aren't going to throw me in the air, are you?"

"Only if you want." He winked. Why did Yankee men always do that?

"Please don't," she said as he whipped her from one side to the other. "I'm afraid of flying."

"The daredevil is afraid of something?" His serious look returned. "Then I won't make you fly."

Something about that look felt as cozy and secure as her favorite wool jumper. She flung that security away and concentrated on her feet. It didn't fit, didn't belong to her, and she didn't want it. Not at all.

The music slowed. Thank goodness. Now she could sit down and escape.

However, Wyatt guided her into the dance position, respectful but unyielding.

The band played "You'd Be So Nice to Come Home To." No, he wouldn't be nice to come home to. This fun wouldn't last, and life would be plodding routines. In fact, was it even fair of him to offer a taste of excitement when it wasn't in his nature?

She hefted up her chin so she could see the other dancers over the navy blue ridge of his shoulder. Time to end the fun and return to their usual conversational topics. "If you aren't going to let me rest, I won't let you rest either."

"Hmm?" He turned his face to her.

Oh dear. Too close. She could feel the warmth of him, and she eased away. "I won't let you rest. You miss your family, so you should write them."

His mouth thinned. "After I've paid my debt."

"Surely they want to know where you are."

"I'm sure Adler does, so he can finish what he started." He released her hand and rubbed the scar on his cheek. "See this? From the day Oralee died. When Adler tried to kill me."

"Didn't you say her death was an accident? Why did he blame you?"

Wyatt continued to dance, but his gaze wandered away. "He knew I loved her."

"Oh dear."

A muscle twitched in his cheek. "I met her first, the summer before my senior year. I was crazy about her. But as soon as she met Adler, she fell for him."

"Oh no. How dreadful."

He shook his head. "No. They were right for each other. They were. I tried to conceal my feelings, but Adler knew I was jealous."

Dorothy held her breath, but she had to hear the rest. "And the accident?"

His arm tensed around her waist. "We were climbing the hill, the three of us boys and Clay and Adler's girlfriends. Adler coaxed Oralee to cross a footbridge in her high heels. He's always talking folks into doing things they don't want to, and it irks me."

Dorothy murmured and swayed with the music.

"Well, Oralee didn't want to, and I took her side. Adler and I, we started fighting. Oralee—she pleaded with us to stop, but we didn't. So she started 'cross that bridge to make us stop. But she didn't have good footing. I grabbed her, but she was mad at me and pulled away." Wyatt uncoiled his fingers from around Dorothy's, and he stared down as if his hand were empty, as if he could see the woman he loved plunging to her death.

"Oh, Wyatt. How awful."

He blinked and closed his hand around hers. "Adler blamed me and rightly so."

"Please don't say that. There's nothing you could have done."

"I couldn't protect her." His eyes swam between blue grief and gray regret. "Adler knew. He knew my jealousy started the whole thing. He threw a rock at me. He might have finished the job if Clay hadn't stopped him."

"I'm sorry." The words felt inadequate, but they were all she had.

His eyes cleared. "Do you see why I can't write home until my debt is paid?"

She caught herself chewing off her lipstick, one of her least sophisticated habits. "Will it make a difference?"

His step faltered for a beat, then resumed. "Can't go home empty-handed. I want to show I'm contrite. Like the Prodigal Son, I want to go home saying, 'Father, I have sinned against heaven, and in thy sight, and am no more worthy to be called thy son.'"

Dorothy hadn't read that story in years, but . . . "Didn't the Prodigal Son return home empty-handed?"

Wyatt stared at her, then his brow furrowed. "Yeah, but he offered himself as a slave. I can't do that."

"His father didn't want that anyway. He ran to him. I'm sure your parents would do the same. They must be sick with worry, not knowing if you're dead or alive."

His lips mashed together. "I suppose."

She fought the urge to rub his shoulder. "If this war has taught me anything, it's that life is short and family is dear."

Everything in his expression softened. "I—I know."

The throatiness of his voice unnerved her, but she forged ahead. "Perhaps you could write your parents, but not your brothers."

"I'll pray about it. In the meantime, the band has issued an order, and we must obey."

She tuned her ears to the music—a song called "Let's Dance"—and she smiled. "Very good, Lieutenant."

He whirled her into a swing dance, and soon the fog lifted from his expression.

For the rest of the evening, she and her friends danced with Wyatt and Jack and Jerry, and they told stories around the table. Wyatt was always serious on duty, and it was good to see him sporting with his friends.

"Oh dear!" Gwen glanced at her wristwatch. "It's past eleven."

How had she lost track of time? "We should leave. The Tube closes at midnight."

Jack stood. "We'll escort you home."

"Wouldn't we be safer alone than with Yankee sailors?" Muriel gave him a teasing look.

"We're gentlemen," Wyatt said. "Dorothy, why don't I take you home, since your dad already knows me?"

She hesitated, but she had to agree. Besides, he was chivalrous and knew her heart belonged to Lawrence.

The party scurried to the Leicester Square station and down to the Piccadilly Line. Before long, Dorothy and Wyatt parted with the others at the South Kensington station.

As they climbed the stairs to the street, a keening sound pierced Dorothy's heart. "The air raid siren."

Wyatt stopped. "Back down we go."

"No." Dorothy dashed up, dodging the people who were returning underground. She had to get home before the bombs started falling.

"Where are you going?" Footsteps thumped behind her.

"Papa—I need to get him to the shelter." She burst out onto the street and paused. Already the roar of aircraft engines overrode the whine of the siren.

"Dorothy, wait." Wyatt circled in front of her and grasped her arm. "You need to get back into the station and fast."

"He won't go to the shelter without me. You saw. I need to go to him." Her voice shook, her head shook, and she tried to shake off his grip.

"It's too late." He gazed overhead, where searchlights crisscrossed the black sky. "I won't stop you, but it's too late."

True to his word, he loosened his grip. Dorothy stepped around him.

A whistling sound, and the earth rumbled, jarring her bones.

"Please, Dorothy. It isn't safe out here. Your father's in God's hands."

That was what she feared most. She covered her mouth and gulped down a sob.

"Come on." Wyatt laid his hand on her shoulder. "Let's get you to safety, and we'll pray for him."

More whistles and closer. Men, women, and children in nightclothes streamed past her down the stairs in orderly fashion. Wyatt was right. She could get buried in rubble before she reached the house, so she joined the stream.

The platform was already filling, but Wyatt and Dorothy found a spot by the tiled wall and sat amongst the crowd.

Wyatt crossed his hands on his bent knees and bowed his head. "Father God, we pray for Mr. Fairfax. Please help him get to the shelter in time, and Charlie too. Keep him safe in your mighty hands, and give him peace that Dorothy is safe as well."

Oh dear. One simply didn't pray out loud in public. She glanced around, but no one seemed to pay Wyatt any attention.

"Lord, we pray for the whole city. Shield us from those bombs, let them fall where they do no harm, and comfort the wounded and those who lose their homes. And Lord, please be with the RAF pilots and the antiaircraft gunners. Give them accuracy and help them protect this great city and her people."

He kept praying, his voice low but strong and driven. He prayed for the Allies, that they'd prevail and soon. He even prayed for the Germans, that they'd see the light and overthrow Hitler and the evil men in power.

It didn't seem proper, the way he prayed, and yet something about that prayer stirred calm into her soul.

Finally he said *amen*, and he leaned his head back against the wall. His smile—such peace. How was it possible?

Questions jumbled in her stomach. Everything British in her said to keep her mouth shut, but something pried it open. "I don't understand."

"Hmm?"

"You—you've lost so much, yet you pray as if the Lord listened, as if he cared."

Understanding flickered in his eyes, then he closed them and nodded slowly. He said nothing.

Dorothy folded her arms over her middle, her jaw tight and her eyes prickling. No one—no one could answer that question.

"When you were a little girl," Wyatt said, his eyes still closed, "did your parents give you everything you asked for?"

"Of course not, but it's hardly the same."

"Did you understand why they refused?"

"No, but—"

"Hear me out." He settled his gaze on her. "Now that you're grown up, do you understand? You couldn't have all the toys, or you'd be spoiled rotten. You couldn't eat nothing but candy, or you wouldn't grow right. You couldn't play in the street, or you could get killed."

All around, Londoners prepared their pillows and blankets, hunkering down for another long night of death and destruction. "I fail to see how losing my mum and brothers was good for me."

"I don't know either. But I do know God is good, and he loves you, and his heart is breaking for you and your daddy."

"You sound like the rector." Her voice quivered too much.

"You go to church?" A simple question without surprise or judgment.

"Not since Mum was killed."

"You should go back."

"I'd rather not."

Wyatt fell silent, thank goodness, because she refused to give in to the indignity of tears. How much longer would the raid last? How long until she could check on Papa and escape from Wyatt?

"Seems both of us are avoiding contact with loved ones."

"Pardon?"

One corner of his mouth flicked up. "You told me to write home, but I don't want to. And I told you to go to church, but you don't want to. Seems we're both avoiding those who love us."

A major difference, but she managed a slight smile.

"How about we cut a deal?" He poked his thumb to his chest. "I'll write my parents if you go to church."

Her mouth flopped open, quite unladylike, and she closed it. He really needed to write home. His parents had to be worried, and he missed them so. But church?

Wyatt's gaze didn't flinch. He seemed to think she needed church as much as he needed his parents. She didn't. However, sitting through one service would be a small price to pay.

"Very good, Lieutenant. I'll cut that deal."

He shook her hand and grinned as if he'd won the greater victory. Oh, but the victory was hers.

12

Wyatt could hardly keep up with Dorothy as she darted around the broken glass on the sidewalk. Kensington had been hit, and orange-red fires pulsed in the distance. The worst he'd seen.

Dorothy rounded a corner and halted. "Oh, thank goodness."

The Fairfax home stood, and Dorothy ran up the steps and flung open the door. "Papa?"

Wyatt followed, breathing hard, his eyes straining in the darkness.

Dorothy turned on a lamp, but the parlor and hallway were empty.

"He must be in the shelter," Wyatt said.

"No, he's in his room."

Unlikely when his daughter was out in a major air raid. "I'll check out back." He headed down the hall and out the back door. No damage in the yard, and he pushed open the door to the shelter. Dark. Empty.

Had Mr. Fairfax gone to a public shelter? Wyatt went back inside. The skittering of tiny toenails on the wooden floor greeted him. "Charlie?"

A paw on his shin, and Wyatt scooped up the pup. "There you are, little buddy. Where's your master?"

"Fast asleep in bed." Dorothy's voice was barely audible as she came downstairs.

Wyatt met her near the front door. "I'm surprised he didn't wait up for you."

"I'm not." Her voice was stoic, but the dim light didn't conceal the hurt.

He wanted to say her father must love her, but why would she believe him?

Dorothy took Charlie and burrowed her face in his black fur. "Would your father wait up for you?"

It hurt to say yes, but he couldn't lie. "Yeah."

"Then write home."

"I will."

She glanced upstairs. "I'll make up a room for you."

"Uh, no. Thanks, but no. I've got to get back to quarters. I'm already in trouble, but they'll let me off because of the air raid. Can I call for a taxi?"

"I'll ring one for you. It may take a while due to the air raid."

"Thanks." While she made the call, Wyatt wandered into the parlor. A desk drew him.

Write home.

He'd promised. Besides, Dorothy had a point. What if something happened to Wyatt during Operation Neptune? In an air raid? His family would be notified of his death and they'd receive his savings and his life insurance—but they'd never hear how sorry he was.

"They answered on the first ring. A taxi will be here in ten minutes."

In ten minutes he could get a good start. "May I have a piece of stationery, maybe two?"

Dorothy's eyes widened. "You don't mean to start now, do you? It's after two o'clock."

"Yes, ma'am."

"All right." She opened a drawer and pulled out a box. "Exactly two sheets left."

"May I have the empty box? Then I can write in the cab."

"Of course."

"Thanks." Wyatt sat at the desk and pulled his pen from the breast pocket of his shirt. How could he do this? What could he say?

He prayed for the right words, for wisdom, for his parents' hearts to soften.

Then he opened his eyes. Dorothy sat curled up in an armchair, peeking through the blackout curtains. Charlie sat beside Wyatt's chair, staring at him with a stern expression.

"I promised to write, Charlie, and I will."

Charlie didn't leave his post, so Wyatt gritted his teeth and plunged in headlong.

Dear Daddy and Mama,

I can't imagine how you feel receiving this letter, but I had to write it. A friend reminded me tonight that life is short and family is dear. These are dangerous times, and for me they'll get more dangerous. I'm serving as a naval officer in that city overseas I always wanted to visit. When you hear of a big operation in this part of the world, I'll be at sea in the thick of it. If something should happen to me, I want to make sure you've heard everything in this letter.

I'll never be able to tell you how sorry I am for my actions that night. Although Oralee's death was an accident, my rivalry with Adler was a contributing factor. I understand why he blames me. Please know I grieve for Oralee, for Adler's loss, and for the future they should have had together.

While my role in her death was unintentional, I claim no such thing in stealing Clay's savings. I feared for my life, and in my panic I betrayed my brother. I'd never thought myself capable of such sin, but I was, and I'm truly sorry. I only meant to borrow it. I planned to repay him before classes started, but I made a foolish business investment and lost every penny.

That's when I joined the Navy. Since then I've scrimped and saved to repay Clay, plus interest and a penalty. I'm only $350 from my goal. I didn't plan to write home until I could enclose the complete check—didn't dare to—but the war and my friend intervened.

Wyatt leaned back and ran his hand through his hair.

Dorothy rested her head on the window, the golden lamplight illuminating her sad, beautiful face. "It's difficult for you, isn't it?"

"Yeah."

"I'm sorry."

"Don't be. I need to do this."

She gazed outside. "The taxi's here."

Wyatt gathered his things, said good-bye, and headed into the cold night. In the taxi, he told the driver his address and settled back.

The cabby pulled away from the curb. "Might take a while, guv'nor, with all the bomb damage. Haven't seen naught like it since '41. If I were a young lad like you, I'd give those old Nasties a taste of the red, white, and blue, I would."

"I reckon you would." Wyatt pulled out his letter. He could barely make out his words in the flickering orange light, but he forged ahead.

Like the Prodigal Son, I come to you broken and contrite and empty-handed, saying, "I have sinned against heaven, and in thy sight, and am no more worthy to be called thy son." The Lord has forgiven my sins, but I can only hope you'll forgive me, and I fear Adler and Clay's forgiveness

*may be too much to ask. Please don't tell them where I am,
but do tell them how sorry I am. In a few months, after my
debt is paid, I'll write them as well.*

*I also can't begin to tell you how much I miss you, but
losing my family is part of my punishment. Daddy, I miss
your strength and wisdom. Mama, I miss your chile rellenos
and tamales, but mostly I miss you. I hear your encouraging,
chiding, loving voice in my head, but I wish I could hear it
in my ears.*

The taxi stopped, and the driver leaned out the window.

Wyatt gasped. Smoke and flame poured out of a building
ahead of them, and firemen directed great streams of water at
the inferno.

An Air Raid Precautions volunteer with a tin helmet and a
white ARP armband waved them off. "You'll have to go another
way, bloke."

"Sorry, guv'nor," the cabby called to Wyatt over his shoulder,
and he drove in reverse.

"That's all right," Wyatt stammered. He slammed his eyes shut
and prayed for the people inside, those who'd escaped, the firemen,
and the ARP volunteers. A bomb like that could hit his quarters
someday. That's why he had to finish the letter.

*You should also know how much I miss my brothers. I
love them, and I'm torn up without them. Adler must be
done with college and helping with the business. I'm sorry I
didn't stay home to help as I'd promised, but he'll do a better
job than I would have. He's a gifted and able businessman,
and I know he's making you proud.*

*Clay must be almost done with his bachelor's degree. He's
a born healer, so I'm glad his pre-med schooling will exempt
him from the draft. I apologize for the financial burden I*

heaped on you. The money will be there soon and will pay for medical school.

After all I've done, I don't deserve to be doing well, but I am. Navy life agrees with me, and I'm glad I can serve our country. Ironically, my faith has grown. Coming face to face with just how wretched a sinner I am has humbled me and made me acutely grateful for Christ's sacrifice.

One night's actions, both unintentional and intentional, have brought nothing but heartbreak and chaos to our family. Even if forgiven, I'll always regret what I did. You created a strong and loving family, and I upended it. I don't know if you will ever welcome me home again, but please accept my apologies and know I will love you forever with all my heart.

Outside the taxi window, fires flickered in windows, buildings crumbled, and water sprayed.

So much destruction. So much loss. So needless.

Wyatt's letter pulsed in the fiery light.

He'd mail it first thing in the morning.

13

Dorothy came downstairs to the smell of roasted potatoes and the sound of the BBC on the wireless. The announcer spoke of the air raid in broad terms, censored so the Germans wouldn't know the Luftwaffe's effectiveness.

If only Dorothy could turn it off.

She'd hoped those days were behind them, but last night's raid appeared to be as large as at the peak of the Blitz. How many had died? How many had lost their homes? Their loved ones?

Papa sat at the dining room table with his newspaper. He didn't look up.

"Good morning, Papa."

He turned a page. "You finally came home."

She stiffened at his tone. "The Luftwaffe delayed me. I sheltered in the Tube and came home straightaway after the all clear."

"I heard a man's voice. Was it Eaton? When did *he* leave?"

Was he insinuating she'd lost her moral standards? While she lowered herself to her chair, she forced her temper to behave. "It was Wyatt. I ran into him at the All-Services Club. He escorted me home, insisted I take shelter, and left ten minutes after he arrived, the time it took a taxi to arrive."

Papa looked at her for the first time, his expression open and pleased. "I'm glad you're finally seeing Wyatt's merit."

Dorothy scooped potatoes onto her plate and swallowed her impatience. "It isn't like that. I'm interested in Lawrence, not Wyatt, and that won't change."

The newspaper rose back into position.

"Oh, Papa, be reasonable. You know I'm like Mum. I need excitement, and Lawrence is exciting."

The paper lowered, and Papa's gaze pierced.

She gave him a gentle smile. "How could I be happy with a quiet, steady chap like Wyatt? I'd be bored and restless."

Something impossibly sad passed through her father's eyes.

Oh bother. How could she be so callous? Mum had craved excitement, but she'd married quiet, steady Papa. She'd been bored. Restless. Contemptuous. Poor Papa had never been able to please her except when he took her to Paris or Edinburgh.

Edinburgh! That was how she could make it up to him.

She grinned at her father. "I have the most glorious idea. London is dreadful now with the air raids, and I have leave coming to me. Why don't you and I take a little holiday next weekend to Edinburgh?"

"Edin—no." He slapped the newspaper together, not in his usual sharp, measured folds.

"It'd be good for us. Such happy mem—"

"No. I have no desire to go there again." He stood and sniffed. "Dark, dirty, contemptible place. I daresay you'd not find it as charming as you remember."

"But—"

"I'll hear no more of it." He marched out of the dining room and up to his study.

Dorothy sighed at his full plate. What had she been thinking? Revisiting memories only made Papa more melancholy.

She poked at her potatoes. But memories were all she had.

Normandy, Edinburgh, Paris. When Mum was at her happiest and most delightful. The only times the family felt whole.

A swelling in her throat, and she pressed her hand over her mouth. The only times Dorothy had felt loved.

WESTERN NAVAL TASK FORCE HEADQUARTERS
19 GROSVENOR SQUARE, LONDON
MONDAY, FEBRUARY 21, 1944

Wyatt laid the report on Commander Marino's desk, his portion of next week's Naval Outline Plan to supplement the Initial Joint Plan for Operation Neptune.

The commander motioned Wyatt and Geier to chairs in front of his desk, and he flipped through the report, puffing on his cigarette.

Framed pictures of the commander's wife and two daughters sat on his desk, overseeing neat stacks of papers.

"Looks good." Marino set down the report. "Anything important to note?"

"No, sir." Geier crossed his ankle over his knee.

Wyatt stared at his colleague. Not true at all.

The commander narrowed dark eyes at Geier. "You must have found something new."

"Yes, sir," Wyatt said.

"Nothing really important." Geier shrugged. "It's all in the report."

It was all important. Wyatt had to contradict Geier, not out of spite but for the sake of the mission. He opened his mouth.

"Our work is crucial." Commander Marino ground his cigarette in the ashtray. "I was at Salerno in Italy. We didn't bombard in the American sector before the invasion, we didn't secure the beaches right away, and the Germans almost drove us into the sea. And now at Anzio. Are you following the situation? We bombarded well and secured the beaches, but then we didn't send reinforcements and went to the defensive instead of driving inland. Now the Germans are counterattacking, and it's bad."

Wyatt's face tingled. "Yes, sir."

"Don't you see?" Marino leveled a hard gaze at them. "Eisenhower refuses to repeat those mistakes. We have to secure the beaches on D-day, flood Normandy with reinforcements, and drive inland. In order to do that, the Navy absolutely must knock out those guns and strongpoints, but first we have to know where they are. It is *all* important."

Wyatt's mouth soured from the venom directed at him as well as at Geier.

"I repeat—anything important to report?"

"Yes, sir." Wyatt stood and opened the report to the first diagram. "Here at the D-1 draw at Vierville, a lot of construction— and destruction. They razed three villas here." He tapped the spot on the map.

"Hardly surprising," Geier said with a chuckle. "We knew they'd fortify that position. It's a beach exit."

"But we're getting specific coordinates." Wyatt turned a page. "And here between the E-1 and E-3 draws, a lot of activity about half a mile inland. Could be they're bringing in a new company or sending one out. Hard to say yet. Also a sudden appearance of shrubbery here by the bluff, camouflaging something, most likely. I'm no infantryman, but the slope of the bluff is shallower here. Maybe Rommel's thinking we'll drive up in this location to encircle the draw at Les Moulins. We should keep an eye on it."

Geier sighed. "As I said, it's all in the report, sir. I didn't want to waste your time repeating what we'd written."

Marino leaned back in his chair. "It's not a waste of time if I asked you to do it."

Wyatt returned to his seat. First time he'd heard the commander upbraid Geier, but he didn't feel the temptation to gloat. Maybe now Geier would do his share of the work so he'd know the material too.

Marino shoved the report aside. "In early March, we're conducting an amphibious landing exercise down at Slapton Sands in Lyme Bay—Exercise Fox. The Royal Navy will conduct the bombardment, then the US 1st Infantry Division will land. I want one of you there on a destroyer as a naval gunfire liaison officer, working with the British gunnery officer."

Wyatt sat up straighter. What a great opportunity. But only for one of them.

"I'd love to go, sir," Geier said.

"So would I, sir."

Marino crossed one arm over his chest, and he tapped his knuckles against his chin as he studied his lieutenants. The hesitation was an improvement, a sign Wyatt had done well today. Yesterday, Marino would have picked Geier without blinking.

Marino pulled a thick folder from a desk drawer. "I need one of you here to keep up with the intelligence, the reports. Mr. Paxton, can you pick up the load, stay on top of things?"

He still didn't think Wyatt was capable, had no idea what he did. "Yes, sir."

The commander handed the folder to Geier. "Here are your briefing materials. Pack your sea bag, and on Saturday you'll take a train down to Portsmouth."

Geier sprang to his feet and shook the commander's hand with a big grin. "Aye aye, sir."

Wyatt's teeth pressed hard together. At least the reports would get done. Those were vital to the war effort. But so were the training exercises, and Geier would botch them up. He needed to do something.

Commander Marino dismissed them, and Geier strode out the door.

An idea percolated, and Wyatt hung back. "Sir, may I have a word with you?"

"Very well."

A measured breath. "Sir, I request permission to meet with the destroyer's gunnery officer beforehand. Not long. I could go down on a Saturday and not disrupt the work here."

Marino's brow furrowed over his dark eyes. "That's Mr. Geier's job."

"Yes, sir. But I . . . I'm more familiar with the details—the maps, the targets—"

"Listen, I'm glad you're carrying more of your weight, but Mr. Geier has everything he needs in his briefing materials."

Wyatt's breath leached out. Would the man read them?

"If that's all, Mr. Paxton . . . ?"

To go further would be to wander into slander. "Yes, sir. That's all."

As for the training exercise, all he could do was pray.

14

ALLIED NAVAL EXPEDITIONARY FORCE HEADQUARTERS
FRIDAY, MARCH 3, 1944

As soon as Dorothy entered the office after lunch, Gwen Hamilton grabbed her by the arm.

"You won't believe what happened." A mix of shock and fascination infused Gwen's gray eyes. "Old Blissy transferred Helen."

Dorothy stared at her friend. "Helen Woolford? In intelligence?"

"I ran into her on her way out—in tears. Blissy accused her of flirting on duty, engaging in behavior unbecoming of the Royal Navy, casting a bad light on us Wrens."

How could Dorothy think with her head spinning? "Oh no. She—she's jealous because Helen stepped out with Lawrence."

"If she finds out you two stepped out, that you carry a torch for him . . ."

Dorothy's lips went dry. Papa had perked up after Wyatt's last visit and after showing him Fairfax & Sons, but now the silent hermit had returned. In the past two weeks, the Luftwaffe had bombed London more nights than not, including a heavy raid on Kensington. Dorothy slept in the damp and chilly Anderson shelter, but Papa stayed in his room. He ate next to nothing. He hadn't gone to the office once this week. And Mr. Montague had sent another foreboding note.

She couldn't afford to leave London. She wet her lips. "But Helen has family here."

"Blissy gave her a choice," Gwen said in a fierce whisper. "Be disciplined and demoted, or transfer to Liverpool, the Western Approaches Command."

"Oh dear." Dorothy pressed her free hand to her forehead. She hadn't known her commanding officer to be manipulative.

"Be careful." Gwen squeezed her arm. "You're more subtle than Helen—she always acted besotted—but still, be careful."

"I will. Thank you for the warning." She gave Gwen a weak smile and went to her desk.

A report lay on top, freshly typed by the Wren writers, ready to be delivered to Lawrence.

Dorothy groaned. Did she dare? Her commanding officer wasn't present. If she were still at lunch, this would be the ideal time. And if Dorothy saw her in intelligence, she'd turn right around and give Lawrence the report later.

She gathered the papers and her senses. From now on she'd be subdued on duty, professional, and not even droll. Why take chances?

Perhaps if she were distant, Lawrence would find her irresistible. A smile threatened, but she hauled it in.

In intelligence, she scanned the office. No sign of Blissy or Lawrence, but Wyatt sat at a table with stereo glasses, photographs, maps, and papers. Just an ordinary man, quiet and steady. When he was hard at work, it was easy to forget how attractive he'd been when dancing.

"Good afternoon, Lieutenant Paxton."

He looked up from the stereo glasses. An ordinary man with an extraordinary smile. "Good afternoon, Second Officer Fairfax."

She gave him a nod and made her way to Lawrence's office.

Empty. Oh bother. Was he dining with Bliss-Baldwin? Or was Dorothy in danger of being as jealous as Old Blissy?

Dorothy gave her head a quick, cleansing shake and turned for her office, passing Wyatt—but Mr. Montague's invitation needed to be issued. It would be rude to ignore it. "Lieutenant Paxton, may I ask a favor?"

"Well, sure."

She sat beside him and lowered her voice. "Do you remember when I told you about the situation at my father's company, how my father's manager wrote to me?"

"Sure do." His eyes were the softest shade of gray blue. "I met Mr. Montague when your dad gave me the tour. Nice fellow."

"He is. Well, when Papa introduced you as my friend and as an accountant, Mr. Montague realized you were the man who made the suggestion."

"To bring in an outside accountant?"

Issuing the invitation was not only polite, it was vital for Papa. "He'd like to meet with us."

Wyatt's eyebrows bounced high. "Me? I'm not qualified."

"He only wants to discuss the idea. He invited us to his home for dinner on Monday."

He leaned back, his face scrunched up. "Doesn't seem right to go over your dad's head."

"My dad's head is buried in the sand. The only way to save that head is to go over it. Mr. Montague only wants to talk to you." Dorothy laid her hand on Wyatt's forearm, but it was too thick and solid, so she withdrew.

Wyatt's gaze wavered and his mouth worked back and forth, but then his gaze steadied. "All right."

"Oh, thank you." She snatched a scrap of paper and Wyatt's pen from the table, and she scribbled down the address. "Eight o'clock on Monday. Please don't get lost this time."

He grinned. "I won't. I'm learning my way around town."

Dorothy glanced around. "Where's your noisier shadow? I haven't seen him lately."

"Mr. Geier? Commander Marino chose him to participate in Exercise Fox down in Lyme Bay, directing fire from a destroyer."

And he didn't choose Wyatt. How awful that Commander Marino didn't appreciate Wyatt's diligence and conscientiousness. Dorothy frowned at the veiled disappointment on the Texan's face. "And he left you to do all the work here by yourself?"

He dipped his chin and chuckled. "That isn't a problem."

She smiled at his modest good humor. "I suppose Lieutenant Geier is the sort of chap who only gets in the way."

Wyatt pulled over a stack of photographs, and his gaze slid to her. "For the record, you said it. I didn't."

The door opened, and Lawrence strolled in. Alone, thank goodness.

Dorothy wanted to spring to her feet, but she rose sedately.

Oh dear. It would also be rude not to say good-bye to Wyatt. "I'll see you Monday. Thank you again."

"Glad to do it." Wyatt pressed his face to the stereo glasses. "Then you can tell me all about church."

Dorothy grimaced. Last Sunday she'd used the extensive bomb damage as an excuse to stay home, but could she use the same excuse this week? And how beastly that she hadn't kept her end of the bargain after Wyatt had written that soul-wrenching letter.

Lawrence smiled at her and continued on his way.

She stopped him right outside his office. "Excuse me, sir. I have a report for you."

"Very good." He took the report and skimmed it. "This also gives me the opportunity to ask if you're free this evening."

Why was he free this evening? Because Helen was leaving for Liverpool? She wanted to leap at the offer, but sophisticated women didn't leap. And they didn't accept hand-me-downs. "It's rather late notice."

"Please, Dorothy." He cupped her elbow in his hand and slacked one hip closer to her, his hazel eyes warm and apologetic. "I've been dreadfully busy, but I'm dying to see you."

Dorothy's heart raced, but for the wrong reasons. What if Blissy saw them in such an intimate pose? She eased her elbow free. "Did you hear what happened to Third Officer Woolford?"

Lawrence's eye twitched. "She transferred to Liverpool, if I heard right."

"First Officer Bliss-Baldwin forced her to do so, because Helen stepped out with you. I can't afford to make the same mistake. Papa needs me here."

"So you won't see me tonight?"

His forlorn expression pressed on her heart. She had to refuse the man she'd loved forever. For Papa's sake. "It's too dangerous."

"I thought you liked danger." Mischief lifted his tone.

"I—I do." Not quite true. She liked excitement, not danger. "But not tonight. I can't take the risk of being seen."

"Very good, then." He gave her an understanding smile and entered his office.

A groan flowed up, but she stifled it. Would she ever have another chance?

15

Wyatt wiped the palm of his free hand on his trousers and rang the doorbell. Dining with strangers? Again? Only for Dorothy.

Granted, he had no foolish notions. The other day he'd seen how close she stood to Eaton, the looks that passed between them, and he knew full well how she felt about the man. But Eaton's skirt-chasing soothed Wyatt's conscience and validated his pursuit.

The door opened to a tiny lady in her forties wearing a dark floral dress. "Oh! You must be Lieutenant Paxton. I'm Wilma Montague. Please come in. We're so glad you could come."

"Thank you, ma'am. This is for you." He stepped inside and handed her the little cardboard box. "My mama would pitch a fit if she saw how I wrapped a hostess gift. Just some things from the store in quarters, things I know you folks are short on here."

Mrs. Montague poked around in the box. "Oh my. Sweets. Soap. What a treat. If my friends hear, you and your colleagues will be inundated with invitations. But I'll keep you my little secret." Light brown eyes twinkled at him.

"Thank you, ma'am."

She tipped her head to one side. "Why don't you join Dorothy in the drawing room while I fetch Mr. Montague?"

He thanked her and stepped into the next room.

Dorothy stood by the fireplace in her navy blue uniform, smiling at him. "I wasn't sure you'd come."

"I promised, didn't I?" If only he could keep that smile directed at him forever. "Speaking of promises, how was church yesterday?"

"Oh." She inspected the family portraits on the mantel. "I'm afraid I was unable to attend."

Second week in a row, and this time she didn't even bother with an excuse. He injected his voice with a hint of teasing. "Hey, now. I kept my end of the deal. I mailed that letter two weeks ago." Had it reached Texas yet? What would his parents think?

"I'm sorry, Wyatt." Her voice caught. "I know that was difficult for you, but I simply can't abide the thought . . . walking in alone, how people will stare. It's been so long. And the rector, how he'll fuss over me."

How could he be annoyed when her pretty eyes washed with regret, pain . . . fear? Fear of being conspicuous? More likely fear of facing the Lord. For now, he'd let her off the hook.

Mr. and Mrs. Montague entered the room and exchanged greetings.

Mrs. Montague squeezed Dorothy's hand. "It's good to see you after all these years, Dolly."

"Dorothy, please." She offered an apologetic smile.

"Of course. You have grown up. So like your dear mother in every way." Mrs. Montague faced Wyatt with watery eyes. "If only you could have known Margaret Fairfax. Such high spirits, such charm."

Wyatt swallowed hard, determined not to botch the chance at a compliment. "If she was anything like her daughter, she must have been lovely."

Both ladies smiled. Dorothy lowered her chin, and Wyatt's chest filled with an unfamiliar joy.

Mrs. Montague ushered them into the dining room, smaller

than at the Fairfax home and not as fancy, but nice enough to make Wyatt feel all elbows and knees.

Potato soup was served. Small talk. War talk. Apologies for the rations. Apologies for the air raids. Apologies for the weather.

Mrs. Montague excused herself and brought in the main course. "I do apologize for the service. Our cook is doing war work now, of course."

"I don't mind, ma'am." Wyatt shrugged off apologies again. "Where I come from, we're really casual."

Mrs. Montague gave him a warm smile and set the platter in front of her husband.

Leg of mutton. Wyatt's stomach lurched. Not only did he hate using up meat rations when the US Navy fed him well, but he didn't like mutton. However, if he complained, somehow Mama would find out and chap his hide. "Smells good."

Mr. Montague sliced the meat. "So, Lieutenant, Dorothy tells me you're an accountant."

"Yes, sir."

"Is your father an accountant too?"

"No, sir. He runs a trucking business. He wanted me to work for him."

One eyebrow rose on the man's thin face. "You didn't want to?"

"No, sir. I did. I do, I suppose." He glanced to Dorothy, and she gave him an encouraging smile. "I helped with the business when I was in high school, but I didn't feel ready to help run the company. I thought a business degree would help. My dad disagreed. He never went to college and he runs the company just fine."

"In my opinion, university is always good for a man." Mr. Montague passed him a plate of mutton, potatoes, and brussels sprouts.

"I think so too, sir. So my dad and I cut a deal. I'd work for him for two years, earn my tuition money. Then my brother Adler would be out of high school and could take my place. My dad made the same deal with both my brothers." A twinge in his gut.

When he ran away from home, he'd left Paxton Trucking without a son for two years.

"Wise man, your father." Mr. Montague's smile lifted the ends of his mustache.

"Yes, sir."

"Did your education accomplish your goals?"

Wyatt took a bite of mutton and sorted his thoughts while he chewed. "I'm good with figures. I like the books, the scheduling, figuring out loads and routes. Adler's my opposite. He likes working with clients, vendors, truckers. I was hoping my degree would fill in the holes."

"Did it?"

Daddy's face flashed in his mind. *"I don't need fancy number tricks. I need a leader."*

Wyatt's jaw clenched, and he pressed the tines of his fork into his mashed potatoes, avoiding Dorothy. "Now I'm even better with figures, but no better with people."

Mr. Montague chuckled. "I'm sure your father is pleased to have a good accountant."

"I didn't go to work for him." He didn't feel like talking about his sins tonight, but he would if he had to.

"Ah, the war, yes. So many plans put on hold. Our Harry is with the Eighth Army in Italy."

"We're so proud of him." Mrs. Montague's face lit up.

"As you should be." Wyatt smiled from the evidence of parental love and from the merciful reprieve.

"Let me explain why I invited you here tonight." Mr. Montague sipped his tea. "Something isn't right at Fairfax & Sons. Business is stronger than ever, but we're losing money. Like your brother, my strength is with personnel not mathematics. I've inspected the books but can't locate the source of the loss. And Mr. Fairfax . . ."

"He rarely goes to the office, especially since this 'Little Blitz' began." Dorothy fingered the linen napkin in her lap. "He denies there's a problem."

"But there is," Mr. Montague said. "If the situation doesn't change, our coffers will soon be empty, and we'll be forced to cut back. Since we already run a tight ship, any cuts would only curtail business. I'm afraid the company is in dire straits."

Wyatt frowned at the concern on all the faces. "And your accountants . . . ?"

"They haven't found the source either."

"What if they *are* the source?" Mrs. Montague leaned closer to Dorothy with an eager look in her eye. "I do love a good mystery, don't you, dear?"

Dorothy's smile looked feeble.

Mr. Montague fixed an appraising look on Wyatt. "Dorothy told me you suggested having an outside accountant investigate."

Wyatt shoveled in a brussels sprout so he'd have time to choose his words. Nasty vegetable. What he wouldn't give for a bottle of hot sauce. "Yes, sir. An experienced man who could look at the books with fresh eyes."

"Are you willing?"

"Me, sir? I'm not experienced."

"But you are an accountant. If word of scandal leaks out, our contracts with the crown will be endangered. I wanted to keep the investigation within the company, but we're small. It would be best to engage someone without links to the British business world. Someone like you."

Wyatt shook his head. If he'd told even a bit of his history, the offer never would have been made. "You don't understand, sir. I failed in business. After college, a buddy and I started a company. It failed within six months. We lost every penny."

Mr. Montague's eyes hooded. "What was the cause of the failure?"

Good, now the offer would be rescinded. "My friend had an

117

idea for a toy, a clever idea. I was concerned because a crucial part was made of rubber, and there was talk of shortages. That was the summer of '41. Milt had a good supply, but then the government confiscated it for defense, and then came Pearl Harbor. Rubber was the first thing rationed. We went belly-up."

His host chewed in silence for a minute.

Wyatt gave Dorothy a shrug, but her gaze was warmer than he deserved.

Mr. Montague dabbed at his mouth with his napkin. "Did your business fail due to your accounting?"

"No, sir. I did everything I could, but we still went bankrupt. When it comes down to it, I made a foolhardy investment."

Mr. Montague leaned back and folded his hands on his trim belly. "Lieutenant, I don't want an investor. I want an accountant with fresh eyes. I am willing to give you a chance. In fact, I'm as close to begging as an Englishman dares."

Wyatt set down his fork, his stomach squirming. "Sir, I'm not comfortable going behind Mr. Fairfax's back. He—"

"Please, Wyatt." Dorothy rested her hand on his forearm, her eyebrows twisted. "If we lose the business or if there's a scandal, Papa—I don't know if he'd survive."

Everything inside him went as mushy as the potatoes. Did she already know she was his weakness? How could he let anything happen to Mr. Fairfax? If Dorothy lost him, she might lose her last shred of faith.

Silver clinked on china as Mr. Montague sliced his mutton. "No one is in the office on Sundays. Each week we could spend an hour or two on the books after church and before lunch. I do reserve the right to my Sunday afternoon nap."

Wyatt couldn't tear his gaze from those pleading blue eyes, and a plan aligned. "You said you don't want to go to church alone. How about I go with you, then we go to the office?"

"I . . ." How could those eyes possibly get any wider?

His plan solidified. "You also said your father wants to see me. We could have lunch with him afterward."

Her hand retreated to her lap. "I don't know."

"That's the deal." A surge of confidence and victory. He could spend time with Dorothy as a friend and protect her by protecting what she loved most. This was his best opportunity to win her affection. Besides, it was the right thing to do.

Mr. Montague cleared his throat. "It seems a most reasonable deal, Dorothy."

She glanced at Wyatt, wary yet weakening.

He unfurled a grin. "All or nothing at all."

Dorothy straightened and lifted her chin. "All right, then. You Americans are a stubborn lot."

He winked at her. "Where do you think we learned it?"

Color rose in her cheeks, and she turned to Mr. Montague. "What time shall we meet you on Sunday?"

"Ten o'clock at the back entrance."

Even mutton tasted good now. He had a weekly date with Dorothy Fairfax.

16

So much in the sanctuary had changed—the boarded-up windows where stained glass had once glinted, the swag of canvas covering a bombed-out gap in the ancient stone walls, and the solid presence of an American officer beside her.

Yet so much remained unchanged. Reverend Bernard Young's face shone as if there were no war, no death, no destruction. And his words from the tenth chapter of the Gospel of St. John, familiar words she'd once found inspiring.

"'I am the door,'" the rector quoted Christ. "'By me if any man enter in, he shall be saved, and shall go in and out, and find pasture.'" Pasture—Dorothy had once found peaceful rest in her faith.

"'I am come that they might have life, and that they might have it more abundantly.'" She'd once felt the overflowing joy of abundant life.

"'I am the good shepherd: the good shepherd giveth his life for the sheep.'" She'd once felt safe and protected in the Lord's care.

Now the harsh truth of life jerked at her. She was no longer naïve. But if she knew better, why didn't she feel better? She'd lost that sense of peace and joy and safety.

Wyatt nodded and murmured beside her, his Bible open on his

lap. At least he didn't dance in the aisle and cry "hallelujah" as some did in American cinema.

The rector's round face glowed, and his arms stretched wide as if to embrace the entire congregation. "Hear the comforting words of our Lord: 'My sheep hear my voice, and I know them, and they follow me: And I give unto them eternal life; and they shall never perish, neither shall any man pluck them out of my hand. My Father, which gave them me, is greater than all; and no man is able to pluck them out of my Father's hand.'"

A panicky feeling fluttered inside her, but fleeing the sanctuary would be more conspicuous than arriving after so many years' absence.

Thank goodness the rector began praying. It would soon be over and she could escape in a dignified manner.

"Our closing hymn . . . number 54."

Wyatt opened the hymnal and held it for Dorothy.

> Savior, like a shepherd lead us, much we need Thy tender
> care;
> In Thy pleasant pastures feed us, for our use Thy folds
> prepare.
> Blessed Jesus, Blessed Jesus, Thou hast bought us, Thine
> we are;
> Blessed Jesus, Blessed Jesus, Thou hast bought us, Thine
> we are.
>
> We are Thine, do Thou befriend us, be the Guardian of
> our way;
> Keep Thy flock, from sin defend us, seek us when we go
> astray.
> Blessed Jesus, Blessed Jesus, hear, O hear us when we
> pray;
> Blessed Jesus, Blessed Jesus, hear, O hear us when we
> pray.

Thou hast promised to receive us, poor and sinful tho' we be;
Thou hast mercy to relieve us, grace to cleanse and pow'r
to free.
Blessed Jesus, Blessed Jesus, early let us turn to Thee;
Blessed Jesus, Blessed Jesus, early let us turn to Thee.

After the rector pronounced the benediction, Wyatt gestured for Dorothy to lead the way down the aisle. "That was a right nice sermon."

Thank goodness she was good at playacting. She steadied her voice. "Yes, it was."

A few people greeted her in the aisle with some surprise, some inquiries after her father, and some praise for her service—not as beastly as she'd imagined.

The rector beamed at everyone from his post by the door. Despite fewer hairs on his head, he didn't look any older than the last time she'd seen him. Yet she knew him to be Papa's age. He brightened even more when Dorothy approached, and he gripped her hand with both of his. "Oh, my Dorothy. It does my heart good to see you."

No mention of her absence, but the intensity of his grip said it hadn't gone unnoticed. "Thank you, Mr. Young. I'm glad to see you too."

How could he have so much light in those eyes? Eyes that shifted to the man beside her.

"May I introduce Lt. Wyatt Paxton of the United States Navy?"

The rector freed one hand to grip Wyatt's. "I do hope your stay in London has been pleasant."

"Very much so, sir." Wyatt shook the man's hand. "I really enjoyed your sermon today. In dark times like these, it's comforting to know we're safe in Jesus's hands. The Nazis may pluck away this earthly life, but no one can touch our souls."

"So true, young man. Dorothy has chosen well."

She choked back a gasp.

Wyatt simply chuckled. "Sorry for the confusion, sir. She's dating someone else."

His gaze bounced between the two of them. Then he gazed heavenward and shrugged. "Young people."

Dorothy smiled, relieved that rumors might be prevented.

The rector squeezed her fingers. "Go in peace, and may the Lord's hand be upon you."

The squeezing spread to her chest, and she could only nod her good-bye. She trotted down the steps, her heart slamming around in its tight confines. The last thing she wanted was the Lord's hand upon her.

Wyatt caught up to her on the pavement. "How do we get to Fairfax & Sons?"

"Bus." The word snagged in her throat.

He glanced up to the dreary gray sky. "Speaking of Eaton, did you go out this weekend?"

"No." She pulled in a breath to compose herself. "Although he did ask." For the second week in a row, she'd been compelled to refuse.

"I don't understand."

Dorothy crossed the road. "Did you hear what happened to Helen Woolford?"

"Who?" He made a face. "Sorry. I'm no good with names."

"She's a Wren in intelligence. She stepped out with Lawrence, so First Officer Bliss-Baldwin transferred her." At the bus stop, Dorothy pulled herself tall.

Wyatt's eyebrows rose. "He's dating other women?"

Dorothy's cheeks burned. "It isn't against the law. He hasn't settled down yet."

"Sure. But still . . ." He glanced down the street, but the wrong way. "Why ask a girl out unless you really like her? And if you really like her, why go out with others?"

He made it sound so simple. If only it could be so.

Wyatt turned back with a frown. "So this Wren broke a rule by dating him?"

"No." Dorothy scanned for the bus in the proper direction. "But Bliss—she stepped out with Lawrence too, and she wants him to herself."

Wyatt whistled, another strange American habit. "Never knew there was so much intrigue at Norfolk House."

Dorothy winced from the unpleasantness of being trapped in a love polygon. "Do you see my quandary? If Bliss finds out I care for Lawrence—if we're seen together—she could transfer me as well."

"You can't leave your dad." His voice softened. "I'm sure Eaton understands."

Where was that bus? Dorothy fiddled with her handbag strap. "He thinks I'm being rather cautious. He likes my sense of daring, but oh dear. I can't."

Wyatt was mercifully quiet for a long moment. "If he cares about you, he'll listen to your concerns. He'd want to protect you, and he'd never do anything to endanger you."

There was such simplicity and security in his words, his voice, his expression. Appealing, and yet . . . how could Lawrence come to care about her unless she stepped out with him? Unless he saw she'd become the woman he wanted?

The rumble of a motor caught her attention. A red double-deck bus lumbered toward them, and Dorothy opened her handbag for her coins.

Why had she agreed to Lawrence's plan to curry Blissy's favor? If he hadn't turned the woman's head his way, Dorothy might be able to see him freely. But then her commanding officer might never have let up her annoying campaign for her girls to tour the Empire.

"Um . . . ?" Wyatt stared at copper and silver coins in his hand.

"Here." Dorothy picked out the correct change for him, then

boarded the bus. She handed the driver her coins, and the woman gave her a ticket. Then Dorothy climbed the steep spiral stairs to the second deck.

Wyatt followed. "I don't know how much good I'll do with those books if I can't figure out your money."

"It's quite simple." She sat on the wooden seat. "Twelve pence in a shilling, two shillings in a half crown, twenty shillings in a pound."

"Not as simple as the decimal system. Hundred cents in a dollar."

"Yet another rebellion against tradition."

A smile rose on the rebel's face as he joined her on the bench. The bus trundled down the road.

"I'm surprised you like the upper level," Wyatt said. "You said you were afraid of flying. I assumed that meant you were afraid of heights."

Dorothy searched her memories. Oh yes. When they were dancing. "I'm surprised you remember."

"It struck me. I'd pegged you as the fearless daredevil, climbing statues and seawalls."

She relished the sway of the bus and the downward view on the street, just the right amount of excitement. "My fearlessness has limits."

"Glad to hear. There's fearless, then there's foolhardy."

She smiled. "True."

He nudged her with his elbow. "But hey, you overcame one fear today. You went to church and survived."

"Shocking, since the hand of the Lord is upon me." She mimicked the rector's tones, but with a sarcastic edge.

"What do you mean?"

Down below, an older couple picked through the rubble of their home, while ARP wardens assisted. "The hand of the Lord only slaps me around. I prefer to stay out of slapping range."

Wyatt chuckled.

Stunned, she faced him.

Crinkles fanned out around his eyes. "Don't you know he's everywhere? You can't get out of his reach, and that's good. You heard the preacher—if you belong to Jesus, nothing can pluck you from his hand."

Her throat tightened. "Then my mother and brothers must not have belonged to him."

One shoulder rose. "That doesn't mean you'll never die. Of course not. We all die, but we're never away from God's care. Wait . . . yes. Psalm 139." He opened his Bible.

Dorothy squirmed. Hadn't she had enough Scripture for the day?

"Wow. This is perfect." Wyatt grinned and handed her the Bible. "Read this out loud. I want you to see it and hear it for yourself. Start at verse 5, but it's all good, of course."

She hesitated, then obeyed in a low voice. "'Thou hast beset me behind and before, and laid thine hand upon me. Such knowledge is too wonderful for me; it is high, I cannot attain unto it. Whither shall I go from thy spirit? or whither shall I flee from thy presence? If I ascend up into heaven, thou art there: if I make my bed in hell, behold, thou art there. If I take the wings of the morning, and dwell in the uttermost parts of the sea; Even there shall thy hand lead me, and thy right hand shall hold me.'"

"Do you see? Isn't it incredible?" Wyatt's voice shook with excitement. "No matter what—when life feels as light as the morning or as dark as the depths of the sea, he's there. His hand leads us and holds us."

The words prickled and poked and rearranged things inside her, a most unsettling feeling, but it didn't unsettle Wyatt. It energized him. "You never—you never turned away."

He shifted on the bus seat. "Didn't want to. He was all I had. In a few short hours, I'd lost everything—my family, my home, my self-respect. All I had was stolen money and the Lord."

He'd even lost the money. But not his faith. "How? How did you not lose faith?"

"I clung to it." He took back his Bible and caressed the black leather. "Like the Prodigal, I looked at myself and hated what I saw. I'd never really thought of myself as a sinner. Sure, I'd sinned, but sinners—those were the other fellows. But then I *knew* I was a sinner and always had been. I needed Jesus. I clung to him, and I've never let go."

On the street corner below, a lady sold flowers in every hue. Some clung to hope, and Dorothy—she'd flung it away.

"Even now." Wyatt's voice deepened, and he cleared his throat.

"Hmm?"

He faced forward, and his Adam's apple slid from the knot of his tie to his strong chin and back again. "I don't know what the next few months hold. The war, my family. My letter—it's got to be in Texas by now. I don't know if I'll be welcomed home or rejected forever. But I do know the Lord will get me through."

"I—I'm glad."

Then he faced her, his eyes earnest yet filled with that baffling light. "Don't you see? He doesn't make the hard things in life go away, but he gets you through if you lean on him."

"If you lean on him . . . ," she whispered. "And I leaned away."

"You don't have to anymore. And when you lean, the Lord won't give way." Speaking of leaning, Wyatt pressed his shoulder to hers. "He's a solid rock."

So was Wyatt's shoulder. Solid and warm and strong.

The familiar sign of Fairfax & Sons rescued her. "Here's our stop." She sprang to her feet and practically pushed Wyatt into the aisle. "Come along, Lieutenant. At the double."

"Careful now." He let her lead the way. "We move a mite slower in Texas."

She trotted down the stairs. "Perhaps you learn a mite slower too. Repeat after me, 'Twelve pence in a shilling, two shillings in a half crown, twenty shillings in a pound.'"

Wyatt didn't repeat after her, but he stepped off the bus with a long, slow stride and a long, slow smile.

For some reason, the only thing she could think about was a long, slow kiss.

She turned on her heel and marched to the back entrance. She simply had to stop making deals.

17

The yeoman took the handwritten pages from Wyatt. "It'll be about fifteen minutes, sir."

He wasn't scheduled to meet with Commander Marino for half an hour. "Very well. I'll wait."

The yeoman retreated into the office. In the background, typewriters filled the air with clicks and clacks.

Wyatt leaned back against the counter. If only he had his book. He was reading *David Copperfield* again. Not only was it fun to read Dickens in London, but he was studying Uriah Heep, the villain who defrauded his employer.

Perhaps he could gain insight into the embezzler at Fairfax & Sons. Yesterday, he'd spent two hours going over the books with Mr. Montague. A fiasco. How could he find an embezzler when he couldn't even count bus change?

Not only was the monetary system confusing, but the British wrote their dates backward and didn't form their numbers right. They used commas instead of decimals, and they wrote the numerals one and seven funny.

Mr. Montague had been patient, and he wanted Wyatt to return next Sunday. But what good could he do?

However, he couldn't afford to fail. Dorothy trusted him—he saw it in her eyes. He wanted to protect her, protect her father, protect the company, but how?

Wyatt crossed his ankles and breathed a prayer for insight. He imagined finding the perpetrator, Dorothy's joy, Mr. Fairfax's relief—

Or would he be angry? Furious that they'd gone over his head? He'd told Mr. Montague nothing was wrong. Why didn't he want his manager to investigate?

A sick feeling coiled up inside. What if Mr. Fairfax was the embezzler?

He shook his head. Ridiculous. Mr. Fairfax might not be the best father, but he was a good man. And how could he embezzle if he never went to the office?

The door opened, and Jack Vale entered.

Wyatt grinned and shook his friend's hand. "You're back. How was Exercise Fox?"

"Just got in at noon." Jack's cheeks looked tanner, hard to do in England. "It was a great experience. They put me with a Shore Fire Control Party. We landed on the beach with British naval fire flying overhead."

Sure, Wyatt wished he'd been there, but he was happy for his friend. "Sounds fun."

"It was." Jack handed his report to the yeoman and gave the man instructions. Then he leaned his elbow on the counter. "I tell you though, for the real deal I'll be glad to be on a destroyer rather than the beach."

"Me too. So, did the SFCPs work as they were supposed to?"

"The parties did fine, but we had radio problems. The destroyers were on their own. Some did great. Some . . . ?" He whistled. "I wish you'd been there."

Wyatt shrugged. "I had duties here."

"If you'd been there, we would have hit those targets."

"Thanks." But Geier had gunnery experience too. He'd probably done fine.

"Say . . ." Jack gave him a nudge and a wink. "How about you? Hitting your target?"

"Target?"

"The redhead."

Wyatt chuckled. "I'm not planning to shell her."

"Hope not. Any progress?"

"Yes and no." He paused, not at liberty to disclose the problems at Fairfax & Sons. "Remember how I cut a deal with her the night we went dancing—I'd write home if she went to church?"

"Yeah. She convinced you after I'd failed."

"What can I say? She's a better dancer."

"Hey, now!" Jack gave him a mock glare. The man took too much pride in his dancing skills.

"Anyway, she didn't keep her end of the deal. She didn't want to go to church alone. So I went with her yesterday, and then we had lunch with her dad."

Open admiration lit Jack's brown eyes. "Wyatt the churchgoing family man versus Eaton the skirt-chasing heel."

If only Dorothy saw it that way. "More like Wyatt the big brother versus Eaton the heartthrob, but we're doing the same thing next Sunday."

"Maybe she'll see you in a new light."

Maybe not. More importantly, he hoped she'd see the Lord in a new light. If he could help reunite those two . . . well, that would be even better than winning her heart.

"Mr. Paxton?" The yeoman handed him the typed report.

"Thanks. Looks great." He smiled at the man, then at Jack. "See you in quarters."

"So long, Casanova."

Wyatt laughed and left. Nothing romantic about Sunday, but he'd enjoyed the sermon, the close conversation with Dorothy, and perking up her dad with business talk.

If only every part of the day had gone that well.

Fairfax & Sons.

Eaton.

Wyatt's steps sounded harder on the tile floor, and he turned up the staircase. One woman had been transferred, and Dorothy could be next. Didn't Eaton care? Selfish twit.

And she adored him.

Wyatt paused at the top of the stairs and took a deep breath. He'd promised himself he wouldn't get jealous, and there he was. Why did he always fall for women who preferred rogues?

He continued down the hall. That wasn't fair. Adler wasn't a rogue. He was ambitious and competitive, but he'd been better suited for Oralee. He'd won her heart through strong character as well as charm.

If Dorothy preferred Eaton, what could he do? Nothing. In the meantime, he'd keep doing what he was doing.

Wyatt entered Commander Marino's office. "Good afternoon, sir. Here's my report."

"Have a seat." The commander's voice and eyes were hard.

What on earth? What had he done? Wyatt lowered himself into a chair.

Commander Marino held up folders in both hands. "This report was written in February when Mr. Geier was here. This was written last week when he was gone."

"Yes, sir." He couldn't keep the question mark out of his voice.

Commander Marino shook one folder. "Tell me, how much of the first report did you write?"

He didn't want to get Geier in trouble, but he couldn't lie. "A good deal, sir."

"Reading them, you'd think they'd been written by the same man, every word. You wrote them all yourself, didn't you?"

Wyatt fiddled with the hem of his jacket. "Not entirely, sir. Except last week's, of course."

The commander flopped the papers down, his gaze hard as ebony. "Give me a percent."

Numbers left no room for fudging. He sighed. "Ninety, maybe ninety-five."

He jerked his head to the side and slapped his hands on the armrests of his chair. "What did Mr. Geier do while you wrote the reports?"

He had no idea, so he chose Geier's own words. "He—he talks to people, makes connections, builds bridges."

"And left you to do all the work."

"I wanted to do it, do it right. I enjoy it, and it's vital."

Marino raked his hand through his black hair. "He lied, took all the credit, and bamboozled me, the low-down . . ."

Wyatt stared at the emotions racing across his CO's face. What had happened to make him see the truth?

Marino's gaze snapped to Wyatt. "Exercise Fox did not go well from our standpoint. Mr. Geier made us look like fools. He didn't know Royal Navy terminology, the differences between their guns and ours. It was all in his briefing papers. Then they couldn't make radio contact with the SFCPs—not Geier's fault, but he should have been able to pick out targets of opportunity based on the maps. He failed. The gunnery officer was furious."

"Oh no."

"Can you do what he was supposed to do?"

"Well, yes, sir. I—I'd study the materials. I already know the maps inside out, and last year I helped direct fire at Amchitka, Attu, Kiska, the Battle of the Komandorski Islands."

"Good." He stacked the old reports to the side. "Our role has become more important than ever. Admiral Ramsay agreed with this department's assessment that we didn't have enough escort and fire support ships in the American sector—partly thanks to *your* work, I now know."

His shoulders squirmed, but he allowed the praise to settle down like a cloak. "Thank you, sir."

"He asked the US to send three battleships, two cruisers, and thirty-four destroyers."

The map in Wyatt's mind lit up with dozens of ships, hundreds of guns. "That's great, sir."

"Granted, they'll strip away some of the British ships, but we'll still be ahead."

"Yes, sir. Miles ahead."

"But that means we'll have more work—complete bombardment plans for each ship."

That was the kind of work Wyatt liked. "Yes, sir."

"I'm bringing in a new man, Lt. Irwin Slobodsky. I served with him in the Mediterranean. He's hardworking and reliable. This week you'll bring him up to speed so he can keep up with the intelligence and reports, and next week you'll head down to Plymouth."

A huge break, and all he could think about was missing a couple of Sundays with Dorothy.

Marino shoved a folder to Wyatt. "Unfortunately, Fox was the last big exercise until the end of April. Exercise Beaver starts March 27—only two regiments, but you'll get your feet wet."

Wyatt flipped through the thick stack of papers. "Two weeks. I'll be ready."

"I know you will." His voice lowered to a growl. "As for Geier, he'll be transferred and disciplined."

How was he supposed to respond? "Good" would sound vindictive. "Thank you" would sound pitiful. "I'm sorry to hear" would sound lenient. So Wyatt just nodded, his head bent over the folders.

"You're dismissed."

"Thank you, sir." Wyatt stood and turned the doorknob.

"And Mr. Paxton?"

"Yes, sir?"

Marino's forehead pinched together. "You told me you were doing your share, and I didn't believe you. I'm sorry."

"All forgiven, sir." He gave his CO a warm gaze. "And I won't let you down."

"I know you won't."

Wyatt headed down the hallway, his mind tumbling. Success fit like a shirt cut off-kilter. But it wasn't about him—it was about the Allied cause.

He accepted it into his empty hands.

18

In the backseat of the taxi, Dorothy strained to see through the blindfold. "Lawrence, please tell me where we're going. And why did you insist I wear trousers?"

"What a naughty girl. As I said, you must pay a price for each question." With a finger to her chin, he turned her head. Warm lips pressed to hers.

She'd ask a hundred questions if she could. "But don't I have a right—"

Another kiss. "No, my dear, or it wouldn't be the thrilling surprise I planned."

Dorothy pretended to pout, but she felt giddy. A second date at last, and on her terms. He'd promised to take her somewhere Bliss-Baldwin would never know about.

Lawrence's finger ran from her chin up her jawline to her ear. A shiver ran through her, but she allowed only a tiny smile.

A masculine sigh. "Your complexion is incomparable. I'm glad you outgrew those freckles. Dreadful things."

Her stomach jolted. When she'd eavesdropped on his conversation with her brothers, he'd used the same adjective. *"Such a shame about Dolly. If she lost that baby fat and those dreadful freckles, she might be a pretty girl."*

Well, she'd lost the fat, but she could never lose the freckles. She could only cover them.

"And what pretty little ears you have." He nibbled on one.

She gave him a playful nudge with her shoulder. "No more of that until you tell me where we're going."

His arm snaked around her shoulder. "That counts as a question."

He drew her close and kissed her so well, she could barely think. She reached to her blindfold—she needed to see what she could of his face in the moonlight—but he gripped her hand and threaded his fingers through hers.

She was floating away to Neverland. Was this how Wendy felt, being whisked away on an adventure? "Do you always kidnap young ladies and ravage them like this?"

"Only the daring ones."

An invitation and a warning. Be daring and sophisticated.

His kiss continued. Had he kissed Helen like this? First Officer Bliss-Baldwin? Any other Wrens? A twinge in her chest, and she pulled away.

The taxi seat creaked, and she felt Lawrence lean forward. "Park there, past the gate. We'll be back in a couple of hours."

Then the door opened, letting in the cool night air, and Lawrence tugged her hand. "Don't remove the blindfold. It's best you not know where we are."

She stood. "Why not?"

"Because we're not supposed to be here." Mischief lit up his voice.

"Hey ho, Bumps, old chap!" a male voice called.

"Hey ho, Coxy!" Lawrence replied.

Dorothy followed, peering down her nose. Art and Gil had often called Lawrence "Bumps," a nickname from rowing crew.

An oily smell greeted her as in a port, but no scent of seawater or sound of waves.

"They're with me. Let them in," Coxy said. "Here's a quid for your trouble."

"Yes, sir!" Another man's voice, obviously pleased with the one-pound note.

Where on earth were they?

Lawrence guided her forward about fifty paces. "All right. You may remove your blindfold."

Dorothy wasted no time. Lawrence chatted with this Coxy by an American Lend-Lease jeep. A short man, Coxy wore the leather jacket and flying helmet of an RAF pilot.

"Dorothy, may I introduce Lt. Cosmo Blythe of the Royal Air Force? Coxy, may I present Second Officer Dorothy Fairfax? You remember Art and Gil."

Coxy's broad face clouded. "I remember them well. Splendid chaps. I'm so sorry."

"Thank you, sir." She gazed around in the darkness. "Are we at an RAF field?"

"We are, but it's best you don't know which one." Coxy helped her into the jeep.

She chewed on her lower lip. "We aren't supposed to be here, are we?"

"Absolutely not." Lawrence hopped into the back. "That's the fun of it."

Coxy sat in the driver's seat. "Which reminds me, old chap. Pay up. I could get in big trouble for this."

Lawrence passed him a whiskey bottle. "Scotland's finest."

Coxy kissed the bottle, then started the jeep.

Oh dear. Dorothy loved adventure, but not when it involved breaking rules and not when it involved danger. The Luftwaffe loved to target RAF fields. The air raids had decreased in March but hadn't stopped. And as the jeep bounded over the field past the slumbering aircraft, a ghastly feeling filled her gut. Please no. Anything but that.

The jeep halted beside a plane with two motors. "The Bristol Blenheim," Coxy said. "A medium bomber. Not as glamorous as the Spitfire or as gloried as the Lancaster, but she gets the job done."

Lawrence didn't bring her here to see the plane as in a museum, did he? "Why are we here?" Dorothy's voice came out small and strained.

He grinned. "We're going flying."

Dorothy clamped her arm over her stomach. "I—I'd rather not."

"Nonsense." Lawrence climbed out of the jeep. "I promise we won't get in trouble."

Coxy stepped out too. "And if we do, old Bumps will take the blame."

Dorothy's breath came fast and shallow as two fears collided— displeasing Lawrence and . . . and . . .

"Let's fly." Lawrence extended a hand and that devilish smile, Peter Pan coaxing Wendy.

Unlike Wendy, she couldn't move. "I—I can't."

"Of course you can. Coxy might not be the best-looking chap, but he's an excellent pilot."

Even pixie dust couldn't help. "I've always—always been afraid of flying."

Coxy groaned. "Did you ever think she might have a stomach like Gil's? Do you remember what happened when I took him up?"

"Nonsense. Gil could be a boring old codger. Not our Dorothy. She's a daredevil."

She'd always been a daredevil, hadn't she? So why was her breath erratic, her face clammy? She'd always been brave, always loved adventure.

Disappointment lowered Lawrence's smile.

No, she couldn't let that happen. She had to overcome her silly fear. "All right. I'll give it a go."

"That's the girl I know." Lawrence helped her out of the jeep. "Now you understand why I asked you to wear trousers."

A ladder stood by the wing. Coxy climbed up, then Dorothy. Coxy slid open the window on top of the cockpit and lowered himself through the hole.

Dorothy sat on the rim, and Coxy guided her down into the cramped plane. The pilot's seat sat to the left of center. There were no other seats. "Where do I . . . ?"

Coxy swung into the pilot's seat. "Down there, the navigator's seat. The best view." He pointed to an open doorway to the right side of the cockpit. "Don't touch anything."

"I won't." She squirmed through the doorway and sat on a stool. Windows curved up and around her, close to her head. Worst of all, a window by her feet angled to allow the navigator to see the ground. The last thing Dorothy wanted to see.

"Dorothy?" Coxy's gaze was solemn. "If you have any problems, inform me straightaway."

"Thank you." She gripped the rim of the stool by her hips, the only thing she could touch.

Lawrence dropped down into the cockpit. "She'll be fine."

"I daresay. I'm afraid the only remaining seat is for the gunner toward the rear. Or you can crouch where you are."

"Here will do." Lawrence squatted and flashed Dorothy a grin. "Smashing, isn't it?"

She managed a smile. Smashing. Crashing. She mustn't think of such things.

Down on the ground, a few men scurried about.

Behind Dorothy came the sound of switches and buttons. "I told my squadron commander I was taking Rogers up for a training flight. I promised Rogers a few nips of that scotch. The ground crew received a quid each."

Paper rustled behind her. "Two fivers for you," Lawrence said.

Dorothy cringed. This date might be more expensive than their dinner at the Savoy. And far more dangerous. She forced herself to breathe evenly.

More switches, and a motor started, loud and throaty. The vibrations shook her to the core.

Coxy talked on the wireless, code words she could barely hear over the din. Then the second motor started, rattling her.

Perhaps this would be a good time to start praying again.

The plane rolled forward. No worse than an automobile. In fact, it was kind of fun, like the top deck of a bus, like the last time she'd talked about her fear of flying. With Wyatt. What had she told him? Her fearlessness had limits? Tonight she'd find out the precise location of those limits.

The plane picked up speed, bouncing and jerking over the field. Dorothy slammed her eyes shut and clung to the stool.

"I clung to him, and I've never let go." Wyatt's voice filled her mind with its soft drawl.

Her fingers hurt from the clinging. *Dear Lord, please let me live.*

The jerking stopped, but then came a sickening feeling, like dropping and rising all at once.

Dorothy stifled a cry and opened her eyes. She couldn't see a thing in the night sky, but she knew she was hurtling through the air, untethered to anything safe and secure. "Oh, Lord," she whispered. "Please help me."

The plane rocked and swayed. How could Coxy see where he was going? See the divide between land and sky, between life and death?

The plane tilted to the left, and Dorothy almost slipped off her seat. She couldn't stifle her cry this time.

"Only a shallow turn," Coxy called. "How are you doing?"

"I'm fine." But her strangled voice betrayed her.

"Are you sure? I can go back at any time."

"Nonsense," Lawrence said in a loud voice over the roar of the motors. "She's fine."

Fine, fine, fine. How could she be fine when the motors rumbled through her, when the smell of petrol sank in her belly, when the plane's incessant motion made her dizzy?

Nausea billowed, reminding her of taking the ferry across the Channel and heaving over the side.

Even the risk of losing her perch on her stool paled in that green light, and she pressed one hand over her stomach.

"Are you feeling sick, Dorothy?"

How could she admit such a thing? But how could she deny it? She tried to shake her head, but that only increased the vertigo, and she groaned.

Coxy cursed. "Please pardon my language. I'll head back."

"Balderdash," Lawrence said. "She's not sick. No self-respecting member of His Majesty's Royal Navy would dare get seasick."

"But she might get airsick." Coxy put the plane into another supposedly shallow turn. "My ground crew will have my head if I have a mess. Sorry, old chap, but I'm in charge up here."

Up. Too far up. How could air be bumpy? She clapped her hand over her mouth. *Please, Lord. Don't let me embarrass myself in here.*

The air bumps were soon replaced by ground bumps. The plane's rapid deceleration was both terrifying and comforting.

But the nausea didn't stop. Why wouldn't it stop?

The motors quieted.

"Dorothy? How are you?"

She wanted out. Immediately. She faced him, her hand hard over her mouth.

Coxy's eyes widened. "Let's get you out of here. Bumps, out of the way."

Somehow she moved, her legs weak and wobbly. Coxy hoisted her up through the top window. Dorothy had to use both hands to climb out, so she squeezed her mouth shut, willing her stomach to behave.

She crawled along the wing toward the ladder, and then her body betrayed her. She leaned over the edge of the wing and retched, over and over.

The plane rocked, and she sensed the two men joining her on the wing.

"Blast it all, Bumps. You should have listened to her."

"It never occurred to me." Footsteps descended the ladder.

Dorothy gripped the wing, head down. How could she ever raise it again?

"Are you finished?" Coxy squatted beside her with compassion in his voice. "Do you feel better?"

Only her stomach felt better. Everything else felt worse. She groped in her trouser pocket for her handkerchief and wiped her mouth.

"Here." Coxy handed her another.

She used that one to dab her eyes. Tears would ruin her makeup. But what were freckles compared to the revolting mess she'd made?

"Are you ready to leave?"

She nodded, miserable inside and out, and she backed down the ladder, hands shaking. *"If he cares about you at all, he'll listen to your concerns,"* Wyatt had said.

How could Lawrence care about a wretched, retching girl like her? Why couldn't she be the woman she wanted to be?

19

On the bridge of the British destroyer *Seavington*, Wyatt compared the map to the landscape before him. The Slapton Sands area had been chosen for the American amphibious training exercises because its shingle beach, bluffs, and rolling green farmland resembled the US landing beaches in Normandy.

The residents had been evacuated from the region in December, and the Americans had invaded with a big amphibious training center.

He lifted his binoculars. The two British cruisers and four destroyers had lifted their fire from the initial bombardment, and the dust kicked up by their shells obscured the landmarks, but . . . "There it is."

The square lines of the abandoned Royal Sands Hotel disrupted the smoke. Wyatt skirted around some sailors to the pelorus, found the bearing, and glanced at his watch. "Captain, the hotel is at bearing one-one-two. We have nine more minutes before we have to hold our fire."

"Very good, Lieutenant." Captain Willoughby issued orders to fire on the target.

As the American naval gunfire liaison officer aboard the *Seaving-*

ton, Wyatt had spent the past few days meeting with the British gunners and gunnery officers. Although Exercise Beaver was an American operation, the US destroyers hadn't arrived in England yet, so British help was needed to protect the convoy and for gunfire support during the landings.

Out on the gray waters of Lyme Bay, dozens of little LCVP landing craft darted toward the beach, carrying two regiments of the US 4th Infantry Division.

Wyatt glanced at his watch again. Timing and accuracy were vital to knock out enemy positions without hitting GIs. Those fake gun positions offered no danger, but the Allies had to take the exercises seriously to be prepared for the actual invasion.

Only two months away.

The *Seavington*'s four 4-inch guns cranked into position, and Wyatt bent his knees to steady himself. Light and smoke and noise assaulted his eyes and ears, and the concussion took his breath. The guns on the Hunt-class destroyers were smaller than on American destroyers, but the salvo was still impressive. He grinned at the navigator beside him. "Jolly good show, old chap."

"Mighty fine shootin' there, Tex." Lieutenant Langley's Texas accent was even worse than Wyatt's English accent.

Smiling, Wyatt peered through the binoculars. A new tuft of smoke appeared about a hundred yards west of the hotel. He picked up the telephone and discussed adjustments with Lieutenant Foster, the gunnery officer. New coordinates were ordered, and Wyatt braced himself as another salvo disrupted the English country morning.

In battle they'd be unlikely to destroy an actual gun battery, since the Germans encased them in thick reinforced concrete casemates. But persistent fire could rattle the gun crew and drive them underground to seek shelter, and it could damage the supply lines—anything to keep them from firing on the troops on the beach.

A new pillar of smoke rose. The hotel . . . was it Wyatt's imagination or had it just lost a chunk of roof?

The LCVPs drew closer to the shore. Time remained for one more salvo.

Wyatt made pencil marks on his map for each hit. He paused when the guns fired again.

Once the troops landed, the ships would hold fire until directed by a Shore Fire Control Party on the beach.

Wyatt didn't envy those fellows in the landing craft. Sure, no one shot at them from shore, but live naval fire whizzed over their heads, getting the men used to the noise of battle.

A geyser of dust rose from the hotel—a solid hit, and Wyatt whistled.

The captain ordered the guns to hold fire. Wyatt made an X on his map and anticipated where the SFCPs might direct fire—at the draw, at the causeway, and at the hotel again, where enemy snipers were supposed to be located. He'd noted his landmarks and knew the coordinates.

Since the SFCPs wouldn't call in fire for a while, Wyatt wandered out to the wing of the bridge. Barely above freezing, the sea air spun around him.

The British ships had a different scent, but a good one. Funny how every ship had her own unique perfume.

Thank you, Lord, for letting me be here. Not only was it fun, but he was helping prepare both the American soldiers and the British sailors for the coming battle. He felt bad for Geier, but the man had his chance.

Wyatt raised his binoculars. Tiny landing craft rode the white-tipped waves onto the beaches, and tiny soldiers ambled over the beach. Wyatt had a hunch they'd move a bit faster when they landed on Utah Beach on D-day.

"Hey, boys," he muttered. "Take this seriously. It's your duty."

Duty. A little pang of guilt. By fulfilling his duty to his country,

Wyatt was breaking his promise to help at Fairfax & Sons. Last Sunday he'd made progress. He'd figured out the departments and the flow of money. Next he needed to look for something fishy. That would have to wait.

Wyatt frowned and rested his elbows on the railing. He could still see Dorothy's face when he told her he was going to Plymouth. She'd said all the right words—she was thrilled he had this opportunity and that Marino had seen Wyatt's worth—but she'd been quiet and distant on the bus ride from church to the office.

That wasn't like her. Was it because Wyatt wouldn't be investigating for a while? Or was it something the preacher said? Something Wyatt said? Or another matter entirely?

He'd asked about her weekend, and she'd said she had a date with Eaton. Instead of gushing about him and every fancy detail, she'd said she didn't want to bore Wyatt. And she got even quieter, a bit pale.

Maybe she'd had a fight with Eaton. Compassion for her beat out elation for himself. Besides, even if she'd had it out with Eaton, that didn't mean she'd turn to Wyatt. If she wasn't attracted to him, she wasn't attracted to him. He refused to fool himself.

His breath tumbled white before him. Up went the binoculars. Couldn't let himself be distracted.

On the beach, figures in khaki field jackets and olive drab trousers covered the beach and climbed over the seawall. Faint stuttering of machine-gun fire crossed the water.

Wyatt returned to the bridge and called down to the radio room—the British called it wireless telegraphy. They hadn't heard from the SFCP, so he bided his time, his foot tapping on the deck. He couldn't fire until coordinates were called in. He couldn't risk hitting the troops.

On D-day they'd have to make dozens of decisions like this— where to fire, when to fire, when to hold fire.

For the sake of those men on the ground, he couldn't afford to fail.

"Lieutenant Paxton?" a talker called. "Wireless, sir."

"Thanks." He grabbed the phone. The Shore Fire Control Party on the beach had called in coordinates, and Wyatt studied his map. Right where he'd predicted a gun position.

"Let's blow that gun to kingdom come." Wyatt grinned. Today he wouldn't fail.

20

Gwen Hamilton leaned over Dorothy's desk and patted a folder. "Aren't you supposed to deliver this to Lieutenant Commander Eaton?"

Dorothy groaned. "I'll wait until he leaves at five. I should have delivered it when he was away at lunch, but I forgot."

Gwen perched her hip on the edge of the desk. "It's been two weeks."

Two weeks since she'd looked him in the eye. She waited until he was out of the office to place reports on his desk. When it was necessary to discuss something with him, she fixed her gaze on the documents, her voice cool and professional.

For the first week he'd seemed just as eager to avoid her, but this past week he'd tried to engage her. If he wanted an apology, she refused. She hadn't done anything wrong. She'd told him she didn't want to fly, and he'd ignored her.

Dorothy flipped through the folder, avoiding Gwen's gaze. The only thing she'd done wrong was to fail to be the woman Lawrence wanted.

On Tuesday evening, she'd had tea with Johanna Katin and blurted out the entire mortifying story. Johanna thought it might be for the best. Her sweet friend thought Dorothy deserved a man she didn't have to playact with. But Johanna didn't understand the decade-long hold Lawrence had on her heart. She didn't know what it was like not to be lovable as she was, not even to be loved by her own father. Playacting was her only hope.

"I'm still here, Dorothy." Amusement colored Gwen's voice.

"I've noticed."

"Well, do you want to give it another go with Lawrence or not?"

Dorothy sighed and pushed the folder away. "Of course I do, but he—"

"But he wants a woman who is daring and sophisticated, and you're acting like a mouse." Gwen picked up the folder and shoved it in Dorothy's face. "Hold your head high and deliver this with that darling droll smile of yours."

First Officer Bliss-Baldwin passed and stopped to talk to Stella Dodds, not ten feet away.

This was ridiculous, the pining, the jealousy, the intrigue. Something hardened inside her. "No more of this," she whispered. "I'm a Wren. I'm not here to win a man but to win a war."

Gwen wiggled the report. "All the more reason to deliver this, oh brave warrior princess."

Dorothy's chin edged forward, and she snatched the folder. "I shall."

She marched through the door into intelligence. Instinctively, she glanced to the worktable, but Wyatt wasn't there, of course. He'd been gone almost two weeks now. A pang in her chest—again. She was surprised how much she missed him at headquarters and this past Sunday.

She'd almost skipped church, but the thought of Wyatt's gentle reprimand led her to attend alone. Something else had drawn her too, a disconcerting tug inside. The sermon, the hymns, the Scriptures—they had an odd calming effect, a strange stirring, not unlike when Wyatt had prayed in the Tube during the air raid.

But right now she didn't have the time or inclination to explore those emotions. She had duties.

Dorothy steeled herself, entered Lawrence's office, and laid the folder on the desk before him. "The latest reports, sir."

He looked her full in the eye, but she didn't waver. She kept her expression strong but not one bit droll. She was here to work, not to flirt.

"Very good." He stood and closed the door. "I'm glad you came. I've wanted to speak with you privately all week. I owe you an apology."

Her mind stalled, and her lips parted.

Lawrence leaned back against the door and crossed his arms. "Time has a chastening effect on me. Yes, even on me."

Dorothy let one corner of her mouth rise.

He frowned and tilted his head. "I'm afraid I allowed the . . . incident to color my opinion of you, which wasn't right. It didn't occur because of a weak will. Indeed, you agreed to fly despite your fears, which shows great strength of will. Rather, it occurred because of a weak stomach, and it wasn't fitting of me to hold that against you. I acted the cad, and I apologize."

A few pounds lifted from her shoulders. "Apology accepted."

"Thank you."

"And I apologize for ruining what should have been a lovely evening."

"Apology accepted but unnecessary." His gaze reached to her, beseeched her. "Do I dare hope you'll honor me with your company again?"

The last bit of weight fell away. "Oh yes. I'm free this weekend."

He winced and glanced away. "I have plans."

Oh dear. Why did she always have to be so impulsive and eager?

"Perhaps next weekend?" he asked.

"I'm afraid I have plans," she said in a bored tone. And now she'd lied, just so she could look sophisticated.

"Another time, then." He stepped away from the door and opened it. "I do hope it's soon."

To leave, she had to squeeze between him and the open door. She looked up into those handsome hazel eyes that promised excitement and thrills. "We'll see." She lifted one eyebrow, perfectly droll, and swung away—

And she almost bumped into First Officer Bliss-Baldwin.

The woman's face went pale, and her gaze darted between Lawrence and Dorothy. "Why are you here, Second Officer?"

Although her heart raced, Dorothy kept her expression nonchalant. "I delivered a report, ma'am."

"May I help you, First Officer?" Lawrence asked, warm and welcoming.

"I do have something to discuss with you." Blissy brushed past Dorothy and into the office, shutting the door behind her.

Dorothy blew out a stiff breath and strode through intelligence. That could have been a disaster. At least Old Blissy's reaction would show Lawrence the need for discretion.

For the first time, she wished he were stationed elsewhere.

Back at her desk, she finished the last of the day's work. The French Resistance was becoming bolder each day, and they provided more and more intelligence about German fortifications, increasing and refining the details on Dorothy's diagrams and maps.

So many of the sweet homes in the Vierville area had been demolished by the Nazis, to open the line of sight for their guns and also to ransack the lumber. Yet her holiday home stood, perhaps because it was built of solid ancient stone.

At five o'clock, Dorothy straightened her materials, grabbed her handbag, and headed out into the main passageway.

The door to intelligence opened, and Lawrence stepped out and smiled at her. "What fortuitous timing."

She gave him a warning look. "Not if my commanding officer sees me."

Lawrence strolled beside her, his overcoat draped over his arm. "Nonsense. I reminded Julia of what I told her at the start. You and I are old family friends."

Did he kiss all his family friends the way he'd kissed her? Jealousy twined inside, but she unwound it. He'd made his opinion quite clear. A teasing smile rose. "I thought you found jealous women tiresome." Oh, just the right amount of lilt in her voice.

Lawrence chuckled. "I reminded Julia of that. I do wish all women could be as modern-minded as you."

"Thank you." But her pleasure at his compliment dissolved. She'd given him permission to see as many women as he wanted, hadn't she? Why did romance have to be so complicated?

They rounded the corner. A dark-haired American naval officer closed a door in the passageway before them.

"Good evening, Commander Marino."

He smiled and shook Lawrence's hand. "Good evening, Lieutenant Commander Eaton."

"May I introduce Second Officer Fairfax?"

"We've already met." He shook Dorothy's hand. "Can't tell you how much we appreciate the work your department does. It really helps."

"Thank you, sir."

"Any word from your boys down at Slapton Sands?" Lawrence asked. "I certainly hope they're doing better with Exercise Beaver than with Fox."

"Much better." Marino rubbed the back of his neck. "I sent Mr. Paxton this time, and he did a bang-up job. Hit two of the targets right on the nose."

Dorothy couldn't restrain her smile. Oh, good for Wyatt.

Lawrence cocked his head to the side. "Paxton? Is he new? I haven't met him."

She blinked at him. Wyatt had been in the intelligence office several times a week for almost three months.

"Sure, you have. He's quiet, but don't make the mistake of overlooking him as I did." Commander Marino shook his head and closed his eyes.

Thank goodness he'd seen Wyatt's merits. Dorothy smiled at Lawrence. "You've met him. Tall, sandy hair, has a Texas accent."

"Oh yes." Lawrence nodded. "I suppose cowboys do know a thing or two about shooting."

Commander Marino's smile flattened.

Lawrence had sounded a bit condescending, but Dorothy didn't dare give him the reprimanding scowl he deserved. Instead, she grasped her chance to escape before Old Blissy could see them together again. "Excuse me, gentlemen. I must run. Good evening."

After they said good-bye, she strode toward the main staircase.

What smashing good news. Bully for Wyatt. Commander Marino would never overlook him again. And if the training exercise was over, he'd return to London soon.

She trotted down the stairs. She couldn't wait to congratulate him. He'd smile, but he'd duck his chin in that modest way of his. What a good man.

A little trill in her chest, similar to when she'd danced with him.

Dorothy paused, her hand curled around the banister, her breath snared in her lungs. Yes, he was a good man and an attractive man, but not for her. They were friends, dear friends, but nothing more.

He wasn't the right kind of man for her, and she must never fall for an American and leave Papa.

A hint of Lawrence's voice drifted down the stairs, and she glanced up. Now that her hope with him had been renewed, why would she want anyone else?

21

Wyatt strolled through Hyde Park with Mr. Fairfax, Dorothy, and Bonnie Prince Charlie. He'd rather have Dorothy right by his side than her father, but how could he complain on an Easter afternoon with a full dinner in his belly and the smell of flowers tickling his nose?

No complaints at all. Even though Exercise Beaver had revealed problems with communication and organization, Wyatt had succeeded and Commander Marino had praised his work.

Now Commander Marino, Wyatt, and Slobodsky—whom Wyatt liked immensely—were busy divvying up targets for the individual warships. The US task force would start arriving in a few weeks, and they'd need to be trained and briefed.

"I can't help but think of William Wordsworth." Dorothy leaned over and trailed her fingers over a patch of yellow daffodils, setting them bobbing. "'I wandered lonely as a cloud that floats on high o'er vales and hills, when all at once I saw a crowd, a host, of golden daffodils; beside the lake, beneath the trees, fluttering and dancing in the breeze.'"

Wyatt smiled at the back of her head. She was as bright as those flowers, breaking up the loneliness of his life the past few years.

She straightened up. "That's an unfashionably sentimental poem nowadays, but I loved it as a child."

Wyatt shrugged. "If it's unfashionable to enjoy God's creation, count me out."

Mr. Fairfax led Charlie around a Victorian statue of a boy with a large fish, and then down a path out of the sunken garden. "Onward."

Dorothy fell in on her father's left. Wyatt didn't have room on her left, so he fell in to the right.

When Mr. Fairfax had asked to accompany them to church that morning, Dorothy looked shocked. Since they weren't meeting with Mr. Montague that afternoon, it worked out fine. But Wyatt was torn. The man needed to be at church too, but if he came along in the future, what excuse could Wyatt and Dorothy give to leave him and go to his office?

Gray clouds threatened showers, and Wyatt frowned at them. Last Sunday's investigation hadn't turned up any leads, and a nasty suspicion hung as heavy as the overcast. Why couldn't the accountants at Fairfax & Sons find the leak? Why couldn't Wyatt? And why did Mr. Fairfax insist there wasn't a problem? What if he was involved?

Wyatt stifled a groan. How could he think such things?

"I do love Hyde Park on Easter, don't you, Papa?" Dorothy reached up to a low-hanging tree branch. "Such lovely memories."

Mr. Fairfax grunted, and his eyelid twitched.

As always, these two broke Wyatt's heart. Dorothy wanted to reclaim her lost family through memories, and Mr. Fairfax wanted to forget. Both grieving in different, clashing ways.

The path led through a tunnel of tall trees, with open fields to the right.

"I used to love the Easter Parade here." Dorothy turned in a little circle as she walked. "Mum and I decorated our Easter bonnets with as many fresh flowers as they could bear. Then we'd watch the others in their finery. I'm so tired of this war. It's beastly to wear navy blue on Easter—and these horrid black stockings."

Wouldn't she cut a pretty picture in a flowery dress, silk stockings, and her hair flowing free? "Well, I think you look pretty in uniform."

"Thank you." She gave him a polite smile as if he'd given the compliment only to be courteous. She didn't know how much he meant it.

"She doesn't need frippery anyway." Mr. Fairfax clucked his tongue and pulled Charlie away from something questionable on the path.

Dorothy leaned around her father and smiled at Wyatt. "Papa never had patience for fashions and flowers. While Mum and I pranced around in our bonnets, he and the boys always stole away to find a cricket match."

Pain zinged across Mr. Fairfax's face, but then he turned to Wyatt and his face cleared. "You don't happen to play cricket, do you, son?"

Son? Again? Wyatt held his breath and ventured a look at Dorothy, but she kept smiling, so he relaxed. "Afraid not. But I do play a mean game of baseball."

Mr. Fairfax turned right onto a path across the open fields, and he flapped his hand. "Bah. Baseball. Barbaric game, all about power and speed. Now cricket is a game of finesse and accuracy. You play with your mind, not brute strength."

Wyatt chuckled. "You'd be surprised. A lot of strategy in baseball, a lot of psychology, reading the other players' minds."

He'd been a solid player in high school, a reliable heavy hitter and a consistent second baseman. Not the star Adler turned out to be, but at least Wyatt had his time in the sun before his younger brother smashed his records.

"We'll have to teach you cricket." Mr. Fairfax gestured to men playing in an open spot between two antiaircraft batteries. "A fine sport."

"Ah, what could be finer than hitting a home run?" Wyatt swung an imaginary bat. "Hearing the crack, watching the ball soar, seeing the infielders gawk, the outfielders run and jump and flail? Now that's a fine feeling. Y'all don't know what you're missing."

"Yanks." Mr. Fairfax's eyes glowed with the joy of a good argument.

As they crossed the field, the man explained cricket with his face lit up. Lots of talk about wickets and pitches and creases and bowlers. Complicated game, but intriguing. Wyatt asked plenty of questions to keep him talking, to keep Dorothy smiling.

His protective urge was satisfied. Wyatt might not be able to heal the Paxtons, but befriending the Fairfax family gave him a taste of redemption.

They followed the path into another clump of trees. A silver band of water shimmered just beyond.

"Do you suppose the ducklings will be out?" Dorothy asked.

"Ducklings." Mr. Fairfax's face brightened again, in a soft, nostalgic sort of way.

"Let's go see, Papa."

Even Charlie's ears perked up.

Wyatt laughed. "Doesn't Charlie chase them away?"

"Oh no." Dorothy shuddered in mock offense. "As a member of His Majesty's Royal Highlanders, he knows all ducks are loyal British subjects."

"So only the squirrels are Nazis."

Dorothy tipped her head to one side. "Possibly the geese. He hasn't quite decided. He growls at them to let them know he's watching."

Wyatt smiled down at the alert little dog. "Carry on, Highlander."

A whole bunch of pathways intersected in a hub straight ahead, and Wyatt stepped behind Mr. Fairfax to let the crowds pass.

From the left, a group of American airmen sauntered in front of them onto the path, wearing crush caps and waist-length olive drab jackets with the Eighth Air Force patch on the sleeve.

A trio of British girls strolled past in floral dresses, and the airmen whistled and called out, all but two pilots, the lone gentlemen of the group.

"Typical Yanks." Dorothy cast Wyatt a teasing glance over her shoulder.

He would have chuckled, but there was something about one of the pilots, the taller of the two who hadn't whistled. Something about the set of his shoulders and hips, something about his walk, something about the way he shook his blond head when his buddies ribbed him for not flirting.

Something about the throaty laugh that tumbled back to him through the air, through the years.

His blood froze into icicles prickling all his veins.

Adler.

No, it couldn't be. Adler was home helping with the business. It was vital to the war effort, so he wouldn't be drafted.

"Wyatt? What's the matter?" Dorothy asked. "Wyatt?"

His name? No! Not his name.

"Shh!" He pressed his finger to his lips, wheeled around, and marched away. There—a bubbler. He leaned over it, his breath galloping.

"I don't trust those contraptions," Mr. Fairfax said. "Don't seem quite hygienic."

Wyatt didn't take a drink. He gripped the sides of the basin. A rusty stain darkened the stone around the drain, and a drop of water plopped down, splattering on the drain shield.

"Wyatt?" Dorothy's small hand settled on his shoulder. "Are you—are you all right?"

159

He was making a fool of himself, but he couldn't stand tall, couldn't look at her, couldn't speak.

"He looks pale," Mr. Fairfax said. "Perhaps Mrs. Bromley used a bad bit of cream in the sauce."

Wyatt shook his head, heavy and slow. Adler would be long gone, but it took a few breaths for Wyatt to gather words. "I think I just—I just saw my brother. Adler."

"You did?" Dorothy squeezed his shoulder. "Maybe it's a sign. You can make up."

"No!" He stood straight, dislodging her hand and looking down into her stunned face, as close as when they were dancing. "Not now. I'm not ready."

Her expression softened. "Because you haven't paid off your debt?"

Wyatt sneaked a glance over his shoulder. No sign of those airmen, thank goodness. "I can never pay off that debt. I'm responsible for the death of the woman he loved."

"It was an accident, and you know it."

"I know. But he doesn't."

"Are you sure?" She gave him a small, sad smile. "What if he realizes it was an accident now? What if he's aching to tell you he's forgiven you? What if he wants to apologize for blaming you, for trying to kill you?"

His cheek twitched the length of the scar. "I doubt it."

"Poor, sweet Wyatt." That tiny hand patted his forearm. "You talk about God forgiving you, but you can't forgive yourself."

His mouth opened to tell her it was about Adler forgiving him, about Clay forgiving him, not about forgiving himself, but the words crumbled on his tongue.

She was right.

His eyes slammed shut, and he groaned.

"Didn't the rector talk about that this morning?" Her voice was so soft and low. "How we try to atone for our own sins, but how Christ made the ultimate atonement and we can do nothing. We don't need to."

This desperate need to pay off every penny. This drive to heal and reconcile. This self-flagellation of depriving himself, of isolating himself from his family.

He gripped the basin so hard the pebbles hurt his fingers. Deep inside it bothered him that God had let him off the hook so easily. He didn't deserve such mercy. So he'd put himself right back on that hook, punishing himself, as Jack kept saying.

He was trying to pay the price Jesus had already paid.

But how could he forgive himself for what he'd done?

On the other hand, how could he not?

"Lord, I'm sorry," he muttered. "Forgive me for trying to do your job. Help me forgive myself."

Tree branches rustled overhead. Children's laughter floated toward him. Charlie snuffled in the grass. Dorothy's hand lay gentle on his arm. And the stone warmed in his touch.

Mr. Fairfax cleared his throat. Not loud, not rude, just getting his attention. Wyatt needed to pull himself together.

He drew a deep breath. He'd thought he was helping Dorothy spiritually by coaxing her to church. Yet she was the one who'd spoken God's truth today.

Wyatt opened his eyes. Dorothy looked up at him with compassion and conviction, her lips bent with a bit of amused understanding.

So kissable.

If her father weren't there . . .

But he was. And Wyatt didn't have the right.

Instead, he covered her hand with his own, squeezed, and let go. "Thanks."

Then he spun to Mr. Fairfax and spread his arms wide. "Didn't you promise to show me some ducklings? Can't be as cute as the ducks in Texas, mind you, but I'll give them a chance."

Mr. Fairfax chuckled. "Why we let you braggarts onto our island, I'll never know."

"Haven't you heard? We're here to win the war for y'all." Then he winked to let them know he was kidding.

Dorothy walked backward toward the lake, beckoning with her finger. "Your misguided sense of superiority will dissolve when you see English ducklings. Utterly adorable."

He followed, completely dissolved. Utterly adorable. And wise and funny and wonderful. Yes, she was.

22

Dorothy turned onto her street. "I'm sorry Mr. Montague couldn't meet us until after lunch, Wyatt. I hate to waste your entire Sunday."

He shrugged. "I don't mind."

"Papa won't mind either. He'll be glad to have more time with you, especially since we won't be in London much longer." Her stomach clenched.

"I don't have my orders yet, but it'll be soon."

"I don't either." Allied Naval Expeditionary Force Headquarters would soon transfer to battle headquarters near Portsmouth.

"Your dad will be fine." Wyatt's voice was so soothing.

Dorothy gave him a grateful smile and opened the door. "Papa! I'm home, and Wyatt's with me." That ought to bring him running.

Only silence greeted her.

"Here's a note." Wyatt picked up a slip of paper from the table. "He's gone to the park to feed the ducks. He took Charlie."

"Feed the ducks?" Dorothy snatched the note and read it herself. "How wonderful. He hasn't done that in years. It used to be his favorite pastime." How Mum had needled him about it. Such a dull hobby, she insisted. But it made Papa so happy.

"It's good he went, then. You see? He'll be fine."

She clutched the note to her chest. "You're good for him."

Wyatt lowered his chin and mumbled something unintelligible.

"You are. Since you've been visiting, he's eating better, he's going to the office three or four days a week, and now he's feeding the ducks."

"Shucks. It's not me. You know what they say about time healing all wounds."

Such sweet modesty. "I wish I had that effect on him. I tried—"

"Hey, now." He locked his gaze on her. "You're a good daughter. No one could be better for him. He may not see it now, but he'll come to his senses."

Even another twenty-four years was unlikely to shift her father's affections. She glanced around the empty house. "Well. We have two hours before lunch. What shall we do?"

"What would you normally do with two free hours?"

"Paint, but you don't seem like the artistic sort."

"Nope, but you could show me your work. I like the sketches you do at headquarters."

"My paintings are rather awful." She wrinkled her nose and headed up the stairs. "But you'll like the conservatory."

"I'm sure I will." He followed her upstairs. "A lot of floors. Everything in London is tall and narrow."

"And in Texas?"

"Wide and open." He stretched out his arms. "Our house is two stories, but all spread out with a big old wraparound porch and plenty of land."

"You miss it, don't you?"

"Sure, but London's grown on me. I love it here."

Dorothy opened the door to the conservatory. "Oh bother. It's awfully stuffy. I usually keep the door open this time of year. The dormer windows let in the sun."

Wyatt stepped inside and smiled around the crowded room. "Conservatory, huh?"

"It started as our playroom, but our toys changed as we grew older."

He removed his jacket and cap, tossed them on a chair, and circled the room, passing the profusion of art supplies, musical instruments, and insect collections. He paused in the corner. "Whose guitar?"

"Gil's. He picked it up on a school holiday in Spain before the Civil War."

Wyatt squatted in front of it and stroked the wood. "Beautiful. Great workmanship. Must have nice tone."

"Do you play?"

"Mm-hmm." He stood and gazed at the wall. "These your paintings?"

Why did she keep those old things up? "I painted those when I was young. Nothing but fairies and ferns and flowers. Pure poppycock."

Wyatt sank his hands in his trouser pockets and tilted his head. "I like them. They're bright and happy."

Too much so. "I liked watercolors then, so sheer and ephemeral. But they're naïve."

"Naïve? A young girl should be naïve."

"But a woman needs to grow up. That's when I started using oils." She knelt by the canvases stacked against the wall and flipped through them.

Wyatt knelt beside her. "After the Blitz?"

Black buildings, red fires, jagged ruins. "I prefer oils, the density, the truthfulness."

"Truthfulness?"

She stared at the painting of a façade piercing the sky and the black crater beyond, where her mother and her mother's friend had been reduced to ash by an incendiary bomb while sipping tea. Only Mum's handbag and hat by the door had survived.

Dorothy's jaw ached. "Truthfulness. Oils show the world the way it is. Watercolors show the world the way we want it to be."

"I don't know." Wyatt frowned at the painting overhead with its patch of golden daffodils. "That's truthful too. Those up there—light and joy and life. These down here—darkness and ruin and death. One isn't truer than another. Just different aspects of truth."

Her mind reeled, and she stared at him.

His gaze settled on her, his eyes blending blue and gray. "When times are dark, it's hard to see the light, but it doesn't mean the light is less real."

There was truth in his words, in the rector's words, in the Scriptures—the painful truth of the sun hitting night-shadowed eyes.

"In Psalm 139 . . ." She swallowed away the rasp in her voice and fingered the blackest black in her painting. "It says, 'Yea, the darkness hideth not from thee; but the night shineth as the day: the darkness and the light are both alike to thee.'"

"You read more of it." Pleasure lent even more music to his drawl.

Too much light hurt, so she pushed to standing. "Would you like to see what I'm working on now?" Her voice sounded tight and unnatural.

"Sure."

She whisked off her jacket, donned a paint-dappled smock, and studied her easel. "Thank goodness I had a good stock of paper and canvas before the war, but I'm running low on oil paints."

Wyatt stood behind her. "I like it."

"I'm experimenting." She dipped a brush into a cup of water, then swirled it in emerald green. "I do the basic work in watercolors—I have plenty of those. After it dries, I add accents in oil. Quite improper, mixing media, but I rather like the effect."

"The real and the ideal together." He reached around her and ran a finger down a streak of brown oil paint on the roof. "And you're letting in the light. I like it."

His chest had to be mere inches from her back, and warmth tingled between them. A naughty impulse made her want to lean back into his security, but everything reasonable inside told her to lean forward, away.

She couldn't move, paralyzed between impulse and reason.

"Say, it's your house in Normandy," he said. "In Vierville."

"Yes." Her voice squeaked. She leaned away and added more leaves to the tree.

"Well." He stepped to the side. "Since you're painting, mind if I play the guitar?"

Dorothy's brush paused above the tree branches where she'd climbed with her brothers. Music hadn't graced the room for years. "That would be lovely. Will you play a cowboy tune?"

"If you'd like, but I'm fixing to play something Latin."

"All right."

After he fetched the guitar from the corner, he sat on a stool a few feet in front of her. He wiggled down the knot on his black tie and unbuttoned the top button of his white shirt. "My Paw-paw Ramirez taught me the guitar, Uncle Emilio taught Adler the trumpet, and Mama taught Clay the violin."

When he rolled up his sleeves, revealing his thick forearms, Dorothy added yet more leaves. Simply because he was an extraordinarily attractive man didn't mean he was the right man for her. "Did you ever play with your brothers?"

"Sure." He plucked strings and twisted the tuning knobs. "We played in a trio, the Gringo Mariachis, we called ourselves. *Gringo* means white boy, and not in a nice way."

"Oh? Were you any good?"

"Not bad for gringos, they'd say. Which means, yeah, we were good." He flashed a quick smile. "It's been a while, so don't expect much."

"Gil only tinkered. Even if you're out of practice, that poor guitar is thrilled to be played."

"Hope so. Has real nice tone." He plucked out an intricate rhythm. "Recognize the song?"

It sounded vaguely familiar, beautiful and exotic. The Americans and their big bands did like the Latin tunes. "What's the title?"

"'Bésame Mucho.' Know what that means?"

"No. I don't speak Spanish."

"Good." He flicked her a little smile, and then he sang.

Oh my, did he sing, cradling the neck of the guitar, crooning to the instrument, the Spanish words caressing the air, rumbling low in her belly, the high notes trembling in her heart.

And Wyatt? This was the same quiet naval officer who precisely filled in his tables and charts. But now with his sleeves rolled up, his fingers dancing over the strings, his voice full of passion, his eyes closed as he lost himself in his music. Oh my. More thrilling than all Lawrence's kisses combined—and Wyatt hadn't even touched her.

Goodness, what had come over her? She wrenched her gaze to her palette and dabbed some color or another onto the canvas, everything a blur.

She loved Lawrence. Didn't she? Well, maybe not love. She didn't know him well enough to love him. But for over a decade he'd been her ideal man with his witty words, debonair looks, and love of adventure.

Everyone always said Dorothy was just like her mother. And Mum always said Dorothy should never settle for safety but should strive for a man like Lawrence who'd provide the excitement she craved. Mum had been miserable, and she didn't want Dorothy to suffer the same fate.

Lawrence was the right kind of man for her. So why were things so very difficult with him? Why were things so easy with Wyatt?

The timbre of Wyatt's voice changed, and she glanced up.

He looked right at her, belting out the title phrase, his eyes hooded as if—as if he longed for her.

No, it couldn't be. He was a friend, a dear friend, but only a friend.

She focused on her painting, although nothing made sense. He was only a friend.

A friend who volunteered to spend every Sunday with her. A friend she could always be herself with. A friend who knew all her secrets and had told her all of his.

Or had he? Was he becoming infatuated with her?

Nonsense. No one had ever loved her but her brothers. And he knew she was set on Lawrence. Wyatt was the old-fashioned sort who wouldn't flirt with another man's girlfriend.

Except she wasn't Lawrence's girlfriend. He was involved with several women, and Wyatt knew it.

The music changed to another Latin-flavored song, and Wyatt stopped singing.

After Dorothy composed herself and her vision cleared, she inspected her painting.

In the grass—tiny splotches of purple, white, yellow. Wildflowers? When was the last time she'd painted a flower? Part of her wanted to paint over them, but they looked right. Not naïve, but another part of the truth.

"I'm getting the hang of it again." Wyatt held up one hand. "But I miss my calluses."

"It sounds very good." Remarkably, so did her voice.

Something wistful passed over his face. "Sounded better with Adler and Clay."

In that room, she felt the same wistfulness. "I miss Art and Gil too."

"I know. I'm glad you were still close when they—when they were killed."

She was too. How could she endure it if they'd been estranged like the Paxton brothers?

"You know . . ." Wyatt strummed a slow tune. "I was convinced my brothers weren't in danger. Then I saw Adler last week. Airmen—they don't live long."

He was on the right path, but she sensed he needed a little push. "What if he dies before you have a chance to apologize? Or what if . . . what if something happened to you?"

"I doubt they'd mind. Plus, my life insurance would wipe out my debt."

How could he not see? "Wyatt, they haven't had a chance to forgive you. If something happened to you, they'd never have that chance. They'd have to live with that the rest of their lives. I couldn't endure it if my brothers had died when we weren't on good terms. Please think about it, think about contacting them."

Wyatt strummed the guitar, his lips tucked in, his brow creased.

Dorothy turned to her easel and added a few strokes of dark gold to the grass.

"You're a wise woman." His voice sounded husky.

"Oh, I don't know about that."

"And a good friend."

His smile was so affectionate, she had to return it. "You're a good friend too." She'd only known him . . . three months now. How had he become such an important part of her life?

He lowered his chin and picked out a new tune. "Say, I've been thinking. I won't be in London much longer, and I've never taken in a big show, had a fancy dinner."

Dorothy's mind whirled. He was going to ask her out. Oh no. She couldn't step out with him, but how could she reject him? If only she could find an escape that wouldn't hurt him. Then she found it. "That's awfully expensive, and you're so close to paying off your debt."

"I refuse to punish myself any longer. And sometimes a fellow has to splurge." His Adam's apple dipped and rose. "I was wondering—"

"Oh! You can't go alone, can you? I'll help you find a date."

His eyes widened with shock, then darkened with understanding.

170

She pretended not to notice, although pain squished her heart. "I know just the girl—Louise."

"Lou—Louise?"

"Third Officer Randall in intelligence. She's the right sort of woman for you—quiet and serious and very sweet. You'll get on famously."

Wyatt cranked one of the tuning keys. "I barely know her."

"Silly goose. That's why you go out, so you can get acquainted."

"That's not how I do things." His voice was stiff.

She'd hurt his feelings, but it was necessary. He wasn't the right man for her, and besides . . . "Maybe you shouldn't get involved with an English girl anyway. Many of us don't wish to leave the country. Many of us aren't free to do so."

He shot her a look, then blinked and returned to his music. "True."

Her breath eased out. He understood better than anyone that she could never leave her father. He wouldn't ask her out again.

She frowned at the patch of dry grass she'd just painted. Whenever she thought Lawrence wouldn't ask her out again, she was filled with grasping desperation. But with Wyatt, it was a sad sense of loss.

"What shall I play next? Any requests?" He gave her a confident, nonchalant look.

What a good friend he was. "You haven't played a cowboy song."

"All right, then." He started a new rhythm, lazy and rocking, and he bobbed his head as he sang "Jingle, Jangle, Jingle."

Dorothy smiled and turned her attention to the house in the painting. The lyrics spoke of a cowboy who loved being single. Wyatt must have asked her out on a passing whim.

Thank goodness, because she didn't know what she'd do without their friendship.

23

Wyatt dodged sailors toting boxes down the passageways of Norfolk House. Adm. Sir Bertram Ramsay, the Allied Naval Commander, had issued the naval orders for Operation Neptune that morning, and his headquarters was packing to move to Portsmouth on the southern coast.

He had to find Dorothy and say good-bye, say what he hadn't been ready to say the day before. The last two visits to Fairfax & Sons hadn't yielded leads, only suspicions he'd never be able to investigate.

He entered her office. There she was, directing Wrens as they removed photographs from the huge wall map.

The aching sensation hadn't left him in the week since she'd shot him down. At least she'd interrupted him before he'd actually asked her out and made a bigger fool of himself. That courtesy allowed them to maintain their friendship with minimal strain.

The more he thought about it, the more he knew it was for the best. After today, he didn't know when—or if—he'd see her again. And how could he ask her to start a relationship that might pull her away from her father permanently?

Why did he always fall in love with women who weren't available?

Dorothy smiled and waved. "Good day, Lieutenant Paxton. Come to help us pack?"

"If you'd like." He ambled over. "My train doesn't leave until 1500."

"Good." She examined the wall. "That's all, ladies. Let's take the boxes down to the lorry." She plunked a box in Wyatt's arms and picked up another. "Follow me."

"Aye aye, ma'am. When's your train?" He followed her into the crowded passageway.

"Tomorrow afternoon. Headquarters opens at Southwick House on Wednesday. Tonight I pack and—and say good-bye to Papa." Her voice quivered.

"He'll be fine. He's doing much better. And the Little Blitz seems to be over."

She glanced over her shoulder, and worry zigzagged across her forehead. "But will he continue to do well after you leave, after I leave? We'll be gone over a month."

He steeled himself. "Actually, I doubt I'll be back. That's why I came today, to say good-bye."

She faced him by the railing overlooking the staircase, her blue eyes enormous. "To me? But I'll see you in Portsmouth."

Wyatt took in every one of her facial features, committing them to memory. "The Western Naval Task Force is based in Plymouth. That's where I'm going, then straight out to sea for a training exercise. After that the American destroyers should be here, and I'll get assigned to one. Then . . . well, you know what's coming."

"But—but afterward—afterward you'll return to London, won't you?" Her eyes. How could he take it?

"We'll be on the far shore a while, gunfire support, antisubmarine patrols, all that. When we're done, I'll get new orders. Don't know where they'll send me."

The emotions on her face took him back to her conservatory when he was playing guitar, the connection that fooled him into thinking she might have feelings for him beyond friendship. It was only friendship, but it had been a good one.

"Oh." Her voice squeaked. "I'll miss you."

"I'll miss you too." Everything in him wanted to ask her to write, but the sooner he got over her, the better. He kept women too long in his heart as it was.

Two Wrens passed them.

Wyatt adjusted his grip on the box and tilted his head to the stairs. "We should get—"

"Yes, we should." She headed downstairs.

Rats, he still had to tell her. But how could he without breaking her heart?

Outside, a truck sat parked by the curb. Wyatt hoisted his box inside, then Dorothy's box, and a sailor stacked them.

Wyatt backed out of the way and turned to Dorothy. "Listen, I feel bad I won't be able to do any more investigating."

She blinked. "Oh yes. I hadn't thought of that."

"I'm sorry. I let you down and Mr. Montague too."

"Nonsense. You did your best. You simply didn't have enough time."

"I don't know if more time would have helped." He lifted empty palms. "Everything's clean. All I have is a couple of hunches."

"Hunches? You didn't say anything yesterday."

"Thought I might have another Sunday. Then today I got my orders."

Dorothy clasped her hands in front of her stomach. "What are your hunches?"

Wyatt tilted his head toward the north. "There's something about the Edinburgh office. The budget is out of proportion to its size. Don't know how I could have gotten up to Scotland to look at those books though."

"I'll mention it to Mr. Montague. What's the other hunch?"

"You won't like it." He took her arm and guided her to the wall, far from the other sailors and Wrens.

"I won't like it? What do you mean?"

Wyatt's stomach balled up. "Because everything's clean, it looks like the embezzlement is coming from pretty high up. The head of accounting, Mr. Montague . . . your father."

Her face went white. "My father?"

"I know. I don't like it either. But I doubt it's Mr. Montague, since he's the one who's investigating. And remember, your dad denies there's a problem and he didn't want Mr. Montague to look into it."

"How could you say such things?" Dorothy tugged her arm from his grasp, but she kept her voice low. "He extended hospitality to you."

"I know." He clamped his lips together, but he had to keep going. "As I said, I don't like it. It's out of character for him."

"He practically thinks of you as another son." Each word tight and crisp.

The pain made him wince. "I know. And I really like him, respect him. I don't think he's capable of it. But that's how it looks from the outside. I wanted to warn you in case something happens. If someone looks into it and suspects your dad, I want you to be prepared."

He ventured a glance.

Her face was as pale as marble, cool and indifferent. She looked down her nose at him. "If you should ever return to London, there will be no more investigating. And no more hospitality."

"Dorothy—"

"Good day." She marched away and into the building.

Wyatt sagged back against the wall and bonked his head on stone. Not only had he failed in the investigation, but he'd failed in his friendship with Dorothy. And he'd never see her again.

Wyatt sat squashed by the train window next to Ted Kelvin and Jerry Hobson, who were working a crossword puzzle. Jack Vale and Irwin Slobodsky sat across from him, lulled to sleep by the train's motions. The officers' sea bags were crammed into the overhead racks.

The English countryside rolled by under an overcast sky. Wyatt gripped his copy of *Hard Times* with the letter burning inside.

Why did it have to arrive today after the fiasco with Dorothy? He was already torn up inside. He'd wanted to warn her, prepare her, protect her, but all he'd done was hurt her. And he'd severed their friendship.

And now the letter.

He didn't get much mail. A few letters from buddies in the Pacific Fleet, but this was his first from Kerrville. Over two months had passed since he'd mailed his letter. He'd assumed they didn't want anything to do with him.

Now this. He cracked open the book. Daddy's handwriting hurt his eyes with its hard, slanting script.

He ought to wait for some privacy to read it, but curiosity and a masochistic urge drove him to open the envelope. A single sheet of Paxton Trucking stationery, covered both sides in his dad's hand. He closed his eyes and braced himself to hear from his father for the first time in almost three years. *Lord . . .*

He didn't even know how to pray, so he read.

Dear Wyatt,

Your mama and I were overjoyed to receive your letter. We haven't stopped worrying about you—or praying for you—since that horrible night. We're relieved to hear you're alive and well, and even more that you've repented.

Mind you, no one but Adler blamed you for Oralee's death. Clay vouched for you, and that's good enough for Mama and me. The sheriff officially ruled it an accident, and Oralee's family accepts it as such.

As for the theft, we can't begin to tell you how shocked and angry we were, and how Clay felt betrayed. We're glad you're sorry for what you did and are working to make amends. Mama and I have forgiven you, and we'll always welcome you home.

Wyatt squeezed his eyes shut, overwhelmed by the image of Daddy and Mama running down the road to their Prodigal. He didn't deserve it. But he'd take it.

We wish we could tell you Adler saw the light, but we have no way of knowing. He ran away that night also, and we haven't heard from him since. We pray he's all right and pray he'll be led to write to us as you did.

Wyatt stared at the paragraph. Adler ran away? Why? To hunt down Wyatt and kill him? Nonsense. He might have done so the first night—but three years later? He might hold a grudge, but not murderous intent.

So why? He stared out the window, at a village in the distance. Had Adler been so overcome with grief that he couldn't bear to see the places that reminded him of Oralee? He could understand not going home for three years—that made sense. But not even writing? That made no sense at all.

Wyatt held a puzzle piece his parents lacked—Adler had joined the Army Air Forces. But was that good news or bad?

As for Clay, we wish we'd had the means to pay for his college, but our biggest client went bankrupt in the spring of

'41. Paxton Trucking took a big hit. Besides, with you and Adler gone and so many of our men enlisting, we couldn't spare him from the business.

We held onto him as long as possible, but last February the government got rid of occupational draft deferments for men twenty-two and younger. The Army snatched Clay right up. He volunteered for the Rangers, and he's now in your neck of the woods.

Wyatt pressed his fist to his mouth to stifle a moan. Clay never went to college? He was supposed to be a physician, a good one. The best. But Wyatt had stolen that from him. Clay hated the trucking business, but Wyatt had dumped it on him when he ran away.

Oh Lord, no. Now Clay was in the Army, in the Rangers, in England?

The map of Normandy flashed in his mind, of the German gun battery at Pointe du Hoc, where the Rangers would storm the cliffs in a daring commando raid. Dangerous. Deadly.

Oh Lord. No, no, no. Had Wyatt sentenced his little brother to death? Clay with his sweet smile and warm brown eyes and caring disposition? He didn't deserve it, any of it.

Wyatt could barely read the last few lines.

There's more with Adler and Clay, but those aren't our tales to tell.

Mama sends her love and lots of it. She's too emotional to write to you right now. You understand. But she'll write soon.

We're praying hard for all our boys. Please join us in praying for your brothers. Mama believes you'll all be reconciled someday and come home to us, but as far as I'm concerned it'll take a miracle.

Before he could make a fool of himself, Wyatt excused himself and stepped over all the blue-clad legs to leave the compartment.

He strode down the swaying passageway, vision blurred. *Lord, forgive me! Forgive me!*

He'd destroyed what he loved most—his family. He'd violated his most cherished principle—loyalty.

At the end of the railway car, he leaned his forehead against a window. His eyes, his fists, his stomach, all clenched shut.

No money could repay those debts. How could Clay forgive him for wrecking his life?

And Adler? What had driven him to cut every tie to home?

All Wyatt knew was that he'd started it. With his jealousy for Adler's success. With arrogant interference. With greedy self-preservation. With cowardly flight.

And his brothers paid the price. Wyatt had shattered their dreams, and now they were both in harm's way.

All he'd ever wanted was to protect his loved ones—and he'd ruined them.

The letter turned damp in his fist. Like a flash flood, the news had washed away his road to redemption.

24

Dorothy hauled the box out of the operations room at Southwick House. Two dozen officers and enlisted personnel, British and American, Army and Navy, men and women—gathered around tables, pointed to diagrams, and stood on ladders by a painted wooden map of southern England and Normandy that filled one wall.

Once an elegant drawing room, it had been transformed for Neptune. The only clues to its refined past were the Georgian woodwork and the white-and-gold wallpaper.

Dorothy passed through the adjoining sitting room with walls the same gray blue as Wyatt's eyes.

She harrumphed and crossed the hallway to the staircase. The carpet on the stairs muffled the sharpness of her steps. Wyatt—the traitor. How could he accuse her father of embezzling? She thought he'd had her father's best interests at heart, but it was all a lie. What could she expect from a man who betrayed his own brother?

She paused on the landing to let two Wrens pass—and to correct herself. That wasn't true or fair. He'd stolen from his brother out of fear, not malice, and he was deeply sorry and he worked hard to make amends.

Regardless, he'd betrayed her and her father.

She hiked the stairs to her departmental office. To her right, First Officer Bliss-Baldwin conferred with Lawrence, Commander Pringle, and several other male officers over a table. To her left, Gwen, Muriel, and the enlisted Wrens unpacked boxes.

Dorothy set her box on the table where Muriel worked and hummed. The tune's Latin lilt took her back to the conservatory, to a dreamy-eyed Texan crooning as if she were the only woman in the world, to his invitation that she'd torpedoed just in time.

She ripped open the box and unloaded the contents. Bother that man. How dare he ask her out when he harbored such an opinion about her father? How could he . . .

Her thoughts hovered over a different memory. Hadn't he said, "Why ask a girl out unless you really like her?" His invitation hadn't been a passing whim after all, had it? But accepting would have been a grave mistake given what she now knew about his character. Besides, she'd probably never see him again, thank goodness.

Gwen sorted folders into piles. "What are you humming, Muriel?"

"The song's called 'Amor.'" She sang a few lines in purring Spanish.

"Do you speak Spanish?" Dorothy asked.

"*Si, si, señorita.*" Muriel struck a pose like a flamenco dancer.

Dorothy tucked in her lips. Wyatt had asked her that question, and he'd been glad when she'd said no. "Do you know what 'Bésame Mucho' means?"

"Ooh. Such a romantic song. *Bésame* means 'kiss me,' and *mucho* means 'a lot.'"

Kiss me? A lot? Wyatt sang that to her?

Gwen leaned over the table, her gray eyes sparkling. "Did Lieutenant Commander Eaton sing it to you?"

"No." She spun away to conceal the telling heat in her cheeks. "Simply curious. I heard it recently and wondered what it meant."

Bother that man indeed. She busied herself with a box on the next table. Who was Wyatt after all? An unassuming accountant? A passionate romantic? Or a heartless cad who ate from a man's table and then accused him of theft? Whatever made him think such a thing?

Her mind ached.

But she was on duty, an invasion was scheduled in early June, and she had more important things to consider than Wyatt Paxton.

Bliss-Baldwin strode across the room, her cheeks bright pink. "The latest reconnaissance photos. So much for your vaunted eyes, Second Officer Fairfax."

"Pardon?"

She slapped a photograph onto the table in front of Dorothy. "You missed something."

"I don't understand." Her face felt numb, and she scrutinized the photograph taken from a low-flying airplane. "It's the house in Vierville where we took our holidays."

"You never mentioned a shack under that tree. How could you overlook it?"

"There wasn't a shack . . ." But now there was, crystal clear under the tree. "That—that wasn't there when we visited."

Bliss-Baldwin sniffed. "I highly doubt it. Look how dilapidated it is."

"But I climbed this tree every day. I'd remember."

"Apparently memories can be as faulty as eyesight."

Gwen handed Dorothy an envelope. "Here are the photographs from that sector."

Dorothy spread out the images on the table. Her family photograph—the tree was rather far away, but no shack was visible, thank goodness. The later photographs neither condemned her nor vindicated her. The angle was wrong in this one, the rise of the land obscured the area in that one, the next was blurry, and the next was from straight above. Dorothy scrutinized the previous week's photograph. The space under the tree was dark and unclear. Was that a shack underneath? Or an illusion created by distance and shadow?

"I'm very disappointed in you, Second Officer Fairfax. Please be more observant in the future." Her blonde head high, Blissy marched back to the male officers.

All the air leached from her lungs. She always recorded even the slightest detail.

Gwen and Muriel inspected the photographs.

"I don't see it either," Muriel said. "Who could?"

Gwen squinted at the shadowy picture. "If you knew what to look for, you could imagine that was a shack, but I wouldn't have thought anything of it."

Muriel peered over Gwen's shoulder. "I never would have suspected a shack."

"Thank you, but I should have." Dorothy slipped the evidence back into its envelope.

"Don't take it so hard." Gwen patted her arm. "Old Blissy's a martinet. But you—I'm concerned about you. You've been quiet the last few days."

Of course she was. A close friend had wreaked havoc with her emotions and then betrayed her. And she'd had to leave London. She returned the envelope to its file. "I'm concerned about my father, all alone."

"If it's any comfort," Muriel said, "the Little Blitz seems to be over. The Luftwaffe has turned its ugly eyes from London to the southern ports. They know something is brewing."

The previous night's air raid on Portsmouth had rattled Dorothy more than it should have. "Small comfort indeed."

"Second Officer Fairfax, may I have a word?" Lawrence's voice, as refined as the Georgian mansion.

"Aye aye, sir." She followed him out of the room.

He gestured for her to lead the way down the stairs. "Have you seen the grounds?"

"Not yet."

"Let's explore. We'll have some privacy."

Dorothy headed outside, under the colonnaded portico and onto the manicured lawn, but her stomach squirmed. After the last few days, she couldn't muster the proper sophistication to banter with Lawrence, and she certainly didn't want to risk having her CO see her with him.

"I talked with First Officer Bliss-Baldwin earlier."

She faced him on the sloping lawn. "Oh dear. That shack. I'm certain it wasn't there when I was a girl. How could—"

"It isn't about that." He motioned for her to keep walking. "First, I vouched for you. I was well acquainted with the grounds, and there was no shack."

"Thank you." But Dorothy frowned. If Lawrence had validated her observations, why had Blissy ranted at her?

"Second, not one soul in aerial reconnaissance identified that shack from earlier photographs. The angles and lighting were wrong. It was impossible to sight. No one blames you. Julia was in a flurry because Commander Pringle blamed her, so she had to pass the blame to someone beneath her. As a woman, Julia has a difficult time being taken seriously."

"I understand." But Dorothy would never pass the blame to someone beneath her.

"I hope this next bit of news will help you see Julia in a more favorable light."

"Oh?"

He stepped close, his hazel eyes warm in the sunshine. "I told her how distraught you were to leave your father, how he has a poor constitution and is in low spirits, and how you're the only balm to his weary old soul."

Her chin drew back. For the second time this week, someone she trusted had spoken ill of her father. "That isn't true."

He gave her a pinched smile. "You must admit, it's partly true. And I must admit, I exaggerated to make my point. Your father needs you."

Dorothy glanced back at Southwick House. Yes, her father needed her, but her work here was vital to the war effort. "Am I being transferred back to London? I'd rather not."

"Of course not. The Admiralty can spare you even less than your father can. But Julia agreed to grant you leave each weekend until we're locked down for D-day. You can take the train home on Friday evening and return on Sunday."

"Every weekend?" Lightness lifted her chest. How thoughtful of Lawrence to think of the arrangement.

He wore a satisfied smile. "Julia saw my point and agreed to my plan."

Of course, she did. She'd have Lawrence to herself every weekend.

"In all honesty, my motives weren't entirely unselfish." He edged closer with that roguish look that usually sent her heart to pattering. "If I should happen to have business in London—and I'll make sure I do—you shall have no excuse not to be seen in public with me."

Her emotions were too wrung out for her to respond with enthusiasm, but enthusiasm wasn't sophisticated anyway. She sauntered back toward Southwick House. "You sly fox."

"The slyest."

Once inside, she and Lawrence parted ways, and Dorothy returned to the upstairs office.

First Officer Bliss-Baldwin met her right inside the door. "I'd like a word."

"Aye aye, ma'am." She followed her to a small office. Was she going to receive another reprimand, or an apology?

Dorothy closed the door. "I do apologize for not noticing that shack in earlier photographs."

First Officer Bliss-Baldwin gazed out the window, every blonde hair rolled in place. "While I'm disappointed in your professional performance, I called you in here about your personal behavior."

Dorothy clenched her hands together. "My personal . . . ?"

"Several months ago, Lieutenant Commander Eaton made an impassioned plea for you to remain in London with your ailing father. And this morning, he made an even more impassioned plea for you to return home on the weekends for the welfare of that same ailing father."

"Yes, ma'am." She eyed her commander cautiously. "Thank you for agreeing. He needs me."

"Your father? Or the lieutenant commander?"

Her breath swished in. "My—my father, of course."

The first officer rested her slender hand on the window frame. "I happened to look out this window a few minutes ago, and I saw you and Lieutenant Commander Eaton talking rather close and chummy."

Dorothy swallowed the nasty taste in her mouth. "We're old family friends. My brothers went to Cambridge with him."

"And he took a holiday in Normandy with you. Quite romantic."

"Romantic? Not at all, ma'am. I was only a schoolgirl—thirteen, fourteen."

First Officer Bliss-Baldwin turned to her with a regal smile. "Are you aware that he and I are walking out together?"

"Yes, ma'am. He told me."

"Did he? Did he also tell you I don't appreciate it when people take advantage of me?"

Dorothy squeezed her fingers hard and kept the alarm off her face. "Advantage? I don't know what you mean."

The first officer pressed her fingertips to the desktop. "I can't help but wonder if he will suddenly have meetings in London. I can't help but wonder if he is feigning interest in me to keep his true lover close at hand."

Dorothy gasped. Such a tawdry word. Why, she'd had only two dates with the man, and one was a disaster. "I assure you, I'm not his—his lover."

"Good." She tugged the hem of her double-breasted navy jacket. "If I were to find out you two were making a fool of me . . ."

Behind the woman's imperious pride, Dorothy glimpsed pain that pricked at her heart. Julia Bliss-Baldwin was a live, feeling woman, and she didn't deserve to be deceived or hurt.

Dorothy's posture softened. "I would never do that to you, ma'am. To anyone."

"Very good. You're dismissed." She waved to the door.

Dorothy stepped outside, closed the door behind her, and sighed. Lawrence thought he was helping, but he'd made things more complicated. And far more difficult.

25

Only Wyatt's sense of duty allowed him to focus on the briefing. On the darkened bridge of the HMS *Seavington*, lit by red bulbs to maintain night vision, Lieutenant Foster described the night's activity as Wyatt prepared to take the morning watch at 0400.

Daytime busyness kept his mind occupied, but at night his failures swamped him and disturbed his sleep. Thank goodness he'd been alert enough for Exercise Tiger the day before.

Foster pointed to the nautical chart, indicating the *Seavington*'s coordinates in Lyme Bay and her designated course back to Slapton Sands.

The previous day, the bulk of the US 4th Infantry Division had landed at Slapton, practicing for the upcoming landings on Utah Beach, with a follow-up convoy due this morning. Over two hundred American landing craft, from the enormous LST "Landing Ship, Tanks" to the small LCVP "Landing Craft, Vehicle or Personnel," were transporting twenty-five thousand troops.

Along with six other British destroyers and two British cruisers, the *Seavington* had bombarded the landing beaches. All had gone fairly well. Confusion had arisen when Adm. Don Moon, commander of the US Navy's Force U, had decided at the last minute to postpone H-hour by an hour when a flotilla of landing craft was delayed.

Wyatt trained his mind and his gaze on the chart. He shared Admiral Moon's traits of cautiousness and attention to detail, and now he saw the danger of those traits, not only in his own life but in command.

"At 0106, we heard from Commander in Chief Plymouth." Foster turned to the ship's log. "The *Onslow* sighted a German E-boat off Portland."

"An E-boat? Just one?" That jolted Wyatt awake. The small German torpedo boats were capable of forty knots and usually travelled in packs to devastate Allied shipping. Admiral Kirk had warned of the dangers of German air, surface, or submarine attacks during the exercises, but none had materialized so far.

"Only one, but at 0224, C in C Plymouth notified us of three E-boat groups in the area. However, all has been quiet since."

"Good." The warning from the Plymouth Home Command would alert the slow-moving convoy of LSTs and its escort ships.

Wyatt settled in at his station and made the change-of-watch notations in the log, careful to use British terminology. Weariness dragged at his eyelids, but this watch shouldn't demand much of him. Today's portion of Exercise Tiger involved landing the follow-up troops and unloading supplies. With yesterday's assault troops well on their way inland, the destroyers would only serve to screen the naval force.

On Saturday the destroyers would return to Plymouth, and Wyatt would report to US Destroyer Squadron 18, due to arrive from Boston today.

"Captain, we have new orders." An officer strode onto the bridge and handed a paper to Captain Willoughby. "We are to proceed to these coordinates posthaste for a rescue operation."

Rescue operation? Wyatt inched closer. What had happened? An

E-boat attack on merchant shipping? A grounded fishing trawler? An LST torpedoed by a U-boat?

After the captain read the dispatch, he bent over the plotting table with the navigator, Lieutenant Langley. "Fifty degrees, twenty-eight minutes north. Two degrees, fifty-one minutes west. Plot our course."

"Aye aye, Captain." The navigator worked with ruler and pencil.

Wyatt peered over Langley's shoulder. The new coordinates were about twenty miles northeast of their current position—which was already a good fifteen miles east of Slapton Sands. The *Seavington* was due to arrive at Slapton by sunrise at 0441. "Captain, I assume Force U has been informed we have new orders?"

The captain didn't even look Wyatt's direction. "We are not under Admiral Moon's command, but under Adm. Sir Ralph Leatham. We take orders from Plymouth, not Washington, DC."

"Yes, sir." As a junior officer and the only American on board, Wyatt knew to hold his tongue.

Langley sent Wyatt an understanding glance over his shoulder. "I'm certain C in C Plymouth will inform the Yanks."

"Thanks. Reckon he will." Wyatt recorded the orders in the log—but did not record his thoughts. Poor communication between the commands had caused several problems and headaches throughout the exercises.

"Too many cooks spoil the broth." He could hear Daddy lecturing on the importance of simplicity of organization, clear lines of communication, and straight talk.

Applied to the military as well.

Daddy would pace the cluttered office, his blue eyes sparking with frustration. *"You get bogged down in details, Wy. Yeah, you've got to know the figures, but you've got to know the men even more. The men—they're the heart of this operation. Talk, Wy. Talk."*

Wyatt rolled the pen in clenched fingers. Even before that June night in 1941, he'd failed his father. Since that night, his failures had accumulated more steadily than compound interest.

Adler should have been in Texas, helping with the business. Instead, he was getting shot at by the Luftwaffe.

Clay should have been in college, training to be a doctor, to save lives. Instead, he was training to take lives.

And Dorothy. As the ship headed into the morning twilight, the ship's log turned the same grayish-purple as a bruise. Not only had he failed to find out who was bankrupting Fairfax & Sons, but he'd shattered her trust. He had a hunch, only a hunch without a lick of evidence, and he'd accused her father of embezzling. How arrogant. In his quest to protect her, he'd wounded her.

Outside the portholes, the sea was calm and the sky was clear and brightening. But not for Dorothy. She had so little to lean on. Her father couldn't support his own weight, much less his daughter's. Her faith was tentative, just beginning to grow. Had he brought her lower? Pushed her farther from God?

Forgive me, Lord. How many times would he have to pray that this week?

Cries rang out from the main deck, relayed up to the bridge. The lookouts had sighted something, and the captain ordered the destroyer to reduce speed.

Wyatt peered between heads to the portholes. When the *Seavington* rose on the waves, a jagged black shape was silhouetted on the band of pink light on the horizon. His breath caught and turned to ice. A sinking ship and a big one.

More cries, and sailors on the main deck leaned on the rails and pointed down to the water.

The waves were no longer smooth. Lumps speckled the ocean, a few nearby, multiplying in quantity closer to the wreck. Dozens upon dozens. Dark lumps on the gray sea.

"Oh, good Lord, no." Bodies.

"Full stop!" the captain shouted. "Full stop! Away rescue parties!"

Wyatt clutched the log table, his mind tumbling. He'd helped rescue men from sunken ships in the Aleutians. Few survived the icy waters. The English Channel was warmer, but not by much. And he'd never seen so many. So very many.

"Ahoy! A lifeboat!" a lookout called.

"Thank you, Lord. Survivors." In the distance, a tiny boat bobbed, crammed with men, bristling with waving hands.

"Hail them. Tell them to come to us," the captain said. "I will not endanger the men in the water."

Wyatt cringed at the thought of what the destroyer's screws could do.

On the main deck, sailors clambered down the rope net and hauled one of the dark shapes up over the rails.

In a moment, the talker turned from the voice tube to the captain. "Sir, it's an American soldier. He's dead."

An American soldier? Wyatt examined the ship's hulk on the horizon. Was that the bow of an LST? The giant tank landing ships carried almost five hundred soldiers plus a naval crew of over a hundred. "Captain, may I have permission to—"

"Granted, Lieutenant." The captain shot him a look filled with worry and compassion. "Go down to the main deck. Interrogate the survivors."

"Aye aye, Captain." He scrambled down ladders and jogged across the deck in the cool air. A knot of sailors clustered around the American soldier.

Wyatt knelt on the deck, and the puddle of cold seawater soaked through the knees of his khaki trousers.

The soldier's face was pale but striking, so real with his dark-stubbled chin and crooked nose, but so lifeless. He wore a helmet, Parson's field jacket, olive drab trousers, and a full pack. Instead of a life vest, he wore what looked like a bicycle tube around his waist.

"Oh no," Wyatt murmured. With a full pack and the inflatable tube so low, he would have tipped headfirst in the water and drowned.

He stood and looked down into the water turning gold in the sunrise. Half a dozen bodies floated within view. All with life belts around their waists. Why hadn't they worn them higher? Why had they been allowed to go into the water with their packs?

The lifeboat neared, low in the water with men hanging off the sides. A few broke free and swam toward the *Seavington*.

British sailors climbed down the net to help them on board.

Wyatt reached over the side and grabbed the first hand he could reach, clammy but strong, and he helped the man up onto the deck.

"Where were you?" Dark eyes pierced Wyatt's.

"Pardon? What happened?"

"You're an American? Isn't this a British destroyer?" The man—a naval ensign—hunkered shivering on the deck.

"I'm a liaison officer." Wyatt grabbed a blanket offered by a sailor and draped it over the ensign's shoulders. "What happened?"

"I repeat—where were you?" His jaw chattered, but that didn't decrease the ferocity of his glare. "C in C Plymouth sent out our convoy of eight LSTs with only a lousy little corvette to escort us. The destroyer never showed."

Wyatt sucked in a breath. Only one escort ship? Even two wasn't enough. "Was it an E-boat? We were told they were in the area."

The man barked out a laugh and downed the rum a sailor thrust into his hand. Then he wiped his mouth with the back of his hand. "Glad someone was warned. We weren't."

So Plymouth failed to tell the ships most vulnerable to attack. "E-boats? How many?"

"Five, ten, who knows? It was dark." He clutched the blanket under his chin. "Their green tracers flying every which way. Our red tracers. Torpedoes, bullets, men jumping in the water. It was bedlam."

Wyatt clamped his hand on his jaw, cutting off a cuss word he'd never uttered in his life. "Your ship?"

"The *LST-507*. We were hit first, then the *531* went up in a fireball. They sank before we did."

"Two LSTs?" Over a thousand men in the water, and his mouth went dry. And Jerry Hobson—which LST was he commanding again?

"Another LST was damaged. Think they got away. Our escort? Fine good she did. Never even turned back."

Wyatt's fingers dug into his cheek. The ensign would know the corvette's duty was to escort the remaining ships to safety, not to rescue survivors, but Wyatt knew better than to remind him.

"So where were you?" That dark gaze bore down on him. "No one protected us. No one helped us. And hundreds of men died. Hundreds."

Where was the *Seavington*? Following her orders to screen Force U off Slapton Sands, totally unaware of the tragedy unfolding nearby.

However, the ensign would bite off his head if Wyatt said that. Instead, he set his hand on the man's shaking shoulder. "I'm sorry. I'm so sorry."

"Come along, sir." A sailor tugged on the ensign's elbow. "Let's get you below decks to warm up."

The man struggled to his feet and stumbled along beside the sailor.

Wyatt remained squatting on the deck, his jaw aching in his grip. Two dozen dripping, shivering men huddled in blankets.

The logical part of his brain said it wasn't his fault. How could he have helped when he hadn't known, when he hadn't been near, when it wasn't his responsibility?

Yet that knowledge only intensified the feeling of helplessness.

Hundreds of men had died. And he hadn't been able to protect them.

26

Dorothy climbed the narrow staircase to Johanna Katin's apartment. Papa had insisted that Dorothy visit her friend after church, since she'd spent all Saturday at home.

Even Saturday evening, to Lawrence's consternation.

She huffed. He'd offered to meet her in London for a posh night on the town, just as Blissy had suspected he would. Dorothy had insisted he stay in Portsmouth. Stepping out with him didn't break regulations, but it didn't seem quite right. And it put Dorothy's position at headquarters at risk.

The risk only seemed to heighten Lawrence's interest.

Why did the risk always have to be to her concerns, not his?

She knocked on Johanna's door, hoping the sharp rap would drive the man out of her head.

"Dorothy!" Johanna kissed her cheek. "I'm happy to see you."

She kissed her friend back and stepped inside, savoring the smells, foreign and rich. She held up a paper sack. "I brought you a lovely piece of cheddar, a few ounces of sugar, and a tin of tea. It'll be good for your grandmother."

"Thank you. You are very kind." Her pretty brown eyes clouded. "But Oma is in hospital again."

195

"I'm sorry. I'll pray for her." Dorothy gripped Johanna's hand. Oma was the only family Johanna had in England, possibly in the whole world. She couldn't imagine how devastated Johanna would be when her grandmother passed away.

"I'll make a spot of tea." Johanna set the sack on the table and pulled out the tin. "I have not heard you talk about praying before."

Dorothy lowered herself into a chair at the table. "I started attending church again."

"Good. Faith is important, yes?" Johanna took a teapot from a cupboard. "When I'm afraid, the Lord is a strong tower."

Dorothy studied Johanna's face as she measured tea leaves into the pot, the slight upward curve of the lips, the relaxed forehead. Despite the horrendous losses Johanna had endured, she had the same peace Wyatt did.

Johanna filled the teapot with hot water from the kettle on the stove. "What sent you back to church?"

"A . . . friend." Or so she'd thought.

"Lawrence?"

"No." They'd never discussed faith. Come to think of it, they'd never discussed anything personal or serious.

"Then who?" Johanna set the teapot on the table to steep.

"Wyatt Paxton. He's an American naval officer."

"You've mentioned him." Johanna took the cheese and sugar from the sack. "But never with a frown."

Dorothy smoothed the box pleats in her skirt. "I'm not happy with him."

"Why not?"

Oh, why did she have to speak so impulsively? She couldn't talk about the investigation. She fiddled with one of the light blue stripes on the cuff of her sleeve. "He's an accountant. I told him what you'd relayed about the situation at Fairfax & Sons. I—I've heard more rumors, and I wanted his opinion."

Johanna nodded and tucked the food in the pantry.

Dorothy's mouth set. "Wyatt had the audacity to suggest my father might be embezzling."

"Mm-hmm."

Her jaw lowered. "Why don't you sound shocked?"

Johanna slid her gaze to Dorothy. "As I said, there are rumors. I don't believe them though."

"You said there are rumors the company's losing money, but Papa . . . ?"

Johanna's face stretched long, but she nodded again.

Dorothy hugged herself. "How could they say such things?"

"They are only rumors. You know how people talk. And your father was absent so long. Now he is in the office more often, but he—he is not as warm and friendly as he used to be. Money is disappearing, and no one knows why. So they blame him."

"But he's never . . . he's always . . ." Her stomach flipped end over end.

"I do not believe the gossip. Your father is a good man. But it looks bad from the outside."

Dorothy gasped. The same words Wyatt had used. "It can't be. There must be another explanation."

"I'm sure there is."

Edinburgh! Wyatt said he'd had two hunches, and he'd named Edinburgh first. That had to be the answer. If she could convince Papa to visit Edinburgh . . .

"Oh no." All hope drained away. Hadn't Papa dismissed her suggestion to visit the Scottish capital? *I have no desire to go there again. I daresay you'd not find it as charming as you remember.*

What if Papa were using the Edinburgh office for the embezzlement? What if he had a partner there embezzling on his behalf?

"Don't worry." Johanna set a teacup and saucer before her. "Your father is a good man, yes? He'd never steal."

"What if you're wrong? What if he's guilty? Papa—he'd go to prison." Her voice cracked.

"Then you must be calm and strong for him. You must be ready."

Ready, prepared. As Wyatt had said. Dorothy rested her forehead in her palms. "Oh dear. Poor Wyatt. He was only being honest with me, telling me how others might see the situation. And I—I was cruel to him."

"He will understand. He knows how much you love your father, yes?"

"I won't see him again. He has new orders. It's for the best though."

"For the best? Do you not want to apologize?" The chair creaked as Johanna sat down.

Dorothy raised her head. "I do, but it's best we don't see each other again. I'm afraid he might be . . . infatuated."

A dimple formed in Johanna's cheek. "And you love Lawrence."

Her nose wrinkled. "I don't love him. I . . . I suppose I've been infatuated. I hardly know Lawrence. In fact, I know Wyatt better, and he knows me better. We talk about everything."

"But he is not attractive to you?"

That would be a lie. Dorothy stood and circled the room. "He isn't the right sort of man for me. He's a quiet, steady sort, and I need an exciting man."

"Why?"

Dorothy stopped by the mantel and blinked at her friend. Wasn't it obvious? "Because I love excitement and fun and novelty."

With a small smile, Johanna rested her chin in her hand. "Yet I'm your friend."

"Oh yes. You're the dearest of friends."

"I am quiet and steady and not exciting at all."

She stared at her friend, one of her closest friends, and she couldn't disagree. Yet something was missing in the argument. "I like quiet friends, but a quiet husband? I'd become frightfully bored, and then I'd be mean and snippy and ruin the poor man."

Johanna's eyes crinkled with amusement. "You are too sweet to do that."

Was she? She'd been snippy to Wyatt when he'd only been honest. It must have been difficult for him to raise his concerns, knowing it might anger her. And still he'd spoken. A man of integrity.

Dorothy groaned and faced the mantel, graced with photographs of Johanna's parents, brothers, aunts, and uncles—all trapped in Hitler's Germany, probably sent to one of those hideous concentration camps. Dorothy's concerns were trivial and petty in comparison.

She traced her finger over a heavy ornate silver picture frame, so lovely. The Katin family had been quite wealthy in Germany, and the treasures Johanna's grandmother had brought with her spoke of old continental charm.

One photograph was propped loose against a frame. Dorothy held it up. "Oh dear. Was the frame broken in an air raid?"

Pain ripped across Johanna's face. "I sold it last week."

"Sold it? Why?" Every item in the flat was a family heirloom.

Johanna stirred her tea, although she certainly hadn't added sugar. "The doctor must be paid."

Dorothy scanned the flat—where were the silver candlesticks that normally sat on the table? "How much have you sold?"

"I am fine." She sipped her tea but didn't meet Dorothy's gaze.

"No, you are not." She breathed hard. What if Hitler had his way and annihilated Europe's Jews? All that would remain of the Katin family would be Oma, Johanna, and these priceless objects. Once they were sold, they could never be recovered. Johanna would lose her heritage along with everything else.

"I won't have it." Dorothy marched to the table and wrenched open her handbag. "You must never sell another heirloom. Never."

"Oma is more precious to me than—"

"Yes. The doctor must be paid." Dorothy pulled out the envelope stuffed with her pay for the month of April. If she were frugal, the remaining cash from her March paycheck would cover expenses until she was paid again at the end of May.

Dorothy set the envelope in front of Johanna.

Her eyes stretched wide. "No, I couldn't. I can't."

"You can and you will." Dorothy's voice quivered. "You mustn't sell your heirlooms. I won't hear of it. Consider it a loan, if you must, but you will never, never sell another piece of your family again. Do you hear me?"

Johanna covered her mouth with her hand, and her face crumpled and turned red. "I—I'll pay you back."

"I know you will." Dorothy swiped at a tickle on her cheek, and her finger came back damp.

So much loss in this war. Too much loss.

WEYMOUTH, ENGLAND

Under a clear blue sky the British motor launch zipped toward the nine ships of US Destroyer Squadron 18 moored in Weymouth Harbor.

Sitting next to Wyatt in the boat, Jack grinned. "Finally get on an American ship again where we'll understand the lingo."

Wyatt nodded and screened his eyes against the early afternoon sun, but he couldn't work up any enthusiasm after the Slapton Sands disaster.

The HMS *Seavington* had taken her load of survivors to Portland, and the crew had been sworn to secrecy. Nine German E-boats had attacked Convoy T-4, sinking two LSTs bound for Exercise Tiger and seriously damaging a third. Jerry Hobson hadn't been there, thank goodness, but hundreds had perished—possibly over seven hundred.

Secrecy was required. Not to cover up the disaster, but to protect the security of Operation Neptune and to blind the Germans to the extent of the damage they'd wrought so easily.

Blame whipped around like the winds in Weymouth Harbor. The Army blamed the Navy for not training the soldiers how to wear life belts and how to abandon ship. The Americans blamed the British for not sending enough escort ships with the convoy, for not notifying the Americans when one of the escorts returned to Plymouth after being damaged in a collision, and for not alerting the Americans about the E-boat sightings. And the British blamed the Americans for using the wrong radio frequency.

Too many cooks indeed.

Jack nudged Wyatt. "All right, buddy. You've moped long enough."

Wyatt lifted his face to the breeze. "It's a lot to handle. Slapton, Dad's letter, Dorothy."

"Ready to tell me about her?"

Exercise Tiger had allowed him to postpone this talk. "I started to ask her out, told her I wanted to take in a big show in town, and she offered to find me a date."

"Ouch."

"Mm-hmm. Then she said maybe I shouldn't date English girls. They might not want to leave the country."

Jack's cheeks puffed up with air. "She certainly let you know where you stand."

"Yep. She can't leave her father. I know that. I should've thought of that."

"Well, now you know. Still friends?"

The motor launch slowed and drew alongside the destroyer USS *Oglesby*. "Would be if I hadn't been a jerk. A few days later I said something stupid. Hurt her feelings. She'll be glad not to see me again."

Jack whistled. "You really know how to burn bridges."

He was an expert at that, and his chest seized.

"Sorry, buddy. That was below the belt."

"No, it's true."

"Still . . ."

The two Wren coxswains heaved the launch to, grabbing lines tossed down from the *Oglesby*, and they beckoned for Wyatt and Jack to board their new ship.

"Thank you for the ride, ladies." Wyatt tipped his cover to the Wrens, slung his sea bag over his shoulder, and climbed the rope ladder.

Jack followed. "Maybe your brothers . . . ?"

Wyatt dropped him a skeptical look. He appreciated the effort, but it was impossible.

"Okay, your dad's right. It'll take a miracle. But miracles are God's specialty."

Too bad he didn't deserve a miracle. Wyatt gripped the manila line as he climbed. But who did? Who deserved mercy or grace or miracles? No one. They were God's to give. Hadn't Job asked why he should receive good from God's hand and not evil? So why was Wyatt willing to receive evil from God's hand and not good?

He hauled himself onto the deck and straightened his navy overcoat and his attitude. *Lord, I'll accept whatever you give me.*

On the quarterdeck Wyatt and Jack faced aft and saluted the national ensign, then saluted the officer of the deck. "Lt. Wyatt Paxton, reporting for duty, sir."

"Lt. John Vale, reporting for duty, sir."

The officer of the deck reviewed their orders. "Very well. I'm Lt. Grover Ellis, the executive officer. Captain Adams is in the wardroom. Report to him."

"Aye aye, sir." They headed forward, past sailors on duty in good old US Navy dungarees and white "Dixie cup" covers.

"Smells good," Jack said. "It was fun serving on the British ships, but it's good to come home."

It was. The *Oglesby* was a Gleaves-class destroyer, same as the USS *Coghlan*, the ship they'd served on together in the Aleutians.

Wyatt pointed to the array of radar antennae on the mast. "Looks like you've got some new toys to play with."

"So do you." Jack pointed to the Bofors 40-mm antiaircraft guns.

"Hope we won't need those." But the way the Luftwaffe had been bombing the southern ports almost nightly diluted his hope.

In the deckhouse they went down the ladder and entered the wardroom.

Two officers sat at the table, and Wyatt and Jack saluted, reported for duty, and presented their orders.

"I'm Lt. Cdr. Edwin Adams, captain of the *Oglesby*. Welcome aboard." The captain wasn't much older than Wyatt, with jet-black hair and a strong-featured face.

"I'm Lt. Wayne Holoch, the gunnery officer." He had a wide, friendly grin and eyes full of laughter. Wyatt would enjoy working with him.

Wyatt and Jack stashed their sea bags in the corner and joined the officers at the table.

Captain Adams looked over their orders. "We're glad to have you here. As liaison officers, you'll report to both Commander Marino and to me. Here on the *Oglesby*, you'll be considered full members of the crew."

"Thank you, sir," Wyatt and Jack said together.

"You bring unique knowledge of targets and communications, as well as experience from the amphibious exercises that we lack." The captain shook his head. "Can't believe they couldn't get us over here in time."

"Exercise Fabius is coming up," Jack said.

"That's the only full-scale rehearsal we'll get."

Wyatt's stomach soured. What if the Germans attacked during Fabius as they had during Tiger? And what about on D-day itself?

If a handful of little E-boats could cause such destruction, what would happen when the full strength of the German naval, air, and ground forces rained down on the Allies?

"Very well, gentlemen." Captain Adams gave them a welcoming smile. "Get settled in your cabin, and then go meet the men. Mr. Paxton, I see you have a courier mission this afternoon, so don't linger."

"Aye aye, sir." Wyatt rose and followed Jack to their cabin.

That sickening feeling persisted. Faced with enemy opposition, would Wyatt be able to protect the ship's crew? The troops storming the beaches? His own brothers?

He plopped his sea bag on his bunk. *Lord, help me. I can't do it on my own.*

27

Was Johanna right? Late that afternoon, Dorothy leaned her temple against the window of the railway car as it chugged south from London.

All her life, Dorothy had gravitated toward quiet girls for friends. Gwen had become livelier, but how much of that had been due to Dorothy's influence? Not only did quiet girls keep Dorothy's more outrageous impulses in check, but she enjoyed drawing them in to her fun, encouraging them to try new things, and watching them grow in confidence.

Could it be the same with a husband?

Her sigh fogged the window, blurring Hampshire's scenery. No, it couldn't. Mum and Papa had been so ill-matched.

Papa liked solving crosswords and feeding ducks. He'd tried to make Mum happy by taking her to Edinburgh and France, but it was never enough for her.

Over the years Mum had grown disdainful and she'd turned to her friends for stimulation. Over the years Papa had grown aloof and he'd turned to his sons for companionship.

Dorothy had watched, excluded and helpless. She'd hated seeing

Mum so unhappy, hated seeing Papa treated so poorly, hated watching their love turn to distant contempt.

She refused to make the same mistake.

The train pulled into Cosham Railway Station just north of Portsmouth.

Valise in hand, Dorothy ducked out of the railway car and headed down the platform toward the bus stop. She climbed the stairs to the little bridge and crossed the tracks. Underneath, two trains departed, one in each direction, and the wind ruffled the hem of her skirt.

Down on the far platform, a tall American naval officer walked amongst the travelers who'd disembarked from the eastbound train. Her breath caught. If it weren't for the slump of his shoulders, she'd think it was Wyatt.

Then the man glanced up at the bridge and stopped. "Dorothy?"

"Wyatt!" She scrambled down the stairs as fast as she dared. "Oh, Wyatt, I'm so sorry. Please forgive me. I was abominably rude, and you were only trying to help."

"What? I'm the one who needs to apologize."

"You?"

He stepped to the far side of the platform away from the passersby. "I shouldn't have talked that way about your dad. I had no evidence. Not one bit. And it doesn't fit his character. Can you forgive me?"

The devastation in his blue eyes melted her. The poor man, always seeking forgiveness. "Of course I do. Besides, you were right."

"Right?" His eyebrows sprang to the rim of his officer's cap. "Your—your dad?"

"No, no. I don't think he's guilty, but you're right about how it looks to others." She lowered her voice, even though the last passengers were departing the station. "My friend Johanna says there's gossip at the office about him."

"Sorry to hear that."

"Do you suppose—I doubt it's possible with us down here—but would you be willing to keep investigating? Please?"

His mouth shifted to one side. "Are you sure you want to keep digging? What if the rumors are true?"

She pulled herself taller. She'd had plenty of time to think on the train. "If he's guilty, we're ruined already. The truth will come out, whether or not we investigate. And if he's innocent and no one investigates, the embezzler will drive the company to bankruptcy. The only chance to save the company and my father is to find the embezzler."

"All right. I'll see what I can do." Wyatt nodded a few times, gazing over her head. "It's a long shot, but I'd like to check out the Edinburgh office. Don't know how I could get up there."

"I think—" Her throat clamped shut, and she swallowed hard. "Recently I suggested Papa and I take a trip to Edinburgh. We used to love it so, but we haven't been there for years—1937, '38 perhaps. Papa refused. He said he never wanted to go back. Do you think . . . ?" The swelling in her throat rose to her tongue.

Wyatt switched his attaché case from one hand to the other. "Hard to say. He's grieving. Maybe it just hurts to see the old places."

She nodded, not trusting her voice.

"Listen, Dorothy. I'm sorry about this. I got involved because I wanted to help your family. I hate to think I could destroy it."

"He—he's all I have left." The swelling rose to her eyes and shoved tears to the surface. Bother. She lowered her valise to the platform and groped in her pocket for a handkerchief.

"Hey, now." Wyatt patted her shoulder in an awkward manner. Something about that fumbling masculine compassion shattered a barrier inside her. Grief yanked at her facial muscles, and she slapped the handkerchief over her mouth. But a hideous little sob erupted, and she swayed toward that manly comfort.

"Hey, now. There, there." His attaché case thumped to the ground, and he gathered her in his arms.

What on earth was she doing? How could she fall apart like this? And in public? She pushed back against his solid chest. "I need to—"

"No, you need to cry." He gently pressed her head to his shoulder, knocking her cap askew. "My mama says women need to cry every once in a while. Washes away all the weakness so you can stay strong. Always let a lady cry, she says."

Everything British in her rebelled. What would her mother say to see her like this?

Nothing. Her mother would say nothing. Her mother was dead.

So were Art and Gil. And poor Papa was drowning in his own grief, unable to see Dorothy's.

Another sob welled up, and another.

"That's it. Atta girl." Wyatt rubbed her back.

She couldn't stop the tears any more than she could stop the war. With both hands, she flattened the handkerchief over her eyes and mouth to muffle her sobs and to spare Wyatt's coat.

For three years she'd held herself together so she could hold Papa together.

So alone. No one to lean on.

A deeper sob ripped up. No, she'd been alone longer than that. Papa only cared about her brothers, and Mum cared only about . . . ? If Dorothy were honest, Mum had cared only about herself. Her brothers had loved her, but they'd gone away to university and then the Navy. She'd been so alone.

"There now. I've got you."

In Wyatt's arms she felt small, but safe and hidden. And not alone.

Her eyes opened in the light muted by the handkerchief and Wyatt's embrace.

He caressed her back, his movements firm but respectful, and his murmurs sent soothing waves through her entire being.

A magnetic impulse told her to relax fully, to wrap her arms around him, to lift her face to him. *Bésame mucho.*

What was happening to her?

"All better?" he asked.

She held her breath. Indeed, the tears had stopped. The timing couldn't be better. "Yes. Yes, thank you." Her voice trembled. She backed away, set her cap right, and patted her face with her damp handkerchief.

"Been a while?" He straightened his tie and gave her a soft smile.

"Ages." Maybe his mother was correct. Although Dorothy felt limp, somehow she felt stronger.

His mouth twitched up on one side, then he broke into a full smile. "You have freckles."

She gasped and covered her cheeks. Her powder! She'd cried it off.

"Looks cute," he said. "Looks right. Redheads ought to have freckles."

"Nonsense. They're dreadful things." She stuffed her handkerchief into her handbag, pulled out her compact, and turned her back on him and the platform. "Please pardon my manners. I simply can't be seen like this."

"Don't see why not. God made your freckles."

She dabbed powder on her nose and cheeks. "The Lord must have dreadful taste."

"Then so do I. Always liked freckles."

Dorothy checked her image in the tiny mirror, patted on more powder, and pinned up a loose strand of hair. Thank goodness Lawrence hadn't seen her like that—crying, freckled, undone. She could imagine the disdain warping his features, and her stomach shriveled.

She angled her mirror toward Wyatt. He gazed down the platform, hands in his pockets, with a hint of a smile. No disdain. Only acceptance.

Dorothy snapped her compact shut. It wasn't fair to compare Lawrence to Wyatt. Lawrence had his faults, but he was everything she wanted in a man and he wouldn't steal her away to the Wild West.

She returned her compact to her handbag, spun around with a smile, and grabbed her valise. "Shall we be on our . . . wait. Why are you here?"

He chuckled and picked up his attaché case. "I'm delivering papers to Southwick House." He pronounced it "South-wick."

"Suth-ick," she corrected him.

Wyatt shook his head as if scolding a small child. "Y'all really know how to mangle the English language."

Her laugh came out shaky. "The bus stop is this way."

He fell in step beside her. "So where have you been?"

"London. Lawrence persuaded First Officer Bliss-Baldwin to grant me leave each weekend to see Papa."

"That was right nice of him."

"It was." Papa had been so touched, he'd finally asked her to invite Lawrence to dinner. But she frowned at Lawrence's true motives.

Regardless, she whipped up a smile for Wyatt. "Are the papers about the training exercise? How was it?"

He looked as if a cold wave had slapped him in the face. "Reckon you haven't heard."

Appalled, she hung back a distance from the half-dozen people at the bus stop. "Oh dear. What happened?"

"Don't know how much I can tell you." He sent her a cautious look. "It was bad. Men died—a lot of men. I couldn't protect them, couldn't save them."

Dorothy hugged his arm, his need for comfort overriding her need to smother her attraction. "I'm so sorry. It wasn't your fault, was it?" *Please, Lord. Please don't let it be his fault.*

He drew a long breath. "Honestly, no. I just wish . . . but it was too late."

Questions crowded her mind, questions she didn't dare ask.

He'd probably told her too much already. "You've had a perfectly frightful week, you poor thing."

"You have no idea." His voice sank to the cellar. "Got a letter from my dad."

From the despondency in his eyes, she knew the news wasn't good. How dare that man! Wyatt was so sweet, so contrite. "He hasn't forgiven you?"

"No, he did. He did forgive me. So did Mama. But my brothers . . ."

The bus pulled to the curb, and Dorothy and Wyatt boarded. She found a quiet seat toward the back, then coaxed the story out of him, how grief-stricken Adler had run away from home and how Clay hadn't been able to become a doctor.

"Now all three of you are over here." She lowered her voice to a whisper. "All three will fight on D-day."

"On the sea, in the air, and on the ground." Wyatt sagged in the bus seat. "It's all my fault."

"You mustn't say that."

"But it's true." His face was too close, too unbearably sad. "If I hadn't done what I did, Adler would be working at Paxton Trucking. He's older than Clay, so he'd still be deferred. And Clay would be in college, also deferred because he'd be studying medicine."

"Oh, Wyatt." She clutched his arm again. How awful. He'd been determined to forgive himself and stop punishing himself, and now this.

"Don't see how they can ever forgive me. Even Daddy said it'll take a miracle."

Somehow she had to elevate his spirits. "Would a good cry help?"

A smile crept up, fanning around his eyes. "Only works for girls."

"Well, if you ever change your mind . . ." She kept her voice light and patted her shoulder.

211

Gratitude deepened his smile, and he squeezed her hand. "Thanks."

Oh dear. Anyone watching would think they were an item. She gave his arm one last hug and returned her hands to her lap where they belonged.

If only it were as easy to return her emotions where they belonged.

28

LYME BAY OFF SLAPTON SANDS, SOUTH DEVON
THURSDAY, MAY 4, 1944

From the gun director high on the bridge superstructure of the USS *Oglesby*, Wyatt stuck his head out the top hatch. A southerly force 3 wind roughened his face and the waters off Slapton Sands.

Under an overcast sky, five of the ships of Destroyer Squadron 18 steamed toward the beaches to provide fire support for Exercise Fabius. The remaining four destroyers of DesRon 18 remained ten miles offshore in a protective screen.

Wyatt's stomach hardened at the memory of the disaster during Exercise Tiger. To avoid another tragedy, the US Navy had provided plenty of warships to escort the convoy from Weymouth the night before.

Fabius had been planned for May 3, but poor weather had postponed the exercise to May 4. While the weather still wasn't ideal, it might not be ideal for the actual invasion either. Wyatt agreed with Admiral Kirk's order to proceed.

Along with Wyatt in the cramped steel compartment, five sailors were ready for action. Gunnery officer Lt. Wayne Holoch was stationed several decks below in the plotting room with the Mark I mechanical computer.

The *Oglesby* and most of her crew hadn't served in combat, and this was the first time the men of the *"Ogie"* were working together in an exercise of this size. Even Wyatt hadn't sat in a gun director in six months. Could be an interesting day.

Muffled booms rose to the north and south, the opening bombardment by the heavy cruiser USS *Augusta* and the light cruiser HMS *Glasgow*.

A flash in the sky stole Wyatt's breath. *Our planes or theirs?*

No air raid alert had sounded, and US B-26 Marauder medium bombers were supposed to bomb the beaches before the landings. Nine bombers flew west in a V formation. Wyatt glanced at his watch—0705. The B-26s, right on schedule.

Was Adler up there?

Wyatt took a steadying breath. No, he wasn't. Wrong aircraft.

A letter from Mama had arrived yesterday, as long and emotional as Daddy's had been short and blunt. Adler had written home not long after Wyatt had, and Mama was thrilled to hear from both her lost boys.

Adler was indeed a pilot based in England, flying a P-51 Mustang fighter plane. Although concerned for his safety, Mama was elated that all three boys were alive and serving their country. She didn't mention why Adler had run away, but that was none of Wyatt's business.

She'd enclosed addresses for both Adler and Clay and begged Wyatt to write, but he had no inclination to contact them yet. Part of him wanted to avoid their replies—or worse, a lack of reply. Only cold, bitter, unforgiving silence.

But mostly, he just wasn't ready. The shock of Daddy's letter was too fresh, and words failed him.

The *Ogie*'s engines slowed, and the gun director rocked slightly forward. They must be nearing the fire support area.

In the cold air, Wyatt adjusted his headphones over his cover. Exercise Fabius closely followed the orders for Operation Neptune. The US Navy's Force O was landing American troops at Slapton as if on Omaha Beach. Meanwhile, other English beaches were mimicking Juno, Gold, and Sword beaches with Royal Navy Forces J, G, and S landing British and Canadian troops.

At Slapton, the 1st and 29th Divisions would land in the same order as they would at Omaha. A few miles to the north, the Army Rangers were scheduled to land at Blackpool Beach.

If only the *Oglesby* were stationed off Blackpool. Clay had to be there. If Wyatt could protect his youngest brother . . .

He sighed and slipped back inside the compartment. Once again, he was trying to earn love and forgiveness. It was all up to Adler and Clay and the Lord.

The general quarters alarm sounded. "All hands to battle stations," a voice said over the loudspeaker. "All stations report when manned and ready."

The gunnery department had been ready for hours, but Wyatt glanced around.

"Ready, sir," said the pointer, the trainer, the talker, the range-finder operator, and the range talker.

"Director manned and ready," Wyatt said on the intercom.

After Wyatt received the ship's coordinates, he marked his chart and performed his calculations for the assigned target—bearing eighty-five degrees, range fifty-one hundred yards. "Start tracking. Target angle eight-five. Range five-one-double-oh."

The pointer and trainer repeated his orders and turned the hand wheels on their equipment. The entire director compartment swiveled on its ball-bearing ring to face the target.

"On target," the trainer said.

"Target sighted." The rangefinder operator peered through the giant horizontal tube of his instrument.

The corrected bearing and range were automatically transmitted to the computer down in the plotting room.

Within a minute, Holoch's voice came through the intercom. "Firing solution computed and transmitted to guns."

Wyatt flipped the intercom switch to speak to the pilothouse right underneath him. "Director to captain. Target sighted. Solution computed and transmitted to guns."

"Acknowledged. Stand by." On the amphibious command ship USS *Ancon*, Rear Adm. John Hall, commander of Force O, would call the shots.

Wyatt stood to look out the hatch. The *Ogie*'s starboard side faced the coast. To Wyatt's left, guns number one and two rotated toward the target, operated automatically by the computer. To his right past the ship's two funnels, guns number three and four did likewise.

Another glance at his watch—0721. The first troops were scheduled to land at 0730, and the naval bombardment needed to finish before then.

Another minute and the intercom went live. "Commence firing. Two salvos, four minutes apart."

"Aye aye, sir. Fire salvo." He braced himself.

Bright orange light, and then the boom and concussion shook the compartment. Wyatt grinned. He hadn't heard the sound of 5-inch guns in months, and it still thrilled him.

He pressed his eyes to the binoculars in his slewing sight and located the concrete bunker on shore. Plumes of smoke and earth rose slightly inland and to the left, not enough to knock out any guns inside but enough to shake up the gunners—if the bunker had held either.

"Down oh-three-oh. Right zero-eight." He called out corrections, and the trainer and pointer cranked their hand wheels. Those movements would transmit electrical signals to the computer, which would make the adjustments.

"Plot to director, we have a new solution," Holoch said on the intercom.

"Acknowledged." Wyatt counted off the time. "Fire salvo."

A giant roar and four more 5-inch projectiles shot toward shore, the last live ammunition the *Ogie* would fire today.

More smoke and dirt obscured the target as the shells landed. A bit short, but the bearing was true.

Wyatt ducked inside and smiled at his crew, kicking himself for not knowing their names yet. "Good job, men."

The pointer grinned at him. "We gave our boys a good show, sir."

"Sure did." He looked out the hatch again. On Lyme Bay, dozens of small LCVP landing craft bounced over the waves. The day's bombardment provided the ships some gunnery practice, but more importantly it acclimated the soldiers to the scream of shells overhead.

Now the *Oglesby* waited. After the troops landed, the Shore Fire Control Parties would contact the destroyers to call in targets. Only simulated fire this time, but it would be good practice.

Wyatt eyed the spectacle. First in the line of assault came the strange-looking duplex drive tanks—tanks fitted with a propeller for propulsion and a canvas shield to keep out the sea.

"Sure hope those things work," he muttered. After the warships lifted the bombardment and before the SFCPs could call in naval gunfire, the troops on the ground would depend on tanks for fire support.

Even though the exercise was only a dress rehearsal, the sight of twenty-five thousand men on the move made Wyatt's throat clamp shut.

Ever since the Battle of Dunkirk in June 1940, the British had longed to return to France and drive out the Germans. For over a year, the Allies had made plans for Operation Overlord. And for the past four months, Wyatt had done his bit in the planning. Soon he'd watch those plans come to fruition.

Dorothy wouldn't see her work come to pass before her eyes.

He smiled at the memory of her sorting photographs and plotting her findings on the map, enthusiasm lighting up her pretty face.

Then came a sweeter memory of that same face pressed to his

chest as she wept. Sweet forgiveness, sweet healing tears, sweet intimacy.

If only that intimacy meant more than friendship. But it didn't.

Just as Mr. Fairfax almost saw Wyatt as a son, Dorothy saw him as a brother. And she was crazy about Eaton. The man might be dating others, but he wasn't a cad, as much as Wyatt longed to cast him in the role. He'd been plenty kind to Mr. Fairfax, and Wyatt could always depend on the British officer's competence and fairness.

In time, Eaton would fall hard for Dorothy. Why wouldn't he? Wyatt's heart hadn't accepted it, but his mind had. Even if he did see her again, he'd be transferred after Operation Neptune. Besides, he loved her too much to take her away from her father.

Just as well she hadn't fallen for him.

"Mr. Paxton, CIC's on the intercom," the talker said from behind Wyatt.

"Thanks." Wyatt flipped the switch to connect to Jack Vale in the Combat Information Center. "Director."

"CIC here. We haven't been able to make radio contact with the SFCP." Disappointment lowered Jack's voice.

"Acknowledged." Wyatt didn't need to tell Jack to keep trying. On the beach, the tanks sat silently at water's edge, according to the day's plan. GIs scrambled over the sands, dodged beach obstacles, and cut barbed wire. Far inland, P-47 fighter planes strafed targets.

What if the SFCPs couldn't make contact on D-day? The destroyers would be blinded, unable to help the men ashore.

Panicky helplessness gripped his gut, but he prayed it away. He couldn't control everything. He could only do his part.

29

Trees, hedges, and flower beds displayed their spring glory, the blooms bobbing in the warm breeze. But Dorothy didn't sketch them.

She sat on the lawn of Southwick House with her feet tucked to one side, a yellowed old sketchbook on her lap, and a tin of colored pencils beside her. Thank goodness she'd indulged in a pencil set before the war broke out, because they were no longer being manufactured and they fit so neatly in her valise.

She'd skipped lunch to draw. Blissy had been in an infernal mood, and Dorothy wanted to avoid gossiping with her friends. It wasn't fitting to make sport of her CO, no matter what a tempting target she made.

What did Lawrence see in her anyway? The woman was a jealous, manipulative harpy.

Dorothy set aside her green pencil and her green attitude. First Officer Julia Bliss-Baldwin was beautiful, accomplished, well traveled, and she came from a family with titles, land, and money.

The Fairfaxes had only money, and if the embezzler wasn't caught soon—or if Papa were the embezzler—they wouldn't even have that.

Besides, Dorothy was the one with the date with Lawrence this weekend—even if it wasn't the type of date she wanted.

"Hi there." A man plopped onto the grass beside her.

"Wyatt!" She grinned. "What are you doing here?"

He removed his cap, stretched out his legs, and leaned back on his elbows. "Such a nice day. Thought I'd go for a drive along the seashore."

She laughed. "Even if you could obtain petrol . . ."

"Can't fool you. Took the train and delivered some reports. Your friend—the blonde—she said you were outside sketching."

Her cheeks warmed. He came looking for her.

"What are you drawing?" He sat up and scooted closer. "The house in Vierville again."

"Your target." She grabbed a red pencil and drew a bull's-eye on the front door.

"You know I'll spare it if possible." Then he tapped the shack. "I don't remember that in the other painting."

"It wasn't there, because it wasn't there when I was a girl. Lawrence agrees, but Bliss-Baldwin thinks I made a grave mistake."

"I doubt that."

Dorothy switched the red for black and filled in the few bare spots on the shack. "It isn't my fault, but in the last reconnaissance photos, there it was. In the earlier photos, it was shielded by the tree, by shadows. No one saw it."

"Maybe the Germans built it to hide a gun. Maybe that's why they painted it black."

"Oh, it isn't black and it isn't German. It's unfinished wood and weathered, from what we can see. It must have been built not long after our last holiday in '37."

Wyatt rested his forearms on his bent knees. "So, why did you color it black?"

"I don't know." She nibbled on the end of the pencil. "I keep trying to change it, but I can't. Maybe it's black because it hid from me in the shadows or because I'm ashamed I missed it."

"Hey." He nudged her with his elbow. "Don't be hard on yourself. You aren't the only one looking at those photos."

"I know." She closed the sketchbook. "No more wallowing. You'll regret visiting me."

"Nope." The sun turned his hair golden. "You're the reason I came to Southwick."

Her heart performed a strange little trill. "Me?"

"I begged Marino to let me be his errand boy. I have good news for you. You'll never guess where I was this past week."

Had she ever seen his eyes so bright? "At sea?"

"Yep. Up to Greenock and back. We escorted some transports."

"That's nice." As glad as she was to see him, why would he come all the way to Southwick to tell her that?

"Soon we're heading back to train in the Firth of Clyde. We'll be there about two weeks, almost up till D-day."

Why was that good news? She'd have no chance to see him, possibly forever.

"Don't you see?" His grin grew. "It's not far from Edinburgh. Not far at all. That's no coincidence—that's God's providence. Both Marino and Adams said I could have a forty-eight-hour leave. Do you think you can get to Scotland?"

"To investigate . . ." Her voice came out in a whisper.

"It's our best chance to clear your dad."

Or condemn him. She rubbed her forehead. "It takes a full day on the train. I have every weekend free, but I'd need an additional day for travel."

"Would First Officer what's-her-name give it to you?"

"Gladly." Anything to separate Dorothy from Lawrence.

"Could Mr. Montague meet us? Or figure out a way to get us in?"

"I'll try to ring him. If I can't, I'll send him a telegram."

221

"How's this weekend? We're supposed to arrive late Saturday. If you took the train on Saturday, we could investigate on Sunday—"

"This Saturday? I have a date with Lawrence." She clamped her mouth shut. What was wrong with her—putting Lawrence above her father? She could reschedule. She should. She would. And why did she feel so awful mentioning her date to Wyatt?

His smile fell a bit, then rose again. "How about the following weekend?"

"Much better." To break her gaze, she set her sketchbook on the grass. "It would be easier to take Friday off. I could take the train on Friday, we could investigate on Saturday, and I could return—" No. No, she couldn't.

"What's the matter?"

"Oh no. I can't go."

He winced. "The weekend after that will be too late for sure."

Dorothy groaned. "No, I can't go at all. I don't have the money for the fare, the hotel. I gave it all away."

"What do you mean?"

"Have I told you about my friend Johanna? The Jewish refugee? Her grandmother's ill, and she couldn't pay the doctor, so I gave her all my pay for April. I won't be paid again until the end of May. I have enough for a trip or two to London, but not Edinburgh. Oh, Wyatt, I'm so sorry."

He frowned. "Do you have enough in the bank?"

"I do, but it's in London. By the time I arrive on Fridays, the bank is closed."

"Could you ask your dad to—oh, you can't ask him, huh?"

She shook her head. "I'm sorry. Why do I always have to be so impulsive?"

"Stop it." He bumped his shoulder against hers. "What you did was kind and generous. Never resist an impulse to be kind."

Now he was the one being kind. "But I ruined your plans."

Wyatt draped his arms on his knees, nodding slightly, his eyes narrowed at the landscape. Oh dear. Was he angry? He had every right to be. But he didn't look angry, merely pensive.

Then he leaned onto one hip and pulled his wallet out of his pocket. "How much do you need?"

She gasped. "No, you can't do that. You're so close to paying off your debt."

He drew out some pound notes. "Not punishing myself, remember? And a few bucks won't make a difference."

Dorothy pushed his hand away. "I can't take it. I know what it means to you."

"And I know what clearing your dad's name means to you." He slipped the notes into her sketchbook. "There's a main train station in Edinburgh, isn't there? I'll meet you there at 0900 on Saturday the twentieth. If you're not there, I'll know your CO didn't give you leave. I'll go sightseeing instead. I've always wanted to see Edinburgh."

She rested one hand on the grass. He was willing to waste his leave looking at dusty old account books and to spend his precious money, not just on her fare and lodging, but on his as well. Such generosity. For . . . her?

Dorothy's eyes tingled, and she cleared her throat. "Why are you doing this? Sacrificing your time, your money?"

He put his wallet back in his pocket. "It's the right thing to do."

How many times had she heard him say those words? He meant them. He was a man of honor, and her heart felt full.

Wyatt sat forward, his hands gripped between his knees. The tendons stood out on the back of his hands, his mouth pursed, and his forehead drew up.

"Oh dear. You're having second thoughts about the money. I'll—"

"No. Not that. No regrets." His head swung back and forth, heavy and slow. "I just—I wasn't honest."

Her lips parted. He'd lied to her? In what way? "What—"

"I didn't tell a lie. Nothing like that. But I didn't tell the whole truth. Sometimes it's wise to hold things back. It is. But sometimes it's dishonest."

Her mind reeled. When had he ever been less than honest with her? "I don't understand."

"I said I was doing this because it's right. It is, but that's not the whole truth. Pretending that's the only reason—well, it makes me look nobler than I really am."

Her fingers curled into the grass blades. What did he mean? Why wouldn't he look at her?

His chest puffed out, and then he blew out a long breath. "I had other motives for wanting to help with the business. I wanted to spend more time with you, hoped you'd—well, I hoped you'd fall for me."

"Oh . . ." She barely heard her own voice. Not only had he become infatuated, but he was willing to admit it. It was too marvelous, too horrible.

His face reddened, and his chin dipped. "Because I've fallen for you. Hard. I—I love you. There, I've said it, but it doesn't change a thing. You're crazy about Lawrence, and it looks like he's crazy about you. So I'll be happy for you. I will. I want what's best for you."

Dorothy clamped her hand over her mouth. He . . . he loved her?

"I wasn't thinking anyway." He jerked his head to one side. "You can't leave your dad. I know that. It was a foolish dream."

Her emotions crashed into one another like waves in a storm, swelling in her chest, filling her mouth. "Oh, Wyatt. I'm so sorry."

"Don't pity me. Please," he said in a sharp tone, and he pushed himself to standing. "I'd better go. I'll see you in Edinburgh. May 20, 0900."

The sun behind his head blinded her and obscured his features. "You—you still want to go?"

"I promised, didn't I? I'll see you then." He put on his cap and strode across the lawn, his shoulders straight and broad.

Dorothy buried her face in her hands and moaned. He loved her? Love? Not infatuation, but actual love?

"*I love you.*" Had anyone ever said those words to her? Ever? Her chest heaved. No. No one. Not that she could remember. Not her father. Not her mother. Her brothers had loved her, but they never would have said so. And her beaus? She'd always thrown them over quickly because they weren't Lawrence Eaton, her ideal man.

And what about Lawrence? Why, he didn't know her well enough to love her. And if he did fall for her, he'd fall for her sophisticated persona, not the real Dorothy.

But Wyatt . . . Wyatt loved *her.*

A little sob burst out. "Why, Lord? Why?"

All the words she longed to hear came from the wrong mouth.

30

USS *Oglesby*, St. George's Channel
Saturday, May 13, 1944

"I can't believe you told her." Jack Vale buttoned up his khaki shirt.

"I know." Wyatt gritted his teeth and pulled on his heavy mackinaw, changing out of the dress blues he'd worn for dinner on the first dog watch. "Now she knows I'm a lovelorn fool, but I had to be honest."

Jack grabbed his cover from the bottom bunk. "On the bright side, now that she knows you love her, maybe she'll come to look at you in a new light."

"That's what I like about you, Vale—your optimism."

With a flourish of his cover, Jack swept a low bow. "At your service."

"Wish it were warranted." Wyatt took his own cover off the top bunk. "She's been crazy about Eaton since she was a girl. He went on their family vacations, and she keeps painting the house where they stayed. He's got a hold on her—and a date with her tonight."

Jack let out a low whistle. "You sure know how to pick them, Wy."

"I sure do." Dorothy's shocked face when he'd confessed his love wouldn't leave his mind—her hand over her mouth, her eyes wide with dismay, her forehead pinched with pity.

Wyatt slammed his eyes shut as if he could wipe his memory

226

clean, but he of all people knew the past couldn't be undone. Better to follow Dorothy's example—no more wallowing.

He pulled his stationery box from a desk drawer, then led the way out of the cabin, down the passageway, through the wardroom, and up the ladder.

Jack kept climbing, up to the Combat Information Center for duty, but Wyatt stepped out onto the main deck. He was off duty for the second dog watch, but he had an important personal duty to attend to.

He stood at the rails and inhaled the cool air. The sun brightened the clouds above the Irish coast in the distance before him, promising almost two good hours of daylight.

Four destroyers of DesRon 18 steamed in a column through a narrow channel kept swept of mines. The ships would spend the next two weeks at Belfast, Northern Ireland, at Greenock, Scotland, and in the waters in between. The crews would keep busy with antiaircraft, antisubmarine, and gunnery drills, and would work with the Shore Fire Control Parties.

He strode aft down the deck. Time to write Adler and Clay.

D-day was less than a month away, and he wanted his brothers to receive the letters before. Dorothy had said she couldn't have borne it if she and her brothers had been estranged when they died. If one of the Paxton boys—or all of them—should die during the invasion, he wanted them to go out on good terms. If nothing else, Wyatt would know he'd done his part.

Above him, the two stacks of the *Oglesby* puffed out steam as the ship made eighteen knots. Sailors bustled around changing watch, and Wyatt nodded to the men as they went to the mess.

He had to admit the main reason he hadn't written earlier was fear. Not only fear he'd never be forgiven, but the greater fear that his family would never be restored.

Wyatt passed the aft superstructure, crowned with the 40-mm guns.

Sure, paying off his debt was right and necessary, but he'd used the debt as an excuse to avoid confrontation.

Wyatt worked his hand inside his mackinaw and slipped his notepad out of his breast pocket. Pages and pages of neat figures showed the huge sum being whittled down. Even with what he'd given Dorothy, he only had $42.57 left to repay, which would be brought to zero when he was paid at the end of the month. Right before D-day.

He sat on the deck astern of the number four gun, a quiet place since no gunnery drills were scheduled tonight.

Resting back against the heavy steel gun enclosure, he drew up his knees. The barrel of the gun stretched over his head, pointing south. In front of him, two depth-charge racks sat at the stern, ready to dump depth charges on any U-boats that dared navigate the narrow St. George's Channel between Wales and Ireland.

His hands clamped around the stationery box. "Lord, give me the words," he whispered. "Let me bring peace, not anger. Reconciliation, not further division. Put my family back together, Lord. Please. Only you can do that."

No more procrastinating. No more excuses. Wyatt set a sheet of stationery on top of the box and uncapped his pen.

Dear Adler,

I'm sure you're surprised to hear from me, but I pray you'll read this and consider what I have to say. I need to apologize and ask your forgiveness.

Sounds like you and I finally wrote home about the same time. Mama gave me your address and begged me to write you. She said you're a fighter pilot. I'm a naval officer based on the same island. Looks like all three of us are preparing for the same operation. On Easter Sunday, I believe I saw you in the park. I couldn't face you then, but I choose to do so now.

I can't begin to tell you how sorry I am about Oralee. Although her death was an accident and there was no malice in my actions, my role wasn't completely innocent. We have a long history of competition, you and I, and I resented how my younger brother bested me in everything. But Oralee rightfully chose you over me. You two were meant to be together, and I was wrong to let jealousy take root.

When she didn't want to cross that bridge and you kept coaxing her, all that resentment boiled up. My pride started that argument. My anger made Oralee cross the bridge just to stop our fighting. And my jealousy led her to refuse my help even as she teetered on the edge.

So no, I didn't kill her in the eyes of God or the law, but my actions did lead to her death. Even though the Lord has forgiven me, I will always live with the regret that her life ended far too early and that your life together never began.

Please know I am deeply sorry for the grief I caused you. If you should choose to forgive me, I'll be forever grateful. But if you don't, I'll understand.

I've never blamed you for wanting to kill me that day, and I forgave you for that long ago. How can I do otherwise when I recognize the depth of my own sins against you and Clay and while I accept Jesus's astounding mercy?

As this war heats up, only God knows what will happen to us. I can't head into battle without telling you everything in my heart. As much as we competed and fought, I miss you. I miss how you challenged me. I miss your sunny spirit, your passionate drive, and how you inspire everyone to do their best. You're a good man, and I admire you, respect you, and love you. I'm a better man for having you as my brother.

I pray we can be reconciled and can meet again. I'm enclosing my address, and I hope you write me. Whatever you have

*to say, I can take it. Even if we're never reconciled, please
know I'll pray for you all the days of my life.*

Your brother, Wyatt

His head sagged back against the gun's cold steel. If only he
could refill his drained soul before writing the next letter. But the
war wouldn't wait for one man to catch his breath, so he exchanged
the written letter for a blank sheet of stationery and sent up another
prayer. This letter would be even more difficult.

Dear Clay,

*I'm sure Daddy and Mama told you that I finally wrote
home. Now I've worked up the courage to write you and tell
you how very sorry I am.*

*The only reason Adler didn't kill me that day was because
you held him back so I could escape. Thank you for saving my
life and for saving Adler from the consequences of murder.
You deserved my gratitude. Instead, I betrayed you.*

*I could make excuses and say that panic and fear messed up
my thinking, but there's no excuse for stealing your savings.*

*Like a coward, I stole and I ran. I went to stay with a college
buddy in Charleston. I intended to send back the remainder of
your money, get a job, and pay back what I'd spent. Instead, I
let my friend talk me into investing your money—without your
permission—in his company. I thought I'd double your money
in months. Not only would you receive your college savings,
but you'd receive full tuition for medical school as well.*

*But the company failed. I lost every penny, plus we owed
our creditors.*

*Since I no longer trusted my business skills, I didn't dare
take an accounting job. When I saw a Navy recruitment*

office, I signed up for officer training. I'm now in the same part of the world as you, preparing for the same operation.

For the past three years, I've deeply regretted how I betrayed you. But Daddy's letter showed me the truth. I didn't just steal your money—I stole your lifelong dream. I wasn't aware that Paxton Trucking was in poor financial straits and that Daddy couldn't afford your tuition. I know how much you hated working in the office, how much you wanted to be a physician, and what a good doctor you would have been.

It breaks my heart that my selfish actions prevented you from doing what God created you to do. Knowing you were drafted because you weren't studying medicine only deepens my remorse.

For what it's worth, I'm almost done paying off my debt, not just what I stole but interest and a large fine. At the end of the month, my paycheck will cover the last of it. I'll send a check home for Daddy to deposit. If something should happen to me before then, my will states that my full bank account goes to you, plus a third of my life insurance.

I have no right to ask for forgiveness, but I do want you to know how sorry I am. I take full responsibility for the sins I committed against you and God. The Lord has seen fit to forgive me, but I'll understand if you don't.

Before we head into battle, I need to tell you how much I love and miss you. As much as Adler and I fought, we rarely fought with you. Somehow we knew you were the best of the Paxton boys, and we always protected you. Until the night I betrayed you.

Please know that hideous act doesn't reflect how I truly feel about you. You're always kind, always generous, always cheerful. A born healer, concerned not just with the body but with the heart and soul. I pray that when this war is over, you can fulfill your dream and have the life God meant for you.

I also pray we can be reconciled one day. If you choose, please write me at the address below. Don't hold anything back. You deserve to have your say.

No matter what happens to us in the coming days, please know I'll love you and pray for you till the Lord takes me home.

Your brother, Wyatt

To the west, the lowering sun turned the clouds golden. Wyatt slipped the letter inside the stationery box. He'd mail both when the destroyers returned to Weymouth. Most likely, he'd find gaps to fill and he wanted them to be perfect.

Wyatt drew his notepad from his pocket. The little pages fluttered in the wind, cataloguing each lash of self-flagellation. He did have to mail the letters and pay his debt because it was right, but he also had to forgive himself—whether or not his brothers ever forgave him.

God already knew the full consequences of Wyatt's actions when he forgave him, when he built the road to redemption on the cross. Nothing could wash away that road. Nothing.

Cool salty air filled Wyatt's lungs. For three years he'd refused to forgive himself, as if doing so would dishonor his brothers. Instead, his refusal only dishonored Jesus's sacrifice.

"Lord, no more," he whispered. "I won't do it anymore. What I did that night was wrong, but living in shame is wrong too. You never excused my actions, but you forgave me. And I—I forgive me too."

The notepad bent in half in his grip. In Greenock, he'd toss it in the scrap paper bin.

31

Simply smashing. Dorothy held the peacock-blue dress up to her chin, let her hair fall over her shoulder in long waves, and gazed through her eyelashes at her reflection. So sophisticated. Lawrence would love the look.

Groaning, Dorothy hung the dress back in her wardrobe. As a member of the Women's Royal Naval Service, she'd wear her uniform and pin up her hair as always. Utility, not glamour. Besides, she'd lost so much weight, the blue dress needed alterations.

She coiled her hair into a chignon, adding pin curls to her usual coiffure.

The stairs creaked one floor down, and the door to Papa's study opened and shut. He was going to sequester himself and not greet Lawrence.

Irritation prickled in her chest, not at Papa, but at Lawrence. Papa had finally asked her to extend a dinner invitation, and Dorothy had been thrilled. She could have had time with Lawrence, Papa could have become acquainted with Lawrence as a man, and a platonic family dinner seemed more respectful of her commanding officer.

But Lawrence had declined, insisting he wanted time alone with

Dorothy before the lockdown for D-day. Reluctant to refuse him once too often, she'd agreed as long as he picked a quiet, out-of-the-way restaurant.

Dorothy buttoned her white blouse over her slip. A compromise. Why must she do all the compromising? Why must he push her to defy First Officer Bliss-Baldwin? Why didn't he take her concerns seriously? Why would he risk her position for a thrill?

She knotted her tie too tight and wiggled it looser. Wyatt always considered her concerns. He'd never put her at risk.

Bother that man. Why did he have to tell her he loved her? Why did he have to be so thoughtful and protective when he wasn't the right man for her? He was an American, and he wasn't exciting. Not like Lawrence.

Lawrence—whose idea of excitement was to put Dorothy in danger.

Bother *that* man.

She pulled her navy blue skirt up over her hips. It was so hard to please Lawrence. So hard to be droll and sophisticated. So hard to tamp down her enthusiasm and chattiness. She never had to work hard with Wyatt. And Wyatt loved her.

Dorothy plopped onto the chair in front of her dressing table and stared at her freckled face. Wyatt even liked her freckles.

The spots had faded and lessened over time, but they still darkened her cheeks and nose and speckled her forehead. Dreadful things.

Those were Lawrence's words. The freckles blurred to beige, and she wiped her eyes clear with a handkerchief.

Bother, bother, bother that Wyatt Paxton. If he'd kept his mouth shut, she wouldn't be so unsettled.

She lifted her powder puff to her cheek and paused.

"God made your freckles," Wyatt had said.

She'd assumed God made them to spite her, but Wyatt said

it with warmth, as if God made them because he liked freckles, because he specifically liked them on her.

"That verse," she whispered. "Psalm 139. 'I am fearfully and wonderfully made: marvelous are thy works.'"

That light stirring returned, and she peered at her image. Marvelous, not dreadful. "God likes my freckles. He likes . . . me."

Since Mum's death, she'd seen God's love like Papa's. Her father tolerated her because she was flesh and blood, but he couldn't abide looking at her. He never sought her company.

That wasn't the sort of fatherly love the Bible ascribed to the Lord. Like the best of fathers, God doted on his children while still holding them to his standards.

"God loves me," she said to her dazed-eyed reflection. "God *likes* me. Freckles and all."

Her hand had settled down to the dressing table with the powder puff in her palm. She stared at it, then at her reflection, at the growing resolution in her eyes.

Dorothy closed the tin. Mascara to brighten her eyes. Lipstick to look like a grown woman. And no powder. She felt naked, exposed . . . and free.

She tugged on her navy blue jacket, buttoned it, and trotted downstairs just as the doorbell rang. "Good night, Papa! I'll see you later."

"Fine" came muffled from behind his study door.

Dorothy swung open the front door. "Good evening, Lawrence."

His handsome smile froze. "Good evening. I . . . I'll make myself comfortable while you finish getting ready."

Feeling cheeky, she set on her cap and grabbed her handbag. "I'm ready."

He winced and lowered himself into a chair in the drawing room. "You might want to check the mirror."

Cheekiness hardened to contrariness. She whirled to the mirror, adjusted a single hairpin, and spun back with a smile. "There. That's better."

His hands clamped on the armrests. "I thought you outgrew your freckles."

"I never said that."

"You'll . . . take care of it, will you not?"

She stood tall and clutched the strap of her handbag. "My appearance meets naval regulations, and I don't feel like wearing powder tonight."

Lawrence's lips squirmed. "I made reservations at a quiet little place—as you requested—but it is rather posh."

Was he embarrassed to be seen with her in public? She forced a smile. "Sounds lovely."

He raised one pleading eyebrow. He was—he was embarrassed.

Was she willing to send him away over so trivial a matter? She'd worn powder daily since she was sixteen. Why make a fuss tonight?

Then Lawrence's roguish smile returned, and he rose and sauntered over to her. "Why, you little minx."

Minx? She blinked. Never in her life had she played the minx, especially not this evening.

He set his hands on her shoulders and nuzzled a kiss below her ear. "You know I like a modern, daring woman."

Since when was eschewing powder modern and daring? She pulled back to study his face.

Never had he looked so pleased with her. "If you prefer to spend the evening in private rather than public, simply say so."

Her stomach soured. She opened her mouth to ask what he meant, but she dreaded the answer.

His hands slid down to her waist. "My parents are in the country. We shall have the house quite to ourselves."

Her thoughts jumbled and swirled and foamed. She'd adored this man forever. Every man she'd met since had fallen short in comparison. Now she could have him. With one simple yes, she might put Blissy and Helen and all other girls out of his heart. One yes, and she might win him at last.

"No," she said, never more certain of a word in her life.

His eyebrows arched. "No?"

"No. It isn't right." The last word came out as *rawt*, with a Texas accent.

"Pardon?"

Dorothy stepped out of his grasp. "It isn't the right thing to do, and I assure you that wasn't what I meant."

He shook his head. "I don't understand."

"And yet I spoke clearly. The quiet little restaurant sounds lovely, and I don't intend to wear powder. I said precisely what I meant."

His upper lip curled ever so slightly.

She gestured to the door. "Perhaps you should leave."

Lawrence sighed, and his posture softened. "Come now, Dorothy. Let's not be rash. I came all the way up to London to see you."

"And you did see me." She opened the door wide. "I'm sorry you didn't like what you saw."

A startled look, then he lowered his chin. "Good night, Second Officer."

"Good night, Lieutenant Commander." She waited until he descended to the pavement, and then she shut the door and sank back against it.

"Bother, bother, bother."

32

What was he thinking? Wyatt peered out the train window. Dozens of platforms funneled into Edinburgh's Waverley Station. Even if Dorothy decided to come, how would he find her?

The train chugged to a stop. Wyatt scanned the platform for a red-haired Wren—in vain.

He fetched his briefcase from the overhead rack. All right, then. He had a weekend in Edinburgh. He'd see the castle and Holyrood Abbey and the Royal Mile, maybe try some of that famous haggis.

Wyatt stepped out of the compartment onto the platform and tried to get his bearings. Hundreds of people, darting every which way, platforms everywhere. Which way was the exit? Where could he buy a map? Country mouse lost in yet another city.

A woman approached—a redhead in a WRNS uniform, her mouth tiny and her eyes big.

He swallowed hard. "You came."

"So did you."

"All right, then." He put on his most confident face. "Let's go catch an embezzler. Where's the office?"

"Oh." She gazed down the platform, freckles dusting her cheeks. She hadn't worn makeup. Why not? Because he'd said her freckles were cute? Nonsense. But she did look prettier than ever, more genuine somehow. "The office is a few blocks away, off Princes Street."

"I'm glad you know your way around, because I'm lost."

Dorothy turned back with a tiny smile. "Again?"

The teasing cracked through the awkwardness, and he laughed. "Lead on."

"Right this way." She strode away, weaving through the crowd like the lifelong city mouse she was.

When the crowd opened up, he came alongside her. "I have one rule for today."

"A rule?" She glanced up at him. Boy, those freckles were cute.

He nodded. "We're going to ignore everything I said last week. None of that uncomfortable talk. We're friends, and I won't let anything change that. Let's do our job and enjoy our day. Sound fair?"

With a blink, she lowered her gaze and headed up a wide staircase. "It does."

"So how was your date last week with Eaton?"

She stumbled, caught herself, and shot him a startled look. "My date?"

He shrugged and continued up the stairs. "I'd normally ask, wouldn't I?"

Wind swirled down the stairs, and she held on to her hat. "Yes, you would."

"So how was it?"

"We didn't get past my front door."

He studied her profile for a second. "What do you mean?"

"We had a . . . disagreement, and I decided . . ." She let out a single chuckle. "I decided I didn't want to be seen with him."

Daylight opened up at the top of the stairs and in his heart, but he clamped down on his joy for her sake. "I'm sorry."

"Nonsense. None of that uncomfortable talk. Let's do our job and enjoy our day."

"Aye aye, ma'am." Outside, clouds muted the sunlight. So Eaton and Dorothy had a tiff. Didn't mean they were through, and even if they were, it didn't mean she'd fall for him.

Dorothy stopped on the sidewalk. A park lay in front of them. "Up to your left, that's Old Town. You can see Edinburgh Castle at the end of the Royal Mile."

"Wow." The ridge was crowned with dark ancient stone buildings, more rugged and wild than London's polite gray polish. "When the recruiter said 'Join the Navy and see the world,' he wasn't joking. Can't believe I'm in Scotland."

"It's beautiful, isn't it?" She pointed straight ahead to a tall open structure of Gothic spires in the park. "That's the Walter Scott Memorial, and New Town is to our right."

"New?"

"Quite." She headed in that direction. "Neoclassical and Georgian architecture, late eighteenth century, early nineteenth century."

"That's what we call old in my country."

"Newborn babes." Another teasing look, and she crossed a wide street that ran alongside the park. "This is Princes Street. If your work doesn't take long, I'd love to show you the sights. If you'd like, that is."

"I'd like that." He'd like that very much. This would probably be his last time to see her, and he wanted to savor it.

"I'm glad. I haven't been here for years, and I miss it so." She headed down a street lined with "new" buildings, square and solid, but with plenty of ornate stonework. "How was your week?"

"Busy." He eyed the passersby and measured his words. "Ran drills, practiced with our fellows on the ground. And you'll be proud of me—I wrote to my brothers."

"You did?" Her grin lit up the cloudy day. "But you don't have all the money yet."

"Nope. You once told me life is short and family is dear, so I decided not to wait any longer. Besides, I can't earn their forgiveness and love."

Dorothy frowned. "I suppose not."

"And I'm only partly responsible for where they are now. Even with deferments, they might have chosen to enlist. And you have to volunteer for both the Rangers and the Army Air Force."

"I'm glad you stopped blaming yourself."

"No more of that." A pair of American sailors in dress blues passed and snapped salutes, which Wyatt returned. "I'll mail the letters as soon as we return to Weymouth. It feels good. I've apologized and I'm making amends—not to earn their love but because it's the—"

"The right thing to do."

He stared at her.

Her eyes had never looked so warm, or maybe it was an illusion caused by the freckles. "You say that a lot, you know."

He chuckled. "Reckon I do."

Dorothy smiled and waved. "There's Mr. Campbell, the manager of the Edinburgh office. Mr. Montague said he'd let us in."

Wyatt had hoped all the men would wear kilts and tam-o'-shanters, but this man wore trousers and a gray overcoat. At least he wore a blue-and-green plaid scarf.

"My wee lassie." The elderly gentleman clasped Dorothy's shoulders and kissed her cheek. "Look at you, all grown up. How long has it been?"

"I don't know." Her cheeks flushed under the freckles. "Six years, maybe seven."

"Your father has been gone too long." He turned his gaze to Wyatt.

"Mr. Campbell, this is Lt. Wyatt Paxton," Dorothy said.

"Nice to meet you, Mr. Campbell." Wyatt shook his hand as the older man sized him up.

"A pleasure." He unlocked the front door. "Highly irregular

having a foreigner look at our books, much less such a young lad. Highly irregular. But Mr. Montague trusts you, and our Dolly trusts you, so I'm glad to have your help."

Mr. Campbell strode through the lobby. "Well, Lieutenant, I hope you find out what's happening. We're losing money, but Mr. MacLeod insists everything's tip-top."

"Mr. MacLeod?"

"Head of accounting." Mr. Campbell unlocked a door.

"One of my father's oldest friends." Dorothy's voice trailed off.

"School chums, weren't they?" Mr. Campbell swung the door open. "Mr. Montague said to give you free rein, but mind you take care with the books. Mr. MacLeod likes them just so."

Wyatt glanced around the overheated room. "We'll put things back exactly as they were."

"Aye, see that you do. Mr. MacLeod would have a conniption if he knew I let you look at his books." He frowned. "I wish I could show you where things are, but I'm not familiar with this department."

"We'll figure it out."

"Aye." A sharp nod. "I'll return at noon and check on you."

After Mr. Campbell left, Wyatt set down his briefcase, shrugged off his jacket, and rolled up his sleeves.

For the first half hour, he surveyed the files and ledgers to figure out the system. Then he pulled files and got to work at a big rolltop desk.

Slowly, he worked his way through each department's ledgers. Dorothy brought him files, reassembled them neatly, and returned them.

But most of the time, she sat in a chair in the corner. Quiet.

Every once in a while, he could feel that pretty blue gaze, and he'd look up. Sure enough, she was watching him with an unfamiliar expression, but then she'd give him a quick smile and motion him back to work.

Made him uncomfortable. But that unfamiliar look wasn't pity, only . . . well, he didn't know what it was. Her gaze penetrating, her mouth turned down a bit, her cheeks pale.

However, he'd come to Edinburgh to study the books, not Dorothy.

He picked up an invoice from Forthwright Business Services. He'd seen a similar invoice earlier and remembered it because of the W in the middle. "Say, Dorothy. Would you please bring me the last file, the one you just put away? Come to think of it, the last three or four."

She stood and flipped through the file cabinet. "Did you find something?"

"I doubt it." The invoice was strangely nonspecific. "Just a hunch."

"Those hunches of yours . . ." She laid four folders before him.

Wyatt spread them in an arc, then opened them. Sure enough, each contained an invoice from Forthwright Business Services. Several, in fact. One per quarter in each department.

"Look. An invoice in this department dated March 6, in this department March 20, April 3, April 17. The same pattern in December and January."

Dorothy looked over his shoulder. "Each is for well over one hundred pounds."

"What kind of company provides services needed in all these departments, from procurement to personnel to maintenance?"

"Forthwright Business Services. The name doesn't tell you anything."

"Only that the owner can't spell."

Dorothy picked up an invoice. "Edinburgh sits on the Firth of Forth. It must be a play on words. And it sounds quite wholesome and honest."

"A little too much." Wyatt opened the check ledger and skimmed through. "All the invoices paid, each signed by . . . Mr. MacLeod."

"Oh dear."

"He's head of accounting. Nothing unusual there." He scribbled down the company's address. "Do you know where Johnston Terrace is?"

"Oh yes. That's where we used to stay when we visited."

"Is it far?"

"About a mile."

"Let's pay a visit after lunch. We'll put in another hour or two of work, and—"

"An hour? Wyatt, it's noon."

"It is?" Sure enough, footsteps came down the hall and Mr. Campbell entered.

"How are our two sleuths?" he asked.

"Hungry." Wyatt slipped the invoices back in place. No need to tell Mr. Campbell about his hunch until they had more answers. "Suppose we could come back later today, around two?"

"Aye. I'll be here."

"Thank you so much, Mr. Campbell." Dorothy returned the files to the cabinet.

After the office manager left, Wyatt buttoned his jacket. "Know where we can grab a quick lunch?"

"Oh yes." Dorothy's voice lit up. "A little shop on the corner that used to sell the best meat pies. I'm sure they're full of potatoes now, but—"

"Sounds fine to me."

After a quick potato-ey meal, they headed out of New Town and up a long curving road that skirted the park—the Princes Street Gardens, according to Dorothy.

Wyatt filled his eyes with the sight of old Edinburgh rising from the ridge above him, but the mystery wouldn't leave him alone. "Tell me about Mr. MacLeod."

"Do you think he's involved?" Dorothy's eyebrows formed a little tent.

"Don't know, but didn't Mr. Campbell say Mr. MacLeod insisted everything was tip-top?"

"Like Papa." That tent collapsed. "Oh, Wyatt. What if they're working together?"

"Don't get ahead of yourself."

"But he and Papa were the best of friends."

"Were?"

At the top of the hill, Dorothy turned right on a cobblestone road. "That's New College, Edinburgh University."

Wyatt would have pegged the building a medieval cathedral—nothing new about it at all.

"As for Mr. MacLeod, I haven't seen him since the last time we came here, 1937 or so."

"He didn't come to London?"

"Not that I know." Dorothy headed up a steep curving road. "I thought it odd. We used to visit Edinburgh every year. And the MacLeods stayed with us in London several times a year. He was such a charming houseguest, full of stories and games. We always had a jolly time."

The road was banked by moss-covered stone walls and smelled ancient and full of history. "What happened?"

"I don't know. I was surprised when they didn't come for Mum's funeral, but when I asked Papa, he said, 'Why would they?' as if they were mere acquaintances."

"Strange."

Dorothy brushed her fingers along the mossy stones. "How we loved it here. Mum and I would go on adventures, darting in and out of the closes, pretending to be princesses and peasant girls and spies for Bonnie Prince Charlie. Sometimes Art and Gil would join us, and they'd play earls and brigands and fierce Highland warriors."

"Sounds like fun." As much as Mama adored her three boys, Wyatt couldn't remember her ever playing with them. "What role should I play?"

A surprised smile, and then she narrowed one eye at him. "Why, a noble knight, of course."

Wyatt shrugged. "Shucks, not me. Maybe . . . I know. You're the princess, of course, and the king appointed me his guardian to accompany his fair daughter on these dark and treacherous lanes."

"A guardian." Her eyes softened. "And she never saw his merits."

"Why would she when she's so far above his pitiful station?" He swept a low bow, one foot poked forward like Sir Walter Scott in the drawing in his schoolbook.

Silence. Then she snickered. "Do you have any idea how silly medieval speech sounds with your accent?"

He straightened and grinned. "I'd love to hear you try on a Texas accent. Reckon you'd sound mighty silly too."

"Shucks. I reckon I sound mighty fine."

No, she didn't, and he burst out laughing.

"It isn't proper for the guardian to mock the princess." She flicked her chin, spun on her heel, and turned left onto a wider street. "The castle's behind you."

"And beneath me." Wyatt glanced over his shoulder and let out a whistle at the monolithic castle. "Promise me we'll come back."

"After we finish our job." Dorothy strode past a church with spires piercing the clouds. "What do you think of this Forthwright?"

Playtime over. "They send quarterly invoices to several departments, for some vague service. In each department it probably doesn't look strange, all spread out, but in the company as a whole, it's suspicious. Did you notice the invoices were staggered? That means they aren't paid all at once."

"Over time, it's a lot of money." In front of the church, Dorothy turned right, then right again on the other side. "This is Johnston Terrace."

He inspected the buildings for numbers. A bit farther and there it was, a building of the same mottled brown stone he'd seen everywhere in town. But no sign hung above the door. "Doesn't look like a business. Looks like a house."

Dorothy's face went completely white except for the freckles. Then she grabbed his arm and marched back the way they'd come.

"What's the matter?" He craned to look over his shoulder at the house. "Don't tell me—"

"That's the house we used to stay in. It belonged to Mr. MacLeod's parents. When they passed away, he used it as a guesthouse."

"It's Mr. MacLeod's?"

She nodded, her face buckling. "He's the embezzler, isn't he?"

Wyatt stopped so he could think. "Sure looks like it. What if he set up a fake business in his guesthouse? He could send invoices to each department at Fairfax & Sons. When the departments send the bills to accounting, he writes the checks—to his own company."

"Oh, Wyatt. Do you think—could my father be involved?"

"I doubt it. They're estranged." Unless that was an act. He gave her hand a reassuring pat. "Let's see if we can find anything else at the office. I want as much evidence as possible."

Dorothy's expression cleared, then settled into the same unusual look he'd seen back in the office. "Protecting the princess . . . and the king."

"Doing my duty, Your Highness." Anything for the woman he loved.

33

"Come along, Wyatt. I am determined that you shall have fun this evening." Dorothy charged up Edinburgh's Royal Mile.

"Aye aye, ma'am." His voice trailed behind her.

They'd spent the afternoon at Fairfax & Sons, where Wyatt recorded all the invoices from Mr. MacLeod's most un-forthright company. The invoices started in early 1941, only a handful and for small amounts, as if he were testing the waters. Slowly they increased and spread to new departments. Thousands of pounds flowed into Mr. MacLeod's pockets each year.

Dorothy's pace increased. How dare that man betray Papa and profit from his old friend's grief? Papa was too distraught to notice the problem, much less investigate.

The scoundrel hadn't counted on the tenacious hunches of Wyatt Paxton.

But now the American had less than two hours of sunlight remaining in his last leave before D-day. "You deserve some fun after a dreary day slogging over books."

"I like slogging over books. But you—you deserve a reward for sitting still while I slogged."

Heat flowed up Dorothy's cheeks. She'd enjoyed that more than she should have. Wyatt cut a fine figure at work, his broad shoulders bent over the desk, his sleeves rolled up, and his face intent as he analyzed. And the best moments, when he'd glanced her way and raised that slow smile, self-conscious in his love for her, but unapologetic.

"At this rate, we'll see the whole city in ten minutes flat."

Dorothy spun to him. "Am I walking too fast for you?"

"Yes, ma'am." He grinned at the buildings she'd ignored, his arms wide. "Show me the sights. Tell me about them. Tell me your family stories. Tell me make-believe stories."

He wanted to hear her chatter? Her leg muscles melted. He loved her as she was. All her life, she'd tried to earn Papa's love. For the past four months, she'd tried to earn Lawrence's love. And without trying at all, she'd gained Wyatt's love. It was baffling and wondrous.

But she was staring at him like a ninny.

She whirled around and saw her surroundings for the first time since they'd left Holyrood Abbey. "Oh yes. On your left is St. Giles, the High Kirk of Edinburgh, where John Knox used to preach. Isn't it splendid? And that's the Mercat Cross—not the original, but it's still nice."

Wyatt gazed up at the massive cathedral and whistled. "I don't know if I'd ever get used to having so much history around."

"Then let's fill you up before we send you back to the history-barren desert of Texas."

"It's not desert where I come from. Hills and trees. Prettiest land you've ever seen."

She liked hills and trees. "No cactus?"

"No cactus."

Regardless, she could never leave Papa. She continued up the street. "Come along. Let's—oh! A kilt shop." She grabbed Wyatt's arm and pulled him inside, breathing deep the smell of wool.

She flipped through the racks of kilts, rich with color and heritage. If only she knew more about tartans.

"Here." She pulled out a Royal Stewart and held it to Wyatt's waist. The red plaid complemented his naval officer's jacket, so deep in blue it was almost black. "A souvenir? You'd look quite smashing."

He took it from her and inspected it. "Only if you buy one too."

"Aye, laddie." Of course, they were both playacting. Neither had the money or the clothing coupons to buy such a garment. She darted to another rack with kilts for ladies. "I've wanted one ever since I saw Greer Garson wear a little kilt in *Random Harvest*." Someone had once told her she looked like her favorite actress, a high compliment.

What a beautiful tartan—gentle blue shot through with bright threads of red and yellow. She held it up and whirled to face Wyatt, her free hand raised like a highland dancer.

"Aye, a bonny look on you, lassie."

Dorothy stared, then laughed. Wyatt was wearing a green plaid tam-o'-shanter, and he'd rolled up his trouser legs and draped the Stewart tartan around his waist.

An elderly salesman peered over the racks at them with a concerned look, and he made his way over.

"Wyatt!" she said in a fierce whisper. She hung her kilt back up.

Wyatt unwrapped the plaid from his waist and returned it to its hanger.

"May I help you?" the salesman asked.

"Admiring your fine merchandise, sir," Wyatt said.

The salesman frowned at Wyatt's head. "So I see."

Dorothy snatched off the tam-o'-shanter, set it back on the shelf, and led Wyatt out of the shop. "Good day, sir."

The door swung shut behind him. "Where to next, lassie?"

She faced him on the pavement. "The cas—Wyatt, your trousers."

He struck a pose like a model in a men's suit advert—except his trouser legs were still rolled up. "When in Scotland, do as the Scots do."

Dorothy laughed. "You silly goose."

A flash of that sheepish smile, and he bent to fix his trousers.

Mum had always told her life was dull, so you needed to fill it with exciting people. Dorothy had followed that creed all her life. Or had she? Quiet Gwen. Quiet Johanna. How she loved bringing fun into their lives.

Did she need an exciting man—or a man willing to join in her adventures?

"All better?" Other than mild wrinkling around his shins, he looked fine. Better than fine.

"Jolly good. Off we go." Dorothy strode along, prattling off information and stories. But her mind was elsewhere.

Yes, Wyatt loved her, but could she love him? Should she? His confession had turned her world inside out. Falling in love with him might mean leaving England and all she loved.

So why did all the reasons she ought to love him crowd out the reasons she shouldn't? As Papa had begged her to do, she'd seen his merits. He was kind and honest, and he did the right thing even when it hurt. He was humble enough to admit his sins and dedicated enough to make amends. He'd even taken her melancholy father under his wing. And his faith was strong and resilient.

He was quiet but not dull. Steady but not stodgy. And she enjoyed his company immensely.

At the end of the Royal Mile, they passed the Tolbooth Kirk, where Johnston Terrace dipped down to the left to Mr. MacLeod's treacherous lair, but they continued to the right. The road narrowed to medieval width, then opened up to the broad expanse of the Esplanade with Edinburgh Castle looming before them in the late-afternoon light.

"Incredible." Awe lit up Wyatt's face.

She wanted to keep that light there for a lifetime, but could she?

The Esplanade funneled into a narrow bridge that led through the portcullis, flanked by medieval statues. The delicious smell of damp stone enveloped her as they passed through.

"That's the Half-Moon Battery." She pointed to the massive rounded wall before them, built of rough, irregular blocks and topped by cannons.

"Incredible," Wyatt repeated.

Up the curving cobblestone road, through another portcullis under the Argyle Tower, and she dashed to a low crenelated wall. "One of the best views in the British Isles. Isn't it marvelous?"

Wyatt ran his hand over one of the cannons. "Wow. A long way down."

"This represents the limits of my fearlessness." With her fingertips pressed to the stone, she stood at arm's length from the edge. The castle stood high on a sharp crag, the steep cliff repelling invaders from three sides.

He stood beside her. "What am I looking at? Is that New Town below us?"

"Yes, and the Firth of Forth beyond that, and the Highlands on the far side."

"Incredible."

The sun was beginning to set. Tomorrow she'd return to Southwick House and Wyatt to Greenock, and soon he'd go into battle. She might never see him again. And what if something happened to him? How could she endure it?

All those times she'd resisted the impulse to lean into him, but now she let herself relax to the side, resting against his shoulder, her heart pounding.

But Wyatt bent over and set his elbows on the wall.

Dorothy winced, but what did she expect? He had no idea how he was tugging at her heart. Should she tell him? Would it be appropriately honest or ridiculously impulsive? Most important, what was best for him?

He sent a smile over his shoulder. "What's next?"

If only she knew. She gazed around and pointed along the wall. "That's the One O'Clock Gun. It's been silenced by the war though. It doesn't quite feel like Edinburgh without that resounding boom after lunch."

"That must be something."

"The Naval and Military Museum is this way. I don't know if it's open, but you'd like it."

"Worth a look."

The path narrowed between two stone walls, and she smiled. At the lowest point of the wall, right above her knees, she hoisted herself up. The path descended, but the wall stayed level. "I used to love walking these walls."

Wyatt grew shorter and shorter. He smiled up at her. "The little daredevil balancing on the seawall." He raised one hand, prepared to catch her.

She paused, her toes above his head, and her throat thickened. "You always protect me."

His face grew serious. "I—I try."

He'd never deliberately endanger her, never coax her to do something that terrified her or that violated her morals.

Careful to keep her skirt modestly about her knees, Dorothy sat down on the wall. "Would you help me down, please?"

"Sure." His voice sounded brusque, but he rested his hands on her waist.

She set her hands on his shoulders, so strong and capable. Could she ever love him?

"All right, then." He didn't look her in the eye. "Ready?"

Yes, she was ready. She scooted forward, and he lowered her to the ground. He stood close, but not close enough, and he kept the bill of his cap low, obscuring his eyes.

He eased back.

No! Not now. Not when she wanted to fall for him, wanted to

tumble into oblivion. "Thank you." She stretched up and pressed a kiss to his cheek, his warm, rough cheek.

As she settled down to her heels, his eyelids opened, revealing eyes as hazy with longing as when he'd sung to her in the conservatory, but with pain crimping the edges.

Everything inside her turned every which way, what was false becoming true, what was true becoming false. Only one certainty remained—she loved him and she couldn't let him go.

He started to back away, but she slid her hands behind his neck and leaned against his chest, the memory of his song feeding the impulse. "Wyatt?" Her voice feathered into the air between them. "I—I know. I know what *bésame mucho* means."

The smoke drifted away, and his lips parted, and she lifted onto her toes and kissed that wonderful mouth.

A rumble sounded in his throat, and his lips stiffened beneath hers, as if he didn't want her kiss, didn't want to start what he couldn't finish.

But then the rumble deepened, and he gathered her close and kissed her back, as wild as that West of his, as true as his words, yet as gentle as his every action. Cherishing her. Loving her.

She tried to be genuine, to show her full heart, show him how much she loved him and cared for him.

All too soon, he pulled back, his lips as loose and swollen as hers felt, his pupils wide and dark. "It's over, then? With Eaton?"

Dorothy sucked in a breath. Over? Yes, it was, wasn't it? But nothing had been said between them. She'd thrown him out without throwing him over.

Oh dear. She was hesitating too long.

Wyatt pushed away from her, several painful feet away on the sunken cobblestone path, and the smoke in his eyes turned to fire. "I don't want crumbs."

"Crumbs?" She smoothed her jacket. How could she explain herself?

"You might be happy with crumbs, but not me."

His face—she'd never seen him angry before, and she didn't like it at all. "I—I don't know what you're talking about."

"Eaton—he throws you a crumb." He flung his hand to the side, like Papa feeding the ducks. "He throws First Officer Fussbudget a crumb. He throws What's-Her-Face in supply a crumb. And y'all don't mind. Y'all keep coming back for those crumbs."

Dorothy's chin inched up at the unflatteringly accurate description. "I hardly—"

"I don't want crumbs." He jabbed his thumb at his chest. "The whole loaf or nothing at all."

She'd never seen him speak with such passion, such strength, such confidence, and she wavered between admiration and fury. "I—I'm not a loaf of bread."

"Yeah, well, I'm not a duck."

In the distance a woman laughed.

With that laugh, Wyatt and everything else faded away into nothingness, and she searched for that laugh, the sound as ancient to her memory as the stones around her.

Dorothy wandered toward that sound, unbelieving, unseeing.

"Hey, now." Wyatt's voice filtered through the haze. "All right, I shouldn't have said that about you. Don't run off. Come on."

Dorothy shook her head, shook her hearing from the voice behind her to the voice before her, the lilting laugh she'd tried so hard to remember the past three and a half years, a sound she thought she'd never hear again. "Mum?"

"What?" Wyatt said.

"It can't be. My mother?" She scanned the few visitors in the courtyard and picked up her pace. The voice—where was it?

"What are you talking about? Your mother? I thought she was—"

"Dead. She's dead." But that laugh tinkled with life, and down by the Argyle Tower, a woman walked arm in arm with a man.

She had a familiar sway to her gait and a familiar way of gesturing with her free hand.

"Mum?" She broke into a run.

"Dorothy! Wait up!"

Her foot twisted on a cobblestone, her weak ankle gave way, and she went down hard.

"Dorothy!" Wyatt squatted beside her and grasped her shoulder. "You all right?"

She shook her head, pain throbbing in the ankle she'd sprained searching for her mother's body in the charred ruins. "Her body—it wasn't there. It was here."

Wyatt rubbed her shoulder. "Say, why don't we get you back to your hotel?"

"No! Don't stop me. Don't hold me back." She struggled to her feet. Pain shot through her ankle and her heart, and she stifled a cry. "I have to find her."

Unable to run, she limped as fast as she could, under the Argyle Tower, down the curving path, searching for the laughing woman.

"All right, then." Wyatt strode beside her. "I won't stop you, but I won't leave you either."

She nodded to keep him quiet so she could hear. Through the portcullis and onto the Esplanade.

There she was, halfway across, and Dorothy gritted her teeth against the pain as she pounded over the broad expanse. The woman's hat and coat weren't familiar, but all Mum's clothes were in London—or they had been until Papa donated them to Blitz victims, too soon for Dorothy's taste.

"Are you sure it's your mom?"

"Yes." The woman's hair was blonde, not Mum's warm auburn, but the way she moved and the fragments of speech left no doubt.

At the end of the Esplanade, the couple turned right, down the stairs that edged the last set of buildings.

Dorothy followed down the steps, closing the gap despite the pain, driven by the pain. With each step, the woman looked more and more like Margaret Fairfax.

At the bottom of the steps, the couple turned left onto the street, and Dorothy saw the woman's profile, clear as the image in her memory. "Mum!"

The woman paused on a doorstep as the man pulled a key from his pocket.

Dorothy hobble-ran. "Mum! Mum!"

The woman turned. Her mouth fell open, and she braced herself against the door. "Dolly?"

Dorothy gripped the handrail, but the world spun around her, fracturing into pieces. Her mother. Alive and well.

"Dolly, what are you doing here?" Her voice snapped, and her gaze darted around.

"Me?" She stared at the face she thought had left her forever. "What are *you* doing here? You're—dead."

"Let's take this conversation inside." The man opened the door.

"Yes, let's." Mum followed.

But Dorothy couldn't move.

"Come on, Dorothy." A hand grasped her elbow—Wyatt. He was still there.

Somehow she mounted the stairs.

Mum hung up her coat and hat. "Shall I make a pot of tea?"

"Tea? I don't want tea. I want answers."

"You mustn't raise your voice." Her words trembled, but she strolled into the drawing room and sat on the settee. "Please have a seat."

Dorothy stood there. Her mother's bleached hair had a harsh and aging effect.

Mum smiled, but it twitched. "You look well. Have you lost weight?"

"What happened?"

"This is rather unpleasant, isn't it? I never thought you'd find me." She looked at the man on the settee beside her.

For the first time, Dorothy did too, and she gasped. "Mr. MacLeod?"

He gave her a stiff, polite smile. "Good evening, Dolly."

"Dorothy." She sank into a chair. "What happened? I deserve to know."

Mum smoothed the skirt of her dress, her mouth squirming between smiling and pursing. "You know how dreadfully unhappy I was. Your father is such a bore, and I made a terrible mistake marrying him. Terrible. I need an exciting man."

The words slammed into Dorothy's chest. An exciting man? Like Mr. MacLeod—as handsome as ever, and certainly as charming and entertaining. "What happened?" her voice ground out.

"Well, Art's death upset me horribly, and then that dreadful Blitz. I wanted out, but your father refused to give me a divorce. Refused. I needed to get away from London and the bombs and your father."

"And me."

Mum shifted in her seat. "Really, Dolly. You mustn't be so dramatic. You of all people should know why I needed to escape."

"What happened?"

She twisted her hands in her lap. "That day I was on my way to have tea with Mrs. Rayburn when the siren sounded. I didn't care whether I lived or died. So I didn't shelter, hoping a bomb would end my misery. When I arrived at the Rayburns, the house was an inferno. And I knew—I had my chance. So I dodged the wardens and ran to the front door. Then I tossed my handbag and hat inside, where I would have left them if I'd come calling. I caught the first train here, and I've never been so happy." She beamed at Mr. MacLeod.

He gave her that same stiff smile.

Something mean tweaked inside Dorothy. "I'm sorry to hear Mrs. MacLeod passed away."

Two sets of startled eyes turned her way, then Mr. MacLeod gave her a nod as if appreciating her cleverness. "Mrs. MacLeod is very well, thank you."

"Please give her my regards." Then she addressed the woman who'd borne her. "How very strange it must be for everyone in town to see Margaret Fairfax without her husband."

Mum pulled at a strand of her bleached hair, her feeble disguise. "I—I don't go out much. And I go by my maiden name, Margaret Wright. It's best. I'm legally dead, and Reginald mustn't know I'm alive. Dolly, you simply mustn't tell him. I can't go back to him. I can't. Please promise me." Her voice climbed almost to a wail.

"Wright with a *W*," Wyatt said, standing beside her chair.

"Yes, of course." Mum blinked at him as if he weren't too bright. But he was. He was exceedingly bright.

And in that brightness Dorothy saw. She saw the house, the familiar house.

Mr. MacLeod had stolen Papa's money and his wife.

And Mum had betrayed Papa twofold.

34

Wyatt clenched the back of Dorothy's chair, anything to avoid making a fist. Never in his life had he wanted to punch a woman, but Margaret Wright-with-a-W Fairfax kept talking, trying to justify the unjustifiable.

Adultery. Betrayal. Theft. Fraud. Lies.

Her sins were no worse than Wyatt's, but he'd fessed up and tried to make things right. These two saw nothing wrong in their actions.

Had Dorothy put it together yet? He'd better get her out before she did, while she was still dazed by the sight of her dead mother. "Dorothy, I think we should leave now."

"Why, yes. I agree. I don't quite care for the company." She stood, calm and composed, but how long would that last?

"Please, Dolly." Her mother sprang to her feet. "Try to be happy for me. Try to understand."

"Understand? I understand you perfectly." Scorn curled her voice. "I'd like to leave now, Lieutenant."

"Sounds wise." He opened the door. The sun had set and cold air swirled from outside, but it felt better than the air inside.

"Dolly, please. I beg you, don't tell your father."

Dorothy stopped by the door, her back to Wyatt. "Tell him the wife he's grieving is gallivanting around with her married lover—his former best friend? Oh no. I love him too much to do that."

Her mother whimpered and covered her mouth. "You mustn't speak that way."

"Let's go." Wyatt set his hand on Dorothy's waist and guided her down the steps.

"Dolly! Dolly, please?"

A cab! Thank goodness. He hailed it, never releasing his grip on Dorothy's stiff waist, and then helped her inside. "Where's your hotel, darlin'?" Wyatt asked.

She clutched her purse on her lap. "The—the—the North British."

"The North British," he repeated to the driver.

"Aye, sir." The cabby pulled away from the curb and drove into the twilight.

Dorothy sagged against the taxi door, her bun loose and disheveled.

Wyatt set his hand on her shoulder, ready to fold her in his arms.

She shrugged him off and hunkered down in her seat. "How could she? How could she?"

"I don't know." Nowadays, he had a lot more understanding about why people sinned, but some things still baffled him.

"I wish she *were* dead." Her shoulders curved forward. "I don't care if it's awful to say. It's true. I was happier when I thought she was dead."

"I understand."

"Papa." She slapped her hand over her mouth. "Oh, poor Papa."

"Are you going to tell him?"

"Tell him?" She raised stricken eyes. "I couldn't. Grief destroys him—you've seen it. Can you imagine what would happen if he knew she'd betrayed him? That she—that she hated us so much she faked her own death to get away from us?"

His chest collapsed. "Dorothy . . ."

"It's true. She loves excitement more than . . ." She moaned and pulled her feet up onto the seat. Shoulders shaking, she curled into a ball.

Wyatt gripped his hands between his knees so he wouldn't embrace her. *Lord, comfort her. I can't.*

"I—I'm just like her," she mumbled into her knees. "Chasing—chasing after—oh, I'm just like her."

How could she think that? Margaret Fairfax showed nothing but contempt for her family, while Dorothy Fairfax showed nothing but concern, caring for her father even when he ignored her. "You are *nothing* like that woman."

"I am. I've always been like her. Everyone says it. Always. That's why Papa—that's why he can't stand the sight of me. Because I look like her, act like her, *am* like her. She was awful to Papa. Awful."

"See? You're nothing like her."

"But I am." She turned her head on her knee, devastation warping her pretty features. "And you—oh no. You're just like him."

"Him?"

"Papa. Oh no. You are." She sat up straighter, her legs still tucked up. "You're like he used to be. You never knew—he was sweet and kind and happy."

"Dorothy—"

"Don't you see?" She clutched her fists to her chest, her eyes wild. "My parents—they were happy once. They must have been. But he was too quiet and predictable for her. So she carped at him and complained, and he could never make her happy. And she ruined him. Even before the war, he'd become aloof and cold. He was a dear man, and she ruined him."

How could this bighearted woman think herself capable of such pettiness? "You'd never do that. You're nothing like—"

"I am." She slapped her hand on the seat between them. "Don't you see? We'd be awful together. Not now, but someday. I can't let myself do that to you. I won't let myself ruin you. I—I care about you too much." Her voice cracked.

His entire chest ached for her. "Darlin', that'd never happen to us. You're better than that, and I'm stronger than that. And we're good for each other. We're right for each other." He gathered her hand in his.

"No!" She snatched her hand away. "Stop it. For your sake, I beg you. Leave me alone."

Wyatt's hand hovered midair. Again.

"Stop it! Leave me alone." Oralee had said those words to him as she pulled her hand away. Her last words ever.

"Leave me alone," Dorothy muttered, curled up in a ball. "Please, leave me alone."

Wyatt stared at his hand—empty and useless—and returned it to his lap.

He couldn't protect someone who didn't want to be protected.

35

Dorothy hesitated on her front stoop, thoroughly wrung out inside.

But she had to come. Papa needed to know about the embezzler. She'd take Mum's secret to the grave, but she wouldn't let Mum and Mr. MacLeod destroy the company and the man who built it. They'd already hurt him enough.

Lord, please help me.

The doorknob was cold and hard in her grip. The Lord had known Mum was alive, known she was Mr. MacLeod's kept woman, known about the theft. And he'd done nothing. *On the other hand, Lord, stay out of this. I'm better off on my own.*

She opened the door. "Papa? Papa?"

In a moment, the study door opened, and he peeked out. "Dorothy? You said you weren't coming home this weekend. And it's Sunday." He glanced at his watch. "Why, it's six o'clock. Shouldn't you be on your way to Portsmouth?"

Dorothy set down her valise, then laid her handbag on the table, same as she always did. Same as Mum did at Mrs. Rayburn's house. Her empty stomach twisted. "I—I had to come here first."

Charlie skittered down the steps, tiny tail wagging. Mum had bought a Scottish terrier to remind her of her beloved Scotland. Or of her Scottish lover? Dorothy felt ill.

Papa descended the stairs. "Where did you go? You—you don't look well."

She wasn't, but it wasn't poor Charlie's fault, so she scooped him into her arms. "I went to Edinburgh."

"Edinburgh?" He stopped halfway down, his voice as thin as his waist. "Why would you . . . ?"

Dorothy opened her mouth, but all the dreadful words tangled in her mouth and tripped each other.

He grabbed the banister like an elderly man with a cane. "You saw her."

She couldn't breathe, couldn't see, couldn't think. "What?"

"Did you—see her?" His gaze dug in, forceful but fearful.

Everything spun inside, everything she knew falling apart, same as last night when she'd heard Mum's voice. "You—you know?"

Papa collapsed to sitting on the stairs, his hand still gripping the banister. "I knew all along."

Her fingers coiled into Charlie's wiry coat. "But how?"

"She was never happy." Papa set his elbows on his knees and rested his forehead in his hands. "She begged for a divorce, over and over, but I didn't want the scandal. So I refused, even when I found her with . . ."

Nausea squirmed in her belly. "Mr. MacLeod?"

Papa peered at her through his splayed fingers. "She's still at his guesthouse?"

She nodded. Papa found them together? So that was why the friendship and the visits had ended. "But how did you know? The air raid, the fire . . ."

His fingers tousled his graying red hair. "The morning after, you and I went to find her. While you searched the rubble, I found her handbag and hat. The authorities believed it to be evidence that she'd perished, but I knew otherwise. There wasn't a halfpenny inside. You know she stored her best jewelry and the household cash in her handbag, so no one could steal them during an air raid. They were all gone. For her to go across town without them, without even tram fare? Impossible."

"From that . . ." Dorothy's ankle throbbed anew.

"I knew what she'd done." His hands balled up. "I knew where she'd gone, to whom she'd gone, and my solicitor in Edinburgh confirmed it."

She hugged Charlie tighter. "But we—we had a funeral."

Papa raised hardened eyes. "She is legally dead. In my eyes and the eyes of the crown, Margaret Fairfax no longer exists. I no longer have a wife."

"How could you—you let Gil and me think she'd died." She spat out the word.

"Wasn't that better? Gil died believing his mother was a tragic victim of the Blitz. Wasn't it better when you thought she was dead? Why did you have to find her? Why did you go to Edinburgh?"

Her mouth tightened at his deception. "I went to save your company."

"Pardon?"

She stretched her chin high. "A few months ago, Mr. Montague contacted me. The company is losing money, and he was concerned because you hadn't investigated."

"Mr. Montague?" Papa rose to his feet, his fists by his sides. "How dare he?"

"He wanted to save the company, save you, and save his own job, by the way. So we talked to Wyatt, and he—"

"Wyatt? Wyatt Paxton? Whatever made you involve him in such a thing?"

"He's an accountant. We thought he could look at the books with fresh eyes, and he did."

Papa's mouth gaped as if he were trying to swallow too much

at once. "How dare he? How dare *you*? Going behind my back as if I were an invalid, an imbecile. I trusted that man."

"He wanted to help." Her heart wrenched at the thought of the man she loved, the man she could never have. "And he—he did help. He realized something was wrong in the Edinburgh office. That's where we went this weekend, and we found the embezzler."

Papa trudged down the last few stairs and into the drawing room, as bent as the invalid he claimed not to be. He lowered himself into his armchair. "Who is it?"

Dorothy sat across the room in her chair by the window. Charlie squirmed, and she set him on the floor. "Wyatt found multiple invoices from a company called Forthwright Business Services, all rather vague. Wyatt and I went to the address for Forthwright—it's that house. Mr. MacLeod's guesthouse."

Papa's fingers clenched like claws on the armrests, his face like stone, his eyes a stormy sea.

Dorothy leaned forward on her knees. "Don't you see, Papa? Something good came out of this ghastly weekend. Now we can stop the theft. Now we can save your company."

"No, we can't." His words came out in a sharp staccato.

"Of course, we can. And we will."

"He knows I can't stop him. He knows I won't."

She shook her head slightly, trying to clear her ears and her eyes. "What do you mean? You have to stop him before he destroys your company."

His eyes slipped shut. "So that's why he keeps her. I'd wondered. He has plenty of women, all younger than your mother. My solicitor keeps me informed. Why her?"

"He—he loves her?"

Papa snorted. "Hardly. She's insurance. If I expose him as the embezzler, he'll expose her. And the scandal . . ."

Her mind whirled, her mouth dry and empty, her eyes open and hurting.

Papa's hands went limp, and he hung his head. "My wife left me—faked her own death to leave me. Isn't that enough to suffer? If the world knew? I—I couldn't—it would undo me."

"But he'll get away with it. He'll keep stealing. Your company—"

"He'll destroy it, and I'll be ruined."

"So stop him. Have him arrested."

His head swung in refusal. "I can suffer financial ruin better than scandal and humiliation. He knows that, and she does too. It would—it would . . ."

It would kill him. Dorothy clutched her head. Her mother was a part of this. Wasn't it bad enough that she'd cheated on her husband and abandoned him? But to slowly, deliberately bleed him to death? What sort of monster was this woman, this mother of hers?

She gulped back a sob. When the company went bankrupt, Papa would be destitute, dependent on Dorothy's provision for the rest of his life. Didn't Mum think about what her actions would do to Dorothy, the child she'd once called her favorite?

"Mum doesn't love me either," she choked out. No one truly loved her but Wyatt. Now he'd seen her mother, seen what Dorothy had come from, what she could become. He'd lose respect for her, and his love would wither away.

And Lawrence? He'd never love her true self.

Her head, her stomach—everything spun—and her fingers dug into her skull.

No one. No one.

A sob erupted. "My own mother—she doesn't love me. Art and Gil—they loved me, but they're gone. And you—you lost the only two children you loved."

Papa snapped up his head, his eyes stark and wide.

Dorothy struggled to her feet. "I know why you don't love me, why you can't stand the sight of me. Because I remind you of her. I thought it was pain you felt. Now I know it's disgust."

"Dor—Dor—"

"Don't." She stumbled for her valise, her handbag, her hat. "I—I have a train to catch. I have to report for duty. I have duties. I won't be back for—for a while."

"Dorothy!" His voice climbed and warbled.

"Good-bye." She bolted out the door and wiped her eyes so she could see.

See? See? She saw clearly for the first time since the war began, and she longed to be blind again.

36

USS *Oglesby*, Weymouth Bay, England
Sunday, May 28, 1944

By the red light on the bridge of the *Oglesby*, Wyatt studied Map
GSGS 4490, sheet 79, showing the western sector of Omaha Beach
around Vierville-sur-Mer in large 1:7920 scale.

On May 25 while in Belfast, the destroyer crews had been instructed to open *Operation Plan No. 2-44 of the Western Naval
Task Force, Allied Naval Expeditionary Force*—hundreds of pages
of orders and tables and maps for Operation Neptune.

D-day was set for June 5. It had been announced to those who
needed to know. Only eight days away.

As junior officer of the watch for the mid-watch from midnight
to 0400, Wyatt had already completed his first inspection topside.
Now he had little to do but study.

The map was a marvel. Blue for water, black for roads and buildings, green for trees and hedgerows, brown for bluffs, and red for
military features—minefields, barricades, and obstacles. Gridlines
showed the coordinates. Wyatt had marked the map's transparent
overlay with the *Oglesby*'s assigned and potential targets, but he
knew each feature by heart.

In a long band below the main map and above the legend, a

panoramic sketch showed how the landing beaches would look from sea level, noting landmarks and their grid coordinates.

Wyatt traced his finger along the sketch as if he could feel Dorothy's fingerprints. Her work had helped make this possible.

A ring of pain constricted his chest. Only eight days earlier, he'd held her close. The memory of their kiss begged to be savored, begged to be forgotten.

At first he'd resisted her kiss, thinking of Eaton's hold on her. Then he'd decided the kiss meant she'd broken that hold—and he'd returned her kiss with abandon.

His face heated, and he glanced out the porthole to the moonless night sky. He'd been wrong. Dorothy hadn't given up Eaton. She'd meant to have both men. Why? So she could use Wyatt's love to make Eaton jealous?

He rubbed the space between his eyebrows. Of course that wasn't true. He knew her better than that. But still, he had too much self-respect to be one of many. All or nothing at all.

If only he hadn't picked that stupid, insulting bread analogy.

Not that it mattered anymore. The discovery of her mother had wrecked everything.

"Tired, Mr. Paxton?"

He blinked at the executive officer, Lt. Grover Ellis, who had the conn on this watch. "Tired? How could I be tired with the US Navy's finest coffee by my side?" He hefted up his mug of lukewarm coffee and a grin.

"Good to hear." Ellis turned back to the helm. A skeleton crew manned the bridge and the most vital stations while the rest of the crew slept.

In Weymouth Bay, the eight remaining destroyers of DesRon 18 slept darkened at their moorings. On the cruise back from Belfast, the USS *Endicott* had been damaged in a collision with a freighter. The *Emmons* was being sent to replace her for Neptune.

The bay teemed with over five hundred ships preparing for the invasion. Every major port in southern England contained a similar number of ships.

The map drew his attention again, one little black square standing out with a tiny green circle nearby and a bold black line in front of it. Dorothy's house and tree and the seawall she'd climbed when her family was whole.

In eight days, that house would lie in ruins, the symbol joining the reality.

The mother gone. The sons dead. The father broken. The daughter . . .

Wyatt squeezed his eyes shut and prayed hard. Dorothy had been devastated by her mother's double betrayal. Would the crisis draw her to God—or push her away? Everything in him longed to run to Southwick House, but he respected her too much to defy her wishes and he respected himself too much to continue the pursuit. Besides, since the invasion orders had been opened, all personnel were sealed on their ships. No contact, no phone calls, no telegrams.

All he could do—the best thing he could do—was pray.

If only he could have fixed Dorothy's family, but he'd failed.

He'd failed to fix his family too. Why hadn't he mailed the letters to his brothers while he was in Greenock or Belfast? But no, he'd wanted to make the letters perfect. By the time he'd returned to Weymouth, all mail was being held to keep Operation Overlord secret.

Adler and Clay wouldn't receive their letters until after D-day. If they survived.

As usual, Wyatt had failed.

The radio crackled, and the radioman pressed one hand over his earphones. Then he looked up. "Mr. Ellis, sir. Air raid alert."

"Sound general quarters," Mr. Ellis said.

The boatswain's mate of the watch sounded his pipe into the loudspeaker. "All hands, man your battle stations."

Wyatt stashed away his map and made a notation in the log—"0103—Air raid alert."

A quiet, orderly rush consumed the ship as almost three hundred men dashed to their stations. Captain Adams emerged from his sea cabin behind the pilothouse, tugging on his mackinaw.

With Wyatt on the bridge, the gunnery officer, Lt. Wayne Holoch, would head up to the gun director. All four 5-inch guns would be manned, as well as the 40-mm and 20-mm antiaircraft guns.

Wyatt stepped out onto the wing of the bridge and inspected the clear black sky. Temperature in the mid-fifties, gentle breeze from the northeast, and enemy engine sounds overhead.

He gripped the rails. Searchlights slashed the sky, and flashes lit up the shore as German bombs fell and British antiaircraft batteries responded.

When were the ships going to shoot back? Wyatt ducked in the pilothouse.

"All guns manned and ready, Captain," the talker said.

"Stand by." Captain Adams caught Wyatt's eye. "All ships have been ordered to hold fire."

Protests roared inside, but a dreadful understanding took their place. If the ships opened fire, they'd reveal their positions, reveal the enormous invasion fleet sitting helpless at anchor.

Wyatt gave the captain a stiff nod and headed back outside.

A flare descended and landed in the water, about a hundred feet ahead, sending out an illuminating glow. "Rats."

"Lower the whaleboat," Captain Adams shouted. "Get a crew out there and sink that flare."

"Aye aye, Captain." Orders flew, and on the main deck men hoisted the whaleboat down to the water.

A bomb whistled above, and Wyatt clutched the railing. A loud rumble, and a geyser of water shot up a hundred yards off the starboard quarter. The *Oglesby* rocked and creaked from the impact.

"Stand by to up anchor," Adams called.

Scattered bombs fell in the water in the distance, but no fires or explosions marred the harbor. The bombers hadn't hit any ships.

If only Wyatt could say the same about the shore. Multiple fires flickered in yellow and orange. How many innocents would die tonight?

His jaw clenched at the *Ogie*'s silent guns, and his fingers stretched out as if he could man the trigger himself.

If they opened fire, they might down a few planes—but the Germans could sink ships vital to the invasion. And the carefully guarded secret of the invasion and its size could be revealed.

They had to remain silent, invisible, powerless.

Everything in him wanted to reach out and protect the people on shore, but for the greater good, he must not do so.

Grief pooled in his gut, and once again he withdrew his hand.

37

Even with her normal appetite, Dorothy would have found the greasy soup an unappealing lunch. She stirred, taking the occasional spoonful to deflect attention.

"Dorothy, are you all right?" Gwen asked with a wrinkled brow. "You haven't been yourself."

Muriel leaned forward. "Please tell us what's happening."

In the past week, they'd pried half a dozen times. "As I said, private family matters. And this beastly heat."

Gwen sipped her tea. "I'm sorry your father isn't well."

Grief and worry heaved inside. Papa wouldn't be well at all. Not only was he carrying his usual burden, but now he knew his wife and his former best friend were defrauding his company. Dorothy's dismay at discovering her mother's secret would only compound his turmoil.

Due to the lockdown for D-day, Dorothy hadn't been able to go home the past weekend. Had Papa eaten even one morsel since she'd left? The poor man.

Her friends' scrutiny pressed hard and had to be removed.

"My father is English. He will prevail." Dorothy hefted up a smile as false as her confidence in her words.

Gwen and Muriel smiled and returned to their soup.

Dorothy changed her stirring from clockwise to counterclockwise. Papa had to be all right. He was all she had, all she would ever have.

After the company went bankrupt, she'd lose her inheritance and no man of any standing would have her. When the WRNS was disbanded or gutted after the war, she'd have to find employment. But what kind of work? Although she'd studied art, she was no artist, and her wartime skills had no peacetime purpose.

Dorothy forced down soup to avoid the crime of wasting food, and then headed back to the office with her friends.

At the top of the stairs, she almost bumped into Lawrence going the other direction.

"Good day, Second Officer Fairfax."

"Good day, sir." Somehow her voice behaved.

With a crisp nod, he trotted downstairs.

Thank goodness he'd been away from headquarters lately. Despite his assertion that he'd come to London solely for their date, he'd also had meetings and had only returned to Southwick this past weekend.

Muriel grabbed Dorothy's arm and tugged her close by the wall. "What is happening?"

"Did you have an argument?" Gwen whispered.

Dorothy freed her elbow. "Must you know every private detail of my life?"

Her friends edged back, eyes wide.

A sigh washed out. After all, she'd inundated Gwen and Muriel with private details for years. "I apologize. With D-day coming, I don't wish to talk about such trivial matters."

Her friends nodded and stepped into the office.

Dorothy followed. Her problems with Lawrence were indeed trivial. Oddly, she hadn't missed him. They didn't have a true friendship, and his kisses, while tantalizing, were showy and detached. Mere crumbs to keep her at his feet.

The thought wrenched her heart.

Wyatt's kiss was the opposite—rough, unstudied, genuine, his heart and soul poured out for her alone. The whole loaf or nothing at all.

His absence gnawed more than her half-empty stomach. She loved him so much.

But she loved him too much to allow him to be ruined.

She could still see him in the taxi in Edinburgh, pulling his hand away as she'd asked. He hadn't spoken again until his brief good-bye.

He must have seen the truth. Why would he want a melodramatic woman curled up in a sniveling, unseemly ball? Why would he want the daughter of a scheming, thieving adulteress? Mum chased after excitement, after a rogue, and so did Dorothy. Wyatt must have put the puzzle pieces together. In time, he'd be grateful he'd escaped.

Leading Wren Stella Dodds handed her a report, and Dorothy signed where indicated.

"Watch out," Muriel hissed. "Here comes the battleship."

Dorothy sucked in a breath. Ever since the Wrens had learned the Americans used the designation "BB" for their battleships, Bliss-Baldwin had earned a new nickname.

Sure enough, the blonde came steaming full speed, guns blazing at Dorothy. "Second Officer Fairfax, I need a word."

"Yes, ma'am." She hurried to match her commanding officer's pace. Oh dear. Had she made a mistake due to her despondency? In the private office, Dorothy shut the door.

The first officer stood behind her desk, glaring as if Dorothy were a lowly scullery maid caught stealing her mistress's jewels. "How dare you?"

Dorothy's mouth drifted open, bereft of words.

Bliss-Baldwin slapped her desk. "How dare you complain about me to Commander Pringle?"

She searched the woman's face. "I—ma'am, I never—I haven't talked to him in weeks."

Her tiny jaw jutted forward. "Commander Pringle reprimanded me. He received a complaint that I was flirting on duty with an officer, that I'd forced the transfer of a girl under my command out of jealousy over that officer, and that I'd forbidden another Wren to see that same officer. We both know who that Wren is."

Dorothy's lips dried out. Although the accusations were accurate, she'd never do such a thing.

"Don't deny it." Both hands slapped the desk. "You're the only girl under Pringle's command who has any relationship with Lieutenant Commander Eaton. You lied to me about him, then had me reprimanded to eliminate your competition. But I won't have it."

"I—I assure you, ma'am. I never talked to Commander Pringle. I wouldn't dream of doing so."

The first officer's eyes fired a full salvo. "You girls think the war has leveled the classes, but it hasn't. You can't cross a woman of my station and get away with it. I want you out of here. Out of Southwick. Out of England."

Dorothy clenched the hem of her jacket. "But my father—"

"Your father needs to develop a stiff upper lip. Commander Pringle has forbidden me to transfer any more Wrens under my command, so you will request an overseas transfer straightaway."

"But ma'am, I don't want to transfer. My work here—D-day is right around the corner."

She sniffed. "You're hardly indispensable."

Dorothy's breath quickened, but she held her ground. "I will not transfer, ma'am."

"You will. If you don't, I'll rescind all privileges, give you the most menial tasks, and find fault with everything you do. It won't take long to have you demoted and disgraced. I will make your life so utterly miserable, you'll beg for a transfer."

All her life, Dorothy had despised bullies. "Or I could simply tell Commander Pringle about this conversation."

Blissy settled into her chair with a serene smile. "You love your father, do you not?"

Dorothy eyed her, not trusting her. "Yes, ma'am."

"I'm rather fond of my father too. He dotes on me and does anything I want." She relaxed in her chair and inclined her head. "As a Member of Parliament, he has the most useful connections. If I want a person destroyed—or her father—he makes it happen."

Her stomach seized. The embezzlement. Mum. Mr. MacLeod. If Wyatt had discovered the truth in one short day, how long would it take a government minister?

The commanding officer held out some papers. "If you love your father, you won't speak to Commander Pringle. You'll submit the request for overseas duty first thing tomorrow. Think how happy you'll be to get away from me."

With wooden fingers, Dorothy took the papers. Happy? None of the choices before her offered happiness, only different varieties of pain.

38

USS *Oglesby*, SOUTH OF THE ISLE OF WIGHT
MONDAY, JUNE 5, 1944

At the bow of the *Oglesby*, Wyatt gripped the lifeline. "Hard to believe this is really happening."

"I know." Jack Vale tugged his gloves higher on his wrists. "We're a part of it—the greatest invasion fleet the world has ever seen."

Behind the overcast, the setting sun illuminated gray waves and gray ships—troop transports and landing craft and destroyers and Coast Guard rescue ships.

South of the Isle of Wight, over five thousand ships and landing craft were gathering. Here at Point "Z," the convoys turned south and funneled into the "Spout," five lanes, one for each landing beach.

"Tomorrow," Jack said.

"I know." All the months of work coming to fruition at dawn. Adm. Sir Bertram Ramsay, the British commander of the Allied Naval Expeditionary Force, had produced massive quantities of meticulous plans. The plans would fall apart in battle, but at least they gave the Allies something to aim for.

The *Ogie* cut through a wave, and fine sea spray hit Wyatt's face. He wiped it away with the sleeve of his mackinaw. "Glad the weather's improving."

"Thank goodness I'm not in Ike's shoes."

"No kidding." D-day had been scheduled for June 5, but a storm had blown in, forcing Gen. Dwight Eisenhower to postpone operations by one day. The *Ogie* had received the "Post Mike One" order early in the morning of June 4 while they were preparing to get underway. The ships of Force U bound for Utah Beach had already been at sea and had to return to port.

"Guess the general's a gambler." Jack grinned.

"An astute one though. Think about it. We've got a narrow window from June 5 to June 7 with the right moon and tide. It won't happen again until the nineteenth."

"Yep. We can't lock up these men on their ships for another two weeks."

A cool force 5 wind blew from the northwest, visibility was good at five thousand yards, and the seas were moderate. Not great conditions, but better than the day before. "Who knows? Maybe the weather will fool the Germans into thinking we're not fixing to pay them a visit."

Jack chuckled. "That'd be nice."

"No sign of the Luftwaffe. That's good."

"Our flyboys won't let them near." Jack squinted at the gray sky.

"We'll have to keep an eye out, but the minefield should keep the U-boats away, and the full moon and good visibility should keep the E-boats away."

"Hope you're right. I want some shut-eye before tomorrow's festivities."

"Me too." But Wyatt doubted he'd sleep in the four-hour block until he'd report to his station.

The sense of history felt both uplifting and ponderous. Wyatt would have to make decisions in the coming days that could mean life or death for sailors and soldiers and civilians.

He squeezed his eyes shut. *Lord, help me make the right decisions. Live or die, I want to do my best.*

"Tomorrow," Jack repeated, his eyes narrowed but swimming with emotion.

Wyatt swallowed hard. Jack had been his best friend for over two years now. They'd been through battles before, but none like this.

More than the fates of nations would be decided tomorrow. The fates of over a hundred and fifty thousand soldiers and almost two hundred thousand sailors hung in the balance.

The fate of the Paxton family would also be decided as the three brothers converged on the same shore from the sea, the air, and the land.

A solid sense of pride and rightness and peace filled his chest. Adler and Clay would do their best tomorrow, he knew it. And if the Paxton boys could help bring peace to the world, perhaps they could bring peace to their family as well.

Wyatt had done right by his brothers. He'd written the letters and check, all to go out when the mail was released. He'd forgiven himself for the delay—he'd meant well. Besides, Mama had surely told his brothers how sorry he was. At least they'd know that much.

More importantly, he was right with God.

If only he was sure about Dorothy's peace of mind.

Jack clapped Wyatt on the back, his lips in a hard line, his cheeks redder than usual, even in the wind.

It wasn't often that Jack had no words, and Wyatt's throat thickened. Tomorrow they'd have no time to chat, but they'd be on the intercom constantly—Wyatt up in the gun director, Jack down in the Combat Information Center, gathering data from radio, radar, and sonar. Once again, they'd work as a team. Wyatt cleared his throat. "I'm glad we're in this together."

"Me too, buddy." One more clap, and Jack strode down the deck.

Wyatt wasn't ready to go to the cabin. He leaned forward, holding the lifeline. The sharp bow split the water, half streaming to starboard, half to port, foaming froth at the divide.

He didn't envy General Eisenhower his decision to proceed.

On one side, he could be launching the Allies on the final path to victory and peace, liberating Europe from Nazi tyranny. On the other side, the Germans could toss the invaders back into the sea. What then? How long would it take to set up another invasion? At least a year. Morale in Britain and America would plummet, affecting support for the war effort.

Tomorrow would be the frothing divide that would determine the fate of the world.

Tomorrow they had to succeed.

SOUTHWICK HOUSE
TUESDAY, JUNE 6, 1944

In the predawn darkness, Southwick House gleamed with lights that reminded Dorothy of balls and dinner parties. But today there would be no dancing or repartee, only determined, rushed, sober focus on a military operation occurring over a hundred miles away.

She walked down the hallway toward the staircase.

By now, the invasion forces would be assembled off the Norman shore, debarking into landing craft and preparing for the naval bombardment. So many lives at stake, but the only face in her mind was that of a tall Texan with a slow, sweet smile.

An urge to pray for Wyatt tickled inside, but she brushed it aside. Best not to turn the Lord's eye to someone she loved, someone else for him to smite.

Dorothy turned up the staircase, but footsteps approached from behind and a man touched her elbow.

"Second Officer Fairfax?" It was Lawrence.

"Yes, sir?" She turned to him with hooded eyes. Lately she didn't have to playact at being detached and uninterested, given her commanding officer's censure and Dorothy's general annoyance at the man. Early morning fatigue only heightened the effect.

"Might I have a word?" His hazel eyes held earnestness unusual for him.

"Today? D-day? We have duties."

"We're early, and I won't take but a moment. Please, Dorothy." His voice fell low and soft as the carpet underfoot.

She sighed and glanced around for any sign of a certain first officer. "Only a moment."

"Very good." He led her to a quiet alcove under the stairs. "I owe you an apology for how I behaved at your home."

"This isn't the time for a personal conversation." Men and women bustled around, intent on the invasion. Besides, she didn't want to hear yet another apology.

"I can't concentrate on my duties with this on my chest." He pressed his hand over the lapel of his tailored jacket. "I behaved abominably."

Which offense was he referring to? She arched one eyebrow to tell him to get on with it.

He pulled in a long breath, his forehead creased. "In my eagerness to see you as a modern woman, I forgot a crucial fact—you are a lady. And I failed to act like a gentleman."

True. "Thank you for the apology."

"I don't have the right to ask, but would you consider giving me another chance, after all this is over, of course."

Dorothy glimpsed blonde hair across the hall, but it was one of the ratings, not Bliss-Baldwin. The word *no* clamored for air. He'd caused nothing but chaos in her life.

"Please, Dorothy." He wrapped gentle fingers around her forearm. "I—I can't get you out of my thoughts. You're not like any woman I've ever known, and I won't rest until I have another chance with you. Please."

She met his gaze, and something new in his expression struck her. What was it? More than his usual apologetic look, verging on pleading.

Then she knew. The power had shifted from him to her, and she couldn't breathe.

The dreams of a decade swirled together—a lifetime with this cultured man, a lifetime of privilege for both her and Papa. But only if she acted quickly. As soon as the scandal of bankruptcy broke, her chance would evaporate.

Perhaps with an exciting husband, she'd never be tempted to stray as Mum had. She'd never have genuine love, but she'd never expected it. Until Wyatt shattered her expectations.

A rush of pain, and she slammed her eyes shut.

"Please, Dorothy." Lawrence's refined voice offered the comfortable life Mum's betrayal had stolen from her. "I promise I'll behave. I promise to be a gentleman."

This time he said it without the roguish tone. This time he said it with sincerity.

"I don't deserve a second chance," he said, "but will you please think about it?"

With a sigh, she opened her eyes. "I'll think about it."

"Thank you. Now I can concentrate on my duties like a proper officer."

"Then *my* duty is complete." She hadn't meant to sound droll, but she had.

He chuckled. "A jolly good Wren you are. Righto." He strode away.

Dorothy climbed the stairs, her feet heavy. If only she'd never met Wyatt. Then she wouldn't know about her mother and she wouldn't know what it felt like to be loved for who she was. Then she'd be satisfied with Lawrence, overjoyed even.

Why did the man who'd been her paragon of manhood now feel like a consolation prize?

She stepped into the office, and Muriel hauled her into the corner, Gwen on her heels. "What are—?"

"We saw you downstairs." Gwen stood close, eyes lit up. "What happened?"

Dorothy glanced over Gwen's shoulder but didn't spy the battleship. "He wants me to give him another chance."

Muriel let out a quiet squeal, then laughed. "Why do you sound like you're at a funeral? This is what you've always wanted."

"This time it'll happen," Gwen said. "I don't know what you did, but he's frightfully desperate."

Muriel squeezed her arm. "He's been asking about you all week."

"What did you tell him?"

"Nothing." Gwen wrinkled her nose at Dorothy. "Because you told *us* nothing."

"But you'll find the path clear." Muriel raised a smug smile.

"Clear? What do you mean?"

"We snitched on Old Bliss to Commander Pringle. She has no right to treat her girls like this. If she tries to transfer you away, she'll be in big trouble."

Dorothy's chest collapsed. "You're the ones? Why did you do that? She thinks I'm the one who talked to Pringle."

"Oh dear." Gwen's mouth puckered up.

Muriel shrugged one shoulder. "It doesn't matter. She can't do anything to you."

She already had. Dorothy hadn't turned in the transfer request, and Bliss had indeed been making her life miserable. "Just watch."

39

USS *Oglesby*, OMAHA BEACH, NORMANDY
TUESDAY, JUNE 6, 1944

Surreal was the only word to describe it. Eyes pressed to the slewing sight of the gun director, Wyatt observed Omaha Beach only three thousand yards away to his left.

Morning twilight illuminated the landscape. A flat beach about three hundred yards deep led to the seawall with a road right behind it, then grassy flatlands for another hundred yards, then bluffs rising one hundred fifty feet above sea level.

At the right edge of Dog Green Beach, an indentation marked the D-1 draw, the exit leading to the village of Vierville-sur-Mer, its church spire pointing above the bluffs. Sweeping left, villas dotted the flatland behind the seawall. Although muted by the low light, Wyatt knew which one was Dorothy's.

He huffed out a breath and pushed away from the slewing sight. Faint flashes rose inland due to the aerial bombardment. US B-24 Liberators were supposed to bomb the beach defenses, but they were too far inland. That might keep German reinforcements away from the beach, but it wouldn't help the soldiers speeding to shore.

That left the bombardment to the Navy, and they'd only have forty minutes.

Wyatt glanced at his watch—0545. Bombardment was to start

at 0550, sunrise was at 0558, and the first landings were scheduled at 0630.

He checked his headphones and the big steel helmet that fit over them. Nothing to do but wait.

So far the invasion fleet hadn't been detected, even in the rising light. The Channel crossing hadn't been disrupted by attack from air, sea, or under the sea. A miracle.

The *Oglesby* drifted at five knots on a westerly course to compensate for the easterly current, her port side facing Normandy. The destroyers of DesRon 18 were divided, some flanking the east side of the boat lane and some flanking the west—including the *Oglesby*.

"CIC to director." Jack's voice came through the intercom from several decks below. "Radar fix on target tare-six-nine, grid 647916, bearing two-six-five, range three-three-five-oh."

Despite the low light, the *Oglesby* could shoot blind due to her fire control radar. Wyatt repeated the coordinates into the intercom. "Prepare full salvo."

"Plot to director," Wayne Holoch called on the intercom from down in the plotting room. "We have a solution."

"Stand by," Captain Adams ordered from the pilothouse right under the gun director.

At Omaha, two battleships, four light cruisers, and eleven destroyers stood ready—eight destroyers from DesRon 18 and three British destroyers. Similar forces stood off Utah to the west and at Gold, Juno, and Sword Beaches to the east.

In the end, all the planning came down to individuals doing their jobs. Wyatt's was to neutralize three gun batteries near the Vierville draw in the initial bombardment. When the first landing craft touched shore, the *Ogie* would shift to known strongpoints farther inland. From then on, they'd fire on targets called in by their Shore Fire Control Party or on targets of opportunity.

Little direction would come from above. They'd receive some

orders from Capt. Harry Sanders, commander of Destroyer Squadron 18 aboard the USS *Frankford* and from Adm. John Hall of Force O aboard the USS *Ancon*. But they'd have no contact with headquarters at Southwick House.

Still, he liked the thought of Dorothy in the operations room at Southwick, monitoring the day's events. His last connection with her, even if it was only an illusion.

His watch read 0550. Impatience, eagerness, and dread mixed in his belly. It was time.

"We have orders to open fire," Captain Adams said. "Here we go, boys. Godspeed. Commence firing."

Wyatt muttered the quickest prayer of his life. "Fire salvo, interval thirty seconds."

Pointing to port, the *Ogie*'s four big guns fired as one, the concussion rattling every bone of Wyatt's body.

A loud scream overhead—the big shells of the cruiser HMS *Glasgow*, aiming for the same region. Wyatt resisted the urge to duck.

For the next ten minutes, Wyatt let those salvos fly. Chances were, they'd never destroy one of the German guns in their thick reinforced concrete casemates. But at least they could drive the gun crews into their tunnels.

"Check fire!" Wyatt ordered. "Track target tare-seven-zero."

Down in the Combat Information Center, Jack and his crew would be lining up target T-70, using the radar to see through the smoke and dust.

Omaha Beach's bluffs now wore a heavy cloak of smoke. Shells zipped in from the fire support ships with no reply from the Germans.

Made Wyatt nervous.

The Nazis were smart. If the German guns fired, flashes would reveal their positions and allow Allied ships to target them. But after the troops landed, the Allied ships would have to hold fire to

289

avoid hitting their own soldiers. That would be the perfect time for the Germans to shoot.

"CIC to director," Jack said on the intercom. "Target bearing two-five-two, range three-eight-double-oh."

When Holoch reported the computer had a solution, Wyatt ordered another series of salvos at thirty-second intervals.

The ship bucked like a bronco as round after round fired at the batteries.

A loud whistling overhead, then a geyser sprang up a thousand yards off the port quarter. A German shell.

"Well, look at that." Paul Tucker, the pointer, peered through his sight. "Guess we disturbed their beauty sleep."

Wyatt managed a chuckle as the *Ogie* sped up and made a tight starboard turn to throw off the Germans' aim. The computer would compensate for the change in course and adjust the destroyer's fire.

The *Ogie*'s guns kept pumping. Another whistle and splash, this time about a thousand yards ahead. The *Ogie*'s engines went into reverse, and Wyatt held on tight. Those were big splashes, probably from 105-mm or 155-mm coastal artillery. One shell could sink the *Oglesby*.

His pulse hammered, and he searched the landscape for the enemy gun. Through an opening in the haze, light flashed, muted as if from behind a shield.

"Got him!" Wyatt read the markings on his slewing sight. "Bearing one-five-five. Top of the bluff. Range?"

Behind him, Clyde Dabrowski, the rangefinder operator, adjusted dials. "Range three-six-two-oh."

In the seconds it took the computer to get a solution and the guns to align, Wyatt obtained permission to fire. "Open continuous fire."

The thunder from the ship eclipsed the earlier barrages as each gun fired independently, as fast as they could. After five minutes, he ordered, "Check fire."

Smoke rose from around the target, and chunks of concrete lay on the slopes beneath the battery. "We hit it, boys. Good shooting."

"Cease firing," Captain Adams said on the intercom.

In the boat lane to the east, four LCT landing craft chugged toward Dog Green Beach loaded with duplex drive tanks, and then came six little LCA landing craft, each loaded with thirty-two men.

Reality slammed him in the chest. Those men would hit the shore within minutes.

Wyatt had done his best cataloguing targets in the sector. All the personnel at the Allied Naval Expeditionary Force Headquarters had done their best. Would it be good enough?

SOUTHWICK HOUSE

The operations room thrummed with activity. Wrens on ladders moved cutouts of ships on the giant wall map, showing the invasion force approaching Normandy. The clock read 0620. The Americans would begin landing in ten minutes, the British and Canadians at 0730.

Dorothy's throat clamped shut. She had helped create the maps and diagrams that sent those men into battle. Today, men would live or die based on her work.

She grimaced and readied the materials on her clipboard—maps and lists of ships and such. Her Wrens would keep the wall map current as information came in from the battle.

Her area of expertise was Omaha Beach. Where she'd spent her holidays. Where Wyatt Paxton served on the USS *Oglesby*.

Love and worry for him twisted together. She'd never see him again, but she'd do her best by him today.

"Ready?" Gwen asked, her gray eyes full of emotion.

"We are." Dorothy smiled and patted her friend's hand.

"Second Officer Fairfax? Why are you here?" First Officer Bliss-Baldwin's voice sliced the air.

Dorothy gritted her teeth. This was no day for her commanding officer to play her little games. "This is my station, ma'am."

Blissy's eyes were bright and sharp. "Not until you finish your other duties. You haven't turned in the paperwork due a week ago."

"Paperwork, ma'am?" Everything sank inside her. The transfer papers.

The first officer clucked her tongue. "You've forgotten? Shame on you. You've neglected your duties lately, and I'm quite disappointed in you."

Dorothy's cheeks warmed, and Gwen gave her an alarmed look. Old Blissy's voice was loud enough for half the room to hear. "I've never neglected my duties, ma'am."

"Yet the paperwork is overdue. Until it's turned in, I can't have you here in operations."

She'd do that? She'd pull Dorothy from her station if she didn't submit for a transfer? How could Dorothy choose between her duty to her father and her duty to her post?

First Officer Bliss-Baldwin gave her a smile tight with exasperation. "Well, do you have the paperwork?"

"No, ma'am."

"Then I'll turn over your duties to a more responsible girl." She turned to Gwen. "Third Officer Hamilton, you'll take her station as well as your own."

Gwen's gaze darted between Dorothy and Bliss. "But, ma'am, I have plenty of work already."

Dorothy's breath hopped around. "Please, ma'am. I know Omaha. I've walked those beaches—"

"How arrogant." Blissy jerked up her chin. "As I told you before, you're hardly indispensable."

Dorothy stared at her clipboard. She was indeed dispensable. The Wrens were only monitoring the battle today, not fighting it.

Gwen could do Dorothy's job, but only Dorothy could care for her father.

"Unless . . ." Bliss drew the word out. "Unless I receive that paperwork within the hour."

"Dorothy . . . ," Gwen pleaded.

If she transferred, who would watch over Papa? He was barely surviving now. When the company went bankrupt, he'd wither and die without her. She refused to abandon him.

Dorothy shoved the clipboard into Gwen's hands, then raised her chin to her commanding officer. "I don't have the paperwork, ma'am, and I never will."

The first officer stared, blinked, then glared. "I'm disappointed. You seemed like such a promising officer."

Dorothy swallowed back her anger, grief, and humiliation. Whatever punishment she received, she would suffer gladly. For Papa's sake.

40

"Fire up ladder, fifty-yard steps," Wyatt said.

Since the new target lay out of sight 1500 yards inland, the *Oglesby*'s fire was guided by radar. Firing in a ladder, with each salvo fifty yards farther inland, would pepper the area.

The guns roared, and Wyatt made notes in his log. They'd used 320 shells in the initial bombardment, 19 percent of stock, and he had to keep track.

He looked through his slewing sight at the beaches. The sun was up, if invisible behind the overcast, and the green of the land seemed wrong for the day, too happy and full of life.

The gray waters off Dog Green Beach churned as dozens of vessels approached the shore. Special LCT(R) landing craft shot hundreds of rockets at the beaches in slanting, whizzing bursts of white fire.

One of the LCTs carrying tanks had sunk in flames—a mine, most likely. Wyatt's eyes stung from the cold wind and from the losses.

The remaining three LCTs hadn't unloaded their duplex drive tanks offshore as planned. The rough seas would probably have swamped the canvas shields that kept the tanks afloat. Instead, the LCTs drove right onto the beach and flopped down their bow ramps so the tanks could drive off.

Wyatt kept a close eye on his wristwatch. At 0642 he'd cease fire and switch to targets of opportunity until they contacted their Shore Fire Control Party.

In the distance, little LCAs bobbed forward. The 1st Battalion of the 116th Regiment had arrived on a British transport ship and therefore landed in British LCA "Landing Craft, Assault" rather than American LCVPs.

An explosion close to shore, and an LCA disappeared. Just disappeared.

Wyatt gasped. "Lord, help those men." Thirty-two of them. The binoculars in the slewing sight allowed a better view than the naked eye, but he wished he could get closer to see, to help.

Lots of smoke and dust being kicked up on shore. A tank exploded in a fireball.

Beside him, Tucker cussed.

Wyatt didn't blame him. The five remaining LCAs stopped near the beach—but not on it. Yet men in khaki and olive drab swarmed out, falling in the water. "Lord, be with them."

The *Oglesby* fired another salvo. Only one more to go.

Three medium-sized LCM landing craft rode up onto the beach. Those carried the Army engineers and Navy underwater demolition teams to blow up the beach obstacles.

Wyatt checked his watch—0642. "Cease firing!"

The *Oglesby*'s guns fell silent.

And a horrid sound reached his ear, low but unmistakable—staccato machine-gun fire and blasts of bigger guns and mines.

The German guns weren't trained to fire on ships at sea but to send vicious enfilading fire down the length of the beach.

Wyatt ducked inside the hatch and grabbed his map. The batteries at the Vierville draw were positioned for that kind of fire. He'd shot hundreds of shells at them, but it wasn't enough. With the guns close to beach level, the *Ogie* couldn't target them now without endangering GIs.

His tightening fists threatened to crush the valuable map, so he set it aside. Men were dying over there, and he couldn't help them.

"Conn to director. No contact with SFCP. Any targets of opportunity?" Captain Adams asked.

His chest filled with lead. The Shore Fire Control Party should have landed by now, should have been radioing targets. "No, sir."

"Very well." He issued new orders—proceed west at one-third speed, watch for targets, clear the decks of cartridge cases, and distribute rations.

Wyatt poked his head out the hatch again. His chest clenched as Dog Green Beach drifted away to stern, but perhaps they could find some of the big guns raking the sands.

Down on the decks, brass powder cartridge cases lay heaped behind the guns, where they'd been pitched out after each projectile was fired. Now the repair parties hauled them to a clear spot on the deck amidships.

Wyatt turned knobs on his slewing sight. He had to find those guns. Had to.

"K rations? Water?" Dabrowski passed out the provisions stashed in the compartment. The Navy didn't usually use Army rations, but with all the cooks at battle stations, the Navy was experimenting.

"Ration, sir?" Dabrowski nudged Wyatt's leg.

"No, thanks."

"Mr. Paxton. Sir. We could be at general quarters all day. You gotta keep up your strength."

Wyatt glanced down to deep-set brown eyes.

The rangefinder operator shrugged. No apology for ordering an officer around. Sure wouldn't see that on a British ship.

"Aye aye." Wyatt lifted a smile and a mock salute, and he took the little cardboard box. "Y'all eat up. Who knows when we'll get another chance."

Inside the box, he found a tin of ham and eggs, crackers, and a dried fruit bar. He scooped the ham-and-egg mixture with a cracker and looked through the slewing sight while he chewed.

Not a pleasant taste. And not a pleasant sight. Between Charlie Beach west of the Vierville draw and Pointe de la Percée the bluffs came right to the shore, so no landings were taking place there. But they made good locations for artillery.

Where? All around the ship, crewmen would be scouring the landscape. Wyatt had marked potential targets on his map, but nothing confirmed by photo reconnaissance, nothing warranting the use of precious ammunition.

For twenty minutes, the *Ogie* cruised back and forth in Fire Support Area 3. With the brown haze of smoke and dust on the bluffs, Wyatt couldn't see any targets. His insides writhed. How could this great ship with all her guns sit idle when the men on shore needed help? But he couldn't risk hitting those men either.

Blind and helpless as a baby rat.

If only Captain Adams would order them to the far western end of DesRon 18's sector. To Pointe du Hoc. He sure wouldn't mind lobbing a few hundred shells at any Nazis who might be shooting at his baby brother.

Overhead, aircraft engines throbbed. Not Adler's P-51 Mustangs, but P-38 Lightnings, chosen to cover the beachhead because Navy gunners could quickly identify their unique twin-boomed fuselage as friendly.

Booms rose from the west. Off Pointe de la Percée, a destroyer sailed before them, flat and gray, orange flashes around her guns, probably the USS *Thompson*.

Wyatt stashed the fruit bar in his pocket. "Director to conn. Sir, suggest we join the *Thompson*'s party."

"Permission granted. CIC, contact the *Thompson* for coordinates. Director, open fire when ready."

"Aye aye, sir." Finally something to do. He followed the *Thompson*'s line of fire to the top of the bluff. No smoke in that area, and the barrel of a big field gun poked through the brush over a rise.

"CIC to director. Grid 635928, bearing three-two-six, range four-three-five-oh."

Within seconds, Holoch had a solution.

"Fire salvo," Wyatt ordered.

Four projectiles leapt to the cliff. A plume of dirt flew up a bit to the right. "Left five."

"Left five." Frank Zaneti, the trainer, cranked his hand wheels.

"Fire salvo."

The *Oglesby* and the *Thompson* alternated fire, blasting away the brush on the bluff. Then a shell from the *Oglesby* knocked the gun askew—a direct hit! A shell from the *Thompson* followed, and bits of steel exploded into the sky.

Wyatt's crew cheered, and so did he. One fewer gun to harass the soldiers.

The captain ordered the destroyer back to Dog Green Beach. When they arrived, a sick feeling stirred up the fake ham and eggs in Wyatt's belly.

In the distance off Dog White Beach, two big LCI infantry landing ships were in flames. At Dog Green, tanks burned at the water's edge, and LCA landing craft milled about, probably looking for a safe place to come ashore. There were none.

Wyatt pressed his eyes to the slewing sight. "Oh, Lord," he prayed.

GIs huddled behind obstacles and broached landing craft. At the seawall, dozens of men hunched over. No activity at the Vierville draw. And the beach—the beach was littered—guns, equipment, bodies, too many bodies, twisted and motionless. A trio of soldiers dashed across the beach and fell—one, two, three.

Wyatt pushed away, his breath rushing out, his mouth agape. Mayhem. Madness. Slaughter.

"CIC here. I can't contact the SFCP." On the intercom, Jack's voice sounded shrill with panic.

Wyatt coughed to restart his lungs. Without the SFCP to call in targets, they'd have to rely on their eyes. But with the German guns trained to fire down the length of the beach, the gun flashes weren't visible from two thousand yards out.

Everything in him wanted to charge the beaches, but the waters were shallow and infested with mines. Too dangerous for the ship and her crew.

Almost three hundred men served on the destroyer. But how many soldiers were struggling on Omaha? Dying?

Wyatt backed up and pressed fists to his forehead. Protect the soldiers or protect the sailors? Why did his decisions always seem to come at a price?

SOUTHWICK HOUSE

Deep in the cellar of Southwick House, dozens of teleprinters clacked as Wrens transmitted and received dispatches.

Dorothy meandered behind the girls, useless. She wore only a light coat of face powder to mute the freckles rather than conceal them, but not even full stage makeup could have masked the redness of her humiliation.

She wasn't familiar with this department, and Blissy knew it, knew she'd add a failure to Dorothy's record today. How long would it take to become demoted?

"Excuse me, Second Officer?" The lieutenant in charge held up his narrow chin. "You have bigoted clearance, do you not?"

"Yes, sir." What used to be a source of pride—being trusted with classified knowledge of Operation Neptune plans—now only deepened her embarrassment.

He passed her a slip of paper. "Take this to Commander Pringle in operations. He's a short man, rather—"

"I know him, sir."

His eyebrows rose up his high forehead.

Dorothy strode out of the room before he could ask the question—whatever had she done to deserve banishment?

What had she done indeed?

The operations room was even more painful than the teleprinter room, because she'd lost the right to be where she belonged, where her hard work over the past few years had led her.

Gwen darted over, blonde tendrils falling from the roll at the nape of her neck. "Dorothy, please? Whatever the battleship wants, please do it. I'm drowning."

Dorothy's heart ached for her friend, for her own duties, for her father. She brushed a tendril behind Gwen's ear. "You don't know what she asked. I can't. You'll do fine."

"Ma'am?" Leading Wren Stella Dodds handed Gwen a pile of papers.

Gwen's shoulders sagged, she sent Dorothy a beseeching look, and she dashed to her station.

Dorothy sighed and continued across the room. Commander Pringle stood in front of the wall map with two officers in US Army olive drab, and she gave the commander the dispatch.

He read it and muttered a mild curse. "Wait for my reply."

"Aye aye, sir."

Pringle faced the US Army officers. "Your boys are making a poor show of it at Omaha. We finally received a report. Your men aren't advancing off the beach, and the beachmaster has halted further landings."

Dorothy gripped her hands together and studied the map she knew so well, now with tiny ship cutouts along the shore.

One of the Army officers read the dispatch. "Come on, Commander. We all knew Omaha would be the toughest nut to crack."

"That's right." The next officer spoke with a Texas drawl that deepened Dorothy's ache. "The crescent shape of the beach, the guns at both draws and at Percée, the high bluffs. Give us time. You underestimate the sheer guts of the average GI."

"Time." Pringle snorted. "You may not have enough of that."

Dorothy's breath came fast and shallow. She probably knew Omaha Beach better than anyone in this room. She'd played in those sands, climbed those seawalls, dangled from the branches of those trees. She'd painted it, diagrammed it, charted it. She'd breathed it, dreamed it, lived it.

She ought to be at her station. Was she saving Papa's life only to endanger lives on that beach?

"Here's my reply." Commander Pringle handed it to her.

Dorothy blinked. She was nothing but a messenger, and she slipped away.

First Officer Bliss-Baldwin was right when she called Dorothy arrogant. She wasn't endangering a soul. What could she contribute today? With wireless silence, they had little contact with the ships and were only monitoring.

It was best to be away from operations anyway, away from thoughts of Wyatt and the *Oglesby*, away from thoughts of that villa of stone, that house of lies.

She marched downstairs, her eyes hot. The houses in Normandy and Edinburgh were the only places she'd felt her family was whole, where she'd felt loved.

Lies, lies, nothing but lies.

Dorothy delivered the dispatch to the officer in the teleprinter room, then excused herself to use the lavatory.

Lies and more lies. Hands balled up, she made her way to the loo, half-blinded.

That photo at Vierville, the one she'd treasured? A lie. She thought it represented her family happy and whole.

It didn't. She stepped into a stall, latched the door, and pressed her forehead to the door.

That photo . . . Mum stood apart, looking away. Was she seeking her next lover? Papa embraced his sons, but not her. Never her. And fat, freckled Dolly stood alone on the seawall. Always alone. Always the daredevil, seeking attention, acceptance, love. Never finding it.

Her eyes burned and her arms shook. Only Wyatt loved her, and she'd sacrificed his love for his own sake. She'd sacrificed her duty for her father's sake, for the father who'd never loved her.

But she loved him, and she'd fight for him.

He was all she had, and she was all he had, and she wouldn't let anyone take him away from her.

Not even God.

"You'd like that, Lord, wouldn't you? You'd like to take Papa from me too. Well, I won't have it."

Her jaw tightened, her fingers curled before her eyes, and she shook those fists. "I won't let you pluck him from my hands."

41

USS *Oglesby*, Omaha Beach

As far as Wyatt could see, dozens of landing ships waited and dozens of landing craft darted, not approaching the shore. And the men on the beach—the few who remained alive—were pinned down, not advancing up the draw.

Wyatt's jaw hardened. What good would it do to protect the *Oglesby* if the invasion failed?

Even if the landings went well on Utah and the British beaches, Omaha was the vital link between them, and Vierville was the key to Omaha.

But closing the beach wasn't part of the Neptune plan. It was risky. How could he propose the idea to Captain Adams?

A German shell hit a landing craft, and it exploded in a ball of smoke and splinters.

Wyatt gritted his teeth and flipped the switch on his intercom. Failure at Omaha wasn't part of the Neptune plan either. "Director to the captain. Suggest we close the beach."

A pause. "How close?"

"As close as we can without scraping bottom."

Another pause.

Wyatt breathed a quick prayer. "Sir, we could spot more targets, help those men—"

"Checking the tide table, the charts. The *Oglesby* draws thirteen feet of water . . ." The captain's voice drifted off.

Wyatt ducked inside and flipped his map over to the tide table. June 6 . . . 0830 . . . the height above the low-water mark was seventeen feet, with high tide at 1052. He flipped back to the map and read the soundings in small brown numbers, same as the captain would be doing.

"One thousand yards," Captain Adams said. "That'll keep us this side of the sandbars off the draw, and we'll have a good three fathoms beneath us. We can get even closer to the east by those fortified houses."

Dorothy's house. "Suggest we start at the draw."

"Very well." The captain called out a heading and speed, and the *Ogie* surged forward.

Wyatt gazed hard through his slewing sight, the wind cooling his forehead under his helmet. The breeze also blew the smoke from the initial bombardment inland, clearing the view.

"Mr. Paxton, sir," Ralph Jacoby, the talker, said behind him. "Bow lookout reports machine gun bearing zero-three-zero at the top of the bluff."

Wyatt turned his sight. There it was, about a hundred yards east of the draw. "Target sighted. Machine gun bearing zero-three-zero, top of the bluff."

"Left fifteen degrees rudder. Prepare 40-mm automatic fire," Captain Adams said. "Commence firing when ready."

"Aye aye, sir."

Jacoby passed the coordinates to the crews of the two twin-mounted Bofors heavy machine guns located behind the funnels.

"Commence firing," Wyatt said.

The Bofors guns pumped out their giant bullets, 120 rounds per minute. Red tracer fire streaked toward the bluff. Bits of earth spat out below the gun, then the tracers rose, and the German machine gun spun into the air.

"Good job, men." Wyatt grinned. Finally doing some good.

The destroyer zigged and zagged, avoiding other vessels, and Wyatt studied the beach. One machine gun knocked out, but how many remained?

"Captain to director. Bearing three-three-five. See those tanks on the road behind the seawall? They're firing into the bluff."

Sure enough, three tanks had made it across the beach and through the seawall, and they sat on the road aimed west toward the draw. All were firing at a spot on the bluff about fifty feet up—a concealed gun position? "Captain, we can hit it."

"Walk it down."

"Aye aye, sir." He'd aim high to avoid hitting GIs, then walk the fire down to the target. After the trainer and pointer finished their work, Wyatt ordered a single salvo from the 5-inch guns.

The boom resounded through the *Ogie*, and chunks of earth fell from the bluff, about ten yards above the tank fire. Wyatt called out the adjustment and ordered another salvo.

The guns inched down and shot another group of four shells. Right on target.

The three tanks rolled forward, then one fired a single shot at a new spot on the bluff.

"Would you look at that?" Paul Tucker said.

Wyatt's mouth drifted open. "They're giving us directions."

Another two salvos, and the tanks advanced again, then fired at a new spot.

"Well, I'll be." A slow smile rose. They might not have contact with their SFCP, but they were still communicating.

Once more, the *Ogie* talked back. Once more, the tanks advanced. This time they rolled up to three other tanks at the roadblock at the draw. The hatch of the last tank opened, and a tanker rose from inside and waved to seaward.

Wyatt gaped, then remembered his manners and waved back. He popped inside and stared at his men. "I think that was a thank-you."

Tucker's thin face broke into a wide grin. "I think you're right, sir."

Captain Adams ordered an easterly heading. "DesRon 18 ordered us to join the *Carmick* between D-1 and D-3. Troops observed climbing the bluff."

Part of Wyatt wanted to stay at the D-1 draw. They'd done some good in the last half hour. But still no troops were advancing. The roadblocks, strongpoints, and big batteries would take time to crack. The 14-inch shells of the battleship USS *Texas* howled overhead to the draw, much better suited to doing that cracking than the *Ogie*'s shells.

And the fellows on the ground were trying to make an end run, American improvisation and ingenuity at its best. If they could get enough men up those bluffs, they could take Vierville from behind.

Wyatt studied his map, looking for the route the soldiers might take.

His heart fell. Right near Dorothy's house.

He could still see her the day they'd met at Norfolk House, how she'd cupped her hand over the photograph on the table, her forehead furrowed at the mention of target selection.

She'd lost so much. How could he steal away one of her few happy memories? He aimed his slewing sight down the line of stone houses. *Lord, anything but that.*

SOUTHWICK HOUSE

Dorothy's fingernails dug into the palms of her shaking hands. "You can't take Papa from me."

She was sick and tired of God laying his hands on her and those she loved. Wyatt talked about being safe in God's hands, but that was a lie.

In her mind she could see the stained glass window she used to love, long since removed to hide it from German bombs. Jesus the Good Shepherd, cradling a lamb with a serene smile.

"A lie . . ." But her words fizzled, her mind muddled.

What was that verse . . . ? *"I give unto them eternal life; and they shall never perish, neither shall any man pluck them out of my hand."*

With her forehead against the lavatory stall door, she uncurled stiff fingers. White indentations from her fingernails filled in, and truth flooded her.

Her hands were empty. She'd told God he couldn't pluck Papa from her hands, but Papa wasn't in her hands. He never had been.

Her knees wobbled. *"No man is able to pluck them out of my Father's hand."*

Not even you, Dorothy.

She gasped and braced herself against the door. She had everything backward. Papa's life wasn't in her hands, but she acted as if it were, as if his life depended on her. She had no control over his life or her own, just as she'd had no control over Mum's or Art's or Gil's.

Nor was she meant to.

Papa was in the Lord's hands. Whether he lived or died was up to the Lord, not Dorothy.

"But . . . but you failed me." Her voice cracked, and so did her reasoning.

She sounded like a child whining because she didn't get her way. In her childish faith she had loved God only when her life was happy.

Wyatt's faith wasn't like that. He trusted God, not because his life was happy, but because the Lord comforted him and strengthened him through the unhappiness.

Her throat thickened. "Oh, Lord, I want that kind of faith. I want to lean on you instead of away from you."

She'd had such a stirring lately, so many reminders of God's love.

The Good Shepherd cradled her close to his heart—not to protect her earthly life but her eternal life. He wanted to hold her because he loved her and liked her, just as he'd created her.

Her hands splayed before her, blurred in her sight. Hadn't she urged prodigal Wyatt to return to his family empty-handed?

"Oh, Lord, I'm a prodigal too." And she ran home to him as she was—empty-handed, overly talkative, impulsive, freckled, and so very lonely and unloved.

No, not unloved. God loved her. No matter what happened in this world. No matter what she lost, God loved her.

The lavatory door opened, and Dorothy clapped her hands over her mouth.

"Frightfully busy today," a Wren said. "I need a rest."

"Our Tommies won't have a rest today," a second woman said in a snippy voice.

Dorothy sat and waited until they left. It was D-day. Men were fighting and dying, and she was crying in the loo.

She ought to be doing her duty.

But Papa . . .

With her fingers flat over her mouth, she shut her eyes.

Could she give up the illusion of control? Could she trust the Lord with her father's life? Could she continue to trust him even if Papa died?

"He's in your hands, not mine," she whispered.

She pushed herself out of the stall, glimpsed her wet and reddened face in the mirror, and washed up, removing the last traces of face powder.

A few steadying breaths, and she headed upstairs to the operations room, where First Officer Bliss-Baldwin discussed a report with a Wren rating.

Dorothy stood at attention before her. "May I have a word in private, ma'am?"

Her commanding officer's eyes widened, at Dorothy's appearance, no doubt. "Very good."

Blissy led Dorothy into the adjoining sitting room. "Yes?"

Dorothy clutched the hem of her jacket, then released it. "Ma'am, I officially request a transfer. I'll turn in the paperwork this evening after my watch, only please let me serve in operations."

"You—you changed your mind?" The look in her eyes—shock, confusion, pleasure?

"Yes, ma'am." Dorothy shifted her gaze to the woman's forehead. "I'm needed in the operations room more than I'm needed at home."

"But your father . . . ?"

Dorothy pulled in a shaky breath. "I'll trust him in the Lord's hands. I can't think of my personal needs right now, only the needs of my country, of the Allies."

"Very—very good. Relieve Third Officer Hamilton straight-away."

"Thank you, ma'am." Dorothy marched away.

How could her heart feel so heavy and so light at the same time?

42

Movement caught Wyatt's eye, glimpses of khaki, disturbances in the brush, and he traced the GIs' narrow, winding path up the bluff behind Dog White Beach.

Now to help them.

A furrow raced through the brush close to the soldiers. Wyatt followed it back to the face of the bluff. Where were the Germans hiding?

There it was. A patch of concrete gray—small but unmistakable. Wyatt called out the coordinates, and the *Ogie* lobbed 5-inch and 40-mm fire into the position. Trees and bushes exploded, stripping the cover from two machine-gun batteries.

Five more minutes of fire rattled the destroyer. Then the battery on the left blew up from the inside—one of the shells must have found the gun slit.

"Good shooting, men." Wyatt gave them a thumbs-up. The battery on the right was neutralized—even if the gun was undamaged, the soldiers inside would be too rattled to man it for a while.

"Captain to director. Troops pinned down behind a house, bearing oh-seven-five, shooting at the next house down. Let's take it out."

Please don't let it be. Wyatt's stomach sank. It was.

310

He had to demolish Dorothy's house, two stories of charming stone with white shutters.

His tongue dried out, but he moistened it and called out the coordinates. In this crazy, upside-down world he had to destroy to protect.

A dozen GIs crouched behind the house next door, aiming rifle fire at Dorothy's house, which stood between them and the path up the cliff. The French Resistance had reported that the Germans had evacuated the civilians in the remaining beachfront villas in order to fortify the buildings. There would be no innocent victims. Only the cherished memories of the woman he loved.

Lord, forgive me. "Commence firing."

Shells dug into the house, and chunks of stone flew away. Wyatt wanted to close his eyes, but he had to spot the gunfire.

His dilemma was no worse than for the crews of the two French cruisers at the far eastern edge of Omaha, firing on their own homeland, their own countrymen.

The roof of the house collapsed, but Wyatt didn't cringe. He was through beating himself up for decisions he made in good faith. When he decided to help Dorothy with the investigation, he'd made the best decision he could. The fact that the investigation revealed her mother's betrayal wasn't Wyatt's fault.

The destroyer weaved around to throw off German fire, the mechanical computer adjusting for changes in speed and direction.

Shells zinged through the air, leaving concussive paths in the sand and brush and reducing the French villa to rubble.

Wyatt's breath leached out, and he shook his head. But he'd make the same decision again. "Cease firing. Look for other targets."

He scoured the bluffs for signs of enemy activity and found none. The GIs continued their trek up the bluff.

The *Oglesby* zigzagged east about nine hundred yards offshore. The rising tide brought them closer to their targets with each minute. Up and down Omaha Beach, nine US destroyers had closed the beach, all providing close fire support. Captain Sanders's command ship, the *Frankford*, had joined the rest of his destroyers, while the British destroyers had departed for the screening area out to sea. They carried about half the ammunition of the American ships and didn't have advanced fire control systems.

"Captain to director," Captain Adams said. "Troops still pinned down behind that house."

Wyatt swung his slewing sight around. The house was a pile of smoking rubble. So why were the troops pinned down? Where were the Germans?

His shoulders tensed. Had he destroyed Dorothy's house for nothing?

SOUTHWICK HOUSE

"Thank goodness you're back." Gwen thrust the clipboard into Dorothy's hands. "Utah Beach keeps me busy enough."

"What's the situation on Omaha?" She flipped through the papers on her clipboard.

Gwen tucked a loose tendril into place. "We haven't received many reports, and those we have received aren't encouraging. Losses are horrific, and we haven't taken the draws."

"Oh dear." It was 0930, and the troops were meant to be well on their way inland.

Gwen looked over Dorothy's shoulder and pointed at a spot on the map. "Small groups of soldiers have reached the top of the bluff here between St. Laurent and Colleville and here between Vierville and Les Moulins." Right behind Dorothy's holiday home.

"What about the—the ships in our sector?" Her voice quivered more than it should have.

"The destroyers have been magnificent." Gwen's eyes glowed silver. "They've closed the beaches, guns ablaze."

Magnificent. Dorothy's mouth relaxed. "Thank you, Gwen."

"The latest dispatch, ma'am." A Wren rating handed Dorothy a weather report.

Dorothy made notations, then carried the dispatch to Commander Pringle. "The latest meteorological report, sir. By the way, I'm relieving Third Officer Hamilton for the Omaha sector. She'll remain in the Utah sector."

"Very good." He skimmed the dispatch.

While he read, she studied the wall map. The scale was too large to show any but the command ships, but she could picture the destroyers close to shore. How shallow were the waters? Had they been swept for mines?

She rested her fingertips on one of the ship cutouts. *Lord, I know Wyatt is safe in your hands forever, but please—please let him live.*

"Those Yank destroyers." Commander Pringle shook his head. "Running around like gangsters, shooting willy-nilly, closing the beach recklessly."

Dorothy offered him a smile. "Aren't we glad they're on our side?"

A wry smile rose. "Only if they win. At this point it's in doubt."

"The troops broke through here, didn't they, sir?" She pointed to the spots on the map.

"In the wrong places. They're supposed to take the draws first, and too few troops have ascended the cliffs to do any good."

Dorothy knew little about military tactics, but couldn't the troops on the bluff seize Vierville and its draw from behind? If they could only get enough men up that path.

She knew the path behind her house. She'd climbed it often enough.

Something hardened inside her, but in a good way. If the Germans had placed artillery in that house, Wyatt and his friends had better pummel it.

All the houses in the area, more than a dozen, and outbuildings too.

This was no time to be sentimental. The house would live in

her memory and in countless of her paintings. The house and the tree and the . . .

Dorothy's blood stopped cold. And the shack. The ugly, old, new shack.

She'd painted it black. Because she'd missed it. Because it didn't belong.

Of all the aerial photographs, only the latest had shown the shack, and the one prior had shown a darkened area Dorothy had interpreted as a shadow.

What if she had been correct? What if the shack was indeed brand-new, built to look old? What if Wyatt had been correct? What if the Germans had built it to conceal a gun?

Commander Pringle moved down the map, where he talked with Commander Marino.

She oughtn't to be impulsive. On the other hand, perhaps this was the precise time to be impulsive.

She approached the men. When they addressed her, she turned her clipboard to face them. "Sirs, I'm concerned about this area where the soldiers are climbing the bluff. Do you remember last month when we spotted a shack under a tree in this location? I'm convinced we'd never seen it before because it actually *is* brand-new. I'm convinced the enemy is using it."

The men exchanged a glance.

A flat smile crossed Commander Pringle's round face. "Thank you, Second Officer."

"Can we target it, sir? Can we send word to our—"

The commander held up one hand. "Wireless silence. We only break it when absolutely necessary."

Everything in her said this was absolutely necessary, and her mouth opened.

"We have several ships in that sector," Commander Marino said, his dark eyes warm. "If the Nazis are using that shack, our boys will blast it to smithereens."

She chewed her lips, then stopped. "Do you happen to know which ships are there?"

"Fire Support Area Three . . ." He narrowed his eyes. "The *Carmick*, *McCook*, *Oglesby*, and *Thompson* are covering the western sector of Omaha."

Dorothy's chest filled with light and hope. "The *Oglesby*? Wyatt Paxton's ship."

The American's dark eyebrows rose. "That's right."

"Simply smashing. He'll understand, sir. If we send him the coordinates, he could—"

"Can't do that." Commander Marino shook his head. "If we transmit coordinates and then our ships fire on those coordinates, the Germans can use that to break our code."

Dorothy winced, but then hope returned. "Sir, tell him the shack is black."

"The shack—"

"Is black, sir. It doesn't make sense to you, nor will it make sense to the Germans, but Lieutenant Paxton will know exactly what it means."

The men exchanged another glance, then both gave her that amused, long-suffering look reserved for silly but otherwise intelligent women.

Commander Pringle inclined his head at her. "Thank you, Second Officer. Carry on."

"Aye aye, sir." No other reply was allowed.

She returned to her station. If only she could shout across the Channel. Wyatt wouldn't give her that amused, long-suffering look. He'd listen. He'd blow that shack into little black bits.

"Lord," she whispered. "Only you can tell him."

43

USS *Oglesby*, Omaha Beach

The *Oglesby* circled to seaward, reversing course, but Wyatt studied the area where Dorothy's house had stood. Where were the Germans?

"Any contact with SFCP?" Captain Adams asked. "One more minute, and we'll return to the D-1 draw."

"CIC here. No contact with SFCP," Jack said on the intercom.

How could Wyatt leave the job unfinished? He could still see Dorothy drawing a big old bull's-eye on the house, nibbling on a pencil and frowning at the black shack.

The shack. He grabbed the map. They'd never taken the shack seriously as a target. Too small. But what if Dorothy saw inside to a black heart?

A loud whine overhead, then seawater spouted one hundred yards astern. A big shell.

The *Ogie* rode the wake and made a hard turn to port to throw off the Germans' aim.

Captain Adams called out a westerly course back to the Vierville draw.

Not now. "Director to captain, I have the target sighted, a shack near the house we destroyed."

316

"We're taking fire from the battery at grid coordinate 654912. Target it."

Wyatt located the battery on the map. That position had been silenced earlier in the morning, but the Germans must have manned it again. The battery perched on the edge of the bluff halfway between their current position and the D-1 draw.

The ship cruised fifteen hundred yards offshore, heading west.

"Captain, suggest we target the shack first. We can zip in, fire a few salvos, then swing around to the battery."

Silence on the intercom. Had he angered the captain or made his point?

"Split fire." The captain's voice was brisk. "We'll charge straight in. Fire forward guns at shack, aft guns at battery. At nine hundred yards offshore, sharp turn to starboard, all guns target battery."

"Aye aye, sir." Adrenaline and purpose warmed his veins.

"Left full rudder," the captain ordered.

"Aft guns on director control, forward guns to local control, rapid continuous fire." While the ship turned toward the shore, Wyatt called out coordinates for both targets and flipped switches releasing the number one and number two guns from the computer.

Tucker and Zaneti spun their hand wheels, lining up the director with the big battery. Down in the forward 5-inch gun compartments, each individual gun's pointer and trainer would line up the shack in their sights.

Wyatt stuck his head out the hatch so he could watch both targets.

"Plot here. We have a firing solution."

"Number one on target."

"Number two on target."

"Commence firing," Captain Adams ordered. "Steady on course, two-thirds speed."

The *Oglesby* bounded over the waves. The forward guns pumped shells straight ahead at the shack, and the aft guns fired to starboard at the battery.

Acrid brown smoke filled Wyatt's nostrils.

Although he hadn't been named after Wyatt Earp, he felt like that famous lawman riding into town with his six-shooter. The wind buffeted his face, and his Texas blood galloped. "Yee-haw!" he yelled.

Back to work, back to the slewing sight. He brought the demolished house into focus, the tree, the shack. Branches snapped off in a cloud of leaves, and the shells fell lower. Bits of lumber arced into the air, then the shack exploded, a ball of fire and smoke.

No fooling, something had been in there.

He whooped again, then spoke into the intercom. "Forward target destroyed. Forward guns to director control." He flipped switches to reconnect them to the computer so they could target the battery as well.

A loud whine, then two big splashes, one to port and one to starboard. A straddle! The Germans were getting their mark.

The *Oglesby* swung hard to starboard, kicking up a wave, and the 5-inch guns swiveled to port to keep the battery targeted. Wyatt clutched the rim of the hatch to keep his balance.

Those were big shells the Nazis were firing, and that battery would be thick reinforced concrete. The *Ogie* might be able to silence the battery, but they couldn't destroy it.

Unless . . . A strange idea, but it might work. "Director to—"

That whine again, and the *Ogie* lurched. Once. Twice.

Wyatt dropped. The back of his helmet banged the hatch opening, his shoulder banged the rangefinder, and his knees banged the deck.

He cried out, but his voice was drowned by a blast of noise, then another. The concussion pitched him forward, and he flung up his hands and grabbed the base of the slewing sight so he wouldn't smash his face.

Ears ringing, he picked himself up. They'd been hit, but how badly? "Anyone hurt?" he called out.

Tucker clutched his left arm. "I'm fine."

Blood trickled from Zaneti's nose. He groaned but then shook himself. "I'm fine too."

Dabrowski, Jacoby, and Ruiz reported only minor injuries as well.

The *Ogie* had slowed and was dragging low in the stern.

His left shoulder felt hot, and he inspected it. Good-sized gash, mighty sore, but not much blood. His helmet and headphones had been knocked askew, and he righted them.

Urgent voices. Damage in the aft fire room, the aft engine room. Flooding. Two German shells had found their mark.

Wyatt peered out the hatch and up over the back of the director. Heavy black smoke roiled near the aft funnel.

He called down to the guns for reports. Both aft guns had been knocked off their training rings and were unable to rotate. Both crews reported injuries.

But the forward guns were undamaged, and the crew had only cuts and bruises.

More whines, and two more German shells splashed to port. The *Oglesby* made a creaky starboard turn.

Wyatt glared at the battery. The concrete was pockmarked but intact, and big chunks of earth had been knocked out underneath. His original idea flew back into his mind.

"Director to captain. Suggest we resume fire with forward guns."

"No time. We have to abandon ship soon."

Abandon ship? It wasn't that bad, was it?

But the bow of the destroyer tipped up at about a fifteen-degree angle. Wyatt pressed up on his toes to see over the director. The stern was awash.

"Handling room four flooding!" sounded in his ears. "We're evacuating."

Wyatt grimaced. "Very well. Gun four, gun three, evacuate."

Another whine, but softer, then a blast on the shore. The Germans had written off the *Oglesby* and were firing at the soldiers on the beach.

He could take out that battery. Everything in him wanted to stretch out his hand and protect the GIs.

But if he and his gun crews stayed behind after the order to abandon ship, he might condemn them to death.

His mind flashed to the ravine in Texas, to grasping for Oralee's hand. This impulse to protect—was it nothing but pride?

The ship slowed, and the bow rose to a twenty-degree angle.

If he wanted to act, he had to do so now, before the order to abandon ship.

He clutched the rim of the hatch. *Lord, what should I do?*

With his eyes shut, he could picture Oralee tottering on the footbridge. What if he hadn't reached out? She still would have fallen, but Wyatt would have had to live with the knowledge that he hadn't even tried.

His eyes flew open. "Director to captain. Request permission to stay with ship, with forward gun crews."

"We've lost computer control." The intercom crackled. "We're about to lose electrical power."

"Please, Captain. I know how to destroy that gun. Please, sir."

A long pause. "Very well. But no heroics. Get those men out of there."

"Aye aye, Captain. I will." He flipped the switch. "Guns one and two, stay at your stations even when the abandon ship order comes. Captain's orders. Switch to local manual fire. Aim a few yards below the battery. We're going to knock out its foundation. Commence rapid fire when ready."

"Aye aye, sir." Worry colored the gun captain's voice.

The klaxon clanged. "All hands abandon ship."

Wyatt yanked off his helmet and headphones. "Get out of here, boys. I'll see y'all in England."

He followed his men down through the hatch, grabbed a pair of binoculars on the bridge, and scrambled down the ladder to the forecastle deck. A stream of men tightened their life vests and filed to their abandon-ship stations.

Wyatt squirmed past them, climbing the tilted deck to the number two gun, which boomed out its shells.

He flung open the door to the gun compartment. Nine colored men were crammed inside the steel enclosure, pointing and training the gun, sliding projectiles and powder cartridges in the gun's breech, ramming them into place, and firing the gun.

Wyatt gripped the rim of the door and leaned in. "I'm staying here. I'll get y'all out in time. Meanwhile, keep on 'em."

"Aye aye, sir."

He climbed down the ladder on the side of the gun platform to the main deck and repeated his message to the number one crew.

Sailors pushed past him and climbed down the rope nets to the life rings.

Wyatt braced his feet wide and raised his binoculars. American and German shells crossed midair. The German shells tossed up springs of seawater astern, but the American shells dug into the earth below the concrete, dirt and rock gushing out.

Wyatt leaned into the number one compartment. "That's the way, men!"

A scraping sound, and the *Oglesby* vibrated to a stop. She'd grounded in the shallow waters. The bow settled lower, and Wyatt winced. They were running out of time.

Still the two guns fired, faster and faster.

The tilt of the deck lessened, and the water level rose. The men in the number one handling room were below decks—they had to get out now.

He hated to lose that gun, but he couldn't risk those men's lives.

Wyatt poked his head into the compartment.

The gun captain's eyes stretched wide. "Sir, the handling room is flooding."

"Get them out of there. All y'all. Abandon ship."

"Aye aye, sir." Not one sailor argued.

Wyatt stepped over to the number two gun. Since it was elevated above the number one, its handling room was on the main deck with Wyatt.

He peeked inside. Projectiles and cartridges lined racks, and sailors hoisted them to the gun compartment above. "Keep on 'em. It's working. I'll get y'all out in time."

Wyatt raised the binoculars. It was working indeed. The Germans had stopped firing. At the very least, he'd protected the GIs for an hour or so.

More dirt and rocks flew from below the Nazi gun.

His feet—they felt cold.

A thin stream of water flushed over the deck.

"Please, Lord. Just a few more shells."

One. Two. Three.

Wyatt groaned. He couldn't wait any longer. Other than the number two gun crew, not one man remained on the *Oglesby* that he could see.

And water sloshed into his shoes.

"Come on, men," he shouted into the handling room. "Get out of there. Abandon ship."

They hopped through the door and hightailed it to the rails.

Wyatt climbed the ladder to the gun compartment, the rungs slippery under his wet soles. The gun fired, and he lost his grip and fell to the main deck, cold water splashing his face.

"Get out, men! Abandon ship!" He clambered up the ladder and onto the gun platform. "Get out now!"

The men squeezed out the narrow door, and Wyatt clapped them each on the back as they passed. "Good job. We silenced that gun."

"We did more than that, sir." One of the sailors raised his thick, dark arm to the bluff, where the battery teetered over a gaping cavern.

A growling, ripping sound, and the battery tumbled down the cliff.

Wyatt gasped. It worked. It actually worked! He waved his fist in the air. "Yee-haw!"

A great creaking shuddered through the ship and pitched her to starboard.

Wyatt's feet slipped from underneath, and he tumbled over the deck, over the rails, cold water slapping his face, rushing over his head.

Yet only peace flooded his soul. He'd done the right thing and protected those soldiers. He'd done right by his family, and he was right with God. *"If I . . . dwell in the uttermost parts of the sea; Even there . . . thy right hand shall hold me."*

Wyatt reached out to grab hold. It was a good way to die.

44

Dorothy signed the document, her head swimming with resignation and exhaustion. The sunlight through the windows of the intelligence office was only now starting to dim at 2130. Other than visits to the lavatory and a brief break at teatime, she hadn't left her station all day.

"A long day, wasn't it?" Lawrence pulled up a chair beside her.

Dorothy folded the document. "Not as long as for the men on the far shore."

"Indeed not." Lawrence's face darkened, then brightened. "But we've achieved success. All five landing beaches have been secured for the most part, and reinforcements are arriving."

"Thank God." She scooted her chair back to stand.

Lawrence laid his hand on her forearm and gave her one of his famous smiles. "After everything returns to normal, you and I will celebrate over a fine dinner."

Her transfer could take weeks, leaving time for a number of fine dinners, but would it be enough time to gain a wedding ring? Her exhaustion deepened at the thought of those dates.

Lawrence's gaze roamed her bare cheeks.

If she were to marry him, she'd have a lifetime of covering her freckles, doing dangerous things to please him, and stifling her stories and laughter.

Her head shook from side to side, her emotions making the decision before her mind did, but her mind followed suit. Why had she been willing to trust her future in Lawrence's flawed, reckless hands and not in the Lord's perfect, caring hands?

It all became clear. She wouldn't marry this exciting wealthy man or any man of means once the company went bankrupt. After the war, she'd find some sort of job and support Papa as long as the Lord let him live.

Warm peace settled in her chest.

"You must be tired." Lawrence patted her arm.

Her gaze found him. "I'm sorry, but I won't step out with you again. Not ever."

"Pardon?" He blinked rapidly.

Dorothy eased her arm out from under his hand. "You aren't interested in me for who I am, and you never will be. I laugh too much, talk too much, and I'm not one bit sophisticated. I do love excitement, but I don't like danger. And I have gobs of freckles."

Lawrence's mouth hung open. Had the man ever been rendered speechless before?

She patted his arm this time. "If I can't be loved for who I am, I'd rather be alone."

His gaze cut away. "I never mentioned love."

Then he definitely wasn't the man for her. She gave him a warm smile. "I'm so glad I won't leave you heartbroken."

Dorothy stood and crossed the barren office. She had paperwork to deliver.

First Officer Bliss-Baldwin entered, and her gaze darted between Dorothy and Lawrence.

No more of this nonsense. She held out the transfer request. "Ma'am, here's the paperwork."

Bliss marched to her office. "I must confess, I'm surprised you kept your promise."

Dorothy cringed, followed the woman, and closed the door behind her. "You have every right not to trust my word, ma'am."

The first officer faced her, eyes sparking. "You lied to your commanding officer?"

She measured her words. "I didn't tell a falsehood, ma'am, but I allowed you to believe one."

Her mouth opened and shut. "Explain yourself."

Dorothy fingered the papers in her hand. "Lieutenant Commander Eaton is indeed an old family friend, and my father is doing poorly and does need me. But I allowed you to believe there was no romantic interest, which wasn't true."

Her cheeks turned pink. "You—"

"We had precisely three dates. The first was fine, the second was an utter fiasco, and the third ended before it started. Even if I weren't transferring, there would not be a fourth date. I've discovered the lieutenant commander . . . he isn't the right sort of man for me."

Blissy flattened her fingers on her desktop. "You defied my orders."

"With all respect, ma'am, Wrens are not prohibited from dating naval officers. However, for you to forbid me to date the lieutenant commander for personal reasons most definitely violates regulations, as does punishing the girls he steps out with and forcing them to transfer."

The first officer spun to the window and tugged the blackout curtains in place.

"Regardless," Dorothy said, "I apologize, and I'm willing to take the consequences."

"What consequences?" Her voice shook. "If you pursue this, I'll be the one facing consequences."

For the second time that day, the power had shifted to Dorothy, but she didn't want it. Compassion for the woman swelled inside her. She understood the desperation to win Lawrence's heart, the willingness to violate regulations to do so. Hadn't Dorothy been willing to change her own essence?

The swelling constricted her throat, and she swallowed to loosen it. Then she laid the papers on the desk. "Ma'am, here's my transfer request. Please accept it as both my punishment and my apology. Please forgive me."

Bliss-Baldwin lowered her head. She bunched up the blackout curtains in her fingers.

Something built inside Dorothy, roaring to the surface, a combination of indignation and conviction. "Pardon me for speaking freely, ma'am, but what sort of man deliberately puts women in such predicaments?"

Bliss gasped and glanced over her shoulder.

For one moment, something passed between them—the shock of realization and pain and regret—but then the first officer's face went flat. "Dismissed."

"Aye aye, ma'am." Dorothy turned and left.

Thank goodness Lawrence had departed. Dorothy headed downstairs to the operations room. One final check for the latest news and she'd return to quarters.

The large wall map was stagnant. Now that the generals were ashore, the Allied Naval Expeditionary Force had proceeded to its next phase. The warships would provide gunfire support as long as the front lines remained in range, but now the main naval role was to transport troops and supplies in a quick and orderly manner.

On one of the plotting tables, grease pencil arrows on the clear Perspex over the map showed the day's advances. The Americans had taken Vierville at 1100—from behind, by the soldiers climbing the bluffs, but the hold on the beach was tenuous. At the other four beaches, the Allies had made greater progress—but they'd faced far less resistance.

Commanders Pringle and Marino came to the table, and Dorothy inched to the side.

"You Yanks certainly rip plans to pieces." Commander Pringle waved his hand over the map.

Commander Marino clapped the British officer on the back. "You know full well no plan stands after bullets start flying."

He chuckled. "True."

"And when the plans fall apart, you rely on initiative, ingenuity, and sheer guts."

"I'll credit you Yanks for that. And your destroyers—fine work they did today."

"That they did."

Dorothy leaned closer, holding her breath.

"I was skeptical." Commander Pringle crossed his arms. "Charging in, firing willy-nilly—"

"Not willy-nilly. Only at known targets. And they blasted them away."

Commander Pringle chuckled. "Wish I could have seen the *Oglesby* going down shooting. A fine sight that must have been."

Dorothy sucked in a breath. "The—the *Oglesby*?"

The men turned to her and sobered.

She moistened her lips and braced her hand on the table. "The *Oglesby*—she sank?"

"Yes, ma'am." Commander Marino's brown eyes softened. "She was exchanging fire with a gun battery. We believe she took two shells. The Coast Guard cutters rescued most of the men."

"Wyatt?" she choked out. "Wyatt Paxton?"

He rubbed the back of his neck. "We don't have the names of the survivors yet."

Her other hand grasped for the table. The commander hadn't offered any consolation such as "but I'm sure he's fine."

"You said . . . she went down . . . shooting?" Her vision was fuzzy, her mouth dry.

"Yes, ma'am. That's the word. She kept firing until the guns went under. And she knocked that battery clean off the bluff."

Wyatt had gone down shooting.

He'd gone down doing his duty, doing the right thing.

How very like him.

How very fitting.

How horribly, tragically wrong.

45

Wyatt ambled down the passageway in the Nissen hut. "How's it feel to be a survivor of the Gunfight at the *Ogie* Corral?"

Jack sent him a searing look. "Should've let you drown."

Wyatt laughed and thumped his buddy on the back. "I'm glad you didn't."

That was the longest minute of Wyatt's life, tumbling around underwater. Once he'd figured out which way was up, he'd kicked off his shoes and stretched up to the surface. His life vest kept him bobbing for about fifteen minutes in the frigid water until a Coast Guardsman fished him out. Jack was on board the cutter. He'd insisted they stick around and search for the gun crew. They'd found all but one man—Luther Jackson, a mess steward, an ammunition handler, and a hero.

Jack opened the door to Commander Marino's office. The commander leapt to his feet and pumped Jack's and Wyatt's hands. "Good to see you boys."

"Good to see you too, sir," Wyatt said.

"How are you?"

"Not a scratch, sir," Jack said.

Wyatt patted his shoulder and winced. "Few stitches, nothing bad."

"Well, I'm glad to see you both intact. Have a seat." He gestured to two wooden chairs, then sat behind his desk, grinning. "The *Ogie* sure made a name for herself."

Jack pointed his thumb at Wyatt. "All Mr. Paxton's doing."

"Nonsense. The whole crew worked together." Still, he allowed himself to accept the praise and the success. Father God did like to lavish gifts on his returning prodigals.

"I felt useless since we couldn't contact our SFCP," Jack said.

"Few of the destroyers did." Marino's grin collapsed. "Too many of the men were killed. Those who lived—a lot of the radios were lost or damaged. The only place it worked well was at Pointe du Hoc. The *Satterlee* and her SFCP did phenomenal work."

A sharp pain in Wyatt's chest. The Rangers had taken horrendous losses at Pointe du Hoc. How long until he knew if Clay had survived?

Commander Marino rocked his chair onto its back legs, his arms crossed. "You've probably heard the Navy's taking a bit of heat from some, saying we failed in the bombardment."

"Yes, sir." But no shame weighed him down. They'd done the best they could.

Marino huffed. "Given more time, we could have done better, but then we'd have blown our surprise. In the future, we'll have to find a position in the middle."

Jack sighed. "Maybe if we'd had an hour and a half as the British had."

"Maybe." Marino's front chair legs thumped to the floor, and he leaned his forearms on the desk. "But one thing I know, Des-Ron 18 did a bang-up job. Up and down Omaha Beach, charging close to shore, blasting away those guns, finding targets the best you could with little contact with the men on shore. Did you hear what Gerow said? Maj. Gen. Leonard Gerow, commander of US

V Corps? When he landed at Omaha late on D-day, he radioed General Bradley at sea—'Thank God for the United States Navy.'"

Wyatt smiled. "That's right nice to hear, sir."

"It sure is. They know. Our boys on the ground know you helped them get off the beaches when all was lost." Marino slapped the desk. "That is teamwork."

"It was worth it, sir." Wyatt's chest tightened. Fourteen men on the *Oglesby* had been killed, most in the initial explosions. The Navy considered the casualties light, but they felt heavy to Wyatt.

However, no regret accompanied his grief. His decision had led to success. But regardless of results, it was the right decision—even if every man on board had died, even if there hadn't been a gun in that shack, even if they hadn't silenced that battery.

He'd chosen to protect. He'd reached out, and he'd continue to reach out no matter what.

"You'll receive new orders soon." Marino opened a folder on his desk. "You were both meant to be on the far shore a while longer, but we'll straighten things out."

"Thank you, sir." Where would he go next? And when? No word from his brothers yet. Even if the mail had been released, they hadn't had time to receive it and respond. If only he could see them before he left England.

"Mr. Paxton, maybe you can solve a mystery." Marino gave him half a smile.

"A mystery, sir?"

"That shack, the one you blasted away—was it black?"

Memories jumbled together. "Not in color, sir. More like a . . . symbol. How did you know about that?"

"One of the Wrens—Fairfax—she was adamant that the shack was a target. She wanted us to send you a radio message that the shack was black. Said you'd know what it meant."

"I would, sir." It meant Dorothy Fairfax had survived all the blows she'd received and had pulled herself together.

And she'd thought of him.

"She was pretty upset when she found out the *Oglesby* had gone down. Don't worry—yesterday I let her know you survived."

Relief flowed out in a long sigh. "Thank you, sir."

Marino fingered the family portrait on his desk and grinned at Wyatt. "She's a friend?"

A friend. "Yes, sir." His voice sank lower than he'd intended.

An urge rose inside to visit her, to assure her he was alive, to thank her for even thinking of sending him a message.

But reason squelched the urge. Reason and a sense of peace. Dorothy was going to be fine, and that chapter of his life had closed. It was time to move on.

46

In a fine slanting rain in the low evening light, Dorothy stood outside her house. She hadn't been home in almost three weeks, but it felt longer.

The invasion had succeeded. All five beachheads were secure, and the Allies were pushing inland. Her job was almost finished.

In the drawing room window, the curtain swished. In a moment, the door flew open. Papa stood on the threshold, gaping at her. "You came back."

Never once had he met her at the door. "This is my home, and you're my father."

"Well, come in. Come out of the rain." He stepped back, his hand still on the doorknob.

Dorothy climbed the steps. Was it her imagination, or did he have more color in his cheeks? She eased past her father, set her hat on the coatrack, and untied the belt on her raincoat. "How have you been?"

"I didn't think you'd come home." His voice sounded husky. "I wouldn't blame you. Why come home to a father who doesn't love you?"

She cringed at her own words. "I shouldn't have said that." A cold breeze shackled her ankles, and she reached around her father and shut the door. "It's raining, Papa."

He grasped her shoulders, his fingers digging in, his eyes awash with emotions she'd never seen before. "Yes, you should have said that. I needed to hear. I needed to know what I'd done."

Dorothy couldn't speak, and she fumbled for the buttons of her coat. This wasn't like him at all.

Papa's face contorted, and his cheeks reddened. "Oh, my Dolly. My sweet little Dolly." He crushed her in an embrace.

She stared up over his shoulder, stiff and confused, the wooly smell of his jumper pulling her back to her childhood, to her father's knee. When was the last time he'd hugged her, called her Dolly? Her face buckled, and a sob swelled in her throat. "Papa—"

"I do love you," he said in a fierce voice. "I have always loved you. But how could you know? How could you when I barely talked to you, barely looked at you?"

"I—I understand why you didn't."

"No." He pulled back and gripped her shoulders again, his eyes red and blue and intense. "You're wrong."

Her head bobbled back and forth, trying to understand, trying to comprehend this strange sight.

A howl rose from the back door, and a scrabbling sound.

"Charlie." Papa glanced over his shoulder.

"Poor thing's out in the rain. You let him in, I'll get out of my wet things, and then I'll make us a spot of tea. Mrs. Bromley's left for the night, hasn't she?"

"Yes. Yes, she has." Papa darted down the hall to the back door.

Dorothy swiped the moisture from her eyes and took off her coat with shaky fingers. What was happening? Papa loved her? Why did those words only send more questions pinging around in her fuzzy head?

Tea. They both needed tea.

Papa knelt at the back door, toweling off the little black dog.

In the kitchen, Dorothy filled the kettle with water, then set it on the stove to boil.

Tiny taps on the floor behind her, then paws scratched at her calf.

"My poppet." Before he could ruin her stockings, Dorothy crouched down and rubbed him behind his ears. "Have you been a good boy while I was gone?"

"You're wrong about why I ignored you." Papa stood in the kitchen doorway, taller and stronger than she'd seen him in years.

"I'll make the tea." She grabbed her favorite Blue Willow teapot and rinsed it with water.

"Listen to me. It had nothing to do with your mother."

Dorothy's vision blurred, but she popped open the nearest tin of tea. "Darjeeling?"

"I lost my wife, my sons, and my best friend. I couldn't abide the thought of losing you too. I—I loved you too much."

Her fingers found the drawer handle, slid it open, and groped for a teaspoon.

A chair scraped across the floor, then creaked. "I know I never paid you much attention. I didn't know what to do with a girl. I—I didn't have sisters. And you seemed so happy with your nanny and your brothers and your little friends."

Dorothy spooned tea leaves into the pot. Now she had to wait for the water to boil. But she couldn't see, couldn't compose herself. Perhaps there were some biscuits in the larder.

"Suddenly you were all I had." Papa's voice dropped and shattered.

The shards pierced Dorothy's heart, and she spun to face him. "Papa . . ."

He sat hunched over the table, his forehead in his hands, his head shaking. "God had taken everyone I loved. I—maybe if I ignored you, he wouldn't see how much I loved you. Then I wouldn't lose you too."

"Oh, Papa." She dashed to the table and sat across from him. "Sounds preposterous."

"No." She pressed her hand over her quivering mouth. No more preposterous than believing she could stay out of God's reach.

"And I . . . I . . ." His fingers curled in, his knuckles taut. "I was trying to protect myself. If I kept my distance, maybe it wouldn't hurt so much if you died too."

A sob gurgled in her throat, and she stretched her hand across the table, but she couldn't reach her father. Charlie whimpered and pawed at his master's leg.

"I was wrong." Papa lowered his fists to the table and glared at them. "The past few weeks I thought I'd lost you forever. And it hurt. It hurt. I hadn't protected myself at all. I'd only hurt you."

Her fingertips found his fist, and she wrapped her hand around it.

He dragged his gaze up to her, slammed his eyes shut, then opened them—full of remorse. "You—you lost your mother and brothers. Then you lost me too."

She squeezed his fist. "I—I always had you."

His cheeks twitched. "Not as you needed me. You needed me to be warm—I was cold. You needed me to be strong—I was weak. You needed me to provide for you—I didn't. You've been the one holding us together, holding me together, nagging me to eat and go to the office. I am . . . so ashamed."

"Oh, Papa, Papa, Papa." Her heart broke for him, and she grabbed both of his fists, shaking them in her grip.

"No more." His fingers clawed open and enveloped her hands in his. "That has all changed. I'm eating as much as I can. I've gone to work every day. I will be strong again. For you."

That strength poured through his hands to hers, from his eyes to hers, from his heart to hers, and her cheek tickled from a tear she couldn't wipe away.

"What hurt most . . . you thought I couldn't look at you because of your mother." He squeezed so tight her knuckles rubbed together. "My sweet, sweet Dolly, you may look like her, you may have her high spirits, but you're nothing like her inside."

She lowered her chin, wanting to reject his words, wanting even more to accept them.

"That woman is selfish and disloyal. You—you, my girl, are generous and faithful. Look how you've cared for me all these years. You never abandoned me. You never ridiculed me."

Truth coursed warm throughout her. She might be like her mother in many ways, but she'd made better choices. And she would continue to do so.

"Dolly. My Dolly. You are tender and kind and thoughtful. You are nothing—nothing like that woman."

She managed a nod and slid her hands free. "That's what Wyatt said."

"He's a good man."

Dorothy dashed for the larder. Biscuits. Biscuits. Where were the biscuits? There was so little food on the shelves. Papa really had been eating well. "He—he was quite the hero on D-day. His ship sank—but he—he survived."

"Thank goodness. Have you seen him?"

Never again, and her chest convulsed. She grasped the shelf for support.

A little loaf of war bread rested before her, wrapped in a napkin, and she clutched it to her chest. Memories ground up the kind words from the two men she loved and kneaded them into old, cruel truths. "I am like Mum. I am."

"Dorothy?"

She stepped out of the larder and faced her father and her short-comings. "I am like Mum in one horrible way. You—you're a good man, and she threw you over for a rogue. I—Wyatt is a good man, but I ignored him and chased after Lawrence."

Papa's face darkened. "Now there's a rogue."

A whooshing sound rose from the teakettle, and Dorothy removed it from the stove. "You never liked him."

"He had no regard for others. I spent too much time apologizing for his shenanigans in Normandy. I spent too much money paying for the damage he caused on his sprees. He didn't care that he put people at risk. He only cared about his own fun."

As she poured water into the teapot, Dorothy pulled back from the steam and from Papa's words. Lawrence hadn't changed one whit. "You'll be happy to know I've thrown *him* over."

"As I said, you're nothing like your mother. Wyatt is a far better man."

Dorothy stared down at the war bread, still in her hand. "It's too late. I offered him crumbs when he deserves the whole loaf."

"I don't understand."

"I love him, but it's too late. I lost my chance forever."

A soft rumble sounded in Papa's throat. "Don't be so sure. A man like that—his feelings run deep and strong."

So many memories—Wyatt always there, taking her to church, going to the office, singing to her, telling her he loved her, kissing her with wild passion. Why had she waited so long . . . too long? If only she could see him one more time. She'd never told him she loved him.

"Did he really go all the way up to Edinburgh with you?" Papa lifted Charlie to his lap.

Dorothy hauled in a breath, set down the loaf, and pulled two teacups and saucers from the cupboard. "He was training in Greenock and met me there. He's the one who solved the mystery."

"Then I owe him."

Dorothy set the china on the table. "What good does it do if you don't prosecute?"

"I don't want to. Not only do I not want the scandal, but I don't want vengeance. I don't care to see them in prison."

He was far more merciful than they deserved, but she loved him for it. "All right. But even if you don't want vengeance, don't you want justice? The theft needs to stop."

Papa stroked Charlie's fur. "It's impossible to have justice without scandal. Impossible. Mac knows I can't withstand it."

Gears turned in her mind. She fetched the teapot from the stove and the milk from the icebox, and she set them on the table. "You're strong enough to withstand the scandal, I know it. If we lean on each other and we lean on the Lord, we can endure anything."

"You're a good daughter." His voice roughened, and his face fell. "But you have too much faith in me."

"What if . . ." Dorothy plopped into the chair and drummed her fingers on the table in tempo with her ideas. "Mr. MacLeod believes you can't endure scandal. But what if he believed you could? What if you assured him you could endure it very well indeed?"

Papa's face scrunched up in confusion.

Dorothy patted the table and smiled. "He'd lose his power. You could have justice without revenge, without scandal."

"I don't see how."

"I do." She sprang from her chair and flung up her arms in a dramatic pose. "All you need to do is a few minutes of playacting."

47

The lobby of Fairfax & Sons brought up a host of memories of Dorothy—going to church, looking at the accounts, seeing her pretty smile.

Wyatt had told himself he was visiting Mr. Fairfax to say good-bye, but he had to admit the visit was a sneaky way to find out how Dorothy was doing. He just hoped the man was in the office.

A soft-eyed brunette sat behind the desk outside Mr. Fairfax's office, and Wyatt gave her a nod. "Good morning, ma'am. Is Mr. Fairfax here? I was wondering if I could see him."

"He is here." Her accent sounded almost German. "May I ask your name, sir?"

"Lt. Wyatt Paxton."

Her hand hovered over the phone, and she smiled. "Dorothy's friend?"

He searched the limited space for names in his memory bank. "Yes, ma'am."

"I am called Johanna Katin. I'm—"

"Dorothy's friend." He grinned at her. "She speaks highly of you."

"She speaks highly of you too." A light flashed in her dark eyes as if she'd had an idea. Then she lowered her chin and frowned. "But she is sad."

His breath caught. "Sad? Why? What happened?"

"She . . ." Johanna traced her finger over the phone receiver. "She is worried about you."

"Me?" Marino had told her he survived. "Does she think I was hurt?"

"She does not know."

Wyatt eyed Mr. Fairfax's door. "Good thing I came. Her dad can tell her I'm okay."

"Oh. She . . ." Johanna tilted her head, and her fingertip hopped between the holes in the phone dial. "She is sad because she . . . I saw her last weekend, and she was sad. Yes. She wished she could see you again."

"To say good-bye?" His chest constricted. They hadn't had a proper good-bye in Edinburgh.

"She is your friend and you want to see her, yes?"

"Yes." Then he shook his head. He did want to see her, but it wasn't wise.

"Oh! She will be happy. She's at her headquarters. You know where, yes?" She rose from her chair.

Wyatt's mouth hung open. He hadn't said he'd visit Dorothy, but now . . .

Johanna opened the office door. "Excuse me, Mr. Fairfax? Mr. Lieutenant Paxton is here."

"Lieutenant . . ." Mr. Fairfax darted out of the office with a wide smile. "Wyatt, my boy. How good to see you."

"It's good to see you too, sir." He shook the man's hand, amazed. Mr. Fairfax's face had filled out and lost the sallow tone.

"Well, come in. Come in. Thank you, Miss Katin." He ushered Wyatt inside and shut the door. "What brings you here?"

The man seemed almost as sprightly as his daughter. Wyatt lowered himself into a chair. "I had a meeting in London yesterday, stayed the night. I'm leaving England soon. I wanted to say good-bye, thank you for your hospitality and friendship."

"It was my honor." Mr. Fairfax sat behind his desk, his expression serious again. "I'm glad you came. I need to thank you for discovering who was stealing from my company. Quite a rude shock to learn my former friend and my former wife had stooped so low."

Wyatt's mouth flopped open. "She—Dorothy told you all that?"

Mr. Fairfax waved one hand before him. "I already knew Margaret was alive. I've known all along."

"Oh." If the man had known his wife faked her own death to leave him, that explained the depths of his grief.

"But—" Mr. Fairfax raised half a smile—"thanks to your keen mind and my Dorothy's cleverness, the embezzlement has been stopped."

"They've been arrested?"

"No. I had no desire to see them imprisoned, and a trial would have created a scandal. I didn't know if I could withstand it."

"I understand, sir."

Mr. Fairfax leaned his forearms on his desk. "Dorothy realized MacLeod's plan hinged on my fear of scandal. What if we unscrewed the hinges?"

As if he needed any reason to admire Dorothy more. "What did you do?"

"First I rang Mr. Campbell at the Edinburgh office. I had him remove the invoices from Forthwright and the carbon copies of the checks and take them to my solicitor's office for safekeeping. Then I gave my old chum a ring." Mr. Fairfax laid his hand on his phone with a faint smile.

Wyatt echoed that smile. "Surprised to hear from you?"

"Quite. I told him I knew what he and Margaret had done. And I told him in no uncertain terms that I would gladly endure any scandal to see justice served. A tiny bit of playacting."

Dorothy's idea, no doubt. "I reckon that surprised him even more."

Mr. Fairfax laughed, a sound Wyatt had never heard that he could remember. "I must admit, his shock did satisfy my thirst for vengeance."

Wyatt chuckled. He would have enjoyed it too.

"Then I offered him a way out. If he offered his resignation straightaway, that would be the end of it. But if he refused, I'd ring Scotland Yard—and I had the evidence hidden away."

"He took the bait."

"He did. He resigned that moment."

"I'm glad it ended well."

"It did for me and for the company." He ran his hand over his hair, and his expression turned pensive. "MacLeod will make do. He'll find a new position. But Margaret won't fare so well, now that he doesn't need her anymore. She'll be out of a home."

Wyatt puckered his lips. A middle-aged woman on her own without job skills, without proper papers?

"I will provide for her." He smoothed the blotting pad on his desk. "I've set up an account. My solicitor will provide her a modest allowance and a comfortable flat. Not the style she's accustomed to, but that was her choice when she left me."

The hardness of the man's voice couldn't hide the softness of his heart. "That's right kind of you, sir."

He raised one eyebrow at Wyatt. "Truth be told, it's selfish of me. I don't want her to return. I refuse to take her back. She's legally dead, so I no longer have any obligation. However, in the eyes of God, she's my wife, and I will take care of her."

What beautiful, merciful irony—this man providing a livelihood for the woman who'd tried to steal his away.

"I loved her once." He gazed over Wyatt's head. "Very much. I will always be indebted to her for giving me three of the best children to grace this earth."

Wyatt swallowed hard. "That is something to be thankful for."

Mr. Fairfax's gaze drifted to Wyatt, gentle yet strong. "I wish you could have known Art and Gil. You would have gotten on famously. Fine young men."

He'd never heard the sons' names out of the father's mouth before, and Wyatt could only nod.

"And Dorothy . . ." Mr. Fairfax's voice cracked, and redness swept over his face. Then he shook himself. "I don't know what I would have done without her. She's a great gift."

"I hope you tell her that."

"She knows now. She knows how very much I love her." He mashed his lips together, his eyes hazy.

Wyatt's nose stuffed up. Somehow all this madness hadn't destroyed the Fairfax family—somehow it had led to healing.

Mr. Fairfax's eyes cleared. "She also knows I am standing on my own again. I refuse to be a burden to her any longer. I have apologized for neglecting my duties as a man and as a father. I will no longer hold her back. She is free to go where she chooses."

"That—that's good, sir." Why did he feel those words were directed at him? "Knowing her, she'll choose to be where you are."

He nodded, rolling a pen along the top of his desk. "You're leaving England? When?"

"Few weeks, sir."

More nodding, more rolling. "Since you're leaving, I'm in no danger of embarrassing my daughter. I must admit, I once entertained the hope you'd become my son-in-law. And I could always use a good accountant."

A punch to his gut. Wyatt had entertained a similar hope. He raised a polite smile. "Thank you, sir, but it wasn't meant to be."

SOUTHWICK HOUSE

One long day of good-byes. Wyatt climbed the staircase at South-wick House that afternoon. Johanna had put him in a bind. What if she told Dorothy that Wyatt planned to visit her—and he didn't?

But mostly, curiosity drove him. Johanna had painted a portrait of Dorothy in blue, but Mr. Fairfax used tones of sunny daffodil yellow. Which was it?

Besides, Johanna had a point. Dorothy was his friend, and he wanted to see her one last time. After all they'd been through, she deserved a better good-bye than she'd received in Edinburgh.

He paused outside the door to the intelligence office. *Lord, give me the right words.* He had to make it clear he wasn't pursuing her. What good would it do with him leaving soon?

One more prayer and he entered the office.

Dorothy had her back to him, talking with her two friends and waving one hand as if telling a story. And she laughed, like cool water on his dry throat. She didn't look sad at all. She looked mighty good.

Her dark-haired friend—Myrtle?—she spotted Wyatt and tapped Dorothy on the shoulder.

She spun around, eyes and mouth round. "Wy—Lieutenant Paxton. It—it's good to see you." She didn't move.

So Wyatt did. He strolled over to her with a smile, although his heart skittered around like a jackrabbit. "It's good to see you too."

She looked impossibly pretty, her freckles peeking out from under a light coat of face powder. "Why are you here?"

Why? Because he didn't have to be back in Plymouth till Monday. Because he cared more about her than about saving face.

"How silly of me." She lowered her chin. "Of course. You have paperwork, meetings."

"Um, yeah." But not at Southwick. "Thought I'd come say hi."

Dorothy glanced up with a little smile. "I'm glad you did. And I—I'm glad you survived. I'm so sorry about your ship."

"Thank you, but she did her job. Thanks to you."

"Me?" Long eyelashes fluttered. "I didn't do anything."

"But you did. Remember that drawing with the black shack? I remembered it on D-day. There was a big old German gun inside. We blew it to kingdom come."

"Really?" Could those eyes get any bigger, any bluer, any more gorgeous?

"Really. But I—" He winced. "I'm afraid I blew up your house too. I'm real sorry about that."

To his shock, she smiled. "I'm glad you did. It needed to be done."

This was no ordinary woman, and love for her strained inside his chest. "It did need to be done. Once we knocked out the house and the shack, our troops were able to advance."

"I'm glad." Her gaze wandered around his face.

He took the liberty of studying her face as well. She'd never looked better—peaceful, in good spirits, if a bit ruffled to see him.

Seeing her soothed an ache and yet created a deeper ache. How he would miss her.

He cleared his throat. "I also—I came to say good-bye. I got my orders. I'm leaving England soon."

"You are? Where—"

"Well, if it isn't the gunslinger." Commander Pringle marched over and shook Wyatt's hand. "We can't stop talking about how the *Oglesby* went down in a blaze of glory."

"Thank you, sir." It hadn't felt glorious at all.

More officers gathered around, including Eaton, but Wyatt kept his smile propped in place.

"Now we can hear the story from the horse's mouth." Pringle crossed his arms. "Go ahead, my boy. Nothing makes an old sailor happier than a sea yarn."

"Uh . . ." Wyatt glanced around, but Dorothy had disappeared from the room. His shoulders slumped. His presence probably reminded her of the worst night of her life, of a kiss she most likely regretted.

"Less of a sea yarn," Eaton said. "More like one of your Western movies. Tell me, Lieutenant, were you a cowboy back in the States?"

"No, sir. An accountant."

The officers laughed.

The attention made him uncomfortable, but he told his tale. No embellishment, no exaggeration, just the facts. They asked questions, pried for more, and he did his best. If only Dorothy could have told the story with all her voices and gestures and enthusiasm.

But she'd skedaddled.

After a few minutes, the officers shook his hand, told him he'd made a jolly good show of it, and left him alone.

Alone. He drew a long breath and smoothed his jacket. He'd completed his mission. Dorothy was better than fine, and he'd said thank you and good-bye. It was time to leave and open the next chapter of his life.

He turned for the door and stopped.

Dorothy stood in the doorway, staring at him with her eyes stretched wide and her lips tucked in tight.

She looked terrified. Why on earth? He gave her a questioning look, but her eyes only got rounder.

She clutched something in front of her stomach. What was it? Looked like a roll that would make a nice pulled pork sandwich.

A loaf?

A whole loaf.

48

If the loaf of National Wheatmeal hadn't been as stale as a stone, Dorothy would have crushed it to bits. This slithering sense of nakedness and helplessness and fear and mortification—was this how Wyatt had felt when he'd told her he loved her?

He stared at the loaf, furrows dividing his forehead.

Then he snapped his gaze up to her, piercing, unbending, probing.

Oh dear. She couldn't withstand the scrutiny. She dashed to the worktable, where Gwen and Muriel sorted envelopes for filing. She set down the bread and blindly grabbed an envelope.

Gwen chuckled. "Hungry, Dorothy?"

She shook her head and shuffled envelopes. What had she done? What must he be thinking?

Solid footsteps approached. Wyatt's warm presence hovered behind her, and a broad hand settled on the loaf.

Her cheeks flamed, and she rearranged envelopes. All week she'd kept that little loaf in her handbag in her locker downstairs, dreaming of this opportunity. Now he'd come. But now her gesture seemed utterly ridiculous.

"For me?" Wyatt's voice sounded clipped and raspy.

Her chin bobbed in response, but she couldn't look at him.

"Come with me. Please." Then he left the office.

She stifled a groan. Now she'd hear it. But at least she could tell him everything. With a lurch, she followed him.

"Dorothy?" Gwen called after her.

"I'll be back."

Wyatt was already halfway down the stairs.

She scampered after him. "Oh, Wyatt. I'm so sorry. You were right when you said I threw you crumbs, and I was wrong to do so. You're the best sort of man, and I—I'm sorry it took me so long to realize it."

Wyatt didn't glance back at her. He strode down the hallway, and she could barely keep up with his long-legged pace.

She jogged a few steps to close the gap. "I want you to know it's over with Lawrence. I told him most emphatically. If only it hadn't taken me so long to realize how much I love you."

A hitch in his step, then he resumed his pace.

"I do, Wyatt. I love you so very much. You're the kindest, sweetest man, and you're so good to me. You always have been. You deserve more than crumbs. You deserve the whole loaf, the whole bakery."

He flung open the door and paused and looked around.

Dorothy ran to his side. "Please say something."

He shook his head, his gaze darting around the grounds.

"Wyatt, please." She touched his forearm. "Say something. Tell me you hate me, tell me you love me. Something."

He looked her full in the eye, startled, as if he'd forgotten she was there. Then he tugged on his cap, grabbed her hand, and marched across the lawn.

She struggled to keep up. Where was he taking her? Someplace private to give her a piece of his mind? Before he could, she'd give him all the pieces of her heart.

Dorothy watched her footing. "I was wrong when I said I'd ruin you. I was afraid I'd treat you like my mum treated my father. I love you too much to risk that. But Papa showed me the truth. I may be like her in some respects, but I've never been cruel to Papa, and I could never be cruel to you."

Still not a word, still the brisk pace toward a copse of trees.

She held tight to his hand, so strong and warm and firm. "I also want you to know I'd leave England for you. I'd go anywhere to be with you. Papa is doing so well since we stopped Mr. MacLeod. And we did—we did stop him."

Wyatt slowed as they entered the copse.

Dorothy followed him through the trees and over the underbrush. "Papa—well, he's the man he was before the war. He'll be fine on his own, and he wants me to be happy. He told—"

Wyatt wheeled to her.

She bumped into his chest and took a step back. The way he stared at her, so many emotions she couldn't pick one apart from the other. "Oh, would you please say something?"

He nodded a few times, then he folded her in his arms and kissed her.

She gasped from the suddenness of it. But then she melted into his embrace, unwrapping the emotions one at a time, each a gift—the surprise, the joy, the love. He didn't kiss her with the hungry urgency of Edinburgh but with confident assurance. Without a word, he'd told her he'd forgiven her foolishness and he loved her as much as ever.

She drew back so she could see that love in his eyes. A breeze cooled her warm cheeks, and she pulled off his cap and smoothed his soft hair. "Say that again, please."

His smile rose, long and slow, and he kissed her again, long and slow and even better than she'd imagined, accepting her, lingering in her company, and reveling in their love.

Why had she longed for Peter Pan and Neverland? Now she had a grown man with his feet on the earth, a man who'd never endanger her but always protect her, a partner for the adventures and the routines, the joys and the sorrows.

She sighed and rested her cheek on his shoulder, over his heart, and the pounding echoed her own. "Tell me all about Texas."

"You're serious?"

"I'd go anywhere in the world to be with you."

He kissed the top of her bare head. "After this war's over, I'll come back to London and marry you, then . . ."

Marry? She lifted her head. "Are you . . . proposing?"

His face scrunched up. "I—I didn't mean to. Not yet. Not like that."

She stroked his cheek and the long white scar. "But you want to? Oh, Wyatt."

He lowered his forehead to touch hers. "Someday I'll make a more romantic proposal than that. I promise."

He always kept his word, and her mouth quivered. "And someday . . . someday I'll be honored to accept."

"All right, then." He pressed her head back down to his shoulder, his voice husky. "You know my intentions. Reckon there's something to be said for that."

She squeezed him. He loved her enough to want to spend his whole life with her. She'd gladly trade romance for that assurance. "There is."

"So, Lord willing, after the war I'll make you my wife. Then we'll visit Texas so you can meet my daddy and mama."

"And your brothers? Have you heard from them?"

He caressed her hair. "No. The mail was impounded for D-day. But I've been away from Plymouth a few days. Maybe I'll have letters waiting for me. I hope so. I'm worried about Clay. The Rangers took a beating. And Adler—fighter pilots are always in danger."

"I'm sure they're fine, and I know they'll forgive you."

He kissed her forehead. "You know, a man can do a lot in life when the woman he loves has faith in him."

She fingered the gilt buttons on his jacket. "I do."

Another kiss to her forehead, sliding down to the tip of her nose. "Even if my brothers never forgive me, I'll be fine. God forgave me, which is all that matters. And my parents forgave me, which is a gift."

"They'll be so happy to see you."

"It'll be good to go home for a visit."

"A visit?" She frowned and raised her head.

He wore a serious, decisive look that suited him well. "I'm not needed at Paxton Trucking. My dad needs a man like him to take the helm—a man like Adler. I've decided to let him take the place Dad meant for me. He'll do a much better job than I would."

She searched his face for anxiety but saw none. "What will you do?"

Wyatt shrugged, and mischief sparkled in his eyes. "I'll take the job offer I received this morning—from your dad."

"My dad?"

"It wasn't a serious offer, but I reckon he'd be glad to make it serious."

"I don't understand."

"You're cute when you're confused." He pressed a quick kiss to her lips. "I was in London for a meeting. I went to your dad's office to say good-bye. You're right—he looks really good."

"He does." Her lips tingled.

"Well." He ducked his chin in that adorable way of his. "He said he'd hoped to make me his son-in-law."

She kissed that wonderful chin. "He's very fond of you. So tell me about this offer."

"He said he could always use a good accountant."

"Oh! He'd hire you in an instant." She planted a kiss on his lips. "You'd do that? You'd leave Texas and your family?"

"To be with you and make a new family?" One side of his mouth crept up. "In a heartbeat."

"Oh, my love, you'll make it Fairfax & *Sons* again. Papa will be the happiest man in the world."

"He'll have to get in line behind me, darlin'." He squeezed her waist. "God is so good. The ring, the robe, the fatted calf, and the whole wonderful loaf. He sure knows how to throw a party for his prodigals, doesn't he?"

"He does." Dorothy relished the joy in his eyes. If only she could stay in his arms forever . . . but she couldn't. "Oh dear. I'll miss you dreadfully. You said you're leaving England soon, and so am I."

"You?" He scowled. "What happened?"

"It's a long and unpleasant story, and I refuse to ruin this moment. But yes, I received orders the other day. I'll be stationed in Algiers."

"Algiers? North Africa?"

"You know about Operation Anvil, of course."

"The invasion of southern France. They keep arguing about it and postponing it."

"And planning it." She ran her hand along the solid ridge of his shoulder. "I'll be doing what I did here—studying holiday snaps and postcards, creating maps and diagrams."

"You have no idea how much those helped on D-day. All the destroyer men raved about them." A smile wiggled in the corner of his mouth. "Glad I'll benefit from your work again."

She studied the growing grin. "What do you mean?"

"I'm going to Algiers too."

Dorothy squealed and hugged him tight around the neck.

He laughed. "DesRon 18 will be transferred to the Mediterranean as soon as the Allies take Cherbourg. In the meantime, I'll be at Allied Force Headquarters making plans."

"I'm making plans too." She nuzzled in his warm neck. "To spend as much time with you as they'll allow."

"I like those plans a lot." With a deep laugh, he picked her up off her feet and twirled her around.

She was flying, but safe in the protection of his love. The greatest thrill of her life.

Read On for an Excerpt of
Sarah Sundin's Next Book in the

SUNRISE *at* NORMANDY
Series

Wars weren't won with caution, and aces weren't made in straight and level flight.

Lt. Adler Paxton tipped his P-39 Airacobra to the right and peeled away from the poky formation.

"Paxton? Where're you going? We're not in position."

Adler ignored Lt. Stan Mulroney's voice in his headphones and thrust the stick forward.

Five hundred feet below, Lt. Luis Camacho's flight of four P-39s grazed the top of the fog bank moseying toward the Golden Gate Bridge. By the time Mulroney found a position he liked, Cam would spot him and dive away into the fog.

Adler wouldn't wait that long. He lined up the afternoon sun with his tail, the engine thrumming in its strange position behind his seat. Most of the pilots in the 357th Fighter Group didn't like the Airacobra, but Adler had taken to it. They had an understanding.

The fighter plane screeched down to its prey at one o'clock below. Adler pulled out of his dive and aimed his nose just forward of Cam's nose. If he'd had any bullets, Cam would've flown right into them. Maybe the wreckage of his plane would've hurtled out of control and taken out another Airacobra or two like bowling pins. A pilot could dream.

He spoke into the radio. "Howdy, Cammie. Got you. Perfect deflection shot."

"What?" The wings waggled below. "Paxton? Where'd you come from?"

"Out of the sun and into your nightmares." Mama would scold him for cockiness, but it was part of the game. And he'd never see Mama again.

He tightened his chest muscles against the pain, then sent Cam a salute and wheeled away.

Good-natured curses peppered the radio waves, but Camacho would pull the same move on Adler, given half a chance.

Alone again in the sky, Adler got his bearings and headed for base. The twin orange towers of the Golden Gate Bridge tempted him as always.

He'd beaten the fog, and the air and waters were calm for once, so he succumbed.

"Come on, darlin.' This may be our last time." In a few days the 357th was transferring to bases in the Midwest, and soon they'd head overseas. Into combat. Finally Adler could do some good.

He eased the plane into a shallow turning dive, aiming for the center of the bridge between the towers.

Down he went to seventy-five feet, his prop wash whitening the wave tops. Plenty of clearance, but the folks on the bridge wouldn't know that. He shot a glance to the pedestrians pointing and gawking, and he chuckled. Folks needed entertainment with the war on.

The girders rushed by over his clear canopy. He whooped, pulled back the stick, swung over Alcatraz, and did a neat roll over Treasure Island and the Bay Bridge.

Nice day for flying. Strange thing about the San Francisco Bay— autumn was warmer and clearer than summer.

Even though Adler had spent the better part of two years in California, he still hadn't gotten used to the hills in summer, toasted to tan. Not like the green of the Texas Hill Country.

A cheek muscle twitched. Nothing there for him anymore anyway.

Adler contacted the control tower at the Hayward Army Airfield and made a smooth landing. After he and the crew chief finished the postflight check, Adler pulled off his flight helmet and life vest, slung his parachute pack over his shoulder, and strolled toward the equipment shed.

Maj. Morty Shapiro, the squadron commander, ambled toward him, tall and lean and angular. "Good flight? Heard you bounced Cam."

"Sure as shooting."

"Mulroney's not happy with you."

"Neither's Camacho." Adler sent him half a smile.

Shapiro didn't send even a quarter back.

"All right." Adler dipped his head to the side. "But I saw an opportunity and took it. Got in a great deflection shot."

"Your specialty." Why did Shapiro's eyes narrow? "Pull a muscle?"

"Hmm?"

Shapiro pointed to Adler's chest.

He paused, his right hand caressing his left breast pocket as if he'd indeed pulled a muscle. Yes, the scrap remained pinned inside, the fabric that had torn from his fiancée's dress when she fell to her death.

Adler rolled his left shoulder. "Reckon I shouldn't have done those extra forty push-ups in calisthenics this morning."

Shapiro glanced behind him toward two men crossing the field in dress uniform. "There he is. Paxton, I want you to meet our newest pilot."

"Want me to show him the ropes?"

Shapiro's gaze slid back to Adler. "Actually, he's an ace. Nick Westin. He flew a tour in the Pacific."

The competition, then. Adler studied the two men. Westin was a big man, his chin high, a swagger to his step, a plume of cigarette smoke trailing behind him.

Adler had no intention of coming in second again, not that being first would be easy with all the hotshot pilots in the 357th. "Who's the other fellow?"

"New staff officer. Fenelli's the name."

Little guy, clipped step, soft about the face. The squadron needed pencil pushers to keep the planes in the air, and Adler would greet him as warmly as the ace.

"Capt. Nick Westin, I'd like you to meet Lt. Adler Paxton."

The little guy stuck out his hand.

Adler blinked, recovered, and returned the handshake. "Nice to meet you."

The man must have stood on tiptoes to meet the five-foot-four minimum height for fighter pilots, just as Adler had slouched to meet the six-foot maximum.

Westin's smile was soft too, but his handshake was good and firm. "Adler? That's an interesting name."

"Means 'eagle.'" Not only was it true, but it was easier than saying it was his mother's maiden name, given to appease her parents when she died birthing her second son.

Westin's dark eyes crinkled around the edges. "Born to fly, huh?"

"Sure was."

"Good trait in a wingman."

Wingman? Adler's heart stilled. But jostling for position was all part of the game.

Wasn't it?

It wasn't. Shapiro nodded. "You'll be Westin's wingman. Figured he'd be the right man to teach you to work as a team."

A punch to the gut. Wingmen didn't make ace. They were side-kicks. Second class. Never first.

Adler threw on a smile. Nothing to be gained from pouting, and he could learn a few tricks from the veteran. "Looking forward to it. The major says you made a name for yourself in the Pacific. Reckon you have some stories."

"Sure do."

After Shapiro introduced Fenelli, the big, swaggering desk jockey, Adler excused himself to return his flight gear to the equipment shed.

Westin fell in beside him. "So where are you from? Somewhere down South?"

"Texas. And you?" The man's accent pegged him as a Yankee.

"Indiana. Prettiest land you've ever seen." Westin waxed on about the farms and the small town where his family ran a feedlot. Three sisters, two brothers, the prettiest wife, and the prettiest baby girl.

Fighter pilots loved to talk, and Adler loved to encourage them. He'd tell flying stories of his own to entertain, then toss out questions before things got personal.

"How about you?" Westin snugged his cap farther down over his dark hair. "Come from a big family too?"

Out of the sun and into his nightmares. He hadn't talked about his family in over two years, and he wasn't about to start now. Tell people he'd tried to kill his older brother Wyatt for accidentally causing Oralee's death? Tell people his younger brother Clay had tried to kill Adler later that same night? Not in a million years.

Instead he raised a rueful smile and snatched his set answer from the shelf. "Not all families are happy."

Westin's eyelids rose, then settled low in compassion. "So what do you think of the P-39? I flew the P-40 out of New Guinea. Got any pointers? Heard she's dangerous in a stall."

Adler liked the man already. "She can be. We've lost four pilots in stalls. You've got to keep a cool head."

Yes, the deflection shot was Adler's specialty.

New York City, New York
Tuesday, November 23, 1943

This wasn't how Violet Lindstrom had dreamed of sailing overseas.

On the pier in New York Harbor, Violet tried not to lose sight of her fellow Red Cross workers among the thousands of soldiers, but her eyes were drawn to the HMT *Queen Elizabeth*.

Designed to be the most luxurious ocean liner in the world, she had never fulfilled her purpose. Instead, she'd been painted a dull gray and outfitted to pack in over ten thousand troops.

Violet sighed, her unfulfilled longing echoing that of the great ship.

"Are you all right, Violet?"

She smiled down at her new friend, Kitty Kelly. "I couldn't be happier."

"Liar." Kitty winked a pretty brown eye. "I know homesickness when I see it."

Violet tightened her grip on her suitcase. How could she already be homesick? She who dreamed of being a missionary in Africa?

Kitty's teasing gaze wouldn't let up.

So Violet chuckled. "I'll be fine when we get to work in England."

"I can't wait to find out where the Red Cross assigns us."

"Me too." Violet latched on to her friend's eagerness. With her teaching experience, surely she'd be assigned to work with refugee children or orphans. What a lovely way to serve the Lord.

Winnie Nolan glanced back at Violet and Kitty. "I'm hoping for an Aeroclub. Sure wouldn't mind meeting a bunch of dashing pilots." She nodded toward a dozen men in olive drab overcoats and the misshapen "crush caps" favored by airmen.

"I'd rather work at one of the service clubs." Jo Radley adjusted her steel helmet. "Can you imagine living in London? How thrilling."

Violet refrained from wrinkling her nose. Entertaining the able-bodied wasn't serving.

"Lookie here." One of the flyboys worked his way through the crowd, a dark-haired man in need of a shave. "The Red Cross is here to see us off. Where are the donuts, girls?"

"On the other side of the Atlantic," Jo said with a wink.

"How about a kiss instead?"

"You're more likely to get a donut, pal." Kitty spread an empty hand and a saucy smile. "And as you can see—no donuts."

His buddies crowded around, and Violet eased back, glad girls like Kitty could banter.

The pilot slapped a hand over his chest. "Aw, have a heart. We're going to war. We might not come home."

Kitty gave Violet a nudge and a mock pout. "Wouldn't that be a shame?"

"Come on. A fellow needs something to remember the good old US of A." His gaze drifted up to Violet. "Say, I've never kissed an Amazon."

And he never would. She ignored the sting of the familiar barb and opened her mouth to tell him . . . something.

But he grabbed her head, yanked her down, and slammed a kiss onto her mouth. Wet, warm, awful.

She pushed against his chest, but he wouldn't budge. Masculine laughter and feminine protests filled her ears, and everything inside her recoiled. Where was the Red Cross chaperone when she needed him?

Someone wrenched the man away. "What on earth are you doing, Riggs?"

Violet hunched over and wiped her mouth with the back of her sleeve.

"Just getting a good-bye kiss."

"Not by force, you numbskull." Her rescuer had a Texas drawl.

"Whatever made you think a pretty girl like her would want to kiss your ugly mug?"

Violet kept scrubbing at her mouth as if she could scrub away the humiliation.

"Here, sweetie." Kitty handed her a handkerchief. "You'll ruin your coat."

Oh no. Red lipstick smeared the sleeve of her charcoal gray Red Cross topcoat. How would she get it out?

"Listen up, boys." The Texan had to be their commanding officer. "These ladies are going overseas too. They're serving their country. Y'all will treat them with respect, first as ladies and second for wearing a uniform. Is that clear?"

The men grumbled their agreement.

"Now, apologize to her, Riggs."

Violet kept her head bent, the handkerchief over her mouth, her eyes scrunched shut.

"Sorry, miss."

"Apology accepted," she mumbled.

"Now, y'all get along," the Texan said.

Footsteps shuffled away.

"They're gone now." Kitty massaged Violet's lower back.

"Are you all right, miss?" A big hand rested on her shoulder. The Texan? Hadn't he left with the others?

Violet dragged her gaze from his brown oxfords up his olive drab overcoat to sky-blue eyes right at her level. "I—I'm fine."

A smile twitched on his handsome face. "You will be. Any woman strong enough to meet Red Cross standards can handle one unwelcome kiss."

She tried to return his smile. "Thank you, sir. I appreciate your help."

"Anytime, miss. They give you any more trouble, send for me."

It would be handy to know a high-ranking officer. "Your name, sir?"

He swept off his cap and bowed his head, revealing sunny blond hair. "Lt. Adler Paxton, at your service."

A lieutenant? He held the same rank as the others. Why had they listened to him? "You must be a married man."

His head jerked up. "Why—why would you say that?"

She held herself straighter, her dignity returning. "I've found married men are more chivalrous. Your wife is blessed."

"I'm not . . ." His eyelids sagged, clouding the blue. "Was engaged once."

Was? Her mouth drifted open, full of questions.

Then he flashed a grin. "Pleasure meeting you, miss." And he was gone.

Gone before she could tell him her name.

And she wanted to tell him, wanted to tell him she'd been engaged once too.

"Well, he's a looker," Kitty said.

Yes, he was. More importantly, he was a gentleman, like the cowboy heroes in her favorite movies.

"Remember the Red Cross guidelines," Jo said in a singsong. "We're here to offer mercy, a listening ear, and wholesome fun."

Winnie laughed. "If Violet wants to offer it to a handsome pilot, so be it."

"Not on your life, girls." Violet put on a playful smile and held up Kitty's soiled hankie. "I've had enough of flyboys to last a lifetime."

They all laughed.

And yet, Violet searched the sea of olive drab for the tall man with the intriguing blend of chivalry and mystery.

Something told her Adler Paxton needed that listening ear.

Dear Reader,

When most of us think about D-day, we think of GIs and Tommies storming the beaches of Normandy, and with good reason. But when I was researching the US Navy for my Waves of Freedom series, I was struck by the naval role in Operation Neptune. As I dug, I was awed by the stories of the US destroyers. I wanted to tell those stories.

In this novel, both the HMS *Seavington* and the USS *Oglesby* are fictional, as are their crews. However, the *Ogie*'s adventures are based on the real-life heroics of Destroyer Squadron 18, and I relied heavily on the war diaries and action reports of the nine destroyers for my research. Those ships charged within eight hundred yards of the shore, heedless of mines and artillery, all to protect the men on shore. They toppled gun batteries off cliffs, cooperated silently with tanks, and knocked out strongpoints when they noticed pinned-down troops. Truly phenomenal work. No US destroyers were lost off Omaha Beach on D-day, but the destroyer USS *Corry* was sunk by mines and artillery off Utah Beach.

The disaster during Exercise Tiger at Slapton Sands was real. German E-boats sank two LST landing ships early on April 28, 1944, and badly damaged another. The best sources indicate that 749 sailors and soldiers perished. The US VII Corps lost more men that night than on Utah Beach on D-day. The reasons for this tragedy are noted in the story.

Another less-known aspect of World War II that appears in this novel is the "Little Blitz," overshadowed by the Blitz of 1940–41 and the V-1 and V-2 attacks that began later in 1944. The Luftwaffe mounted Operation *Steinbock* from January 21 to April 18, 1944, in retaliation for heavy Allied bombing of German cities. In those three months, about 1,500 Londoners were killed, a rude jolt to a war-weary nation. But in those three months, the Luftwaffe lost about 300 bombers of the 462 available on the Western Front, crippling the force on the eve of the Normandy invasion.

During World War II, 100,000 Wrens served in Britain's Women's Royal Naval Service throughout the world. These women served in ninety different ratings and fifty officer categories, and greatly aided the Allied war effort.

I hope you enjoyed reading about D-day from the sea. Please join Adler Paxton in the skies over Normandy in *The Sky Above Us* (2019) and Clay Paxton on the ground in *The Land Beneath Us* (2020).

If you're on Pinterest, please visit my board for *The Sea Before Us* (www.pinterest.com/sarahsundin) to see pictures of London, Normandy, Wrens, destroyers, and other inspiration for the story.

Acknowledgments

As always, I'm indebted to my family, friends, agent, editors, and publishing team—I love and appreciate you all! As solitary as writing often seems, that is an illusion. It's a team effort, and I have the best team.

An enormous thank-you to the WRNS Association, Weymouth, for answering my questions about the Wrens. Thank you, ladies, for your service—and for helping a perplexed Yankee author.

Five of the character names in this novel were "won" in a raffle for the historic El Campanil Theatre in Antioch, California (www .elcampaniltheatre.com). The stories behind the names touched me, and I wanted to share them with you.

Johanna Katin (pronounced KAY-ten): supplied by Marge Katin. Her father-in-law, Jacques Katin, fled Germany just before the war and served in the US Army. Katin is of Jewish-German origin. Jacques's mother, Johanna, and sister, Leone, were unable to leave and died in the Kovno Ghetto. I'm honored to offer this small tribute to those who perished in the Holocaust and the few who managed to escape.

Jack Vale: supplied by Andres Santamaria, a compilation of his family names from the 1940s. When I mentioned the name to my youngest son, he declared it the best name ever, fitting for my hero's best friend.

Jerry Hobson: supplied by Phyllis Hobson. She chose her husband's name for three reasons. First, they grew up in Antioch and have always loved the El Campanil Theatre—not only did they attend movies there, but Jerry performed on stage as a teenager. Second, Jerry developed an interest in World War II history during high school, especially in classes taught by Mr. Wayne Korsinen. Third, Jerry served ten years in the US Army, five of those in Germany.

Edwin (Ed) Adams: supplied by Merle Whitburn. Ed Adams was his father. He started a trucking business in the 1930s. During World War II, his company hauled supplies and blood plasma, despite shortages of tires and gas. He was president of the California Truck Owners Association. Mr. Whitburn says, "He was a special man."

Wayne Holoch (pronounced Hall-ock): supplied by Nancy Sweet. Her father, Wayne Roy Holoch, served during World War II in the Philippines. Mrs. Sweet says he was scheduled to be among the first to land on mainland Japan if the atomic bomb had not been deployed.

Thank you for these names and these stories!

And thank you to my readers! I appreciate your messages, prayers, and encouragement. Please visit me at www.sarahsundin .com to leave a message, sign up for my email newsletter, read about the history behind the story, and see pictures from my trip to London and Normandy. I hope to hear from you.

Discussion Questions

1. The naval aspect of D-day, Operation Neptune, is often overlooked, yet 195,000 Allied sailors served that day. Have you heard of this aspect of D-day? What parts interested you?

2. Life in Britain was very difficult during World War II, with air raids and severe rationing and shortages. What elements surprised you in this story? How do you think you would have handled this life?

3. Wyatt feels the need to repay his debt to the penny. In what ways is this right? How does he use his debt as an excuse? What does he learn about punishing himself for his sins and forgiving himself?

4. Dorothy is devoted to her father, even though the man ignores her. In what ways is this good? In what ways does she overdo it? How does her longing for love affect her relationship with Lawrence?

5. Wyatt is typical of most Americans of his day, never having left his home state before 1941. Although he has many "country mouse" experiences, he enjoys London. How about you? Are you a homebody, or do you love to travel?

6. Dorothy is trying to remake herself to please Lawrence. How does this cause problems? How does she come to accept herself? Have you ever tried to remake yourself to please a person or a group? Watched a friend do so?

7. More than anything, Wyatt longs to protect those he loves, but his history has led him to doubt that protective urge. Are there times when we "can't protect someone who doesn't want to be protected"? When should we reach out, and when should we withdraw our hands?

8. Wyatt notes that "Dorothy wanted to reclaim her lost family through memories, and Mr. Fairfax wanted to forget. Both grieving in different, clashing ways." In your experience, what's the healthiest way to deal with grief? How does this vary based on personality?

9. Wyatt has a history of jealousy with his brother Adler, and he struggles not to give in to jealousy with Lawrence Eaton. How does he grow in that respect?

10. Dorothy enjoys her friendships with Gwen, Muriel, and Johanna. How do they influence her for the better—and for the worse?

11. Wyatt sees himself as a failure and is quick to see setbacks as evidence of this. How does he grow during the story?

12. Dorothy's holiday home in Vierville-sur-Mer—what does it represent to her? How does her attitude change throughout the story?

13. Dorothy doesn't want to repeat her mother's mistakes. In the beginning of the story, this means one thing—and at the end, something entirely different. Discuss her relationship with her mother.

14. Psalm 139 weaves throughout the story. How does it make you feel to know the Lord is always present? That he created every part of your being? That his hand is always upon you?

15. Discuss Dorothy's paintings—watercolors and oils, light and dark. How does her intuition come into play through her art?

16. Just for fun . . . Squirrels? Adorable jokesters or Nazi spies? Charlie needs to know.

17. From what you've heard about Wyatt's brothers, what might you expect in *The Sky Above Us* (Adler's story, coming in 2019) and *The Land Beneath Us* (Clay's story, coming in 2020)?

Sarah Sundin is the author of the WAVES OF FREEDOM series as well as the WINGS OF THE NIGHTINGALE and the WINGS OF GLORY series. Her novel *Through Waters Deep* was a finalist for the 2016 Carol Award, won the INSPY Award, and was named to Booklist's "101 Best Romance Novels of the Last 10 Years." In 2011, Sarah received the Writer of the Year Award at the Mount Hermon Christian Writers Conference.

A graduate of UC San Francisco School of Pharmacy, she works on-call as a hospital pharmacist. During WWII, her grandfather served as a pharmacist's mate (medic) in the US Navy and her great-uncle flew with the US Eighth Air Force. Sarah and her husband have three adult children—including a sailor in the US Navy! Sarah lives in northern California, and she enjoys speaking for church, community, and writers' groups. Visit www.sarahsundin.com for more information.

War is coming.
Can love carry them through the rough waters that lie ahead?

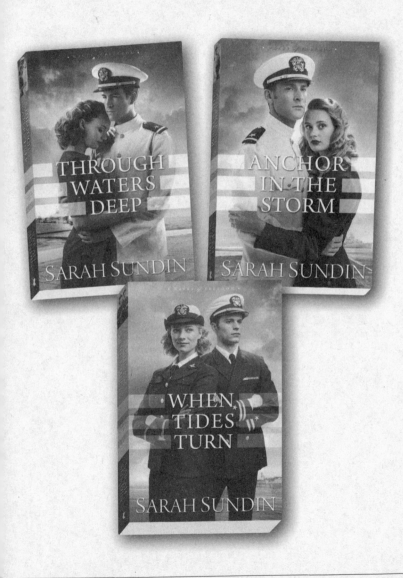

"Sarah Sundin seamlessly weaves together emotion, action, and sweet romance."

—*USA Today's* Happy Ever After blog

"A gripping tale of war, intrigue, and love."

—*RT Book Reviews* review of
A Memory Between Us

GET TO KNOW

SARAH
SUNDIN

★ ★ ★

To Learn More about Sarah,

Read Her Blog, or See

the Inspiration behind the Stories

Visit

SARAHSUNDIN.COM